# WHEN THEY FELL

## FALLING SERIES

### MADI DANIELLE

Copyright © 2022 by Madi Danielle

All rights reserved.

No part of this book may be reproduced in any form or by any electronic or mechanical means, including information storage and retrieval systems, without written permission from the author, except for the use of brief quotations in a book review.

This novel is entirely a work of fiction. The names, characters and incidents portrayed in it are the work of the author's imagination. Any resemblance to actual persons, living or dead, events or localities is entirely coincidental.

Designations used by companies to distinguish their products are often claimed as trademarks. All brand names and product names used in this book and on its cover are trade names, service marks, trademarks and registered trademarks of their respective owners. The publishers and the book are not associated with any product or vendor mentioned in this book. None of the companies referenced within the book have endorsed the book.

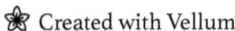 Created with Vellum

# PLAYLIST

Red Flag-Natalie Jane
Everytime- Ariana Grande
Dirty Thoughts-Chloe Adams
Trust Fall- Bebe Rexha
Couple of Kids- Maggie Lindemann
You and I- PVRIS
Yellow- Xana
What a Time- Julia Michaels
Sinner- Dezi
Middle of The Night- Elley Duhe
Feels like shit- Tate McRae
Heaven-Julia Michaels

# 1

**Present**

I can't do this.
   I have been staring at the blank word document for what feels like hours, and I can't come up with a good idea to save my life. I reach over to take a sip of coffee when I realize it's empty. I groan. Great, now I can't even enjoy my coffee while I wallow in self-pity about not being able to come up with any idea to write.

I look over at my phone that I try to avoid when I'm writing. I know myself, I will get distracted in various social media sites, videos, news articles, and anything under the lie I tell myself that I'm "looking for ideas".

Really, I am looking for an excuse not to write. I decide it's not worth the internal battle right now, I'm going to text my best friend Aylin for a real distraction. She's probably studying, I hope. If she's in class or a clinical then I'm shit out of luck for a distraction, and might have to entertain myself.

Aylin and I met our freshmen year of college. We were roommates and ended up being inseparable the remaining four years despite our different study interests; mine being English with a focus in creative writing and hers being human services. She's now working on getting her Doctorate in mental health counseling to be a big fancy therapist. And I'm here questioning my entire existence and career choice as I can't even come up with a single idea to write about.

I decide to text her and hope for the best.

> Mel: Whatcha doing?

I wait a few seconds to see if the bubbles will pop up on the screen, they don't.

I throw my head back and groan loudly even though there's no one to hear me in my tiny studio apartment. Unfortunately, being a writer without many ideas doesn't pay very well. I've written a couple of novellas and one series that did okay and, luckily, continues to do well enough that my bills are paid, but not enough that I'm going to afford a mansion any time soon. I also may have to suck it up and get some other job in a publishing house or something if I can't get another idea to even afford the minimal life I have.

My phone pings and I quickly check to see if it's Aylin, lucky for me it is.

> Aylin: Still no new ideas?

Damn her. She knows I've been struggling, mostly because I've been picking her brain for weeks trying to see if she has any ideas or any interesting stories from her clients. Whenever I ask she usually proceeds to yell at me and say she can't break confidentiality. I tell her it's still confidential if I don't know who they are, but she shoots me down like the good therapist she's going to be. Or already is since I get sessions with her for free.

> Mel: Nope. Can we go do something fun tonight?

I'm not a huge party person, I never have been, but sometimes when I have writer's block this bad, it's best for me to go out, enjoy myself, meet a man or two and forget about my problems.

This also has historically led to me drinking way too much, and not remembering much, but ending up with some crazy dream that leads to a book. That's how my series came to be, so I'm betting 100% on that plan.

I also know Aylin has been going through a lot of stress with school and may want to relax a bit. It is a Friday night. It's Portland, Oregon. We can find fun.

> Aylin: What kind of fun?

> Mel: The kind that includes alcohol, dicks, and bad choices.

> Aylin: How "bad" is bad?

> Mel: Not bad enough for jail, but definitely bad enough for some next morning regret. You in?

> Aylin: Fine, I'll be at your place after my last clinical around 6.

I smile. She's the best.

Now, what to do until six? I look at the clock and it's only eleven. I debate my options for other things that could spark my creative brain.

I could go for a walk, maybe see something to trigger my mind. I could listen to music way too loud since my neighbors are at work. I could make up horrendous dances to really unlock that creative part of my brain.

I could clean.... I look around my desk at the various wrappers and four, no five cups that I've just left here promising to clean up later. I grimace. I hate cleaning.

I could do some self-care and clean myself up, face mask, do my nails, and hey maybe for fun I'll even shave my whole body.

Looking back at the blank document I decide to do a mix of all my ideas.

Reluctantly, I grab as much of the garbage from my cluttered desk as I can to clean it up. I can hear my mom's voice in my head as I do so saying, *"No wonder you can't get anything done when everything is a mess around you!"* I dump the wrappers in my garbage and bring all the cups and mugs to the sink to begin rinsing them out and putting them in the dishwasher.

"No wonder I can't get anything done when everything is a mess inside my head too," I say to myself.

Once all the garbage and dishes are off my desk, I even go the extra mile to wipe down my desk to clear off the crumbs and various spills from the cheap wood.

I rearrange some of my notebooks, my container of pens, and my laptop so it looks more organized. I place my hands on my hips to appreciate my handy work, not that I really did much beyond what I should've done a week ago.

I connect my phone to my Bluetooth speakers and begin to play whatever song decides to come on. I sing along to the upbeat power song, acting like I'm in a music video while I sweep, dust, start my laundry (the reason I picked this apartment because there was no way I was going to a laundromat), and clean up the other various dishes around my apartment and start the dishwasher.

At one point I jump up on the counter acting like I'm starring in my own concert as I scream out the lyrics and end my performance by dramatically laying across the (now clean) counter and playing dead until the next song comes on.

As my final cleaning task, I even make my bed. I usually only do that after I wash my sheets, but I like this feeling of being "put together" I have right now. I'm not planning on bringing anyone back to my apartment tonight, unless it's Aylin, because she can get clingy when she's drunk.

I bring my speaker closer to my bathroom so I can continue listening to my random mix of music as it plays on shuffle. I decide to start my self-care with a shower, continuing to scream the lyrics to every song that comes on.

I take my time in the shower using up all the hot water as I use all my fancy products generally saved for special occasions. I shave every possible part of myself, wash my thick auburn hair, and scrub my face with more than just my moisturizer.

I could be so much more put together if I tried, but I generally have no reason to try. I haven't dated anyone in almost a year because the last relationship broke me, not that the ones before were easy breakups either. I just feel like after so many failed attempts I've essentially stopped trying. I think I have a fucked-up guy picker or something because every single one of them has been a liar, and on occasion a cheater or two, which does wonders for a woman's self-esteem, let me tell ya.

Once I'm out of the shower, I put a face mask on my damp skin while keeping a towel around myself, and my hair piled in a towel at the top of my head. I exit the bathroom to let the steam out before I even start the hours-long task of tackling my hair.

I check my phone for no reason. I know there won't be any notifications and I'm right. I don't talk to many people outside of Aylin. I have a few friends, but no one I talk to as much as her since they all have husbands and kids, which is great for them, but we are just at different times in our lives.

I go to my fridge to grab some water, putting it into a cup with a straw so I'm able to drink it with my face mask on. I *almost* go for the wine, but decide I should probably hydrate instead.

Plus, this is my self-care time and what else is better for

yourself than water? At least that's what I'm telling myself, so I don't go back for the wine.

Over two hours later, my face feels soft as shit from the face mask. My hair is dry and mostly straight; I dried it with some purposeful waves left in because I'm not sure if I want to straighten, curl it or leave it for tonight.

I changed into sweats and a tank top as I stared into my small walk-in closet, the other perk of this apartment. A place to keep my clothes, *and* a place to wash them in the same apartment? Sold.

I grab a pair of jeans with some rips that I know make my ass look fantastic, and a top that is reminiscent of a corset in the way it fits me that makes my tits look like a dream. I also would need a jacket with this outfit since it's April in Oregon and the night is still freezing.

I go through a couple more options. I know I'll end up asking Aylin what she thinks. I pick a dress that's tight at the top, but flares at the bottom so it does not flatter my ass like the jeans, but I would pair this with some fishnets and ankle boots for an edgier look.

I also grab a couple other shirt options to go with the jeans: an over the shoulder t-shirt, a sweater, and a tank top option that would also need a jacket, but fuck it.

Eventually, my music stops giving me the same hype it had earlier, and I settle on my small couch that sits against the edge of my bed so they both face my tv that's bordered in overflowing bookshelves. I grab the romantic comedy I'm currently reading off my nightstand and read through a couple chapters to kill some time while I wait for Aylin to get here.

I don't realize that I passed out on my couch until I'm startled awake by the pounding on the door. I scramble off the small loveseat that isn't even big enough for my five-foot-three frame to lay down on without my feet almost dangling over the armrest. I go to the door to let Aylin in.

"You know I've been knocking for like five minutes, right?" she says as soon as I swing the door open before she walks in.

"Sorry, I passed out reading a book I guess," I shut the door behind her wondering if all of the effort I put into myself earlier was ruined by my little power nap.

"Must be a really good book then, huh?" She jokes, already going through my fridge, probably for snacks, since she rarely eats during her busy days.

"It isn't bad. Nothing on my next best seller though!" I put my hands on my hips proudly.

"Right, the one you would have to start and then finish first?" She looks over at me with one eyebrow raised.

I put my hand over my chest and feign like she physically hurt me, "Ouch! Next time just cut my throat. It would be faster!"

"I'm trying a tough love approach to try and help you get inspired," She takes some pickles out of the fridge before closing it and leans over the counter to dig into her snack of choice.

"I don't think that will work for me, I'm a Pisces and I'm sensitive," I lean on the other side of the small island from her and bat my eyelashes attempting to appear sad and innocent.

"Yeah, you're the epitome of innocence over there, miss 'alcohol, dicks and bad choices,'" she mocks my words from earlier.

"Now you're getting it!" I shoot up and make the short distance to my bed that has my clothes I picked out earlier laid out, "So what are we wearing?"

## 2

**Present**

Another 2 hours went by while Aylin and I fixed our hair. I ended up going with straight, so my thick auburn hair is draped around my shoulders and falling in the middle of my back.

Aylin gave her long brown hair a slight wave, pulling the front pieces back from her face leaving the rest of it to fall around her at a similar length to mine.

We look somewhat related. We've been mistaken for sisters on multiple occasions, despite our different hair colors, my green eyes, and her blue eyes. We are both on the shorter side; Aylin is taller than me by about two inches, but we are both curvy and damn proud of those curves.

We choose our outfits for the night with those curves in mind. Aylin makes me wear the jeans that I picked out because she says I look beyond hot with the black off the shoulder t-shirt. Apparently I look like I'm not trying too hard to look sexy, and that it's just natural. I pair the laid-back look with some white Vans.

I convince Aylin to switch it up and go with the edgier look since she's so put together and I'm feeling chaotic. I have her put on the dress that I picked out which accentuates her tits and her waist, before falling loosely around her hips mid-thigh.

She tries to fight me on the fishnets, but finally gives in when she sees them on. She even agrees to the ankle boots, when I was sure she would say no. She wears her own jacket since the sleeves on the dress are short.

After debating where to go, we decide on one of our go-to bars in downtown Portland, which isn't always the best place to go on a busy night, but I figured we were throwing caution to the wind tonight. We take an Uber there, since finding parking is impossible and I'm not planning on being sober enough to drive home.

By the time we get there, it's close to nine. There's a good amount of people on the streets around the bar. We get a few comments from guys as we walk into the bar including some cat calls and bad pickup lines, but choose to ignore them.

We shared a bottle of wine before we left the house, but that had done nothing to create a buzz for myself.

We squeeze our way into a spot at the bar while the bartender is on the opposite end from us. A guy comes up to us as we turn to see if he has potential...he doesn't.

"Did Christmas come early? Because you two are exactly what I asked Santa for," The random man says.

I don't even attempt to hide my gag before turning away. His face is okay. He has shaggy blonde hair that he didn't even bother to style, a V-neck cut too low, and jeans that look too big. I also hate cheesy pick-up lines.

"Sorry, not interested," Aylin says before turning away. She always has to be the nice one because I certainly won't.

I feel the man standing there a moment longer. I'm about to turn around and tell him to get lost when I feel him walk away muttering something under his breath that sounded like, "whatever".

The bartender finally looks our way, coming over so we can order our drinks. I go for a red bull vodka because that nap earlier made my head feel like I'm still tired, even though my body isn't. Aylin wants to play it safe with more wine, but I convince her to at least get a rum and coke, which she reluctantly agrees to.

I'm not sure how long we have been at the bar. I just know I'm about four drinks in and feeling fantastic. I don't remember what number Aylin is on, but she's become clingy, which means she's feeling just as good as I am.

We have sung along to some of the songs they've played, scoping out the guys and finding ourselves extremely uninterested in anyone around. Some more have tried to talk to us, but we shoo them off. In my case it hasn't been friendly, while Aylin tries to make up for my attitude with letting them down gently. I roll my eyes every time.

The night continues as I feel myself getting drunker and everything around us seems to get louder.

I'm dancing on Aylin jokingly when I feel the phone in my pocket vibrate. I wonder who would be trying to get a hold of me at this time, or maybe it's just some useless social media notification.

I pull my phone out to see it is an Instagram notification, a message. I get various messages about my books from readers, but this one catches my eye once I see the name.

I suddenly can't feel anything anymore, the sounds have gone silent in my ears, and I feel like I'm not here all because of the name peering at me through the phone screen. I haven't seen or heard this name in ten years. I've never forgotten about him. Though, I figured I would never hear from him again. I have accepted we weren't meant to be, but here he is again, messaging me for who-knows-what reason. I truly thought I would never see this name again. Yet here it is.

INSTAGRAM: ZANDER WELLS HAS REQUESTED TO MESSAGE YOU.

# 3

**21 Years Ago**

"You're going to be fine, Mel," My dad tells me in the car in front of my new school.

It's my first day at kindergarten. I've already cried, told him how scared I am, but he's still making me go.

"Can I try again tomorrow?"

Dad just laughs as he gets out of the car, coming around to the back seat where I am. I haven't unbuckled myself because I can't tell if I'm about to cry again or if my tears are empty.

That's what mommy tells me when I see her crying, she says she cries until her tears are empty and then it's done.

Daddy opens the back door, and unbuckles me, "I'm going to walk you inside, if you really hate it then you can try again tomorrow."

I think about it, I know I'm going to really hate it, so I'll get to try tomorrow. I nod as I take his hand to help me down from his big car.

He holds my hand as we walk into my new school. The door

opens, it's loud. I hear a lot of kids and see one of them chasing another one. I hide behind my dad's leg.

A lady with brown hair comes up to us so I hide myself more behind my dad's legs.

"I'm Miss Eve, and what's your name?" The lady asks, leaning down next to me as I try to shield myself more.

"Melody, will you say hi to your new teacher?" I feel my dad try to move me out from behind him, but I hold onto his pant leg.

I don't think my tears are empty because I feel them coming again.

"Your name is Melody? That's beautiful, I would love to see your beautiful face that matches your name," The lady that said her name is Miss Eve whispers

I sniffle and start to move out from behind my dad's leg to see her better. She smiles while she holds out her hand. I move closer to her and put my hand out to hers, she shakes it lightly.

"Melody, do you want to go play with the other kids?" She asks me.

"Mel," I say quietly.

"What was that sweetie?" She asks over the kid's laughter.

"Mel, everyone calls me Mel," I say a little louder.

Miss Eve smiles and then I see a little boy run up behind her. He's not much taller than me, has light brown hair and bright eyes that look like a pretty mix of green and blue.

"Hi! I'm Zander, want to play with us?" The little boy asks.

I look behind me because there's no way he is talking to me; he doesn't know me.

"Zander, this is Mel, you can tell her about the game we are playing if that's okay with you, Mel?" She looks between us and I'm still not sure if the boy was talking to me at first.

"Yeah! Come on!" He says before quickly taking my hand and pulling me toward the other kids.

I look back to my dad who's smiling as I try to keep up with this kid, Zander, practically pulling my arm out of its socket.

We get over to where there's five more kids standing around. Zander lets go of my hand before he talks again. It's clear this kid isn't shy.

"This is Mel!" He says excitedly, putting his arms out to show me off.

I shuffle my feet and look down; my face feels hot. Daddy says when my face feels hot I'm sick and need to stay in bed. I turn around to tell him I'm sick, we need to try again tomorrow, but he's gone.

"Hi Mel! I'm Amber," One girl says, she's taller than everyone else and has long blonde straight hair.

I had long hair like her, but my mommy made me cut it. I don't like my new hair that only goes to my shoulder.

"I'm Jason," Another kid says. He has hair cut really short and is wearing boots even though it's hot outside.

The other three kids introduce themselves and I begin to feel a little more comfortable. Maybe I don't completely hate it. The Zander kid stays close by me all morning, including me in all the games with the other kids. He always smiles at me even when I don't get the game we are playing, and he helps me figure it out. He's nice.

After school, my dad asks me how the rest of my day went. I realize I'm smiling as I tell him about all the games we played today.

He asks if I made any friends so I tell him about Amber and Jason since they were nice to me all day too. He then asks about the first kid to come up to me and I smile as I tell him about Zander. The first kid to be nice to me when I was more scared than I ever have been. I hope we become best friends.

# 4

*Zander*

**Present**

What the fuck am I doing?

I haven't talked to Mel in, what, ten years? She probably barely even remembers me. She's a famous author now and all, at least that's what I see from her Instagram.

She probably won't even see my message; this was a stupid idea. I regret the message the second I press send. She probably has a boyfriend, not that it matters. I'm not expecting anything from her. I just wanted to say hi. And tell her I'm back. If she will even care.

I had to leave ten years ago and haven't reached out since. I've thought about it, but I figured she wouldn't want to hear from me. I mean, she could have reached out too. It wasn't my fault we had to leave, but it was my fault I never reached out.

I throw the phone across my bed and put my hands over my face. I'm an idiot.

I can't sleep, as usual, and as I toss and turn in bed, I figure *what the hell* and log in to Instagram. She just *happens* to pop up on the "discover" page, well her book does. The cover has interesting art that I thought looked cool. I click on the picture and see a username realizing it was her. What are the chances?

I debate for a good thirty minutes before sending the message. What do I say? Do I even say anything?

Then I just do it, and I regret it. I roll over to grab my phone to see if there's a way to unsend a message or send another one saying it's a mistake, when I see she replied.

She must be drunk or on something because her response is jumbled. I keep my message simple and to the point - hers is like a code I need to decipher.

> Zander: Hey Mel, I moved back to Portland if you're still here I would love to see you.

Mel: ZANDERRRRRRRR MUTHERFRUCK WELLS!!! TONORW K? ID RINK NOW

Mel: YU STLL HOT DAMMMMMMMITTTTT

I chuckle at her double response; she must be drunk. I think she's going to regret those in the morning, but I can't help the smile that spreads across my face. We should probably continue this conversation tomorrow when she's sober and I can actually understand her. Assuming she will still want to talk to me.

I put my phone on my nightstand, continuing to smile as I am finally able to drift to sleep.

I wake up when the sun is streaming in through the window right in my face. I need to get curtains or something today.

I just moved into this place yesterday and I have plenty on my to-do list. With how I set my bed up, this moves to the top of the list.

I also have boxes to unpack, not many, since I really don't

have much. Yesterday, I decided my bed and a nightstand were all I needed for the night, so that was all I set up.

My stepbrother, Trent, and I are renting this house. We were really lucky to find this place since it's outside the city and private. We are paying out the ass for it, but it's just money and we will make it. If anything, that's what we are good at.

I remember the messages with Mel last night and quickly check my phone to see if she said anything else, but also so I can reply to her.

She didn't say anything else last night, so I send her a message. She may still be sleeping since it's only eight, and if it weren't for the sun I wouldn't even be awake.

> Zander: Good morning. I hope you feel okay today, I would love to meet up with you later if you're up for it.

I'm not even sure if she will respond now that she's sober and I wouldn't blame her. We both have had ten years to reach out and neither of us has.

We didn't have the happiest goodbye when I moved away. She might still be mad about it, or she's mad that we never talked about it. I didn't want to push it with her, so I left her alone and tried to forget.

I knew she would move on with her life and be completely fine without me in it. If anything, I would drag her down. I knew that even before I got roped into this life I'm in now. Mel was always too good for me, and I knew it.

I set my phone down again face down, so I won't obsess over it if she responds. I sit on the edge of my bed with my elbows on my thighs and my head in my hands. This bed is too low to the ground, my six-foot three frame is practically crouching while I sit like this.

I run my hands over my face before getting up and going to the attached bathroom. That's another perk to this house, the dual master suites, so Trent and I don't have to argue on who gets more privacy. Neither of us have ever been shy about bringing girls home for the night, but it's not something either of us want to hear from the other if we can help it.

After figuring out the new shower and digging through my backpack to dig out my essentials, I find my soap, toothbrush, and toothpaste.

I get in the scalding shower that feels like it might be burning off a layer of skin, but I don't turn it down. I feel like I need to clean off the constant layer of imaginary grime on my skin.

It started when Trent roped me into this life. I didn't want to be involved, but he convinced me and now I'm stuck. At least until I'm able to figure out a way to tell him I'm done and do what I want with my life. I'm only twenty-seven, but sometimes I feel like this will be the rest of my life because of everything I've involved myself in. You can only do so much illegal activity before it catches up to you and it's too late.

As the burning water hits my skin, my mind wanders to Mel.

Once I found her Instagram, I debated messaging her, but opted to look through her pictures. A lot of them have to do with her book series, or the other books she's written. She has over 10,000 followers and seems to be doing well.

I did see some pictures of her which is where my mind begins to wander. She's always been beautiful, but now that she's an adult she's stunning. Her long dark red hair, her nose she always complained about, but I always found perfect, now has a ring in it, her full lips that I remember on mine.

Fuck.

Her body that fit perfectly in my arms the last time I held her, her tits that are more than a handful each pressed against me. The sounds she makes.

FUCK.

My cock is instantly hard remembering everything about her and wondering how every part of her has grown. I wonder how she would feel against me now. I can only imagine she would still fit perfectly against me, every sift inch of her silky skin against my hard planes.

I start rubbing my stiff shaft, close my eyes, and picture how it felt to have her breath on my neck as she whispered in my ear. How she sounded with my name on her lips, her head thrown back, and tits pressed against my bare chest. How perfect her hips felt in my hands as I held onto her so hard. I know I left marks, and she just asked for more.

I remember kissing down her entire body as I claimed every single part of her as mine, because she was. I wasn't sure if it would be forever, but I wanted it to be. It didn't even matter because in those moments she was mine.

"Shit Mel," I groan as I spill out into my hand and immediately wash it away in the shower.

I haven't even seen her in person yet and she's already completely taken over my mind, just like she did ten years ago. This isn't going to go well for either of us because I'm not giving up on her as easily this time. This time, she will be mine and I'm not letting go.

# 5

## Zander

**10 Years Ago**

"Why can't I just finish high school here, it makes no sense." I'm annoyed.

My dad's job moves him around all the time, but I'm about to start my junior year of high school, and I know we will be moving by the time this year is over. Which means I'll have to do my senior year in another new place.

At least we are in Portland for this year, so I'm comfortable here. I would rather just finish here and not have to worry about moving to wherever my dad needs us to go. I can stay where I want, get a job, figure it out.

"Because this is the deal with my job and you're lucky they let us stay in one place until you finish the school year anyway," he says matter-of-factually.

"I get that, but it would just be one more year," I try. "Plus, I'll be eighteen at the beginning of next school year anyway."

"Zander, we've been over this and I'm sorry this is how it is, but I just need you to help me out, bud."

"How about I just stay here, and you move to wherever they

need you. I'll finish high school here on my own," I know it's not going to work with him, I've tried this so many times.

"By yourself?" He laughs.

"No, Nanna will stay with me," I still know this isn't going to work.

My Nanna has lived with us my whole life to help my dad raise me since my mom left when I was too young to even know her. Nanna's health has been getting worse over the years and sometimes she can't even get out of bed on her own. I know I could help take care of her, but my dad doesn't trust me.

To be fair, I guess he doesn't always have much reason to, even if he doesn't know everything I do.

I'm a decent kid, but moving around all the time I've had to develop ways to cope with the constant change and making new friends which has led me to questionable choices before. I've done some stupid shit to try and "fit in". I don't care to be popular; I just don't like to be completely by myself. But my grades have always been good, and I haven't been arrested-yet, so he could try to trust me a little bit.

"And when you forget about her medications?" He asks.

"That was *one* time, and I was fourteen," I say. Not that it's an excuse.

Grandma ended up in the hospital because my dad was gone for a week and I forgot to refill her meds, but I'll never do that again, that's for sure. Shit was scary.

"Zander, I'm sorry. Enjoy this year, maybe you'll catch up with old friends while we are here." He's been trying to use that excuse like it will help any of this.

"I don't even know if any of them still live here, or go to this school, I haven't talked to them in like six years?"

Jason and I "follow" each other on social media but haven't even talked since the last time we saw each other before I had to move when I was ten.That was the last time I saw Amber and

Mel too. We were all so close when we were younger; it's crazy how that went away so easily.

It would be cool if they still lived here. I wonder if we would pick up where we left off or if we are all too different. The one person I'm most curious about is Mel. I wonder how she's grown up, what she's like now. I'm not huge on social media so I've never even looked. That's if she even still lives here.

"Zander," my dad says, pulling me out of my thoughts, "thank you for always putting up with all of this. I wanted a different life for you, but I'm so proud of who you are and how you handle all these changes."

"Thanks, dad," I don't let him see the darker parts of myself that these changes have created, and how I really feel a lot of the time, but he doesn't need to know.

He's proud of the son he thinks he knows and that's okay with me.

We say goodbye as I go out to my car to drive to school. One perk of my dad feeling guilty about all the moves and changes in my life was when I turned sixteen last year, I got to pick out any used car (within reason) that I wanted.

My dad's job may suck for uprooting us all the time, but it pays him well. I picked a black Subaru WRX with all the upgrades possible, which, since it was used, was just a stroke of luck.

Was giving a sixteen-year-old this car the best idea? Probably not, but I also would never dare crash the thing. It's too amazing. I also knew I wouldn't get a chance with another car like this if I fucked up, so maybe it really was a good idea.

Moving back to Portland is bittersweet for me. I know where things are and have a general idea of what to expect so I'm not going in blind. Plus, there's the potential I may already know three people.

Still, it's scary to walk into any place as the "new" kid. Not to brag, but I'm not bad looking and I'm tall so that generally helps along with my natural ability to talk to anyone. Though, it can be exhausting to get to know a bunch of new people.

I take turns a little faster than I probably should, but I'm confident in my driving enough to know I won't crash. I've practiced since I got the car (and even before that with my dad's car) and know what it can handle. Speed and sharp turns are its strong suits, and are also my favorite.

I drive into the student parking lot, finding a spot further from where the rest of the cars are. One thing I know about being the new kid is to not give anyone a reason to target you for any reason, good or bad, until you get a feel for the place. No one likes the new kid showing up and showing off to everyone.

I walk toward the building. I have my schedule on my phone, but I still have to figure out where my classes are. I've never stepped foot in this school, and it's slightly overwhelming.

I walk with confidence, like I know where I'm going, to not make anyone notice me before I'm ready. This school is huge with a lot of other students, so I don't look out of place, especially with my simple black t-shirt, dark jeans, and Converse. Normally, I would have a hoodie, but September in Oregon is still warm, and I don't need to be covered in sweat on my first day.

I finally find my first class, English, and settle into a seat toward the back. I pull out my phone to go through my schedule again. I also to see if certain places I remember are still around so that I can swing by sometime.

I'm not watching the other students come into the room, and I only look up from my phone when the teacher starts talking. I slip my phone back in my pocket and look toward the front of the room. I can't recognize anyone in the room from the backs of their head.

"Welcome back to school, everyone, we are going to start

with attendance so I can start to match names to faces," the teacher says. Her name is written on the board, Mrs. Burns.

She goes through the list. I'm always one of the last to be called no matter if they go by first or last name, since both of mine are at the end of the alphabet. I zone out the names she says until she gets to the middle and one name catches my attention.

"Melody James," Mrs. Burns says. I snap my head up, looking around.

"Here," she says, and I catch sight of her.

Her red hair is darker and longer than when we were young. I watch her side profile as she turns her head slightly. It's her. She's here. She's smiling as she writes something down and I smile, watching her flip her hair over her shoulder so the side of her face is exposed to me now.

I watch her bite her lip while she writes. She can't be doing homework yet, so what is she writing? She's perfect. She's grown up, and even though she's sitting down, I can tell she has some nice curves that I want to just reach out and grab for, even in this room full of people. I wouldn't care.

Mrs. Burns continues to go down her list and I know my name is coming up soon. I wonder how Mel will react once my name is called.

My leg begins to bounce, and I continue to watch her. Her hair falls back over her shoulder, so she pushes it behind her ear. She's still chewing on her bottom lip while she writes. She's too far for me to even begin to guess what she's writing.

"Zander Wells," Mrs. Burns calls out.

I don't say anything, just raise my hand. As soon as my name is called, I watch as Mel snaps her head up like I did.

She looks back and locks eyes with mine. I can see her green eyes that I can't forget, staring right at me. Seeing her full face makes my stomach drop. She's beyond beautiful.

I smile at her and give a little wave. She's staring at me; she looks to be in shock, and she hasn't looked away. I catch her eyes scope down my entire body, though her view is interrupted by the desk in front of me.

I haven't stopped smiling at her, she hasn't looked away. Finally, she does, and I notice she stops writing and just stares forward all class.

I cannot remember anything Mrs. Burns said, but it's the first day and I'm sure it wasn't important.

I was staring at Mel the entire time; she would steal glances back at me every once in a while, like she didn't expect me to still be sitting here. Little Mel Bell, I'm not going anywhere, not yet.

After class, I'm quick to get up so I can catch Mel before she walks out. I'll figure out where my next class is eventually, but I have to talk to her.

She's putting her notebook she was writing in at the beginning of class in her bag. I walk up to her desk, and she doesn't look at me right away.

"Hey Mel Bell," I say using the nickname I came up with for her when we were little. My voice being significantly deeper now makes it sound like a threat, but it catches her attention.

"Am I seeing a ghost or is Zander Wells seriously standing in front of me?" She says finally, standing up to get a good look at me. I have almost a foot on her. Her tone is joking, but I can sense the uncertainty behind it.

"Last I checked I'm not a ghost," I chuckle, bringing my arms up to pretend and inspect them.

Mel chuckles, lightly pushing at my arm, "Some things never change, do they? Except you grew up, what the fuck?" She says, still examining me as we begin to walk out of the classroom.

"I could say the same for you," I can finally see her fully now that she's standing and dammit, I was right.

I try not to be obvious that I'm checking her out, but I am.

Her chest is hard to miss in that V-neck she's wearing. Her shorts may be a gift from the gods as they showcase her thick thighs that lead to her slip-on checkered Vans.

"What's your next class?" She asks suddenly, changing the subject. I'm aware she may have noticed my eyes grazing over her body. I really hope I didn't make her uncomfortable.

"Doesn't matter, I'm not going until I get your number so we can make sure to properly catch up," I say, walking alongside her to who knows where.

"So, you'll stalk me until you get my number? Pretty extreme," She nudges me, chuckling and I can still sense uncertainty behind her joking tone.

"I wouldn't say 'stalk' but I'm saying you might find me outside every one of your classes all day until I get your number. If that still didn't work, then I think I can remember where you live," I smile.

"Okay, fine, but only because I can't have the new kid creeping on me and ruining my rep around here," She steps in front of me, so we stop walking, and winks at me with her joke that I'm not sure is a joke.

"We certainly can't have your rep being ruined, Mel, I take that very seriously," I lean closer into her. I can tell her breathing catches having me so close, I smirk.

I take my phone out of my pocket, handing it to her. There's no code on it because I don't see the need. She puts her number in before handing it back to me. I instantly press call and she looks confused as she pulls her own phone out to see it's me.

"I had to make sure you didn't give me a fake, wasn't sure if you were just trying to get rid of me," I say, hanging up.

She smiles as she puts her own phone back in her pocket, "I'll talk to you later Zander, it's great to see you again." She turns around to continue walking down the hall.

I watch her go as the warning bell sounds, but I don't care.

Mel is here. I have her number. I may only have a year here, but I'm going to get closer to her. I think I might go insane if I don't. She's still got her same attitude and humor that leaves me smiling like a complete idiot in the middle of the hallway.

Shit, I still have no idea where I'm going next. I pull out my phone to see where my next class is, and I see Mel texted me.

> Mel: Our park after school. Meet me there.

My smile is bigger now, maybe she wants to get closer to me too. Maybe this year won't be so awful, but leaving will. I should tell her. I don't want to ruin any of this so maybe I'll wait.

The final bell rings and I'm late to my next class, oh well. Worth it.

# 6

## Mel

**Present**

My head is pounding. I'm pretty sure I can't feel my left arm, and my mouth feels like I chewed on sand and spit it out.

I don't want to get up.

I start to open my eyes which makes the pounding in my head so much worse, as I have to adjust to the sunlit room around me.

Luckily, it's mine since I don't remember getting home, I'm thankful for that. I'm laying stomach down on my bed with my left arm swung over the edge. That explains why I can't feel it, it's completely numb from the lack of blood flow.

I groan as I work to turn onto my back, my head and stomach both have a reaction to the sudden move, and neither are happy.

"Too loud," I hear Aylin say from next to me, neither of us bothered getting under the covers of the bed.

We are also both still dressed in what we wore last night aside from our shoes that I can't even be bothered to think about where they ended up. They could be left on the street somewhere and I wouldn't care.

"We fucked up," I said, looking over at her. She's still facing away from me.

"Why? What else did we do?" She mumbles.

"Oh, I don't know, I'm just saying we fucked up because we feel this shitty."

I'm working on getting the feeling back in my left arm that now feels like it's being stabbed with pins and needles.

"I'm never leaving this bed," Aylin says into the pillow.

"Whatever floats your boat."

I work on swinging my legs over the edge of the bed. I need water, an immense amount of headache pills and coffee, but I'm taking it slow.

My phone pings from where it sits on the kitchen island, and I'm instantly reminded of one of the last things I remember from last night, which was getting a message from Zander fucking Wells. I'm also pretty sure I responded, and I'm scared to know what I said.

Slowly, I make my way into the kitchen, grabbing water first. I down the whole thing to relieve the horrible feeling in my mouth. I also start the pot of coffee for the both of us because I know Aylin will rise from the dead at the smell of coffee.

I go to the bathroom to find headache pills; I take two with another glass of water. I leave the pill bottle on the nightstand next to Aylin for when she's ready.

Once I feel like I've hydrated enough that I can swallow without it feeling like daggers going down my throat, I have my cup of coffee with some sweet cream creamer before I face the music of looking at my phone. I'm terrified of what I'm going to find.

I see I have an unread messages from Zander and when I open the thread, I see my messages to him last night. I instantly want to curl up in a ball and climb into one of these cabinets to never be seen again.

In his first message he said he would love to see me, and in my response, I think I offered tomorrow, which is now today. I also think my next message was saying he's still hot, so that is just fantastic.

I'm also pretty sure I said that just based on his tiny profile picture because when I click on his profile the most recent picture of him is from 3 years ago. It isn't a selfie or anything, it's an artistic shot in front of a sunset on some sort of mountain. Everything else posted is various drawings and scenery. I wonder what he's been up to for the last ten years.

He took my messages with stride though, since he replied this morning saying he would like to meet up later.

Later, like today. Oh my God. No, there's no way I'm going to meet up with Zander, nope. I can't.

But I am curious. Who has he become? What does he do? What does he really look like? Is he married? Girlfriend? Any kids? College?

Fuck, I have too many questions. I know they won't stop. I'll see him once just to settle this curiosity, it'll be fine. We are adults and I can control myself to not have an emotional or mental breakdown, or worse; throw myself at him, falling into old habits. I know I'm stronger than all of that.

> Mel: Hey, sorry about that, I feel fine now. Where would you want to meet later?

I'm biting at my nails waiting for his response.

My hands are shaking, I can't believe this. Maybe he won't even reply, maybe he had a lapse of judgment reaching out to me and he's going to just leave it at that.

I'm not that lucky because his response is almost instant.

> Zander: Could I pick you up around 7? And you can text me your response

He sent his number in the last message. Honestly, I deleted his old number so I'm not sure if it's the same, but it's something I never really considered. Even though my number is the same as it was the last time we talked.

I copy the number and save it as a contact before opening an empty text thread. Is it the smartest idea to agree for him to pick me up? I would have to give him my address which is like "don't get killed 101" to not do.

It's also not like he's a complete stranger. Well, I guess in some ways he is. I just won't give him my apartment number and I'll meet him outside, yeah. No getting murdered today!

> Mel: It's Mel. 7 sounds good. I live at the Waterfront apartments, let me know when you're here I'll meet you outside.

"What are you over there smiling about? There's nothing to be happy about right now," Aylin groans from my bed. I knew the coffee would get her up.

I didn't even realize I was smiling; this is going to be bad.

"Remember that Zander guy I told you about like forever ago?" I ask as I watch her slowly make her way out of my bed like I did just a few minutes before.

"Yeah, high school boyfriend, right?" She says, holding her head as she finds her balance.

I decide to be nice by pouring her a cup of coffee. She drinks her coffee black like a psychopath, but what is it that people say about therapists? They are the most messed up of all? I'm sure something like that has been said before.

"Yeah, pretty much," I shrug.

We were never technically "officially" together, but it felt like we were more than any of the "real" relationships I've ever been in.

"He messaged me last night and wants to meet up tonight."

"What? Hasn't it been forever since you saw him? Also, didn't he break your heart?" She meets me at the island, taking the cup of coffee from me while looking at me skeptically.

"Ten years, but I'm fine now. It's been so long, maybe it'll be nice to catch up," I take a sip of my own drink to avoid her direct eye contact.

"Mel," she says softly. I look up at her again, "be careful."

"Yes, mom, I always am," I roll my eyes at her.

That is not true. I fall fast and I fall hard. She's been the one to pick up the pieces on more than one occasion, but I am truly stronger than I have been in the past. I can handle seeing Zander again without falling apart. I have to.

AYLIN WENT HOME a couple hours ago. I took another long, steaming shower to wash away last night and prepare my strong side. I even force myself to eat some carbs to keep my stomach happy. I only drink water to re-hydrate myself from all the alcohol that I feel sucked up all the moisture from my body.

I'm not sure where Zander is planning on taking us, so I'm not sure how to dress. I decide to lean casual for this occasion. I'm going to border on the line of a little sexy so Zander will realize what he's been missing. Plus, he's the one that asked me to meet up so I'm assuming he's single which is why I'm giving myself permission to show my cleavage more than I would have if this were just me and any old friend meeting up.

I pick a t- shirt with a lower neckline to do exactly what I would like it to do, and jeans without any rips that could be a second skin over my thick thighs. I also choose to go with boots that reach over my calves and give me an inch in height since I know Zander is tall as shit. I throw on a light jacket just in case it's a little cold.

My hair is down, I left it a little wavy and put on some makeup to make my face look less like I blacked out last night. I put some eye shadow on that makes my green eyes pop even more against my pale skin.

I'm not going to do anything with Zander tonight, but I sure as shit want him to wish I would. Yes, I'm going to be a bit of a tease because I want him to know what and who the fuck he lost out on when he walked away all those years ago.

My confidence begins to waver as it gets closer to seven. I'm sitting at my kitchen island practically shaking as I stare at the time with my phone in front of me waiting for Zander to say he's here. Aylin has been texting me, hyping me up, reminding me to stay strong. She tells me I got this and throws in her "Men aren't shit" pep talk. I laugh at her amazing therapeutic advice, but she knows that's exactly what I need to hear.

My phone pings, based on the time I know it's him. I glance at the screen and I'm right. I think my heart is going to actually jump out of my chest.

> Zander: I'm downstairs by the front door of the building, can't wait to see you.

I could ignore him. I could just not reply and stand him up. He doesn't know which apartment is mine.

I don't have to go down there.

Why the fuck did I agree to this in the first place?

I'm an idiot.

I'm actually the biggest idiot I've ever known.

> Mel: On my way down.

Dammit. I wouldn't do that, I'm too curious.

I grab my purse from the counter as I make my way out. I

take the elevator down the five floors to the bottom. Frankly, I'm not sure how my legs are still holding my body up because I feel like I'm about to completely implode. My heart is racing, my vision is blurry, my stomach feels sick. I'm an actual mess, but I look good on the outside.

I reach the bottom of my apartment building. I see the front glass doors that are right in front of me.

I see him.

Holy fuck I see him.

I walk toward the doors slowly, he's facing the street, but I know it's him. He's so tall, as I get closer, he definitely got taller, he now has *at least* a foot on me.

He's wearing dark jeans and a black jacket from what I can see from the back. His brown hair looks lighter in the evening sun. The way the sun continues to hit him as he turns around to face the doors makes me forget to breathe.

His hair that always has a natural curl at the ends is cut shorter than before, so it isn't falling in his eyes like it did before, but now is styled in a disheveled way that's pushed away from his face. His eyes, those damn eyes with the bright mixture of blue and green that I found myself lost in more times than I will ever admit. As soon as he sees me, I notice those perfect thick lips stretch into a smile to reveal his perfectly straight, white smile. I swear I'm going to pass out with him looking at me like that.

I open the door, and smile with a weak, "Hey Zander."

"Hey Mel Bell," he says, his smile widening before he comes over and wraps his arms around me instantly.

I can't help but throw my arms around his neck as he hugs me so tight and picks me up to spin me like I weigh nothing which is definitely not the case.

He sets me down, but doesn't let go of his hands placed on my waist as I hold onto his forearms, which are noticeably bigger and stronger from the last time I felt them. He's looking right at me, and I'm still in shock and don't think I remember how to breathe.

"Sorry if that was too much, I'm just happy to see you, you look amazing," He pulls back slightly, but doesn't fully let go as he looks me up and down. He's still smiling, and I can't look away from his gorgeous face.

"It's fine, this is weird to see you again," I try to say lightly, but I think it comes out more cautious than I want it to because my voice is shaking from my heart not wanting to slow down.

"Weird in a good way, I hope?" He pulls back farther.

It felt like he didn't want to drop his hold from my waist, but he does, so I drop mine from his arms. He has one thick eyebrow raised at me skeptically.

"I haven't decided yet," I say, as my confidence slowly starts to come back now that he's not touching me. My brain is beginning to function again. "So, what's your plan?"

"Getting right down to business little Mel is all grown up now, huh?" He nudges me lightly to be playful. I try to not show my smile coming back. "Well first, we are going to go to dinner and then if you can stand to stay around me a bit longer, I may have a surprise I want to show you."

Now it's my turn to look at him skeptically, what kind of surprise could he want to show me? I think he sees the question on my face as we walk toward his car.

"It's not bad, just give me dinner and we will go from there," he chuckles, probably wondering what I'm thinking.

I'm so glad he can't read my mind to know I'm thinking all the obscene things I would let this Adonis of a man do to me if he just asked even after all these years, and I feel like a pervert.

No, dammit Mel we are staying strong. Nothing is going to happen, yes, he's hot, but my brain is stronger than my vagina.

We get to his car, it's not the same one he had in high school which I remember was way too nice for a seventeen-year-old to have, but this one is nicer. I'm no car expert, but I'm pretty sure this is a Porsche.

He opens the passenger door for me, I step in and feel like I'm practically sitting on the street with how low the black sports car is. I glance around the interior that feels much bigger until he steps in, then I feel like there's barely any air to breathe, which may be because of the tension between us or because Zander has such a large frame.

In the small area I notice his muscles have become bulkier over the years as well. He was in shape when we were younger, but leaner. Now he looks like he could overpower any one without even breaking a sweat.

My mind unwillingly wanders to wondering what he looks like naked now. I need to focus on something else to stop my mind from going to all these dirty places.

"There's no cup holders in here," I blurt out as he starts the car which roars to life with a sound that for some reason doesn't help the arousal I'm already feeling. I'm blaming the close contact with Zander, my damn thoughts and not because of the memories of the last time I was in a car with him. Even though this one doesn't have a backseat so that won't be happening again.

Zander laughs while putting the car in gear, "That's what you notice about the car?"

I don't have time to respond when I'm thrown back against the seat from the speed at which he takes off. I can't help but watch how his left arm grips the wheel and his right seamlessly shifts the gear shift.

I can only imagine the way his muscular forearms bulge when he does so, and the veins that are probably just existing under that stupid jacket I want to rip off his body.

I'm staring at him, I know I am. Zander knows it too because he looks over at me, a smirk on his perfect lips, but doesn't say anything as he shifts the car higher, increasing the speed way beyond the speed limit, but I don't question him.

I clench my thighs together the entire drive and try not to stare at Zander the whole time. I feel his eyes drift to me every once in a while.

I'm so thankful that he doesn't try to talk during the drive because I don't think I can form coherent thoughts with him this close to me right now. I can barely stop my thoughts from drifting to all the various things I would let this man do to me every few seconds until I shut them down.

Stay strong, Mel, you can do this. It's just dinner. He's just a guy. You'll be fine. Maybe if I repeat the words in my head long enough, I'll start to believe them. Seeing this man driving this incredible car like this makes me think about the little boy I met when we were five and I can't forget him.

# 7

## Mel

**21 Years ago**

Daddy is taking me over to Zander's house to hang out. Him, Amber, and Jason have become my best friends over the last three months of school. We all talked about having a sleepover, but our parents all wanted to meet first. So, daddy is hanging out with all their parents while I get to play.

Once we get there Zander opens the door and immediately grabs my hand to pull me to where he has all his toys in a big open room. Another grown up goes up to daddy right away, and I'm guessing he's Zander's dad. They shake hands before going to another room.

"I want to show you something I just got!" Zander is always so excited, and I can't help but be excited when he is like this with me.

He pulls out some Nerf guns and a bunch of Nerf bullets, "Once Amber and Jason get here, we can have a war!" He says, loudly.

"Okay! But we get to pick first since we are here now," I say, picking the biggest gun with lots of space for extra Nerf bullets.

An older lady comes into the room, "Hi there, I'm Zander's Nanna, Mary."

"Nanna, this is Mel!" Zander says before I can say anything.

"Oh, Mel, I've heard so much about you," she says," You and Zander have become really good friends."

I nod because I'm not sure what to say, new people make me nervous. I feel like Zander helps me be a little less shy, but sometimes I still get nervous around strangers.

"I'll leave you two to play and go with the adults, I hope to see you around more, Mel."

She leaves the room. Zander is still smiling as he's putting together his Nerf gun.

"Where's your mommy?" I ask. He never talks about a mommy, and I don't have a grandma that lives with me.

His smile goes away. I feel sad for him already.

"She's not around, I never really met her, it's just my dad, Nanna and me," He shrugs. He won't look up at me. I feel bad for asking.

"That's okay, my mommy isn't around much so at least you have your Nanna!" I try to make him smile again. I like seeing his smile, it makes his eyes light up even brighter than they normally do.

He looks back up at me and I think he was about to cry, but his smile comes back, "Yeah, I don't need her, come on let's hide before Amber and Jason get here!"

We scared both of them when they came over. Then we had a war that turned into kids vs. adults. It seemed like all our parents got along, and when daddy and I were leaving he told me I could have lots of play dates and the sleepover we all wanted with my best friends.

# 8

*Zander*

**Present**

I couldn't help but glance over at Mel every couple seconds as I drove to the restaurant in Lake Oswego. I didn't want to take her to just any place, I wanted to make sure I took her to somewhere nice.

Plus, the drive will take longer since it's a bit out of town, so I'm guaranteed to spend a longer time with her if this will truly be the only time I see her. I'm going to make the most of all the time she's willing to give me. I'm lucky she even agreed to this in the first place, I'm determined not to ruin it.

I chose not to say much during the drive so I could save it all for when I can give her my full and undivided attention, but I can't stop looking over at her.

I didn't plan on grabbing her and hugging her like that when I saw her, but I couldn't help it. Once I did, I didn't want to let go, and I knew that was going to be a problem later. Having her in my arms again felt better than I remembered.

The pictures I saw don't even compare to how she's grown

up. She is more mature in every way, and she's the definition of perfection.

I can tell she's nervous because Mel has never been one to hold her tongue aside when we were little, and she was shy. But she doesn't really say anything during the drive either. One of the many times I glance over at her I notice her trying to subtly glance over at me, and occasionally shift in her seat. I'm glad I'm not the only one of us affected, no matter how indifferent she may seem.

Once I park at the restaurant, I quickly get out of the car to open the door for her. I may not be a gentleman by any means, but I can do a nice thing here and there, especially for her.

She seems shocked once the door is open, and as she steps out, I hold out my hand to help her out of the car. It is ridiculously low, and it was something I questioned myself since I'm so tall, but I'm a sucker for a sport's car, and I had to have it.

Once I have her hand in mine, I intertwine our fingers together, she looks at me, but doesn't make any attempt to pull away. Friends hold hands, it means nothing.

We walk inside, I made sure to make a reservation earlier, so they have a table ready for us. They take us to the table right away, it's toward the back of the dark restaurant where the main source of light comes from the various candles including the ones on each table.

I'm thankful for the privacy since I know we have a lot of things to talk about. I'm expecting Mel not to hold back. We both thank the hostess as we sit down. I wanted to pull out her chair for her, but Mel beat me to it.

I sit across from her almost forgetting everything as I look into her green eyes again. I really forgot how hypnotic they can be, they make me want to drop down on my knees, apologize for everything I ever did wrong to her and then stay on my knees to show her with my mouth just how sorry I am.

"So," Mel speaks first, "what brings you back to Portland?"

"Portland is home. It always has been. I wanted to come back sooner, but other things kept getting in the way, so once I was finally able to, I came back."

I plan to be as honest with her as I can. I may choose to omit some information that I know requires a bigger conversation, but I know not to lie to her anymore, that's what led to everything in our past.

"Hm, and so here you are."

She takes the water that was waiting for us at the table to her lips. I watch her mouth as she drinks the cold liquid. She pulls the glass away and licks her lips as she sets the glass down. I adjust in my seat; I should not be so affected by this woman so easily. I'm a grown man now, I can control myself. We aren't teenagers anymore.

"Here I am," I decide to take over this conversation. I want to control the questions, so she doesn't back me into a corner about what exactly held me back and ask too many questions about what I'm doing now. "What about you big shot author? How's fame treating you?"

She scoffs, "I'm definitely not a big shot author, or famous by any means. I can't even come up with another idea to save my life right now. So, currently my full-time job is looking for inspiration."

"*You* don't have any ideas? I remember you always carried around a notebook and a pen because you said the smallest thing could give you the craziest idea. Then, you had to write it down in that moment or it may go away."

She doesn't say anything, just turns to her purse as she pulls out a notebook with a pen attached.

"Still do, it has just been a bit empty lately," She sighs before putting the notebook back in her bag. "What do you do?"

Shit.

"Sales, I'm in business with my stepbrother," I match her

earlier actions by taking the glass of water and drinking half of it in big gulps.

"Sales? How vague, the ever-mysterious Zander Wells," She rolls her eyes.

"There's an idea for your next book," I try gaining control of the conversation again, "a story about a mysterious, extremely attractive man."

"Don't forget humble," She scoffs, "that would work if I knew the answers to the mystery or else it's just another book without an ending."

"That's where you get to use that creative brain of yours, the mystery can be whatever you want it to be," I wink at her.

This is not how I wanted our night to start off, I wanted to give her comfort about our past before getting into the present since it's more complicated now than it was in the past.

"What about any relationships, you get back with that shithead from high school?" I can't help but ask. I am pretty positive of the answer, but I need the validation.

"Oh wow," She laughs, "Mark and I never got back together after you left. Especially not after what went down at that party."

I lean back, putting my hands behind my head, "Ah, the New Years party, that was a great night."

For me and Mel it was. It was not a good night for Mark.

Mel just lets out a soft laugh before our waitress comes over to take our drink order. I order a Jack and Coke; Mel chooses to stick with water.

"Have enough to drink last night?" I ask, I can't help myself to push her buttons a little bit.

"Oh my God, I'm sorry about that, I rarely go out drinking. My best friend and I just needed it. I'm sorry," she shakes her head and hides her eyes from me. I want them back. I want them looking at me again.

Not thinking, I reach my hand out to take hers that is

resting on the table, because I just need her to look at me again. "Don't be sorry at all, you're here now."

She looks back up at me and doesn't make an instant move to remove her hand. When the waitress comes back with my drink and a refill of water for Mel, I let go so it's not awkward. We tell her our food order before she walks away again.

"So, no boyfriends or husbands I should know about?" I ask, leaning back and taking a sip of my drink that is definitely more Jack than Coke.

Mel laughs, "Definitely not, Mark was not my last shitty boyfriend, not by a long shot. I think my type is perpetual assholes," It hurts to hear her mention other boyfriends. I'm also assuming she's lumping me in the "asshole" category in her mind. "What about you? Any girlfriends or wives going to appear behind me to slit my throat?"

Now it's my turn to laugh, "Nope, as a perpetual asshole, there's no need for you to worry about any other women." I throw her words back at her which may just make me seem a bit more like an asshole. I miss how our relationship was always easy going. I'm hoping that can still be the case, even all these years later.

"Okay, I wasn't totally including you in that. You were never my boyfriend, remember?" She glances over the glass as she takes another sip.

I may not have been officially her boyfriend, but she was mine, and even now she still is. She's always been mine, even if she doesn't realize it.

"Look, Mel, I want to be honest with you that I didn't come here with any expectations about us. I know we were over ten years ago when I left, and I don't expect to come back having everything be the same and for us to be together. I just wanted to see you, apologize, and explain if you would let me. Then if I'm lucky at the end of the night get a nice kiss on the cheek, hoping you will call me again."

I lay all my thoughts out for her to digest, I didn't want to beat around the bush anymore, and I feel like her knowing there's no expectations will help her relax more.

"Good, then I'm waiting for that apology and explanation."

She leans back, folding her arms across her chest. This action only brings more attention to her tits that are already on display, like a constant challenge for me not to stare at. I try to subtly adjust myself in my jeans because clearly, I can't control myself around her, and I really am a teenager again.

"I should have told you that first day at our park in high school that I was only going to be here for the year. I know I should have, but I didn't want to ruin anything with us, and I kept telling myself I have time. That was my excuse for months. By the time I realized I really didn't have time it was too late, and I couldn't hurt you because we had gone through so much. But Mel please know the last thing I wanted to do was leave you. I begged my dad to let me stay with Nanna, but he wouldn't let me."

I have her full attention. She looks like the guard she put up is slowly coming down the more I talk, so I don't stop.

"I'm sorry. I'm so extremely sorry. The last thing I wanted to do was hurt you, and the more we hung out the more I wanted it to be for longer. I was also in denial which is why I didn't tell you."

I take another sip from my drink, even though it's strong it's not going to get me a good buzz. Which is probably good since I'm driving anyway, but fuck I wish I could be a little less sober for this.

"Why didn't you ever reach out after you left?" She asks quietly, and if I wasn't staring at her lips I might have missed it.

"I convinced myself that you hated me and that you would be better off without me. I figured you'd move on with your life, forget about me, and reaching out would just make things worse for you," I say, looking into her eyes slightly pleading for her to understand. "It was stupid, I know that, but the more time past I figured the worse it would be for me to reach out, so I never did."

"I thought you hated me for the shit I said when you left. That's why I never reached out either," she says, and I can tell in the way she says it that it's something that has bothered her all this time.

She did say some mean shit to me that day, but I deserved every single bit of it.

"I never blamed you, and I definitely never hated you. I deserved everything you said to me," I say matter-of- fact because I don't want her feeling like any of this was her fault.

"No, you didn't, I'm sorry." She shakes her head.

"I forgave you as soon as it happened, so don't feel bad. You never did anything wrong to me Mel, I'm the one that fucked up. Big time, and then I've kept fucking up until right now, where I'm trying to fix it all," I'm really hoping she won't question more of my fuck ups because there's been plenty, I can't bear to share with her yet.

Luckily, she doesn't. It just looks like she's trying her hardest not to cry.

"So, is this us starting over then? Truce?" She asks, hopefully. This might be the best-case scenario for us right now and I'll take it.

"Sure, we can start over," I stand up.

She looks up at me with a confused look on her face. I walk back behind her slightly.

"What the hell are you doing?" She asks, turning around in her seat to face me as I'm walking back over to the table.

"Hey, I'm Zander, I'm twenty-seven years old from Portland Oregon, what is your name?" I say holding my hand out for her to shake.

The tears she looked like she was about to shed are gone as she's laughing and putting her hand in mine where I can't ignore the warm buzzing I feel when our skin touches. From her instant blush I think she notices it too.

"Hello Zander, I'm Melody, twenty-seven years old from Portland Oregon. It's nice to meet you," she says matching my joke. I reluctantly let her hand go before sitting down.

"How's that for starting over?" I ask, taking another sip from my drink.

I see her visibly relax before she responds, "I think that's the perfect place to start."

# 9

## Mel

**10 Years Ago**

Zander agreed to meet me at our park after school. I raced out of my last class of the day to drive over to the small park that used to be almost exactly in the middle of where our houses were.

I don't know where he is living now, but I'm still living at the same house I always have, aside from my mom not living there for the last five years after my parents got divorced.

I get to the park and don't see any other cars around, good. I wanted to get here first.

I go to the swings because they have always been my favorite, something about the breeze just makes me feel free, when I close my eyes, I feel like I'm flying. When I have that feeling, I don't have to think about much.

I've come here throughout the years by myself after Zander had to move away. Whenever things were tough, I would come here.

When my parents told me they were getting divorced, when Amber and I fought, any significant time in my life has led me back to this park. This is the park we always considered "our park". It just makes sense this will be where we catch up and I tell him about everything he's missed since he had to leave.

I hear a loud car coming close, as I look up, I see a sleek black car speeding into the parking lot.

Is that him?

I watch as he parks and steps out of the car. It is him.

Even between this morning and now I forgot how much he's changed and honestly, how hot he is now. His light brown hair has a natural curl, more so now than when he was younger, and it falls across his forehead practically in his eyes.

I don't want his eyes covered though; I need to see those bright blue/green eyes looking right at me.

He's so tall, at least over 6 feet so when he's standing next to me, I have to look up to see his face. Through his t-shirt he has been wearing today I see he has lean muscle, and the sleeves are tight around his biceps.

I bet his arms would be so easy to fall into.

No, I can't go there, I have to tell him about Mark. I have to tell him about a lot of things.

He walks closer to me since I haven't moved from the swing and wasn't planning on it anytime soon.

"Hey," he says as he sits on the swing next to me.

"You remembered our park?" I ask. I figured he would, but it's still nice to know that I'm not the only one that has held onto memories.

"Of course I did. This was our place," he leans back on the swing and I notice the bottom of his shirt rides up a little to reveal some of the toned tan skin underneath. I look away quickly because I feel my blush spread across my cheeks.

"Yeah, it was. A lot has changed since you left," *and I just didn't think you'd remember something like this, or me.* I don't say the last part because I don't want to seem weird.

"Well yeah, it's been like six years," He shrugs like it's not a big deal as he moves back and forth on the swing.

"So, what do you want to know about?" I turn to face him because I could word vomit the last six years to him if he really wanted me to, but I figured that might be too much.

"How have you been? What is going on with you?" He asks.

He wants to know about me? I honestly thought he would ask about Jason and maybe Amber first.

"Me? Well, where do I start? I'm clearly the most popular girl at school, prom queen. I light up every room I walk into, and I have guys falling to my feet constantly," I joke as I try and lighten the mood because I still can't believe I'm sitting with him right now and humor is how I approach most things in life.

"Wow, that must get really annoying."

"It is, you have no idea, like come on people I'm just a normal girl, treat me like it!" I throw my hands up for dramatic effect.

Zander laughs, "But really, give me the rundown on your life. Who is Melody James now?"

"Melody James is a sixteen-year-old who likes writing stories, hates math and spends her free time reading books either at home or in this very park that you are currently in."

"You still come here?"

"Every once in a while. My parents got divorced a few years ago so I needed a place to go to just be alone and this place seemed like the best option."

"I'm sorry, I didn't know," he says sympathetically.

"It's fine, why would you know?" I shrug it off, this is too depressing. "Anyway, everything is fine. I live with my dad in the same house as before. My mom moved out and I go to dinner with her once a month because my dad makes me and it's awful every time. She always has some sort of comment to make about something I'm not doing good enough, or whatever she's in a mood about that day. I've just learned to ignore the comments now anyway."

"What could she even comment about? It's not like she did much raising you. If I remember right, she was hardly around, it was always your dad," I know this is something Zander relates to because of his mom, so he actually understands.

"Just comments about how I look and what I could do differently in life, really anything," I try to laugh it off, I don't know why I'm telling him this. It was not what I planned on when I planned for us to meet here.

"How you look? She shouldn't say shit about that. You are beautiful, Mel. Like what the fuck?" Zander says and I'm taken aback.

Did he really just say that? I feel the blush coming back to my cheeks, I guess now would really be the time to tell him.

"Thanks, um, something you should know, though, I do have a boyfriend," I'm looking down at the sand at our feet as I say it. I shouldn't be ashamed to admit it, but for some reason I am.

"That's cool, what's his name?" He doesn't even seem phased by the news. It's like it doesn't even affect him and I don't know why that bothers me that he didn't have more of a reaction to the news.

"Mark, he's a football player which I know is grossly cliché, but I really am not 'popular'," I do air quotes around the word. "I just do my own thing and for some reason he liked me. He's nice, but we've only been together a couple months."

It started right before school was out, and then we spent almost the whole summer together, which was great. For some reason I've never felt any real "spark" with Mark. And I'm already more drawn to Zander in this short time of him being back than I ever have with Mark. That makes me a bit annoyed with myself because I don't know what that means.

"He sees how amazing you are, and he better know that he's the luckiest guy in the world," Zander smiles at me. I can't help the shiver that takes over my body at his words.

"Stop, or I'm going to think you're flirting with me," I shake my head at him. "Do you have a girlfriend or anything? Where have you been anyway? Tell me about you."

"My dad dragged me and Nanna to Las Vegas first, then we spent some time in Phoenix and finally San Francisco before moving back here," he says simply like it's not a big deal. "I don't have a girlfriend, I saw someone briefly in San Francisco, but long distance is not a good idea, and since we kept moving, I just never thought it made sense to have any real girlfriends."

"No real girlfriends, so you just lead them on and then refuse to commit?" I swing the swing to the side to hit him with my body as I'm joking. "Such a player Zander Wells turned out to be."

He laughs, "It's not like that, I just never had anyone that made it worth committing, and I knew we would move anyway so there wasn't a point."

"I get it, but I'm still going to give you shit."

"I wouldn't expect anything different from you Mel Bell."

I groan, "Do you still have to call me that horrible *not* nickname you came up with?"

"What? Am I still the only person to call you that?"

"Yes!"

"Then nope, that's mine only and I'm not going to stop," He smiles at me, and I have to look away again. His perfect smile isn't even fair. It's not fair for him to be this good looking at all.

"You're still annoying, so some things definitely don't change," I roll my eyes as I start to swing forward slightly.

"That'll never change, I will annoy you as much as you let me," he says. I notice he hasn't looked away from me. "What's the deal with Amber and Jason, I didn't see either of them all day."

Ah, this conversation.

"I haven't talked to Jason much since junior high. He's still here as far as I know, just fell out of touch, but Amber is another story." I feel like I need some sort of push to help me through this story and I really hope Zander isn't about to judge me for it.

"Should I guess? I can guess some crazy shit, let's see...she killed someone, and you helped her hide the body and you can never interact again, so they won't lead the murder back to you?" I stop swinging and snap my head over to him.

"What the fuck, no!"

He just starts laughing.

"Okay then whatever the real story is can't be that bad."

I gape at him for a moment before telling him what happened.

"Mark may have technically dated her first, at least that's what everyone thought all last year, but he said that wasn't true. Amber and I haven't been close in years, but we never had any issues. Amber claims they were together all Sophomore year, but Mark says they hooked up a couple of times and she wouldn't leave him alone. Either way he says it was long over before he started talking to me, Amber just doesn't think so," I shrug.

It was a big reason I wrote off Mark for so long, he kept asking me out and I kept saying no because he was with Amber.

"Anyway, stupid drama bullshit, he made things official with me in June, she found out, was pissed, confronted me, and it wasn't pretty."

"Damn...Mel the homewrecker. I'm going to be honest I never saw you as the type, but hey, if that's what you're into, who am I to judge?" I stare daggers at him.

"Fuck you, I'm not a homewrecker, there was no home to wreck! I turned Mark down for months before *finally* giving in when he had enough people convince me that he and Amber were done," Zander is just smiling.

"I'm giving you shit, Mel Bell, chill. I really won't judge

because anything you could've done; I've probably done worse." He still hasn't looked away from me.

"What have you done that's so bad then?" I just shared all my bull shit with him, and he's barely shared anything.

"Oh, where do I start? I stole a pack of gum once."

I fake a gasp.

"I'm going to call the police, I bet there's a huge bounty on your head right now and I'm about to be rich!" I pull out my phone like I'm actually going to call.

Quickly, Zander gets up from the swing and grabs my legs to pull me to him while I'm still sitting. My legs are around his knees, and because of his height my chest is almost touching his belt line.

I look up at him, he still has his joking smile on his face, "I will take that phone from you and I'm not afraid to fight you for it," he says.

I laugh as he lets go of my legs and I instantly miss the warmth his hands brought to my calves. He sits down in the sand right in front of me so if I swing my legs out, I will end up kicking him.

"But really, Mel, I've done some shit things," his smile is gone now and he's looking down. I'm not sure if it's at my legs or the ground, "there were times I knew we were leaving, and some girls were interested in me so I would sleep with them even if they had a boyfriend. It didn't matter to me, I was leaving. I know that's fucked up, I would just be so mad we were leaving again, and I acted out selfishly."

I'm shocked by his confession, for some reason I couldn't see Zander like that, but at the same time, I don't even really know him anymore.

"I wouldn't do something like that to you though, I actually care about you and if you like this Mark guy, I won't become involved in your life," he says, looking at me now.

I see the truth in those beautiful eyes, no matter how badly

I want to tell him Mark doesn't matter and tackle this man in front of me right now I just nod.

"I want you around, you were my best friend, and I would like to have that back," I say even though I don't believe the words because they are only half true.

I want him around, but I think I would like more than just my best friend.

His smile returns, "I'm here for you Mel Bell, until you tell me to fuck off for real, I'm here."

"Speaking of being here, do you know how long you will even be here before your dad makes you move again?" I ask, it seems like the time is random that he has to move, and I don't know if he ever learns about it ahead of time.

He drops his head again and dammit I want him looking at me, "Nope, he doesn't get much notice before a move," He looks back up at me and the sadness that was just in his voice appears to be gone again. "But I'm here now and we are going to cause some trouble."

I smile at him, I'm not sure what trouble we are going to cause, but it doesn't matter. In this moment I think I would walk through fire with Zander if he wanted me to.

The rest of the day at the park was full of laughter, jokes, more catching up, and promises of more days like this.

Once the sun starts to set, I look at my phone for the first time and notice five missed calls from Mark and two from my dad. I text them both that I'm sorry I was catching up with an old friend.

Mark just says he wants me to come over and doesn't question who I'm with.

My dad does ask who I'm with. When I tell him it's Zander, he tells me to enjoy myself and come home before midnight. If I said I was with Mark, he would make me come home by eight.

Weird, considering I think Zander might be more capable of trouble than Mark, at least for me.

# 10

**Present**

The rest of our dinner goes well after we've had our reset and decided we are starting over. I know it's probably for the best since we are completely different people now and it only makes sense to get to know each other that way.

The one thing about Zander that I'm questioning but trying not to bother him about is his job, he says "sales with his stepbrother", but he won't go into more detail. It honestly just makes me more curious and wonder how honest he's being about everything.

He did tell me his dad got remarried and that's how his stepbrother came into his life. His name is Trent, and he's three years older than Zander. They moved here together into some rental outside of town and offered to show me soon.

I asked Zander why he came back now, why not sooner? He explained that his Nanna got really sick. They didn't think she should move again so Zander offered to stay with her to take care of her.

She ended up passing away, which I could tell was still hard for Zander to talk about and I held his hand while he told me. I was glad he let me. He even squeezed my hand to know that he was okay with it.

He then explained that he and Trent had their business in Phoenix, and that Trent didn't want to leave, until Zander was finally able to convince him to move to Portland.

When we finished dinner, I offered to pay because I didn't want to consider this a date, but he wouldn't let me. I asked to at least pay for half, and he just looked at me with narrowed eyes that told me to drop it.

We walk out of the restaurant with Zander's hand on the small of my back, and I feel the skin there warming under his touch. This makes me want to lean into him more to gain more of his warmth. I'm not even cold, but it's like a comforting warmth that makes my skin tingle.

We get to the car, Zander opens the passenger door for me again which I roll my eyes at a bit, he's not a mean guy, but he's not what you would call "chivalrous" either. At least he didn't used to be.

Before I can climb in, Zander places his left hand on my hip to spin me to face him and pushes me against the side of the car, even though it's so small there's not much to lean against.

I'm looking up at Zander's face as he presses his body close to mine, even through all our clothes I feel my skin lighting up from the warmth I was seeking out from just his hand. I feel like I'm on fire, but in the best way.

"So, what do you say? Are you up for the surprise?" He asks, his voice low, and his face so close to me I feel his breath caress my skin.

"You're asking if I can still stand to be around you?" I ask, bringing back his words he used earlier.

"Can you?"

I think his face has inched closer because I can smell mint

mixed with what reminds me of a bonfire on him, it reminds me of summer nights. His scent is like a fire with a hint of spice and I want to be surrounded by it.

"Take me to the surprise," I say without breaking his gaze.

He smiles before taking my hand and helping me step down into the car.

Once he gets in the driver's seat and the car roars to life I turn to him, "The surprise isn't taking me to some secluded place to murder me, is it?"

"Mel, if that was my plan, I wouldn't have taken you somewhere public first, come on I thought you watch true crime," He's joking, and we both smile as he speeds off down the street.

I'm paranoid he's going to get pulled over for speeding, but Zander seems unfazed like he literally owns the roads and doesn't have a care in the world. As we go back toward Portland, I recognize the streets we are on as we get closer to where I assume he is taking me.

"Are we going to our park?" I wonder, which feels weird to still call it that after so long,

I haven't stepped foot there since he left the last time. It used to be my place of solace, but after everything we went through all the memories hurt to think about, so I never came back. But no matter what, it always stayed our park.

"If I tell you then it's not a surprise anymore," He pretends to scowl, but I barely notice because I'm watching the veins in his hand flex as he shifts.

I feel like I might drool at the sight. I adjust in my seat slightly; I should not be this turned on from *veins*. *Pull yourself together, Mel.* I see him smirk in my peripheral vision and I think he noticed how I'm looking at him. Dammit. I roll my eyes before looking out the window, and away from him.

I was right, we pull up to the dark, empty park. Zander turns off his car and it's silent. He turns to face me, I meet his gaze. I don't like the silence, when the car is on there's at least something to use as an excuse not to say anything, but this is too silent.

"Race you to the swings," he says, the smile slowly growing on his face. I match mine.

"Okay, but just know, I play dirty," I say before flying out the passenger door.

Was that cheating? Yes, but I warned him.

I hear his heavy footsteps closing in behind me. I know I won't win so it's time to fight really dirty.

I stop and turn around where I know he's close behind me. He tries to turn to get around me, but he's too close. I stick my foot out to trip him. He sees it too late and grabs me around the waist at the last minute as we both go tumbling to the ground,

Zander breaks my fall. He's lying on his back on the hard asphalt, and I'm laying directly on top of him. My skin is on fire again, especially where his hands are on my waist holding me to him.

"You do play dirty," he says underneath me and I can feel each breath he takes.

"Are you okay?"

He broke the fall for both of us, and he could have really hurt himself.

"In this position I'm better than I've been in ten years," He smiles up at me and I think I can feel him growing hard underneath me. It slams my confidence back into my brain, especially to confirm that I'm not the only one that's been struggling with attraction all night.

I start to lean down so our noses skim each other. I can smell his nostalgic scent again, "Are you going to do anything about it?" My voice is lower and more breathy than I meant it to be.

I feel his hands on my waist tighten as I prepare to pull my last move of racing to the swings because we are still in that race, and like I said, I play dirty.

I begin to prepare my hands and feet subtly, getting ready to jump up and run again, when I feel like Zander is so focused on what I'm hinting at, I try to hop up, but as soon as my hips move off him, his hands tighten hard enough that I can't get away.

In one quick move he switches our positions, so now I'm pinned under him and I can *definitely* feel his erection which is limited by his jeans, in this new position because it's pressed right against my groin.

Now, I'm not saying if this man wanted to fuck me right here in the parking lot I would let him, but I also don't think I'm strong enough to say no right now if he tried.

"I take it back, *now* I'm better than I have been in ten years," he leans over me, holding my hands down by my head and my hips down with his legs.

"And I'm still wondering if you're going to do anything about it," I taunt again now that I'm at his mercy, and I really do wonder if he is going to try anything.

Zander doesn't say anything, he just leans down as close as I did to him, our lips not even an inch apart. I can practically taste him, I feel him everywhere, I'm breathing in his air and I want more, I just want more of everything that's happening right now.

"Yeah, I'm going to win the race," he hops up off me and goes back to running.

What an asshole! I push through my lust filled thoughts to hop up and chase after him. His long legs put him at a huge advantage and he was at the swings way before me.

"You're not the only one that can play dirty," He winks at me as he sits on a swing taunting me with his win. "What's my prize?"

"We never negotiated the terms, so I don't think you get a prize."

"That's not fair, I want to negotiate terms now, then."

"That's not necessarily fair, but fine, what do you want?" I ask as I walk closer to him since there's no point in running now that he already won.

I go to sit on the swing next to him, but he stops me.

"I want you to swing with me," I furrow my eyebrows at him.

"Yeah, that's what I'm trying to do, and you stopped me," I say, confused.

"No, I want you to swing with me on this swing," He points to the seat he's already sitting in.

Zander's muscular build takes up the whole seat and then some, and I'm not small so I'm not sure about his plan here.

I think he notices the question in my face, he gestures to me over to him, I hesitantly move to stand in front of him, and he stands up in front of me, I keep my eyes on his.

He leans down as he reaches behind my thighs, before I can question what he's doing he picks me up and wraps my legs around his waist, which leads me to let out a surprised squeal and he lifts me with ease.

"What are you doing?" I ask with my arms wrapped around his neck as he starts to sit us on the swing together.

He moves my legs, so they hang behind him and I'm straddling his lap which is not helping my arousal. Especially since I can feel his strained cock is right against my core where I want him to be, minus all these clothes.

"Swinging with you," he says simply like none of this is affecting him at all, which annoys me because it very clearly is.

Our faces are only inches apart and I could close the distance so easily to feel his lips on mine. I wonder if it will feel the same as it did before. I want to know, but I refuse to give in first. Especially when he can seem so unaffected all night while I'm practically jumping out of my skin being so close to him again.

He does exactly what he said he was going to do and swings

with me. We don't go very high, but I continue to hold onto him for dear life like we are flying. I can tell he finds my fear about this funny.

"What?" I ask since he hasn't stopped smiling and I just want him to say something.

"It's funny that you think I would let anything happen to you," He's chuckling, and it makes me narrow my eyebrows at him.

"You pulled me to the ground, that could've hurt me," I pointed out, which only made him laugh harder.

"First of all, you tripped me, that could have hurt *me*, and second of all I had you, I wasn't going to let you get hurt," he takes one of his hands to tuck my hair behind my ear.

I didn't notice he stopped swinging, so now we are just sitting on this swing together, but I won't move. His hand that tucked the hair behind my ear has moved down to my jaw, and then to the back of my neck where he's holding me.

"I will never let you get hurt." I don't get a chance to say anything before he pulls me to him and crashes his lips onto mine. I can't help the light sigh I let out into his mouth. Our bodies are completely pressed together.

The warm feeling of our skin together has turned into electricity that starts at our lips and lights up everywhere our bodies are touching. His kiss starts gentle, but quickly changes, his tongue at the seam of my lips wanting entry which I give him immediately.

He pulls me closer, his hand moving from my neck into tangling in my hair. His other hand on my hip pulling me closer even though there's no more room between us. His tongue explores my mouth like it's the first time again and I let him, while I do the same.

I move my hips against him and am reminded of his stiff cock underneath me. I can feel the wetness between my thighs.

I want some relief, anything. I move my hips and moan into his mouth as I find that relief.

Zander feels what I'm doing, pressing his hand harder against my lower back to encourage my movements. I hear his own slight moan in my mouth, but he's so focused on our kiss that hasn't stopped and my movements in his lap.

I feel myself building, and I move a bit faster against him to continue to chase that feeling. Zander continues to pull me closer as he starts to move his own hips to meet my movements.

I'm panting, running out of breath; I swear I'm only surviving on the air that's in Zander's mouth, and I never want to stop. I want more than this. I want to feel him, I want to feel his body.

I move my hands to his chest to feel the hard muscle underneath which makes my eyes roll as he continues his assault on my mouth, biting at my lower lip while our hips are moving without any rhyme or reason anymore.

I move my hands to the back of his neck and pull on the short hair that is there. I am so close, I'm beginning to whimper in his mouth, I want him so fucking badly when suddenly a voice breaks us out of our own world.

"Hey!" Someone calls from the distance, and I see a flashlight and a man coming toward us.

I jump off Zander's lap as gracefully as I can. He has to steady me since my legs are not fully working from the *almost* orgasm that I'm pissed has got interrupted. Now I might actually think about my actions before I let Zander touch me again. Maybe. Probably not, but maybe.

Zander gets off the swing, stepping in front of me as the stranger approaches us. I notice Zander's defensive stand as he shields me, and I already want to jump this man again even with our new audience.

"This park is closed, you kids need to leave," The man who

turned out to be a cop says as he approaches us and shines his flashlight right in Zander's face.

"I'm so sorry officer, this place has special memories for us, so I just wanted to surprise my girlfriend here with a trip down memory lane for our anniversary," Zander says so smoothly, though my head snaps up at "girlfriend". I'm sure he's just putting on a show for the cop, but hearing him say that still sends a flutter in my stomach that I quickly squash back down.

"Mhm, well you both need to leave, I don't want to cite you," The officer says, trying to shine his light at me, but Zander adjusts his stance, so I remain hidden.

"Of course, we will leave now. I'm so sorry, have a great night," Zander says to the officer before turning us both around to head back toward his car.

He keeps me in front of him the whole walk back, so the officer never got to see my face.

Maybe what he said is true and he won't let anything hurt me, maybe he really does want to protect me this time. I just need to make sure I'm protected from him as well.

"You okay Mel Bell?" He leans down to whisper in my ear as we get back to his car, his old nickname for me sending a shiver down my spine. I hate that stupid nickname but hearing him say it in his deep lust filled voice is something I could get used to hearing again.

"Yeah, for the most part I'm fine," I say, turning around to face him once we reach the car.

"For the most part?" He asks, concerned, but it's not what he's thinking.

I just look at him with my eyebrow raised waiting for him to catch up, and he studies me for a second. I make a quick glance down to his crotch before meeting his eyes again.

"Oh, My Mel Bell does play dirty," He winks before kissing me way too quick before gesturing for me to slide in his car which I do, and he shuts the door behind me before climbing in the driver's seat.

"I guess I'm giving you plenty of reasons to call me again after tonight," he says as the car turns on.

I roll my eyes, because I'm not going to give him any more of an ego boost.

Zander drives back to my apartment and I'm giving myself a pep talk the entire drive that I will not be letting him come up to my apartment no matter how badly I want him right now. I'm going to be strong and make him work harder for me.

I just got an apology after what feels like an entire lifetime apart, and I still have so many questions about who this Zander is.

"Can I walk you to your door, so I know you're safe?" He asks once he parks in my lot.

I bite my bottom lip while I think about it, *stay strong Mel!*

"Yes, but you're not coming into my apartment tonight," I made it clear it wouldn't be tonight, if I happen to call him over in the morning though, mind your business.

"Of course, like I said I don't have any expectations I'm just glad you're speaking to me," He smiles before exiting the car.

I see him coming around to open my door, but I open it before he gets the chance and I smirk up at him as I climb out.

We walk into my building like how we walked out of the restaurant, with Zander's hand on the small of my back as we get to the elevator. The feeling between my thighs has not lessened since the park and I know I'm going to have to take care of it myself as soon as I close my front door.

The elevator doors open, and the throbbing between my legs heightens as I realize we have five floors up. I'm hyper aware how Zander is still holding onto me, his hand has now moved to my hip to hold me against him.

We step inside the elevator; I'm pressed against Zander's side. It feels like the doors take ages before they finally close. As soon as they do, I turn to Zander and I'm going to give in, I reach up, but he's ahead of me.

He has me pinned against the wall, and my arms are around his neck pulling his lips to mine again while he gives me exactly what I want. His lips are hungrier than they were at the park, both of us panting in each other's mouth like we can't get enough. I whimper when I feel his warm hand move quickly inside my belt line and under my soaked panties.

"I can't leave you like this," Zander says with lust straining his voice as his lips are on mine again.

His strong fingers start rubbing my clit. I moan loudly in his mouth as my orgasm is even closer now. I feel it building ten-times faster than it was before. Zander's expert fingers working me and I'm coming apart in his arms, he inserts a finger inside me while still working my clit and I explode in his arms. I moan into his mouth while he swallows the noise.

The elevator signals we are at my floor, and he removes his hand from my pants quickly, I watch him as he brings his finger into his mouth, and I feel like I'm going to fall apart again.

"You taste even better than I remember," He winks before leading me out of the elevator.

I'm so fucked for this man. I still can't breathe from what just happened in the elevator, no one has ever made me come so quickly, not even myself. I'm choosing to blame how close I was from the park.

We reach my door, and I turn to him, my back facing my door, "This doesn't change anything, I'm still not inviting you in tonight," I say even though my vagina is screaming at me to let him in and fuck me into next week.

"Of course, I wouldn't come in even if you asked," Zander smirks before putting his arms around my waist to bring me closer to him again.

If he kisses me again, I think all my strength will go away, not that I'll stop him. He presses his lips to my forehead before resting his forehead on mine, "I do hope we get to do this again; I want a chance again Mel. I know I don't deserve it; I know I don't deserve you in any way, but I want to prove myself to you. I just want a chance."

"I'm not promising anything, Zander, but I'm willing to give you a chance to prove yourself. Just so you know, one fuck up and I'm done. I can't be hurt by you again," My voice is shaking as I admit that last part to him.

"I never want to hurt you again Mel, and I'm willing to take anything you'll give to me." He says, and sounds relieved from my words even though I didn't promise anything, I know I'm not letting him go. Not yet.

"Then I'll talk to you later and maybe I'll see you again tomorrow if you're free," I say cautiously as I look up at him with a glimmer of hope in my eyes. I feel like if he agrees he really means what he's saying.

"I will be free any time for you, Mel Bell. Goodnight." He presses a quick kiss to my lips before turning and going toward the elevator again.

I unlock my door but watch him as he steps into the elevator and keep watching until the door shuts. Once he's out of sight I walk into my apartment, shut the door behind me and lean against it.

I am so beyond fucked. There's no way I get out of this without my heart getting hurt again, I just know it.

# 11

**21 Years ago**

I'm so excited, our parents all finally agreed for us to have a sleepover. So Jason, Amber, and Mel are going to come over to my house and spend the night.

I went with Nanna to the store earlier to get all our favorite foods. We are going to have pizza for dinner, and I picked out everyone's favorite candy.

Jason likes gummy worms, Amber likes lollipops, and Mel and I like M & Ms, she likes the peanut ones best, but I like the normal ones.

My dad and I put up our tent in the living room for us all to sleep in. Everyone is going to bring their own sleeping bags. I wanted to set it up in the backyard for us to pretend we are camping, but dad said no.

Everyone comes over and I show them the huge tent hoping they will be just as excited about it as I am, but Amber isn't.

"We all have to sleep on the floor?" She asks.

Amber is always picky about stuff and sometimes she can be annoying when she acts better than us, especially to Mel but I don't know if she notices or if she's too nice to say anything.

"Yeah, it's inside camping!" I tell her, "I wanted to go camping outside, but my dad wouldn't let us."

"Good, I wouldn't sleep outside because there's bugs and animals out there." She folds her arms.

"I'm going to find a bug and put it in your hair while you're sleeping," Jason says to her while he starts to laugh.

"No, you're not!" Amber screams.

She walks into the tent and puts her sleeping bag on the far-right side.

"I'm sleeping all the way over here and you're sleeping all the way over there." She points to the other side of the tent.

"You can't tell me what to do, it's Zander's house he gets to pick." Jason points to me.

"And I say Mel can pick." I say, since Mel hasn't said anything because I think she wants to stay out of any arguments. That's when I notice she gets shy like when I first met her, but really she's not shy at all.

"Why me?" She says, seeming like she's shocked I even said that.

"Because you'll be the fairest," I shrug.

"And because you like her," Amber says, rolling her eyes.

"That's not true, Amber! We are best friends," I argue.

"Okay stop fighting, Amber can be on that side, I'll be next to her, then Zander and Jason on the far side, and no one is putting bugs in anyone's hair while they sleep." Mel says, looking right at Jason.

I'm glad she didn't say anything about Amber saying I like her. I might a little bit, but she's my best friend and that's it.

The rest of the night everyone gets along for the most part. Amber still acts like a spoiled princess most of the time because it's "not her house and it's not how she would have it at home".

After watching a movie, we all get into the tent to go to

sleep for the night. My Nanna checks in to make sure we are all comfortable before turning off the light and going to her room down the hall.

I'm not really tired so I lay on my sleeping bag for a while in the silence. I'm not sure how long it is, but I look over and Jason is definitely asleep. I sit up to see that Amber is too, but as soon as I sit up so does Mel.

"Are you not tired?" She asks me.

"Nope, you?"

"Nope."

"Come on," I try to be careful as I push down my sleeping bag trying not to wake up Jason or Amber and Mel follows as we go toward my room.

I know I have a flashlight, so I find it before turning the lights off in my room again and turn on the flashlight.

"Let's play shadow puppets," I say quietly because I know if my dad or Nanna hears us, they will tell us to go back to bed.

"Okay!" She says as we both lay on my floor, and I turn the flashlight to shine on my ceiling.

We each move our hands in weird ways to make shapes on the ceiling, and have the figures fight or eat each other. We are laughing and have to remind each other to be quiet.

"We should have nicknames for each other," I say because I want us to have something special that Amber and Jason don't share because I think Mel is my best friend out of the four of us.

"Mel is my nickname, dummy, oh! That can be yours." She giggles, and I nudge her with my shoulder.

"But everyone calls you Mel, how about Mel Bell," I smile over at her and she's still laughing at her joke.

"A nickname is supposed to be shorter than your full name, that's longer."

"I like it, I'm going to call you Mel Bell!"

"What would yours be then Zan Bam?" I laugh at her trying to come up with something.

"If that's what you want it to be," I shrug.

"No, I don't like it, I just like calling you Zander, or dummy!" She smiles over at me.

"Well, I'm still calling you Mel Bell."

I look over at her to see her roll her eyes. That was when I was sure that I do like her and definitely more than just my best friend

# 12

**Present**

On my drive home I think about the night I just had. I really didn't expect to touch her, I genuinely didn't have any expectations but something about her draws me to her every time I'm close to her, I just can't help myself. I wasn't even going to kiss her on the swing, but I couldn't take it.

I wanted to go at her pace, but I have no self-control around her. Then how she started to grind against me, I just couldn't take it and I needed to hear her, I needed to give her what she wanted even after we were interrupted by the fucking cop.

I will be replaying that short elevator ride in my mind on repeat forever, especially since my dick is straining in my jeans and has been since she fell on top of me in the parking lot. I don't even think jacking off will help. I want her, but I'm really going to try and go at her pace, I don't want to ruin things with her, not this time.

I already feel bad that I'm not telling her everything, but I can't tell her what Trent and I do. I know that alone will ruin this, even if I'm technically not lying.

In all fairness we do sell, I just didn't tell her *what*. If she asked, I would've told her. I will tell her at some point, just not tonight. I'll tell her anything she wants to know; I'm not making the same mistake twice.

I get home and see that Trent's car is here, we haven't spoken much since we moved in. Not that we talk much about anything other than business lately anyway. I walk inside and see him sitting at the island with a drink in hand. I walk into the kitchen to grab some water.

"What have you been up to, little brother?" He asks, taking a sip of the dark liquid, which I assume is whiskey.

"Oh, fuck off with that shit, I'm bigger than you," I roll my eyes.

He always has to be condescending to me which is one of the many reasons I can't wait until I'm finally able to go do my own thing which I haven't even gotten to tell Mel about. I plan to be a tattoo artist. I noticed she has something on her wrist, but I couldn't tell what it was, I wonder if she has more.

"Whatever, what were you doing because I know it wasn't a run," he says like that's the only thing I could possibly ever do, and to him that's true. He doesn't care about anything outside of our "business".

"Nope, I was with a girl." I don't want to give him much info about Mel, she's mine and the less Trent knows the better.

"Damn, forty-eight hours back in the old stomping grounds and you've already found some pussy? Impressive, little brother."

"It's not like that, but don't waste your time worrying about me and my dick and tell me what you found out from Jason," I move the subject away from Mel and back to business.

Jason was our "in" to come here and start selling, we started before we fully moved here with him as our guy on the ground. He's involved with some guys I plan to stay far away from, but they needed product and we needed sellers. We hadn't talked much since we were kids, but he was someone that could help me get back to Portland, which is exactly what I wanted.

The "business" for us is drugs. Well, for Trent since he started before he roped me into this life which is a life I never wanted, but he pulled me in and made it impossible for me to leave.

I've been stashing money for years preparing for the day I tell him to fuck off, but it always gets pushed off. I really wanted my move to Portland to be alone but wasn't so lucky and now here we are.

Trent started small, selling weed to close friends, then connections were made, and it grew, which was when I reluctantly became involved. Then, weed became legalized and I thought we would be off the hook, but that just isn't how shit worked out for me.

Trent wiggled his way into the world of harder shit, which I was completely against getting involved in, but then suddenly I ended up with some product in my car when I got pulled over. One of the other reason it took me so long to come back to Portland. I had to spend some time locked up. I got lucky, it was only a year, but once I was out I really was limited on my options.

That's another thing I'm afraid to tell Mel, I don't know how she will take it, but I know it's another thing I will have to come clean about eventually if I want to have any sort of future with her.

"Things have been good before we got here, but they will need us on the ground to run product so we can increase sales," he says, finishing off his drink.

"Does that include you or is it just going to be me running product like it always is?"

I can't remember the last time Trent did any of the dirty work, he's like a fucking drug lord that sits on his throne of cash and cocaine while making his ants do all the work. I cut back a while ago on being on the ground for him, but he always has something for me to do and while I'm still getting my shit put together, I'm at his mercy. But I have my light at the end of the tunnel now, a real reason to get out.

"I might help out since you made me come here and build back up from the bottom when we had a good thing going in Phoenix, closer access, reliable buyers, and even more reliable runners."

He stands up and I think he's going to refill his whiskey, but he comes closer to me, acting like he's trying to start something we both know he won't finish. He's slightly shorter than me, and has some muscle, but is nothing on me. I always make sure I look as intimidating as possible because of this world. A gun is scary, but a big guy holding a gun is scarier.

"And I did all the work to make sure we aren't starting from the bottom here since it was my connection that started running and recruiting here," I remind him, and widen my stance, if he really wants to fight me, I will. It wouldn't be the first time, won't be the last.

After staring at me for a few seconds I'm about to take the choice away from him and punch him in his smug face just to see him bleed, but he backs off. He grabs the whiskey and refills his glass.

"You'll learn one day little brother all the shit I've done for you and for our business. You'll thank me," He downs the liquid in one gulp.

Doubt it. I'm going to get out, get an apprenticeship as a tattoo artist, open my own shop, and have people traveling from all over to get my art on their skin. All the while I will have Mel by my side and forget all about this bullshit life.

"You done with this useless pep talk or do you have

anything actually important you want to talk about?" I'm making my way out of the kitchen to head to my room.

I want to call Mel and hear her voice, but I figure that might be too much, but I want to text her.

"Yeah, tomorrow we have a shipment coming into the unit, I need you to go take inventory once it arrives and make sure the guys get their product to run."

"When?"

"I don't know, Zander, it gets there when it gets there, so as soon as I get the call, I need you to go."

"And you can't go inventory yourself because...?"

"Because you do what I ask you to do, and you get paid well for it. Plus, I don't question you about the pussy you get or make you share."

I don't even notice I'm squeezing the water bottle so tight that it breaks open until I feel the cold water on my hands. Trent just laughs as he starts to walk away.

"This one must be something if it has you pretending that water bottle is my neck, can't wait to meet her." He walks away.

I can't move because if I do I know it's going to be to punch him so hard he is out cold on the floor, and I don't think I would stop after that.

He could never make me share Mel, ever. I would break his neck if he got too close to her, safe to say I will do everything I can to make sure they never meet.

I go up to my room and lock the door behind me, I'm done with him. I'm so fucking done with him. The only bright spot for me is when I take my phone out of my pocket and see Mel texted me already.

> Mel: Thank you for tonight, I'm actually excited to see you again tomorrow.

I smile, me too, Mel Bell, I just have to figure out the shit with my brother first. I'm hoping the drop happens in the morning, which it usually does. Since they tend to drive all night because there's less traffic, then unload into the storage unit that's under a fake name in a town over in the early morning so no one else is there. I'll figure it out, I always do.

# 13

*Zander*

**10 Years Ago**

I've been back for three months. I feel like Mel and I have been able to regain our friendship we had before. I also think it's even better now that we are older.

We talk on the phone almost every day and even if we don't then we are texting. We meet up at our park multiple times a week. I've gone over to her house a couple times and have seen her dad, which can be rare since he works nights at the hospital. When he's not working, he's often sleeping. He was so happy to see me when we all had dinner one night he had off work.

The one thing I don't like is how often Mel complains about Mark. I've met him a couple times, and he's the definition of a prick. He's an entitled douche, but I'm keeping all my opinions to myself because I don't want Mel to think I'm sabotaging her relationship or something. I don't need to; Mark is doing that all on his own.

Mel has called me crying multiple times because of a fight

they had, or her being paranoid about something she sees of him on social media.

I'm always there for her. I'm always there to talk her down and comfort her. Even if she's not crying over him, she's complaining about him. I feel like I've heard more negatives about the guy than positives and every time I want to tell her to break up with him. I want to tell her that she's too good for him, but I stick to comforting her because she never asks for advice. I think she knows what I'll say.

It's the night before Thanksgiving which is widely known as the biggest party night, and Mel is stuck at home sick. She called me this morning and I could instantly tell she didn't feel well due to her raspy voice that I refuse to admit was sexy as fuck...but it was.

She didn't come to school today, and I'm heading to my car after my last class when she texts me.

> Mel: Will you come over pretty please?

She didn't even need to say please, if she wants me over then I will be there, but I also can't help to fuck with her a little.

> Zander: No way, you're sick! Keep your germs away from me!

> Mel: I'll tell them to stay away from you, please!

> Zander: As long as they listen, then I'll be over.

I was going over no matter what. I stop at the pharmacy first to bring her some cold medicine, her favorite flavor of Gatorade (orange), and her favorite peanut M&Ms.

When I get to her house, I park behind her car that I know is parked in the garage because she obviously isn't going anywhere.

She must have heard my car pull up because she's opening the front door for me. I grab the pharmacy bag and meet her at the door. She eyes the bag in my hand and looks at me skeptically.

"What's that?" Her raspy voice sends a chill straight to my groin. Fuck she does sound extra sexy like this.

"Poison. Let me in," She gives me just barely enough room to walk past her into her house.

My arm brushes against her as I walk by her. That damn surge of electricity I feel at the slightest touch throws me off like it always does, but I crave more. I'm like an addict, I want more of that feeling though I know it's not going to be good for me, and yet I keep coming back for more anyway.

"Cyanide?" She closes the front door as she turns to face me.

"Top shelf Cyanide, your favorite," I say as I pull out the orange Gatorade.

Mel smiles as she walks over to grab the Gatorade from me and takes a big sip right away.

"You know what I like," She winks and the mixture of that voice and that wink about sends me into a frenzy. I clench my jaw to distract myself from grabbing her and kissing her so hard neither of us can breathe.

"What else do you have in your bag of goodies?" She asks, taking me out of my thoughts.

She pulls out the cold medicine and makes a retching noise before throwing it on the couch. Then she pulls out the candy and looks at me in shock.

"I really hope you are just good at guessing and your memory isn't *that* good," She seems shocked.

I'm also not sure how to decipher what she's thinking because it seems like she doesn't want me to have actually remembered her favorite things.

"Clearly, it all was just a lucky guess," I shrug.

She looks at me like she knows that's not true, and there's a flicker of something in her eyes, but it's gone quickly. I'm pretty sure I imagined it because it almost looked like it could indicate something more than friends.

"Come on, let's watch a movie," She flops down on the couch and starts to turn on the TV to put something on.

I pick up the cold medicine she threw onto the couch and start to open it.

"I'll stay and watch a movie with you if you take this."

"You can't tell me what to do," She folds her arms across her chest and turns her head away.

"You're right, I can't," I say softly as I slowly start to walk toward her, starting opening the medicine, preparing to pour the right amount in the little cup. "But I can force you."

I straddle her lap, and I'm significantly bigger than her so she's instantly trapped under me, the blanket she threw over herself is between us as she starts thrashing trying to push me away.

"You can't make me! I won't take that demon juice!" She's yelling, her voice raspy and swatting me away as I try to hold her back with one hand, the other has the cup of medicine. "I'm going to cough on you and infect you with my germs!"

"I don't even care, you're going to take it so you can feel better."

I finally get both her wrists in one hand, and they feel so small compared to my large hand wrapped around her. I pin them above her head. I'm choosing to ignore the feelings stirring below my waistline.

"No! I don't want to feel better!" She keeps yelling and turning her head away from me.

"What's going on?" I hear her dad say, clearly irritated because he looks like he got woken up as he descends the stairs to the left.

"Dad! Zander is trying to make me take demon juice!" She yells and I can tell her voice is hoarse from the struggle.

"It's cold medicine Mr. James," I say simply, shrugging.

Instantly realizing how this position right now might look bad with me on top of her lap straddling her and holding her wrists above her head.

*I wish it was how it looks.*

"Melody, take the damn medicine so you can feel better, and I can go back to sleep before my shift tonight," he says, definitely annoyed, but more so with his daughter than me.

I smile to have him on my side, him being a nurse probably helps the situation.

"Ugh! Fine, but I need my hands free to do that," She gives me a pointed glare. I reluctantly release her wrists and she snaps the medicine from my hand.

I climb off her lap, settling into the couch next to her as I watch her down the medicine like a shot of alcohol while her dad goes back upstairs to his room. She dramatically gags and retches as she swallows the liquid before grabbing the Gatorade and taking a few big gulps.

"Was that so hard?" I ask sarcastically.

"Yes."

She's still pretending to pout, but I don't miss the slightest curve on her lips.

"So, what are we watching?" I lay my head back on the couch next to her as she throws her blanket over the both of us while we pick what to watch.

We settle on a stupid comedy because laughter is the best medicine for everything, at least that's Mel's reasoning. We are sitting on the couch, and probably closer than we should, but Mel doesn't say anything, and I won't dare move away unless she does.

As we are about to start our second movie, this time it's a horror movie Mel said she wanted to watch, Mel's dad comes downstairs again in slightly better spirits. Well, as good as it can be for him. He's a nice guy, just generally doesn't talk much.

"I'm heading to work, do you two need anything?" He asks, looking between the both of us, appearing genuinely curious.

"Nope," Mel says simply as she clicks on the movie.

"As long as Mel doesn't need to take any more meds, I think we are good, Mr. James," I catch the glare she gives me from the side.

Mel's dad, Dan, chuckles before waving us off and leaving through the garage. Once we hear the garage door close indicating he's gone Mel speaks again.

"Why is he so okay leaving me alone with you, but if Mark were here, he would make him leave?"

"Probably because I'm awesome and he knows it?" I pretend to be offended, like that is the real reason.

"I think you need a whole other couch to hold that ego of yours," She rolls her eyes.

"It's obviously because he's your boyfriend and I'm your friend and he's known me since I was like five."

"I guess, but you're still a guy, and we aren't five anymore."

"No, we definitely aren't."

There's something charged in the air around us, it feels thick and suffocating, but also has that same addicting feeling that makes me feel like I'm going to go insane if I don't get my fix. I don't know if Mel even notices or if it's just me.

We watch the movie in silence, aside from the little gasps Mel makes and I look over a couple times to see her trying to subtly hide her eyes under the blanket we are still sharing, I chuckle.

"You scared?" I finally ask which results in her jumping at my voice.

"No, I'm fine!" She straightens and pretends to not be fazed by the movie or the fear I just accidentally inflicted.

The sun has long set by the time the movie ends. Mel stretches her arms and legs out while still sitting on the couch. I can't help but notice how her chest protrudes as she arches her back and it pushes her tits out. Which I noticed as soon as I came over, she's not wearing a bra, and it's been hard not to focus on that when the blanket would fall beneath her chest and remind me.

Mel picks up her phone that she hadn't touched since I got to her house, and I get up to pick up the trash from her M&Ms and the empty Gatorade bottle to help clean up because I don't want her to have to deal with any of it while she's sick.

"Don't you want to go to any of the parties going on tonight? Biggest party night of the year, woo!" She says with fake enthusiasm so I can only assume she's looking at posts on social media about said parties.

"Nah, this is clearly the best party to be at tonight," I gesture around me to the empty, barely lit house as I take the garbage around to the kitchen.

I come back into the living room and Mel is still looking at her phone, scrolling.

"Seriously Zander, you don't have to stay with me," She shrugs, not looking at me and not sounding convincing.

"You got better plans?" I throw myself back onto the couch next to her and pull the blanket over myself again.

"Well, no, but you might."

"I don't," I look over to her and I want to say something, but I stop myself and say something else instead. "What's the next movie?"

Another movie down and I can tell Mel is getting tired, but she waves me off when I ask if she wants to go to bed.

"I'm not a loser, it's the weekend bitches!"

"Okay, but you're sick," I roll my eyes.

This woman is so stubborn. I love it.

She waves her hand around my face, dismissing me, as she pulls out her phone to look again. I'm wondering if she feels left out even though for these last few months, I've never really known her to go out much.

I chuckle at her and pull out my own phone to make sure my dad or Nanna haven't tried to get ahold of me since there's really no one else that would be checking in on me anyway.

"What the fuck?" I look over at Mel who is staring at the screen, clenching her jaw.

"What's wrong?"

"Mark said he was going to his buddy's house tonight, but I'm pretty sure he's at Amber's which he *distinctly* told me he wouldn't be going to," She's clutching her phone tightly and still not looking at me.

"Why do you think that?" I try not to smile at the possibility that Mark is being a lying tool bag and that maybe she might actually break up with him this time.

Mel holds out her phone that's replaying a video that looks like it's a fancy living room I have vague memories of as a kid, but it's decorated differently. Definitely rich. There's lots of people around so it's hard to make out any specific face, but I notice one in the back that looks like Mark from the little I've interacted with the asshole. I recognize his smug, shit eating grin.

"You're sure this is Amber's house?" I ask since I wouldn't know for sure, but I'm sure she's been there more recently than me.

"Well, she's the one who posted the stupid video so, yeah."

"You still follow her shit?"

"I like to spy," She shrugs.

Well okay then.

Mel looks like she's deep in thought before she finally turns to face me completely, "Go spy on him for me!"

"What? Why? Don't you have all the proof you need right there?"

I'm all for getting into some trouble, but I feel like this should be enough for her.

"I have proof that he lied, sure, but what if he's doing more? I'm fucking done, Zander, but I want to confront him."

"Then, we go together, and you confront him, you don't need me to spy."

"I want you to spy, see if he's doing more, then I will confront. Please."

I swear when she says please I will do anything for her, and that's not a good thing because I mean *anything*.

Mel runs up to her room to get changed from her pajama pants and t-shirt to some jeans and a sweater before she comes downstairs again. I wouldn't even guess she's sick, aside from the slight red tint to the end of her nose and when she talks it sounds like a raspy whisper. Even with all of that she's still beautiful, she always is.

We both get into my car; Mel asks if I remember how to get to Amber's house. I shake my head, so she has to give me a couple reminders until we make our way there. We hear the party down the street and there's no place for me to park. The street is covered in cars.

"You go in, and I'll drive around the block until I hear from you then we'll run," Mel says as she leans over the console to look out my window at the house as we slowly drive by.

I barely hear her because I'm distracted by how she's leaning almost completely into my lap and the scent of her hair, peaches, I think.

"Excuse me? You think you're going to drive my car while I go in to spy on *your* boyfriend?"

"Yeah, there's no place to park and I can't go in or it's not spying!"

"Do you even know how to drive a stick?" I raise my eyebrow at her, I know her little Honda is an automatic, and I'm protective of this car.

"*Yes,* I know how to drive a stick you jerk, pull over up here,"

She points to a spot in front of someone's house for me to get out.

We both get out of the car, and she rounds the front about to get in the driver seat, I grab her arm, that damn heat is there again. She looks at me with her mouth slightly open. She feels it too, I know she does.

"Please be careful, Mel, I'll be in and out within a few minutes."

She rolls her eyes, "Yes, Sir."

I will not acknowledge how those words made my cock twitch. I would say fuck this whole plan and shove her back into my car to fuck her senseless if I didn't already care for her so much. Why does she make me feel like this? It's hard to be a good friend and want more.

I smirk as she climbs in the driver's seat and instantly takes off quickly, little Mel Bell is more reckless than she lets on. I can't wipe the smile off my face until I'm approaching Amber's front door that is open while there's people everywhere.

I lift my hood over my head to hide myself a bit, though I'm sure the majority of these people are too drunk or high on something to notice me.

The music is blaring, voices are blending together and it's like pushing my way through a crowded sweat lodge. I'm taller than ninety-five percent of the people here so I'm just trying to navigate through the tops of people's heads, find my target, hopefully catch him in some deep shit, then leave.

Almost as if it's fate I see the bastard. He is *fucked up*. His eyes almost like they are closed, but he's laughing so loud, and I can hear his slurred speech from across the room. I can't even tell what he's talking about.

As I get closer, I see a girl sitting next to him. I'm not sure who she is, but I hardly know anyone around here. I was worried about him seeing me, but he's so fucked up he wouldn't recognize his right hand if it detached itself and walked up to him.

I step closer to try and understand anything he says, then I see him sling a heavy arm around the blonde next to him and pull her closer to him.

Got you, mother fucker.

I quickly take out my phone and take some pictures. I wait a little longer to see if he's going to do anything else, he brings the girl closer as he whispers in her ear, and she looks at him flirtatiously.

Then suddenly he pulls her in for a sloppy kiss. I take more pictures.

After that I turn away and walk out of the house before I catch him fuck this girl in front of everyone.

Mel is about to be heartbroken, and I feel bad about that. If I didn't want to get back to her I would have beat Mark's ass, but I'll let Mel deal with him first, then I can't promise he will walk away with his face intact if I see him again.

I get outside and appreciate the fresh air while I try to distance myself from this house as much as I can, especially because the noise level is so loud it has to be minutes before the cops come to bust the party. I see my car down the street so I pick up my speed to get to Mel as fast I can.

I reach the driver's door and open it so we can get back to our original spots.

"You know, you're not letting me be a very effective getaway driver," she says looking up at me annoyed.

My heart hurts that I'm about to see her cute annoyed face become something painful.

"I'm driving us back to your house," I keep my voice flat. She rolls her eyes and climbs over to the passenger seat while I climb in the car and speed off right away.

"So, what did you see?" She turns and asks me as soon as we are off Amber's street.

"Too much," I'm gripping the steering wheel so hard my knuckles are white and I'm imagining it's Mark's neck between my hands.

"Did you see Mark? What was he doing?" She asks, and I hear the nerves in her voice, she must notice my anger.

I toss my phone over to her, "See for yourself, Mel."

She unlocks the screen; she's instantly able to get to the photos. I hear her gasp and sniffle.

Fuck. I want to look at her, I want to take her in my arms and comfort her. Her house isn't too much farther so I speed to get us there in half the time.

"Are you fucking serious right now?" She says, not even really talking to me I don't think.

I see her typing something on my phone, "What are you doing?"

"I'm sending these to myself to send to him when I tell him to lose my fucking number."

She's angry. Good, she should be. I glance over and see some tears, but she mostly looks angry. My little Mel Bell is a fighter, and even though it's a shitty night for her I can't help the slight smile that spreads on my lips that I quickly wipe away.

We get to her house, she's been typing on her phone the remainder of the drive after she sent the pictures to herself. I park in her driveway, neither of us getting out right away, I turn to face her.

"Are you okay?" I ask, sincerely. I may hate the guy, but I want her happy no matter what.

She ignores my question. "What do you think?" She asks as she holds out her phone to show me the text, she typed out to accompany the pictures.

> Mel: We are fucking done. Don't talk to me. Don't look at me ever again. You're a piece of shit and I should have broken up with you way before this because you're a shit boyfriend, but I hope her pussy was worth it because if I ever hear from you again, I will cut your dick off and shove it up your ass.

"I'm all for the threat of violence, but is the last part necessary?" I ask, but when she shoots me daggers, I know I should've kept my mouth shut. "It's perfect."

She smiles and presses send.

"You coming inside?" She asks.

It takes me off guard a little bit, I really expected her to tell me to fuck off so she could either go inside to cry or scream in peace.

"You want me to?"

She nods, we both get out of the car to go inside. It's like once we walk through the door the anger she was holding onto is gone, and she's suddenly sobbing.

"I'm sorry, I really didn't want to cry," she says, and I hate that she's apologizing.

I quickly take her in my arms, wrapping her close to my chest while her tears come out stronger and her sobbing increases.

The electricity of having her this close to so much of me is intense. I'm warm and I just want to hold her tighter, longer, I don't want to let her go. She holds my shirt in her fists, holding herself to me as tight as she can while she cries. We stay like this for a while, just her crying and me trying to comfort her, whispering things in her hair.

"You deserve so much better."

"He's a piece of shit."

"You're the strongest person I know."

She doesn't say anything through her tears until I feel her

sobs have subsided a bit and she pulls away slightly, which makes me want to pull her close to me again, but I let her because this is about her, not me.

"Will you stay with me tonight? I really don't want to be all alone," She shuffles on her feet and isn't looking at me as she asks.

My heart flutters at her words. I know it's innocent and she just broke up with her fucking boyfriend for God's sake, but I can't help feeling happy that she doesn't want me to leave.

"What about when your dad gets home? You don't think he'll be mad we stayed the night together...alone?" I don't want to insinuate too much, but she gets what I'm saying.

"Zander, he came downstairs, and you were on top of me, pinning my hands up and he wasn't mad. We are fine."

It's true, plus it's not like anything is going to happen.

"Yeah, I'll stay, I'll let my dad know."

For the first time since we got back, Mel smiles, it's small but it's there. She goes upstairs to change back into her pajamas, and I text my dad to let him know I'm staying the night at Mel's and to not worry. He won't, he trusts me.

"You can come up here, you know?" Mel calls, and I think her voice is almost officially gone because I know she meant to yell what she said, but it was barely audible.

I head up the stairs, this is just two friends staying the night together. Not a big deal. I'll sleep on the floor, and nothing is going to happen, that's okay. I make sure I tell myself that repeatedly, so I make sure I don't do anything stupid.

I reach her room that's around the corner from the top of the stairs. Mel is climbing into her bed while I notice she's just in a t-shirt and panties.

Shit.

She gets into bed and is under the covers instantly, so I don't get to stare at her legs too long before they are out of view.

"You know you can take off your jacket and get comfortable," She chuckles lightly, but the sadness is still there.

She's sitting up in bed and turning on her TV.

I forgot that I'm still wearing my jacket and shoes, so I take them both off. I think I notice Mel glance once at me and take a sharp intake of breath as my jacket slides down my arms. I'm no body builder, but I have some muscle, especially my arms and she clearly notices. I see her shuffle around in the sheets and lay down while trying to focus on the TV.

"Is there somewhere I can get some extra blankets and pillows for the floor?" I ask.

"Oh, um, you don't have to sleep on the floor."

"What? You sure? I could also go downstairs and sleep on the couch, I'm not picky."

"Zander, I don't want to be alone, I want you here," She points to the empty spot next to her on the bed.

*Oh.*

"You sure? I don't want you to be uncomfortable, I know it's been a rough night and I…"

"Zander, just get in my bed."

I would say she doesn't have to tell me twice, but she did.

"Okay."

I climb into her bed, careful to not touch her because I don't want her to think I'm trying to take advantage of her or anything.

"You sleep in your jeans?" She asks, raising an eyebrow at me as I settle next to her, but with enough distance we aren't touching.

"Well, not usually."

"I said, you can get comfortable. Don't be weird." She goes back to looking at the tv and going through the channels.

I catch the smirk on her lips. She's not making it easy on me right now.

I sigh while undoing my belt before slipping off my jeans

and throwing them to the side of the bed so I'm just in my black briefs and *very* aware that she is in a similar state of undress as me.

I feel like I'm a virgin, all excited to be in my underwear with a girl.

Get your shit together, Zander.

I notice Mel is going through the same channels and still hasn't settled on something, I think she's nervous and thinking the same as I am, but too proud to admit it too.

She finally settles on something, and I'm instantly pulled in by what I'm hearing.

"Did you just put on some true crime shit?" I look over to her as I lean back on her headboard.

"Yeah, I have to listen about brutal murders to fall asleep," She shrugs, settling lower under the covers, facing me while she lays on her pillow.

"You are something else, Mel Bell."

She furrows her brows together and starts to bite on her bottom lip, "In a good or bad way?" She whispers.

I can hear the hurt behind her tone. She may be putting on a good face right now, but twenty minutes ago she was sobbing into my chest, and I need to remember that.

I scoot myself lower, so my head is resting on my pillow as I face her as well. I reach my hand up and tuck a piece of her hair behind her ear.

"In the best way."

A small smile shows on her lips, and I just watch her. I drop my hand and bring it back over to my side. Mel reaches over to turn off the lamp next to the bed, so the only light is from the TV.

We are silent for a few minutes just the sound of the story about some murder that I'm not listening to because I can't hear anything over my heartbeat.

"Zander," she says so softly I almost miss it.

"Yeah?"

"Will you hold me? Please?"

My eyes snap open to meet hers in the dark, she's staring right at me.

I won't deny her, so I reach my arms out and she scoots herself closer to me as I wrap my arms around her completely.

She buries her face in my chest like she did downstairs, but now she's not crying. She fists my shirt like she was before to hold me as close as she can.

Our bodies are completely pressed together and I'm painfully aware of the skin on her legs touching mine. Her chest against mine, rising and falling with our breathing. I can't think about how close our hips are because I'm already trying not to make her aware of my erection that is very present, but this is not the time for that to happen.

I hold her close to me, unable to fall asleep, but I finally feel her breathing slow down. The slightest snore coming from her due to her stuffy nose, and it's the cutest sound I've ever heard.

I pull her tighter to me, and finally close my eyes. I wish this didn't feel so perfect, but it does. I have no idea how I could ever let her go.

## 14

Mel

**Present**

I called Aylin as soon as I got back last night and let her know everything that happened. She said she was so happy it went well but reminded me to be careful again.

Yeah, yeah, I am.

I didn't sleep with him so that's a positive! I stayed strong, right?

Did I still let other things happen?

Yeah, but I'm only human, and being around Zander makes my brain break just a little bit.

After I get off the phone with Aylin I change into an oversize t-shirt and some boy short panties which is what I tend to sleep in every night because pants are a joke.

After brushing my teeth and washing my face I climb into bed, and I can't stop replaying the night in my head.

I smile at the memory of how his hands felt on me and briefly in me. God, everything feels so good with him. Just being around him feels good.

Okay, I'm *not* being careful. Zander has been back in my life for like twenty-four hours and I'm already stuck back in my old ways. I need to keep my strength; he hasn't gotten me back yet.

The memories continue until I fall asleep.

I wake up feeling more rested than I did yesterday, which is probably due to the lack of alcohol I had last night, but also could be because I'm excited about seeing Zander again today. I take my phone to see if he's reached out, and he sent me a text really early this morning at around five. It's now nine which is usually the time my internal alarm clock wakes me up.

> Zander: Good morning beautiful, do you want to come over to my house later and I'll make you dinner?

Go over? To his house? Yes. Obviously,

I'm curious about where he lives since I got next to no information on what he does other than "business with his stepbrother" and that they rented this place together.

Also, I need to get more information on that. I can tell he's holding back, and I understand him not wanting to tell me every single thing about himself the first time we see each other again. It just seemed a little weird. It makes me cautious with him since he's hid and lied about important information before.

> Mel: Good morning! That sounds great, tell me when and where.

I vow I'm going to get at least one story idea today, even if it doesn't go anywhere, I'm going to come up with something.

I go make myself my regular coffee while I wait for Zander to reply, though I'm not going to be someone that waits by the phone for him. I've been there and I'm not doing it again.

I take my coffee, wrap a blanket around myself as I sit on the loveseat and read a bit. I hear my phone go off, but I'm not going to acknowledge it. I waited ten years for him to come back. He can wait a few minutes.

I finish a couple chapters and my coffee, so after I take my mug to the sink to clean it out, I check my phone. Zander sends me his address and says he can't wait to see me at five.

> Mel: Seems a little early for dinner, grandpa.

> Zander: I would ask you to come over now if I weren't dealing with some work shit, but that's the soonest I know I'll be done.

I'm tempted to ask more, but I'll keep the actual conversations to in person because that only seems fair.

Though, I do wonder what work shit he's dealing with. Especially on a Sunday. I guess selling stuff isn't limited to the weekdays.

I change into some leggings and a sweatshirt to be comfortable as I sit at my desk, and open up the blank word document I left on Friday that I haven't touched since.

I decide I am going to go with Zander's idea and try something mysterious. I start writing any idea I can think of as a mystery, some with crime, some with secrets, just anything that comes to me, good or bad. I fall into my thoughts and let it all fall onto the keyboard and into the screen. I'll look back later and narrow some things down.

Hours go by that I don't even notice, which is good, this is a good sign I haven't completely lost my creativity. Even if none of these little mysteries go anywhere, at least I wrote something, and maybe this can spring me back into action before I have to start freelancing or looking for an actual job....gross.

I feel like my confidence got boosted by Zander thinking I'm some "famous author". It feels good to know that he thinks that, though I want it to be true.

Finally, I get off my computer when I feel like my head may

explode from all the different thoughts I had swirling around my head all day. None of the ideas stood out to me like crazy, but it's a place to start, and I tend to like my ideas better after I've let them sit anyway.

Zander's house is thirty minutes away from my apartment when I look it up. It looks like it's in the middle of the forest. I really do watch too much true crime because my thoughts always go to getting murdered, but I'm still going to go.

I put on some jeans and a simple black t-shirt. I bring a light jacket just because I know it will be colder when I leave later tonight, definitely not in the morning because I will *not* have sex with him. Definitely not.

As I make the drive through town and toward the more forested areas, I know I was right about him living in the middle of the forest, at least it seems that way. Though this is Oregon so you can drive fifteen minutes away from town and feel like you're in the middle of the forest.

I pull up to the house and it's bigger than I expected. The outside resembles a mix between a cabin and a modern angular house with windows taking up almost the entire front. It looks modern, almost too modern to be where it is, but I like it.

As I get closer I can see into the living room, and I see the open floor plan into the kitchen where Zander looks like he's actually cooking. It makes me smile to see him like this, especially since he can't see me watching him yet.

It doesn't take long before he looks up and out as I pull up to park next to his black sports car. My gray Subaru Crosstrek isn't a bad car by any means, I just bought it two years ago, but next to his sleek Porsche it looks like a piece of shit. I see Zander smile as he leaves the kitchen and appears at the front door to greet me.

He's smiling as he leans against the open doorway. He's wearing a white t-shirt that hugs his muscled body and sweatpants that hang low on his hips. I realize I'm just now seeing him without long sleeves on and his left arm is covered in a black and white tattoos, while his right arm has something on the top of his upper arm that disappears under his sleeve, possibly a half sleeve or the start to another one.

I'm currently trying not to drool over this man's clearly sculpted body, slightly disheveled hair and bright eyes that are focused on me, along with the smile that makes his whole face light up and my legs feel like they may give out from underneath me.

"Hey, Mel Bell," he says as I reach the door, and he softly wraps his arms around my waist while placing a light kiss against my forehead.

"You make me feel like I overdressed," I say as casually as I can while I gesture to his sweatpants. I should've opted for leggings. I really do hate pants.

"You're perfect," he pulls back, but doesn't let go of my waist. I feel my cheeks getting warmer and have to look away so he doesn't see.

He drops his hold on me, and I miss the warmth and the electricity his touch brings, but I follow him inside, examining my surroundings.

The house is big, but not a mansion. There are stairs leading up to a second floor in front of the front door, to the right is a bigger living room than the little, I guess, family room I saw through the windows that leads into the kitchen.

I meet Zander's gaze again after scanning my surroundings. He doesn't look like he ever looked away from me. His eyes are fixed on me, and the look is curious, but there's also fire in his beautiful eyes that makes me weak.

I need to put some distance between us, or some sort of distraction or I'm not even going to make it to dinner without jumping on him, I just won't be able to handle it.

No, Mel, you're stronger than this. I've never been so out of control around a guy before, I don't know what it is about Zander that makes me feel like this and have uncontrollable thoughts, but he does.

"So, is your brother here?" It's the first non-sexual thought I can think of to say, and I know if he is here that nothing will happen anyway and I'll be safe.

"No, he had to take a trip back to Phoenix to deal with some business stuff there," He shrugs, and finally breaks his gaze.

I notice he tenses up at the mention of his brother and I feel like there's more to this than I know.

Zander walks back into the kitchen with me close behind as I sit at the island opposite to where he looks like he's finishing up the food, he takes something out of the oven and pours what looks like some sort of sauce from the stove into the dish fresh out of the oven. It looks like some sort of bake, and it smells amazing.

"Are you ever going to tell me about this elusive 'business' you and your brother are a part of?" I raise my eyebrows at him.

I'm really nosy and I let it slide last night because I didn't want to push for too much information right away, but I really want to know more.

"'Elusive business'? Mel the author using all these fancy words," He jokes, a chuckle coming from him which makes me smirk a bit.

He's avoiding the question, and this makes my curiosity peak more.

"Avoidance does not bode well, Mr. Wells," I narrow my eyes at him.

I'm going to call him out on his shit this time. He wanted me to give him another chance and I am, though he has to earn me back.

He turns back around, leaning on the island across from me, drawing in my eyes to his own again. My heart thumping like crazy again, it just started to calm down once he turned around I feel like I didn't even get a chance to recover.

"You're right, I'm going to tell you tonight which is why I wanted you to come over. I just ask that you hear me out completely before you decide to run away."

That doesn't sound good.

"Why would I run away?"

He smirks, "Call it a hunch. Let's eat first and then we can talk more about it."

I try to push through and not dwell on what he said too much. Why the fuck would I run away? This has to be bad.

We sit in the little family room next to each other as we eat. I try to forget about what he said and just enjoy his company as it is right now. We joke, we reminisce a bit, save for the times we were naked together. Neither of us have brought up that particular part of our history yet.

I'm thankful for how comfortable he makes me feel, we are just like old friends that have never spent any time apart. We laugh so hard when he reminds me of the time, we scared our parents so bad from sneaking off to our park, and they literally called in a search party without us even realizing it. It shouldn't be as funny as it was, but in the eyes of a seven-year-old who had no idea what we did wrong, looking back is hilarious.

Once we are done eating Zander takes our plates back to the sink. He's on his second glass of whiskey, while I'm finishing my third glass of wine because I'm still nervous and whenever I feel the blush rise to my cheeks, I take big sips.

I follow him into the kitchen again and take up the seat I had earlier at the island while I watch his back as he cleans the dishes. I see his very muscular back as he scrubs. I watch his muscles flex and I'm wishing he was doing this particular chore without that damn shirt on.

I bring my thoughts back to what he said earlier and decide

to push forward. If it's really that bad, then I know it will help my dirty mind from its wandering thoughts.

"Okay, it's time. Give me your deep dark secrets, Zander," I lean against the island which I know is pushing out my tits, but I want to tease him a bit. Maybe then he will be more likely to share what he's so afraid to tell me. Plus, then I'm at the advantage since I feel like I'm at a severe disadvantage with him most of the time.

He sighs, turns around and leans against the counter as he holds onto the sides next to him making his arms bulge under the sleeves. I have to force my eyes up to his face, which doesn't help my arousal either way. This man is the walking definition of "everything Mel James finds hot" and it's a problem. I'm going to ask about his tattoos at some point, they look similar to some of the art I saw on his Instagram, and I wonder if it's something he designed.

"Please promise me you will hear me out completely before making any sort of decision about who I am now," he pleads quietly as he looks at the floor.

I sense something sad in his voice, possibly shame.

I shouldn't, but I get out of my seat and go over to where Zander is standing. He doesn't look up until I'm standing in front of him, looking up to get his eyes back on me, which he does. I slowly wrap my arms around his middle, subtly feeling the hard muscle underneath the soft fabric as I lock my arms around him, pressing myself against him.

"I promise."

I lift my toes to press a soft kiss on his lips. I shouldn't, but I just can't help but want to comfort him and make him feel comfortable to tell me this thing that is clearly bothering him.

I also expect him to deepen our kiss, but he doesn't. He keeps it soft before backing me against the island and lifting me effortlessly on top of it. Sitting on the island I'm almost face to face with him.

At least now I'm not needing to strain my neck to meet his eyes. He stands in front of me, his hands on the island essentially caging me in, I would have to slide down his body to jump down. Or fly across the island to where I was sitting before. I'm planted right where I am, at his mercy while I hear him out. Zander looks right into my eyes as he tells me what he's so worried that I'll run away from.

"We moved back to Phoenix after we left Portland. I finished my senior year which was an extremely rough year for me. I was planning on moving back here right away. As soon as I graduated, I was going to get a job here, the shittiest apartment I could find, hope you would still be here and mostly just figure out my life. Once I graduated, as I was looking for jobs out here my Nanna got really sick, her cancer came back. The access to her treatment was so close in Phoenix so even though my dad had to move we knew Nanna would struggle. We didn't want to figure out different doctors for her, so I promised to stay." Zander's struggling through this part of his story, and I'm not sure what this has to do with his business, but I let him talk.

I lightly put my hand on his, rubbing my fingers along his knuckles.

"My dad found someone in Phoenix and remarried pretty quickly. She had a son a few years older than me who was a real asshole, and I don't even know why. I never did anything to him, but we were always at each other's throats. My dad and his new wife moved, but for some reason they let Trent stay with me and Nanna which I was not happy about. Nanna ended up doing well with her treatments and hung on for a few years before she finally passed away. I was by her side the whole time so even though Trent and I had fights and did not get along I focused on taking care of Nanna."

Now, I really don't know where this story is going, him and Trent hate each other yet they are here now?

What?

I think Zander sees the question on my face as he continues.

"After Nanna died, I just needed someone in my corner. Trent and I were able to put aside some of our differences enough to not fight every time we were in a room together. He was trying to get me to join his business which I really had no interest in joining at all. I discovered my love for art and had my eyes set on becoming a tattoo artist. I just want to create pieces people love so much they want on their body. While my dad was okay supporting me while I took care of my Nanna, after she passed, he wanted me on my own to figure out my life without his support. This led to me making some bad decisions, giving me no choice, but to ask Trent for help."

It is so hard to not ask questions as he goes on because everything he says triggers more questions. I just continue to run my fingers along his knuckles, both to soothe him and myself.

"I didn't want to get involved, I really didn't. I swore it would only be a couple years, I would get enough money to start the process of tattooing, find an apprenticeship and forget Trent and all his bullshit. It was like once he had his claws in me, I couldn't escape. Every time I would think I was close, there's another reason to stay. Which is why I was stuck in Phoenix for so long.

"*Finally*, I was ready to leave and tell Trent he could shove it. I was ready for the fight, for everything. I was going to move back here. Then Trent said he was coming with me and the only way I was going to convince him to let me move was if we expanded the business up here, and once I had my distance I would tell him to fuck off. But he came to make sure things continued as they should."

I can feel his anger, his resentment, his everything. He's stuck. He's stuck doing this thing he doesn't want to be involved in, and he doesn't know what to do.

His head drops a bit and I take the opening to ask what he still hasn't said.

"What is the business, Zander?"

His eyes snap up to me, he sighs and hesitates before looking directly into my eyes, his apology already in them, I can see it.

"The business is drugs, Mel, we deal drugs and it's bad. It's everything, every bad, horrible, addicting, toxic piece of shit. We deal with it all. I got out of the groundwork for a while, more like Trent's assistant, doing his dirty work. But being back here, he has me doing more of the old shit that puts me in more danger of getting caught and going ba...going to jail."

My heart drops, he's a drug dealer?

I look around, half expecting the FBI to break down the door and raid the house right now. I can't go to jail; I don't know what to think. He's breaking the law daily. This house is paid for with drug money.

The air is thick, and I feel like I can't get a deep breath in. We are silent as I notice Zander is watching me, gauging my reaction. Waiting for me to say something, anything.

"I don't understand, you're joking, right? This is just a prank you're going to say 'gotcha!' And say you actually sell windows or something, right?" I finally squeak the words out.

He's joking, he has to. It's Zander, he's not a drug dealer.

"No, Mel, I'm serious and I promise you I wouldn't be doing it if I had a choice, I'm doing everything I can to get out. *You give me more of a reason to get out because I don't want you anywhere near this life. I want you safe and away from any danger.*" He's leaning closer into me, making me feel more trapped on this counter. I can't get away from him, but I don't even know yet if I want to.

"I don't get how you don't have a choice? You have money now, tell Trent to fuck off and get away from him," Seems simple to me.

"You don't think I tried? Back in the beginning I tried so many times before I was so deeply involved, but Trent always has a way to make me stay. Blackmail, people threatening to kill me, it depends on his mood which threat he wants to use. I have to have something on him and money he doesn't know about which I have some, but most of what I have he knows about since he's in charge of everything. Including my life."

I guess I just don't understand because I'm not involved in something like this and have never been one to let anyone be in charge of my life. My parents, mostly my dad, raised me to be independent and so I knew I would never be able to have a job with a normal boss which led me down the writer path.

Zander is staring at me. I can tell he's waiting for more of a reaction from me. I wish I could give a good reason as to why I'm not terrified and running out of here right now. I should be, I should be terrified, running for the hills and not looking back no matter how hot Zander is, not even thinking about our history.

This is a lot.

But I'm not even scared. He makes me comfortable. He makes me feel safe, even though common sense tells me I'm probably not safe at all in this house.

"How much danger am I in right now just being here?"

I wonder how much drugs are in this house with us? Are there going to be people coming here trying to rob him? Kill him? The reality is slowly settling in.

"There's no drugs in this house, we don't keep them here. No one knows where we live, we do things with safety in mind because Trent is beyond paranoid about people coming after him. And I told you before I wouldn't let anything happen to you, so with me, you're safe."

His words bring me some comfort. I just can't figure out why I'm not trying to run and never look back.

"You wouldn't let anything happen to me? Ever? That's a big

promise to make in a world full of surprises," I drop my voice so I'm almost whispering.

I lean closer to him on instinct like an invisible rope pulling me closer. Why am I not afraid? I don't know what any of this says about me, but his words have just drawn me closer when they should've pushed me further.

"I never said I promised nothing would happen to you, but I will do everything I can to ensure your safety Mel, and *that* is a promise." Zander is leaning closer to me now, almost like he feels the same invisible pull as I do.

"Scared?" He asks, his voice has gotten impossibly deeper it almost sounded like a growl as he continues to lean into me.

He's between my legs, and I feel him against my center, pressing every part of our bodies closer and I want it.

"Of you?" I breathe out but keep our closeness.

"Of all of this."

"Yes."

I crash my lips onto his.

I don't know why.

I am scared of him.

I'm scared of how I'm feeling, scared of how easily he was able to come into my life and how easily I've let him.

I'm scared of what he told me.

I'm scared he still hasn't told me everything.

I'm scared that we will be in danger.

I'm scared of him breaking my heart again.

I'm scared of everything that's happening.

Even knowing all of that I kiss him hard. His hand is on my back, pulling me closer against him so we are completely pressed together. His other hand is in my hair, pulling my head back to deepen our kiss. His tongue is against mine, like we are both desperate for the other one, wanting more, wanting everything. I never want to stop.

I want to go further, I want more, but I pull away from his

lips, breathless. He looks at me with fear in his eyes, but he doesn't let go of the hold he has on me. He looks afraid that I may say I'm leaving, like that was a goodbye kiss, but that's not what it was.

That was a warning. A silent one. I'm giving him my trust, and if he breaks it, he loses me. I just hope he understands.

## 15

**Present**

I had no idea what I expected when I invited Mel over today.

I just know that as soon as Trent told me he was going back to Phoenix for the night this would be my one chance to take her to my house since I won't dare bring her here while Trent is within the state.

I knew I was going to tell her the truth, I knew I had to before anything else continued because I wasn't going to hide this from her like I hid having to leave before.

She did what I asked. She listened to my complete explanation, and she still didn't run. Little Mel Bell has a fire in her, a recklessness in her I know I've seen before, but I don't even think she realizes it. She might be scared-terrified even, but she's willing to face those fears.

She makes me feel like I'm on fire, and this fire pushes me to be better. This pushes me to really get out of this life and get away from Trent. It's not going to be easy, but I'm going to do it.

Then she kissed me, and I wasn't sure if she was doing it for the last time before she got up and ran, or if she was telling me, it's okay, she's truly giving me a chance.

God, I wanted to push that kiss further. I wanted to lay her back on this island and promise her so many things against her perfect pussy that I'm sure is already soaked under her damn jeans. It's hard for me to hide how I'm feeling in my damn sweats, but she pretends not to notice.

"Come on, do you still love s'mores?" I ask as I look at her swollen lips from our kiss.

I want to bite her bottom lip so bad and just pull her to me again, but I stop myself.

"Duh, who doesn't?" She smiles.

I take her hand and help her hop down from the island so she's back to her normal height where her head doesn't even reach my shoulder. We go out into the backyard that opens up to acres of forest. We have a fire pit that I start to light as she settles on the bench, bringing her legs up in front of her and holding them against her chest.

"Are you cold?" I ask, even though it's technically spring it is a little cold out here.

"No, I'm fine," She clearly lies, watching the fire start to spark to life.

I give her a questioning look before going back inside to grab the marshmallows, roasting sticks, chocolate and graham crackers. I swing by the living room and grab a big blanket too. She's always been stubborn, and I can tell she's cold.

I come back outside, she eyes the blanket in my hand and narrows her eyes at me.

"I said I'm fine, Zander."

"I heard you, maybe this is for me,"

I settle on the bench next to her, with the blanket across my lap as I open the packages, and hand her a marshmallow and roasting stick.

She starts roasting her marshmallow, keeping a good distance away from the flames to not burn it, just enough to get the perfect light brown shade. I watch her as she intently focuses on her task.

Once it's up to her standard, she brings it between the crackers in her lap with chocolate on one side. She smashes it together and before taking a bite she looks over at me.

"What?"

"I just can't believe you're here," I say simply.

I really can't.

I never thought I would actually have her near me again and I'm not letting her go easily now that I do.

"I'm about to stuff food in my mouth, and that's what you're thinking?" She looks like she doesn't believe me.

"I'm also thinking I want to steal that s'more from you, but I was trying to be nice."

She drops her jaw, and holds the treat away from me, "No way, make your own."

I can't help it, I crowd her space, "Come on, you can share with me."

"No! Make your own!"

I am leaning over her trying to take it from her, she's pushing me away, I finally get close and take a big bite out of her creation. She may be onto something with the slightly browned marshmallow. I'm someone that burns mine though, not usually by choice.

"Ugh, you're so annoying," She looks at the bite I took and looks at me through narrowed eyes.

She looks between me, and the now half eaten treat before grabbing the blanket from my lap and throwing it over herself. "Hah!"

"I brought that out here for you anyway, so *hah!*" I counter and she rolls her eyes before finally taking a bite herself.

I make my own s'more, trying to copy what she did, but as

usual I end up burning the marshmallow so mine doesn't turn out as good as hers. I sigh, putting it together anyway.

"Want help?" She asks, a joking condescending tone to her voice.

"Nope, I'm going to accept my failure," I take a bite, and of course it's still good, just not as good as hers.

She chuckles as she cuddles herself tighter under the blanket, the fire continuing to grow.

Once I finish my s'more, Mel looks over at me, and scoots herself closer on the small bench that didn't have too much space between us anyway, throwing the large blanket over both of us. I put my arm around her shoulders to pull her closer to me. She cuddles close into my chest, resting her head against me, her hand on my thigh. I'm painfully aware how close she is to my dick, and it reacts already growing hard beneath my sweats. I try not to show how she's affecting me.

"This reminds me of that time you were sick, when I came over and we watched a bunch of movies and you refused to take your medicine," I say into her hair as I laugh at the memory.

"Oh God, do not remind me of that day," She ducks under the blanket, raising it above her head to hide. "I should not have asked you to go spy on Mark at that party."

"Why not?" I pull the blanket down so she can't keep hiding under it.

"It was stupid, I should've broken up with him long before that."

"I don't disagree with you there, but I was pretty happy with how the night turned out."

"Yeah, the end of it turned out okay," She turns to look up at me, a small smile playing on her lips.

"Did your dad say anything to you the next day by the way?" Even though things progressed with us after that night we never really talked about it.

I don't know why, we just focused on making new memories together and that night never came up between us again, which was okay considering all the nights that surpassed that one.

"Oh, nothing, he asked if he should expect to see you around the house more now." She shrugged like it's not a big deal.

"And what did you say?"

"I told him yeah, I think you'll be around a bit more."

My heart pounds in my chest to know she said that just the next day. It took almost another month for anything to happen between us right before Christmas. Then, the famous New Year's party I know we both remember vividly.

"What about now?" I ask, looking down at her cuddled up against me. I feel so content with her like this.

"What do you mean?" She looks up at me, confused, sitting up a bit more to look directly at me, the blanket falling off her shoulder.

"Am I going to be around a bit more?" I smirk.

After a beat of silence, she finally says, "Yeah, I think you might be."

I can't stop myself. I reach out, tracing my knuckle along her jaw before moving my hand into her hair, tangling my fingers through it, and pulling her lips to mine.

She melts into our kiss immediately, and I deepen the kiss, teasing my tongue in between her lips. She lets me in, I feel her sigh. I pull her bottom lip gently with my teeth, turning her sigh into a moan. I tighten my grip on her hair, and she throws her leg over my lap so she's straddling me. I adjust our position so I'm sitting up straighter and can hold her against me.

She moves her hips against my obviously hard cock thanks to the sweatpants that don't hide anything. I feel her trying to gain the friction as she rubs herself against me. I encourage her movement with my hand on her hip and my other in her hair.

We kiss fiercely, hungry for each other and desperate like

we won't survive with the other's mouth. I feel her movements begin to increase. I want her to get there, but not like this. I want to really feel her.

I lift her up and lay her down on her back on the bench. She gasps at the surprise movement, but I keep kissing her. I move my lips to her neck, nipping and licking as I unbutton and unzip her jeans. I slip my hand under her waistband and into her soaked panties. I run my finger along her seam, and she arches her back, pressing her tits into my chest while she moans.

I take this as her telling me to continue. I raise myself above her, to look into her hooded, lust filled eyes. The desire in them prevents me from stopping even if I wanted to. I move myself down her body to pull off her pants and take her drenched panties with them.

"Zander! What if someone sees us, we are outside."

She finally questions what I'm doing once her pants are almost completely off her legs.

"No one is coming back here, Mel, but I'll stop if you want me to?" I raise my eyebrow at her as I drape her pants over the side of the bench.

I start to lower my mouth to her glistening pussy, my mouth waters in anticipation.

She shakes her head, "No, I don't want you to stop."

I don't give her a chance to say more as I bring my mouth to her clit. She lets out a loud moan that just makes me keep going. I suck her clit into my mouth and suck hard.

Her hands reach down and wrap her fingers in my hair. I continue to flick my tongue against her clit while I bring two fingers to her opening and push them inside. She yelps, and pulls tighter on my hair, pushing me into her.

"Zander," She moans, and I look up to see her head thrown back, her back arched and I groan against her sending the vibrations through her body.

I continue to flick my tongue against her and move my fingers in and out of her opening. I then remove my fingers, replacing my tongue where they were, and spearing her with my tongue before licking up to her clit.

Her taste will be my downfall, I can be here forever, hearing her moans, yelps, and whimpers as I continue to taste her. I'm already addicted to this woman, and I know there's no going back.

Her grip on my hair tightens again, I can tell she's getting close. I go back to focusing on her clit with my tongue while my fingers enter her again, I curl them up to hit a sensitive spot inside. She responds by bucking against my face. I use my free hand to push her hips down.

"You taste like fucking perfection, Mel," I growl into her.

"Zander!" She yells out as she comes. I continue to lick her through her orgasm, and once she's finished, I rise back up to her lips.

My cock is hard as a fucking brick, throbbing and begging to get inside her, but I'm not going to push her farther than she wants to go, no matter how desperate I am to feel her come around my dick.

I kiss her again, she licks my mouth, tasting herself, and I grind my dick against her exposed center, and she groans into my mouth. I can only assume it's from the post orgasm, her taste on my tongue, and the feeling of me against her like this. I feel her bring her hips against me, and her hand reaches down to grab me through my pants. I groan into her mouth and as I grind down harder against her.

A breeze goes by, and honestly, I forgot we were outside for a second. Reluctantly, I pull away from her mouth and look down at her appreciating the view underneath me. Her shirt has ridden up to expose most of her stomach, her tits way too covered by both the shirt and her bra, they will get my full attention next, I swear it. Her lips are red, swollen, and parted as she pants. Her long hair spilling over the bench.

"We should go inside," I say, my voice huskier than it normally is due to the strain I'm feeling.

She nods and smirks, "I think I'll need my pants."

"You sure about that?"

The corner of my lips turning, but I hand her pants back as we both stand up. I adjust my dick, so it isn't completely tenting my pants. She notices the movement and I see her lips curl up slightly.

It's disappointing to see her pull on her pants, and adjust her shirt. I'm not sure if she's going to let anything else happen tonight, but that's okay.

We have time.

I grab the blanket and food as we walk back inside letting the little fire go out on its own.

I set everything on the island while Mel asks where the bathroom is. I let her know it's around the stairs past the living room down the hall before the guest bedroom. I watch as she walks away, appreciating the view of her full ass as she goes.

I hope she's not going in there to talk some sense into herself to run while she still can. No, little Mel Bell, I have you now.

# 16

**10 Years Ago**

> Mel: Whatcha doing?

It's almost midnight and I can't sleep.

School just got let out for winter break today, and to say the last couple weeks have been rough would be an understatement. Mark still tries to talk to me, except when he's talking to shit to his friends which I just roll my eyes at as I walk the other way.

Then, he's texting me that night begging for another chance.

Zander has been there for me this whole time. Every time I feel like I'm being judged or talked about for breaking up with Mark for "no reason" Zander is there for me, making me laugh which comes rarely.

I knew Mark was a piece of shit for a while, but it hurt to see the truth so clearly. I know I do deserve better.

I hate to admit that I think that "better" might be Zander.

He hasn't tried anything, I secretly hoped he would that

night when I asked him to hold me. It almost made me want him more that he didn't take advantage of me being sad and heart broken. I know it was smarter to not do anything that night.

I'm also starting to wonder if maybe Zander does only see me as a friend. I feel like we flirt, at least I am, and he seems to reciprocate, but he hasn't tried anything.

Nothing at all.

Sometimes I catch a lingering look, or there's a graze of some sort, but that's it. He's coming over more lately and my dad seems happy to have him around, often talking about various topics I don't care about, usually sports or cars.

My phone goes off. I see he replied, so either I'm not the only one who can't sleep, or my text woke him up.

> Zander: Laying in bed staring at the ceiling, you?

> Mel: Same. Our park?

This isn't the first time I've texted or called him in the middle of the night.

Sleep has been harder to come by lately for some reason. I don't think it's from sadness, I think some of it has to do with my conflicted feelings about Zander and if he feels the same. I end up lying in bed thinking of different scenarios.

Sometimes I even debate confronting him about it, what would happen? I always chicken out in reality, which sucks.

> Zander: See you in 15.

Yes. I hop out of bed, and don't worry about being quiet since my dad's working yet again.

I pull on some thick fleece leggings since it's freezing outside, a long sleeve sweater and heavy jacket. I opt for Uggs for the warmth. I'm not going for cute in this look. I've done cute and Zander hasn't tried anything no matter what I wear so it doesn't seem like it matters.

I get into my car and think about how Zander and I used to meet at the park when we were like eight and nine. I think about how we would walk there and stay until almost sundown. That's when we would go our separate ways home.

I smile at the memories. I wonder how our lives would've been if he never had to leave in the first place, and is this our second chance? Maybe he won't have to move away again, and we have some sort of future together.

I shake my head at my thoughts. I don't even know if he feels anything more than friendship for me, I'm getting ahead of myself.

I drive the short distance to the park and see Zander's car already parked. I pull up next to him as he steps out of the driver's seat, leaning against the door.

I step out of my own car as I eye him up and down. It's not fair for him to be this good looking. I feel inferior in my bundled clothes and hair I didn't even brush.

I don't doubt he looks this good without any effort since his hair isn't styled in any way, and he's just wearing a hoodie with jeans.

"Trouble sleeping?" He asks after I shut my door behind me.

"Yeah, I guess. What's your excuse?"

"Same," He shrugs as he walks over to me. "I have an idea."

He grabs my hand, the comforting warmth is not new, it happens every time he touches me. I never want the feeling to go away. He's pulling me away from the playground part of the park toward the grass.

"What are you doing?" I ask because we always go to the swings.

"Switching it up tonight," He looks back at me and smiles.

Heat takes over my cheeks and I let him pull me along until we are in the middle of the grass field, which I'm pretty sure is used for little kid's soccer games.

Zander sits right in the grass, and I watch him, twisting my face in concern.

"What's that look for?" He asks from the ground looking up at me, even though he's so tall his head is level with my hips.

"Isn't it wet?" I point to the grass.

It's the winter in Oregon, everything is wet all the time.

"Either you sit next to me, or you sit in my lap," He says seriously.

I take my bottom lip between my teeth thinking about the options. I sigh before sitting on the grass next to him. I was right. It is wet.

"My ass is going to be soaked," I say, annoyed.

"You'll live, lay down." Zander says as he leans back so he's on his back on the freezing grass.

"You're insane, no way!"

"Mel, I'm serious, I will make you lay down if I have to."

"Do it, you won't."

Zander smirks before grabbing me quickly before I have the chance to get away, he pulls me down next to him so I'm in his arms, forced to lay flat on the ground right against him.

I gasp at the movement and yelp as the cold hits my back. He holds me tightly, so I don't have a chance to get away.

"See, not so bad," I hear the humor in his voice.

"Zander, it's freezing what the fuck are we doing?" I ask, arching my head to look up at his face.

"Sh, just lay here in silence for a minute, look at the stars."

I roll my eyes before looking up at the sky. Zander's hold on me doesn't loosen and I feel myself snuggle closer into his heat.

We lay like this in silence, I'm completely focused on the feeling of his arms around me, and how much I like this. It reminds me of the night in my bed a few weeks ago. He hasn't held me like this since and I missed it.

"See those three stars in a line right there?" He finally says and points up to the sky.

It takes me a minute, but then I notice what he's pointing out, there's three stars that are almost in a perfect line.

"Yeah?"

"That's Orion's belt, and if you draw with your mind up around you can see his torso holding a bow and arrow, and below it his legs."

I tilt my head against him trying to picture what he's explaining. I can see it a little, but it's definitely not a guy holding a bow and arrow.

I feel Zander chuckle against me, and I look back at him.

"Are you laughing at me?"

"Yeah, you look so cute trying to see it," He reaches over and takes his thumb to rub across my forehead. I didn't realize I was scrunching in concentration.

He smooths out the lines, continuing to look right at me, even in the darkness I can see the shine in his eyes. They pull me in like they always do, making it so I never want to look away.

I notice his hand moving from my forehead to the side of my face as he lightly runs his fingers against my skin, just barely touching until he gets to my neck, and his hand wraps around the back of my neck, pulling me to him.

My heart is hammering in my chest. Is this really happening?

Zander lowers his face to mine and ghosts his lips against mine, I don't even think it counts as a kiss. His eyes meet mine one more time almost asking for permission. I give the slightest nod before his lips are on mine for real this time.

I melt into every part of him that's touching me, his lips, his hand holding my face to his, his other hand around my back pushing me closer to his side. My entire front pushed against his side.

The kiss is soft at first, testing, feeling, surreal. I lightly feel his tongue against the seam of my lips, and I open to let him in. Even as his tongue explores my mouth the kiss is soft and testing, both taking our time to enjoy this. I match his tongue movements in his mouth, never wanting this to end.

I feel Zander slightly adjust our position so I'm flat on my back, not caring about the freezing ground anymore, he's filling me with more than enough warmth. He presses me against the ground, as he leans over me and we have yet to break apart, probably both unsure of what this means, but enjoying it now.

I feel his hand move to my hip and hold me tightly as his other hand slides down my body. I want him to take things further, but he doesn't. He's just holding me, and my arms are around his neck, holding him. It's perfect.

I couldn't even begin to guess how long we make out for until we pull apart, both breathless and charged between whatever this is developing between us.

Zander's eyes meet mine, and there's so much there, the lust, the desire, the care, everything, it's all in his eyes barely illuminated by the moonlight. His mouth is red from our extended kiss, but it's almost hard to see as it's overshadowed from the smile across his face.

Zander settles back next to me on the ground, pulling me as close as possible. We tangle our legs together as we continue to lay on the freezing ground, staring at the stars a little longer. We don't say much to each other, it's obvious we don't want to break this bubble we've put ourselves in where it's just Mel, Zander, and the stars. Nothing else matters but us, and I don't want that to change.

# 17

## Present

In the bathroom I take a breather. What am I doing?

Zander just told me he's a drug dealer, involved in some weird drug situation with his stepbrother and then I let him eat me out on a bench in his backyard.

I really am losing my mind, that's the only explanation I can think of to explain my actions.

Do I trust Zander?

My brain is screaming no, and to run away and never look back.

My vagina and my heart are screaming yes, give him another chance, he deserves it.

I know which one I'm going to follow, and God help me if this goes badly I don't know what I'll do.

I come out of the bathroom seeing Zander sitting on one of the couches in the bigger living room with another glass of whiskey in his hand.

He's man spreading which I would normally complain about, but something about him and his presence makes it seem so hot. His large muscular body spread out on the large couch, though he makes it look so much smaller than it is.

I catch him looking me up and down as he takes a sip of his drink. His looks linger on my body and it's almost like he didn't get an eyeful earlier. The memory already making me blush.

"You are the most beautiful woman I've ever seen," he says once his eyes meet mine again as I'm slowly walking over to join him on the couch.

"You're just saying that because you want in my pants," I raise my eyebrow at him.

I know how this game works and I'm comfortable enough with Zander to call him out on it.

"That's not true, I was just in your pants and I'm still saying it because I mean it," he winks, and I think I may have just died.

I roll my eyes to pretend his wink didn't just send a lightning bolt through me, "You know what I mean."

He chuckles, "I know, but I really do mean it."

I sit on the couch next to him, he instantly pulls me to him to hold me close and I smile at him wanting me so close all the time, I love it.

"And honestly, I would love to get in your pants again, but when we go further, I plan for the full night and holding you while we sleep through the day. I would love that to be tonight but I don't want you meeting Trent and he will be back in the morning. I do want you here as long as you want to be," Zander says, moving my hair from my face.

My face twists in curiosity, "Why don't you want me to meet Trent?"

"It is not at all whatever you are thinking. I don't want you exposed to Trent and this world more than you already are being around me. Trent can be a real asshole. I will defend you until the end of the Earth, but I don't even want him getting any ideas to put you in potential danger, please believe me." I hear the desperation in his voice with his pleads.

Zander is a huge, strong man that appears to have a heart of glass and he's holding me in it as he tries not to break it, as he tries not to break me.

"I do believe you, and I want to trust you again, Zander. You're off to a decent start," I smile up at him.

He appears to relax a little at my words, he pulls me in for a soft kiss that I'm slightly begging to deepen, to take things further. It remains soft, despite the electricity running through my entire body at the contact. Our lip's part and I settle into him as he holds me closely.

After a few minutes of silence, and neither of us saying anything, I just focus on listening to Zander's heartbeat. He speaks with humor in his voice.

"Am I off to a decent start because you've had two orgasms in two days thanks to me?"

"Who says I haven't had more *not* thanks to you?" I ask, looking up at him.

"Little Mel Bell and your mouth," He shakes his head as he laughs.

"I've never had complaints about my mouth before," I shrug, looking away from his direct gaze but I feel his eyes burning my face that is still in his vision.

I hear him sigh after a few seconds of silence, "You're going to be the death of me."

Not unless he ends up the death of *me* first.

WE END up cuddling on the couch and talking until I could barely keep my eyes open.

Zander offered to drive me home because he didn't want me to drive while I'm so tired and risk getting in an accident. I swore I was okay, he said I could stay the night and we would figure something out when Trent came back. He even offered to sneak me out the back or in a suitcase or something. I don't think I could make myself fit in a suitcase even if I wanted to, but I appreciated the thought.

I let him know I'm really okay, I'll blast music on my drive home and be okay. He's still reluctant to let me go and it makes my stomach flutter that he cares so much.

"Seriously, I'm fine, I've survived on my own for a while now."

I look up at him as he's walking me to my car outside and the temperature has dropped significantly now that it's past midnight. I wrap my arms around myself. Zander holds me close to him. His body heat is more than enough to keep me comfortable.

"But now I'm around so get used to it," He squeezes me tightly and for a second, I feel like he might just throw me over his shoulder and drag me back inside. I'm slightly disappointed he doesn't.

"Yeah, that will take some getting used to for sure," I joke, reaching for the door handle, but Zander's long arms beat me to it.

I roll my eyes, but secretly I love this new side of Zander that I don't remember him having before. There's still so much about him I have to get to know, but everything feels so easy and natural with him. It almost feels like we were never really apart.

"Let me know when you get home, I'll be pacing waiting to make sure you're safe," he says, leaning down to kiss me gently on my mouth.

His gentle kisses almost affect me more than our lust filled, hungry kisses because the emotion I feel behind the gentle ones mixed with the electricity I feel sets my whole body on fire.

I nod as I climb in my car as he shuts the door behind me. Zander watches me drive away, and I don't even see him turn to go back inside before I'm out of view. I feel like his presence gave me energy again as I drove home thinking about the night with my music playing in the background of my thoughts.

I get home in no time, as I'm taking the elevator up, I think about being in here with Zander and I don't think I'll ever be able to be in here without remembering the feel of him on me. His hands, the way his fingers played me so perfectly. His lips, the way they feel against mine and the way I feel whenever he's around.

I am so fucked.

Once my door is shut and locked behind me, I send him a text like I promised I would. He must have truly been waiting by his phone because he replied instantly.

> Mel: In my apartment, door locked, all safe and sound.

> Zander: Good, get some rest and I'll text you when I wake up.

Good morning texts are the best texts to get so if he really means that, my butterflies may take over my entire stomach for this man. Now that I'm back my exhaustion takes over again, so I change into my sleep uniform of t-shirt and boy shorts before climbing into my soft bed, drifting off to sleep shortly after.

He wasn't kidding, and neither was I.

> Zander: Good morning, I hope you slept well, I'm going to have a busy day, but I'll be thinking of you.

And the butterflies in my stomach did, in fact, take over (almost painfully). My heart races thinking about him going about his day doing God knows what.

Ignorance is probably bliss about what he does on the daily, and this is a mystery I think I'll be okay with because this one will prevent me from going to jail.

If I don't know, I can't be arrested, right?

Zander's text wasn't the only one on my phone, I also had one from my dad.

> Dad: Dinner tonight?

My dad is not a man of many words, he's always been that way. Straight, to the point, and no bullshit. We tend to have dinner at least once a month since I moved out. He usually initiates since he has a schedule to follow, and I don't.

> Mel: Sushi?

> Dad: Sure. You know the place. 1800.

I use my fingers to figure out the military time conversion, I've never understood it, but he always uses it because that's what they use at the hospital.

Six, got it. I do know the place, my dad being a man of little words is also predictable. We go to one of the same three restaurants, or his house for our monthly meet ups. I don't mind it though; I know the food is good and it's easy. I reply to Zander next.

> Mel: Try not to think about me too much, don't want you distracted.

> Zander: Trust me, I already am. What are you doing tonight?

I was wondering if he would ask.

> Mel: Going to dinner with my dad, then coming home and possibly having a hot date with Netflix and maybe some ice cream.

Zander: Would you be down to share your hot date?

> Mel: With who?

Zander: I think I know a guy that might be interested. He's funny, handsome, likes ice cream and Netflix

> Mel: Do I know him? Because that's not ringing a bell

Zander: Ha. Ha.

> Mel: I may be persuaded to add to my date

Zander: What do I have to do?

> Mel: Hm....

Zander: Be nice.

> Mel: Dammit. I wasn't going to be.

Zander: Let me know when you're back from your dinner, Trent has me being his fucking errand boy today and if I'm able to escape to see you then I want to.

> Mel: Be safe, please.

Zander: Only because you said please.

I smile at our exchange; everything is so easy with him it's scary. I finally make the effort to roll out of bed. I think I know a mystery I can use to start a new story.

∽

My day consists of writing, writing and more writing.

I take a break to clean myself up, take a shower and put clothes on so I can leave the house to run to Starbucks. My at home coffee was fine, but today is a two-cup day.

I needed to treat myself a bit for no other reason than I think I might actually have a story worth writing about. I'm not going to thank Zander for the inspiration, but he may have helped just a little bit. At least the way he's making me feel has stirred up something in my dormant creative brain.

Later, I drive to the restaurant called Catch to meet my dad. He's already there even though I'm a few minutes early, he's always earlier. I get out of my car and meet him at the front door.

"Hey Mel," he says as he pulls me in for a quick side hug.

"Hey dad, good to see you."

We walk inside and get a table at the sushi bar as usual. The waitresses are all familiar with us as we frequent this place often. He comes here even without me, so they are all more familiar with him.

"Anything new with you?" He asks as he fills out the ordering form with the same things he always gets.

"Yeah, I think I got a new story that might actually go somewhere for the first time in a bit."

He nods as he grunts his approval, handing me the ordering form, though he knows what I get, but I fill it out anyway.

"Good, glad to hear it, kiddo."

"Yeah, also...um," I mark my two choice rolls and debate whether to say this or not. I do it anyway, "Zander Wells moved back, remember him?"

My dad's eyes meet mine, an eyebrow raised, "Zander Wells from when you were a kid?"

"Yeah, and high school, remember?"

He knew something happened between us in high school. We weren't exactly secretive about it, but relationships always felt weird to talk to my dad about, so he doesn't know much about how our relationship became a bit more than friendship.

"Yeah, I always liked him. What's he up to?"

The waitress comes by, so my dad hands her the ordering form, she goes over all our selections before walking away again.

I don't think I should tell him the truth about that. I should be vague. I shouldn't have said anything to begin with. I knew it would open up to some questions I can't answer.

"Sales. Him and his stepbrother own their business and just moved back from Phoenix not too long ago," Lying to my dad has never been easy. I feel like the man can read right through me.

"Nice, good for him, so you've seen him to catch up?"

*If by "catch up" you mean practically fuck him in a swing, then an elevator and let him eat me out on a bench in the forest then yeah, we've caught up.* Jesus, what's wrong with me? Thinking it like this I found like a whore.

"Yeah, we have."

He nods with a quiet, "good" as he drinks his water.

"If you want, he can join us next time."

"Maybe." I shrug.

It's not necessarily awkward with my dad, sometimes I just don't know what all to talk about with him. I never like to talk about my stories before they are finished because I feel like it will jinx the process or something, and he respects that.

Of course, I'm not going to tell my dad about every single thing that happened between Zander and I, past or present and that's the only other interesting thing going on in my life.

My dad knew about Zander leaving last time and that I was upset about it, but he didn't know the feelings I developed for him. He also didn't know about how he lied, and it shattered everything. My dad just accepted that I was having some teenage meltdown, checked on my well being and moved on with life. Which is okay.

My mom knew even less. She met Zander like once when we were younger, I think. I told her about him briefly during one of our obligatory meetings. She asked what we were, and I didn't have a real answer. She asked if I was being careful by using protection because she would not be supporting a teenage mother, and that conversation ended.

"How's Aylin?" My dad asked, finally breaking our silence.

He likes Aylin too, she joined in some family holidays during college because her family is...complicated to say the least.

"She's good, busy as always."

"She's almost done with her degree, right?"

"Yeah, one more year and my girl is a doctor," I say proudly.

I told her I would only refer to her as Dr. Aylin once she finishes and she tells me to shove it.

"Good for her, I'm proud of her."

"I'll let her know, she'll appreciate that."

"I'm proud of you too Mel, you know that right?"

"Yeah, I do."

I know my dad secretly wishes I was doing something else with my life, maybe getting a Doctorate like Aylin, working some nine to five or just something more conventional.

I do know that he is proud of what I have accomplished as a writer, and he never makes me feel less than, unlike my mom who feels the need to tear me down any chance she gets. Which is why now that I'm an adult our correspondences are limited to holidays and birthdays.

Our food comes and we fall into silence again as we eat. I can't help but wonder what Zander is doing, and hoping that he's safe.

# 18

**Present**

I wonder what Mel is doing. I haven't heard from her since this morning. I'm hoping she has been able to write and it's keeping her busy.

I wonder if she will tell me what she's writing. I really should read some of her books she already has out. That's going to be on my list today for sure, to get my hands on some of her books.

"How did it go yesterday?" Trent asks as soon as he walks in the door, returning from Arizona.

I'm annoyed. He never tells me when he will come back because I would've had more than enough time with Mel this morning if she had stayed the night. It's not even about the sex with her, I would've been more than happy to just fall asleep with her in my arms.

"Fine. Product came in, went to the runners and money was dropped," I say simply.

We didn't speak much before he left other than him telling me he was going to Arizona and would be back in the morning.

"Did you go back and check the money?" He asks. I already want him to leave again.

"Not yet, I got caught up in some stuff last night, so I wasn't able to go check. I'm going today," I brush him off.

"What did you get caught up in, I didn't have anything else for you to do?" He's already mad, as always, so I'm annoyed.

"I can have a life outside of this bullshit, you know?"

"It's that piece of ass you mentioned before?" He has a smile spreading across his lips. I know it's not for a good reason.

My fists clench at my sides.

"She's not a piece of ass. I told you don't worry about what I'm doing," I'm seething. "I do what you want for the business, and I get my shit done."

"God, you like her," He rolls his eyes and scoffs.

Trent wouldn't understand, he's never had a woman stick around long enough to even like him, though I think he prefers it that way. He gets his dick wet, moves on, and that's all women are to him.

I don't even think he has the capacity to feel anything for anyone. Not even his own family. I've seen how he treats his mom and, to put it simply, they don't have a great relationship, and he never mentions his dad.

"I'm going to check the money."

I grab my keys and head toward the door. I can't deal with him right now.

"Hold on, I have a few more things for you to do today," he says, still with his stupid smug smile on his face. "After you check, I need you to check in with our runners, remind them who we are and not to fuck with us, don't sample the product, etc."

"There been any issues?" I wonder.

I'm used to being the "muscle" for Trent because he doesn't like to get his hands dirty, but usually he only asks me to do that when there's an actual problem.

"Not yet, but we are still new around here, I just want to make sure everyone knows their place. Then, I want you to do some runs as well, get a feel for the market around here, maybe show some of the rookies how it's done."

"Why don't you show them how it's done since you're the expert in all of this?" I fold my arms across my chest and widen my stance.

"I am the expert, but I taught you everything I know so you can show them. Plus, you've been out of practice for a while, it'll be good for you."

He doesn't take my challenge and it makes me more annoyed with him. There's no winning, there never is with him.

I glare at him for a bit longer than I need before I turn and walk out the door. I hate him, I really do.

I get to the storage center in the next town over and go straight to our unit. I check to make sure there's no one around before opening it and going in, turning on the single light bulb that barely lights up the space. I have to keep the door closed in case anyone comes by.

We have the unit under a fake name and pay in cash so it can't be traced back to us. This is where the drugs go when they are brought in, where the runners pick them up, and drop the cash off once they are done.

I inventoried everything that came in here. I know the price of everything and how much should be expected, and the runners are expected to drop off all the money they made. Then, Trent and I go through to split up what they get paid and once a week they get their cash.

It's a fairly simple process, I just feel like I'm the one having to do it all, even though Trent claims to be in charge of it all.

Whatever, he can be, I don't plan on sticking around.

In the dim light I count the money, separating the bills by value, wrapping every $500 for each because it's easier that way. I calculate how much should be here based on the inventory and sale price and see we are about two grand short.

Fuck.

I hate when Trent is right about something and needing to check in with the runners. Maybe one of them just forgot to come back with their cash. I'll show up, they will get scared, hand it over. I can only hope.

I stuff the cash in my backpack before leaving the unit, triple checking that I locked it behind me. I hate that I'm going to have to tell Trent about this, he's going to want answers.

He's not going to want me home until I have those answers.

"Fuck!" I slam my hands on my steering wheel once I'm in my car.

I hate this. I hate this so much. I don't want to deal with this bull shit anymore. I'm done.

I drive way too recklessly back to our house, which is probably really stupid considering I have tens of thousands of dollars in literal drug money in my passenger seat, but I've done worse.

I pull up to the house, and Trent is still here. I don't know what he did in Arizona or why he went, but he must have still gotten a full night's sleep because I see him on his computer at the island.

I walk in the door, bee lining right to the kitchen where I drop the backpack in front of Trent.

He looks up at me without lifting his head.

"And?" He asks without even opening it.

"Some is missing," I say blankly.

I know where this conversation is going to go, I know what I'm going to have to do, now let's just skip to that without the Trent pep talk.

"How much?"

"Two grand."

"Dammit."

"Any idea who?" I ask, and I know I shouldn't have.

He wants me to go around checking on everyone anyway, so I'll find out one way or another.

"I don't know these guys as well as the ones in Arizona, so no. Check on them all and report back."

There it is. I knew that would be his plan.

I pretend to be a good little errand boy, keep my mouth shut as I walk back out.

In my car I pull out the burner phone from my glove box next to my pistol. I turn the phone on for the first time in days because the contacts for all our runners is in it, names (at least the ones they give us), numbers and addresses. I'm sure some of these addresses will be fake, leading me to some abandoned warehouse or some shit, but these guys usually run around together and hang out at the same spots so I'm sure I'll find them.

The day turns into the afternoon and evening while I go down the list, confronting the runners, making myself as intimidating as I can. When needed, flashing my pistol tucked in my jeans and making threats I'd rather not follow through on, but will if I have to.

So far no one has confessed to forgetting to drop any money, which would make my life easier. Grab the money, "firmly" remind them to not do it again, then bring it back to Trent, and hopefully meet up with Mel.

At this rate I'm not sure if I'll be able to see her tonight, and that bothers me more than it should.

I look at the time, it's already past seven, she might be with her dad still, or headed home. I'm going to check with her after this next "meeting".

I walk up to the shitty run-down house and knock on the front door. There's people here I can tell, but they aren't coming to the door. I'm not even sure of this one's name, they are on the list as "Cee". I knock again, even harder this time and I hear movement inside, but they don't come to the door.

"I will kick this fucking door down if you don't open it!" I yell.

I will admit I am intimidating looking, and I have the voice to match it. That's why Trent has me as his muscle when he needs it. I look the part and I won't back down.

I prepare to do what I said and kick the door down when someone answers. It's a younger looking guy with long hair, hiding the majority of his face. He isn't looking at me so it's hard to guess his age. Late teens? Maybe twenty?

"Cee?" I ask. He looks up and this kid is very clearly high.

Shit.

I push past him to go inside, and the inside matches the out. The house is old, dirty, and falling apart. I can't see a clean spot on the floor, the walls are covered in I don't want to know what, and I've seen at least three cockroaches since I walked in.

Among the trash everywhere, I see some product, open and mostly gone.

Double shit.

I grab the kid by his collar to force his eyes on me, but I don't think he can see me clearly through his high.

"Did you use all this shit?" I ask, shaking him.

Hoping that maybe he will snap out of his drug induced haze if I scare him enough. Doesn't seem like that will work, heroin is quite the drug. Nasty stuff, I really hate being involved at all, it makes me sick.

"You better have two-K in your fucking pockets right now or you're going to wish you overdosed on this shit," I threaten, still holding the kid's collar and barely getting any sort of response from my words.

"I don't have shit," The kid finally says, his head lolling to the side in my grasp. I drop him, not even caring that his feet are not ready to catch his weight.

He falls like a rag doll onto the ground.

I go to where the half-used product is, picking up what's remaining. At least now it's only like a grand missing if I'm looking on the bright side.

"Who's going to pay for all this shit you used?" I ask, possibly to no one. The kid may be passed out on the floor after the fall he took.

I look around for anything of value around the shithole. As long as I come back with the money, I can leave the kid breathing, scared, and knowing he will never hear from us again for any jobs.

There's nothing, I know there's nothing around worth what he owes. The kid is on the floor groaning so I grab him by the back of his neck, lifting him from the ground completely.

"Tell me, Cee, what am I supposed to do to get the money you owe us?"

He looks at me a bit more now, still extremely out of it, but at least maybe digesting what I'm saying.

"I don't know, man, but if you kill me, you'll never get it," He slurs and speaks slowly, it irritates me more.

"Do you know how many people say that, like your life actually has any value?"

They really do all say that, and yet they never get the money either way.

"If I kill you then I don't have to worry about you stealing from me again."

That got his attention.

"No, no, please don't, I'm sorry! I'll pay it back; I swear it won't happen again."

I think the kid is starting to cry now. I'm numb to it all by now. Numb to the pleads. Numb to the tears. Numb to everything these lowlifes try to offer me like it will make any difference.

"Oh, I know it won't happen again. That is a guarantee, but

not one you get to make," I drop him on the floor again. His limbs are still moving slowly so he isn't able to catch himself and falls hard on his face.

"Please, man, I really didn't mean to!" He's fully crying now.

"But you did, so now you have to be handled," I pull out my pistol from my jeans, and show him. "I could kill you, that's one way, or I could leave you so bloody you'll *wish* I had killed you."

Yup. He's definitely crying.

He grabs onto my pant leg, begging, making empty promises and he's hysterical.

It's honestly disgusting. I have no sympathy for these people.

Addicted or not, you fucked up, you stole, and you have to pay. You're playing with fire in this life and it's on borrowed time. I use the butt of my gun to hit him across the face, so he gets off my leg. I don't want him touching me. Blood flies from his nose and mouth.

"I'm not going to kill you, this time. But you're not going to contact us again, not to buy or to do any jobs and if you do then I *will* kill you, understand?" I wave my gun around to remind him I'm serious.

He nods furiously, I kick him directly in the stomach, sending him reeling as I walk out the door with the half-used product.

That's one thing in this life, sometimes we have to eat some of the profit, but that's what happens when you trust unreliable drug addicts to deal drugs. We try to avoid this, but every once in a while, someone slips through.

One side of me feels bad for my actions when it comes to situations like this.

I recognize this guy is young, stupid and desperate. The other part of me doesn't feel bad because he's in charge of what he does, and he chose to do something beyond stupid.

I've never been one to shy away from a fight, sometimes even seeking them out when I was younger.

I leave the nasty house, checking the time on my phone. It's almost eight now, I text Mel to check on her since she hasn't said anything to me, and I need to make sure she's okay.

> Zander: How's dinner with your dad?

I get in my car, putting my gun back in the glove box as she replies.

> Mel: It was good, I'm at the store now picking out ice cream for my hot Netflix date.

> Zander: My favorite is mint chocolate chip in case you were wondering.

The next text comes through as a picture of a cart with mint chocolate chip and chocolate chip cookie dough both already in it.

> Mel: You're not the only one with a good memory.

I smile. She remembers the little shit about me too, for some reason this makes my heart skip.

I drive back to my house now that I have the answers and Trent is not going to be happy about it. I throw the drugs in the front trunk of my car and drive slightly more cautiously than I normally would. I hate driving with product in my car, especially since I've been caught before.

My plan is to go home, give Trent the news, drop the product with another runner to deal with, then go see my little Mel Bell.

I pull up to the house and go meet with Trent.

"What did you find out?" He asks.

This guy is not one for small talk.

"I found out who it was, he used half the product, I took back the other half, roughed him up a bit and let him know we would not sell or work with him again," I tell him everything so casually like we are just talking about the weather.

"Who was it?"

"Cee? I hadn't heard of him before, seemed like a younger guy, not reliable."

"Hm, okay. Sucks to lose a runner, you can go finish running that product, then find someone to replace him."

He waves me off like it's as simple as that.

"What? I was going to drop the product with another runner and then be done for the night?"

"Why would you think that?" He sounds like he has humor in his voice like what I said is funny.

"Because I did my fucking job, and I want to be done for the night," I glare at him.

Just once I would like him to treat me like a fucking human.

"Your job is what I say it is, and you're running that product, then you're finding a new recruit," He's not backing down on this.

Maybe I can still pass it off to another runner, and they will have a friend or something to recruit.

I'm also picturing Trent's face as the perfect target for my fist right now.

"Problem?" He asks like he can read my murderous thoughts toward him.

"Yeah, actually, I don't see you jumping up to do any runs or recruiting,"

I know it's a moot point. Trent does what Trent wants to do.

"And I don't see you stepping up to build this business beyond what it is. Do what I fucking say Zander and we won't have issues."

"Leave me alone to have a life sometimes and we won't have issues, Trent," I spit his name back at him.

"Hah! This is about that girl, isn't it? Jesus Zander, do what I ask, and I won't question you about your little piece, alright?"

His face has never looked so punchable. That's not even a word, but it's a word I would describe Trent.

"Whatever."

I decide I won't rearrange his face tonight, mostly because I don't feel like breaking my knuckles on his face. I want my hands intact so I can appreciate every time I get to touch Mel without worrying about an injured hand.

# 19

### Mel

**10 Years Ago**

"Are you sure you want to go? We could do literally anything else tonight," I tell Zander as he walks into my house.

"Do you want to go?" He questions.

"I mean, I don't know, I haven't gone to many parties and it's New Year's Eve so it just kind of makes sense," I shrug.

I really don't like parties, but Zander and I are always together, just the two of us. I feel like we should spend some time with other people too. Plus some of my other friends have wondered why I haven't been doing much lately. They know about Zander, but I try to keep the extent of my feelings to myself for some reason.

I am more than happy spending time with just us, but I don't want him to get bored of whatever this is. It's been almost two weeks since we first kissed, and it wasn't the last time, not even close.

We haven't gone much farther than that even though I would like to.

I haven't had much experience in the sex department, I lost my virginity last year and it was nothing special by any means, it only happened once with that guy, it was awkward and not fun. We were friends and decided to try. It hurt, didn't last long and no passion.

Then, of course, there's Mark who had more experience than me for sure. He made it a little better, but he's selfish and still missed that spark. The spark I feel with Zander just by touching him.

"Mel, if you want to go then we are going," Zander says, pulling me out of my thoughts. "If you don't want to go then we will do something else, no matter what I'm happy."

"I just don't want Amber, Mark or either of their groups there."

"Okay, how about this," He starts, taking my hands in his, and holding them tightly. Yup, there's that fucking spark. "We go and if you're not having a fun time or we see anyone we don't want to then we leave, and I get you all to myself the rest of the night."

The smile on his lips makes my own appear. I nod in agreement. I'm tempted to say I'm not having a fun time no matter what just so I can get him all to myself for the rest of the night anyway.

Later in the evening we get to the party, which is at a girl Jennifer's house. We aren't really close friends but acquaintances and had some classes together, someone that is cool to talk to, but likely won't stay in contact outside of school. She's someone with those cool parents that don't care if you throw a party at the house.

Her neighborhood is nicer than the one I live in, but it's not mansions down every street like Amber's. This party is also not as loud as Amber's was when I sent Zander in so hopefully the cops don't get called, that's one of the reasons I don't like parties, I'm too paranoid about getting in trouble.

Zander intertwines our fingers as we walk in together. It makes me smile that he is so comfortable holding my hand in front of everyone like he wants people to know we are something, even if we don't know what we are.

The music is louder inside, the living room has a ton of people with familiar faces, but none stand out as anyone I'm trying to avoid so I let out a relieved breath.

Jennifer spots us and walks over. She takes a second to notice Zander's and my hands still holding onto each other but doesn't comment on it.

"Hey Mel and...Zander, right? Glad you're here, there's drinks in the kitchen, obviously music everywhere, I hope you guys have a good time!"

"Thanks, Jennifer," I smile at her as she goes back to the crowd of people, dancing and drinking.

"Want a drink?" Zander leans in my ear to ask over the music. His breath on my sensitive skin sends a shiver down my spine.

I nod, so we make our way to the kitchen together. There are more people in here, some are playing beer pong in the attached dining room. Even though I trust Zander not to drug me I watch as he grabs some different drinks around and mixes them together.

I might trust him not to drug me but watching him make the drink I don't know if I trust him not to kill me with alcohol poisoning.

"What are you making?" I wonder, the amount of different alcohol and mixers he's putting in that one drink cannot be good.

"It'll be good, I promise, and I'll drink it if you won't," He smirks as he continues his shitty bar tending.

"Are you just trying to get me drunk to take advantage of me?" I lean my back against the counter and look up at him.

"Of course not," He leans closer to speak right into my ear

again. "I don't think you need to be drunk to let me do what I want with you."

His breath on my ear along with his words made my legs turn to jelly.

My mouth parts slightly. Zander stands up straight again, smirking.

I want to ask what he wants to do with me then, but I don't think I can form the words.

Maybe I do need to be a little drunk, not sloppy, but just a little. That is if he even means that. He's said other shit to get a reaction from me, this wouldn't be new.

"Here, just try it," he says, handing me the drink he made.

My face contorts in disgust just at the sight of it. Then, I bring it up to my nose to smell, the sense is taken over by the smell of pure alcohol and it stings by nose. I gag at just the smell.

"No, you never smell the drink before you taste it, come on, Mel!" Zander nudges the cup.

"You're a sick bastard, aren't you?" I look at him skeptically. There has to be something wrong with him, and maybe I found it, he's disgusting.

"Just try it," He rolls his eyes at me.

I bring the cup back up, trying my best not to smell it again. I take a tentative sip, the burning liquid hitting my taste buds immediately. I swallow, and it feels like I swallowed liquid fire.

I cough and gag before handing the cup back to him and searching out something to get the taste out of my mouth.

"That's fucking nasty!" I exclaim as I find a water bottle, quickly opening and downing it.

He laughs as he takes the drink and takes a big drink like it's nothing, no reaction after he swallows. I just watch in shock and his Adam apple bobs as the drink goes down his throat, and his face stays completely fine.

"You a sociopath?" I raise my eyebrow at him.

"Not that I'm aware of, just used to some different drink combinations." He shrugs before taking another big gulp.

"You're a big partier, aren't you?" I drink more of the water now that the taste has finally subsided a bit.

"I went to a few at my last school, I did a lot of stupid shit to try and make friends until I realized it wasn't worth it,' he says simply.

"Like what?" I feel like I'm just interrogating him at this point with all my questions, but he doesn't seem to mind.

"The parties, I threw some, drank too much, did stupid dares, tried some drugs, nothing too bad mostly just weed and molly once. None of it is worth some temporary friends."

I had no idea about this side of Zander. He told me about what he did before moving and sleeping with some girls which I won't tell him, hurt to hear about for absolutely no reason because we hadn't been in each other's lives for years.

Even now, we aren't really anything, so I have no reason to be jealous.

"So, you don't miss doing all of that stuff all the time?"

I suddenly feel insecure about all the time we've been spending together since he moved back, and how boring this must be for him to hang out with me. We don't do much of anything. I have been content with it because that's what I do anyway, but I never thought about if he wanted more.

"Not at all, these last few months I've been the happiest I've been in years." He smiles at me, and I know he's telling the truth, though for some reason I still feel like I've been holding him back. "What is something you will actually drink?"

I look around at the options, I find some Dr. Pepper and rum.

Zander grabs a cup which he puts in front of me on the counter. He repositions himself so he's standing behind me, my back pressed against his front as he lightly holds my body, his arms holding the counter on the sides of me, caging me in. I forgot what I was doing. All I can focus on is how his body is completely against mine, and the heat from him is shooting right down to my core, my arousal taking over my mind.

I don't move, so I feel Zander take the can of soda, and pour it in the cup he grabbed for me, then his other hand pours the rum in at the same time. I just watch his hands move in ways I'm currently unable to since my brain has short circuited due to how turned on I am from how his body is against me right now.

Once he's done, he doesn't move from my back as he lifts the cup to my face. My hand remembers how to move again as I take it from him to take a sip. I take a bigger sip than I normally would because I feel like it might be the way to get my brain working again, at least to some capacity.

"Better?" His breath is against my ear again. I fumble with the cup, almost dropping it, but I catch myself.

"Y-Yeah, that's better," I can form words. Look at me go!

I turn around, Zander still hasn't backed up so now the fronts of our bodies are completely pressed together, he's still leaning close to me. When we stand like this, I have to completely look up to meet his eyes.

There's something in his shining eyes that is only making my arousal more apparent. It's like he's burning his eyes into mine, focusing on just me, nothing else around us matters and like that won't stop what he wants.

I need to break the tension, or I might do something stupid in the middle of everyone. I bring my cup up to my lips, taking another big sip. He watches my movements and doesn't move away from me still. I lower the cup from my mouth as I lick the liquid from my lips. His gaze watches my movement and the fire in his eyes increases even more.

He brings his own cup up to his lips and downs the rest of it, though I feel like it hasn't even affected him at all.

"Come on," he says, grabbing my hand and pulling me

behind him, briefly looking around before dragging me upstairs.

"What are we doing?" I ask as I force my feet to keep up with him.

There are people upstairs too, but less than there is downstairs. The music is still loud enough to carry up here as Zander goes to a random door, looks in before pulling me inside and shutting it behind us.

Zander presses me against the door he just shut, my heart is racing. I don't even know what room we are in if it's a bedroom, bathroom or a fucking closet. I'm only aware of Zander's body still pressed against me, my back against the door and his face so close to mine. His breath is a mixture of his normal mint and fire, but with the lingering alcohol on it as well, though I like the smell when it's mixed with his.

"I needed to kiss you," he says, and I feel like all the air in my lungs left. I don't think I'll get it back.

"You couldn't kiss me downstairs?"

I can't help the comment, maybe holding my hand wasn't really him being okay with people seeing us because he doesn't want anyone to see any more than that. I'm not big on PDA, but I also don't want to be his dirty little secret.

"I could have, but not like this."

I don't have a chance to retort when his hands are holding my face as he crushes his lips onto mine, and now I get it.

It would've been pretty uncomfortable to kiss me this deeply, passionately, hungrily in front of so many people. His tongue is in my mouth and there's nothing soft about his actions. My hands are fisting his shirt in front of me, holding him to me. One of his hands slips from my face and slides down my body, grazing my chest, and continues down until his hand is on my waist, pulling my hip to his by my belt loop. I arch my body into his, pressing myself to him completely. His other hand has moved to the back of my head, pulling my hair enough to tilt my head back to deepen our kiss.

He pulls away, both of us panting as he moves to my neck. He's kissing, licking and nipping. I lean my head to the side to give him better access as a light moan escapes my lips. His pull on my hair and waist tighten in reaction to the noise.

It seems like he took my reaction as a challenge. His bites on my neck are getting harder, and I'm arching myself more into him, moaning louder.

He keeps his hold on my hip and thrusts his hip into mine, pushing me against the door. A gasp escapes me at the movement. I can feel the slickness between my thighs, I fucking want him more than I've wanted anything ever.

He breaks away from my neck to look into my eyes again. Lust and desire are overpowering his gaze as he stares into my own, I'm sure mine are doing the same.

"We can stop if you want," he says simply.

"What about any of that makes you think I want to stop?"

I push against his contained erection with my hips. He groans as his lips find mine again.

Zander bites my bottom lip as he pushes himself against me, I moan into his mouth. I throw my arms around his neck to pull his face into mine as he continues to kiss me fiercely. I feel him drop down as his hands move to my ass and down to the back of my thighs, he picks me up, my thighs wrap around his waist as he moves us away from the door.

He throws me down onto something soft, a bed I assume. Thank God it's a bedroom.

He stays between my thighs, grinding into my center. I lift my hips to meet his movements. His hands move to the hem of my shirt and start to lift it. Our lips break apart long enough for him to remove my shirt so I'm just in my bra. He moves down my body, kissing down my throat and chest, he goes to my right tit, pulling down my bra to reveal taut nipples that he takes into his mouth. I throw my head back with a moan as he sucks and licks at my nipple.

I barely notice his left hand releasing my other nipple free until he is rolling it between his thumb and forefinger. I grind my hips harder against him, needing to feel him. His erection is evident, though confined in his jeans. I want them off. I want all these stupid clothes off.

I reach my hand to the collar of his shirt, and start pulling it off him, he lets me, his mouth leaving my nipple as he sheds his shirt. I get my first view of him without it.

Goddammit. He's all lean muscle with strong shoulders that lead to defined biceps. His stomach has defined ab muscles that I want to run my tongue across.

My reaction must be all over my face because Zander looks at me with a slight smirk on his lips and if I wasn't so turned on, I might want to hit him.

He leans down again kissing my mouth fiercely as he continues to grind his erection against my center that I know is completely soaked. I reach my hand down to start unbuttoning his jeans.

I get the button free and start to unzip his jeans when one of his large hands grabs both my wrists, and pins them above my head, stopping me. His lips leave mine and I whimper at both the loss of contact, and him stopping me. I grind my hips against him to tell him what I want without saying anything.

"Mel, I don't have a condom," He growls, breathlessly.

"I'm on birth control, it's fine."

I grind myself against him again, desperate for any contact since I can't reach out and touch him with my hands pinned above me.

"Are you sure? I don't want you regretting anything," His voice is strained from the desire I also see taking over his eyes.

"Zander, stop questioning everything and just fuck me."

I rarely hold my tongue, but I never make demands like

this, so I don't know what has gotten into me, but it seems like my words sent any sort of restraint he had out the window. His mouth is on mine again, biting and licking. I moan into his mouth, which only encourages him further.

His hand is still pinning my hands above my head while his other hand snaps my bra off completely. He uses his free hand to squeeze and mold my breast in his hand before focusing back on my nipple that he takes in his mouth, and sucks hard while he flicks his tongue against it.

I'm ashamed of the noise that comes out of my mouth, I don't think I've ever made such a noise. Zander releases my nipple with a pop. His hand moves down my body and expertly removes my pants with one hand like it's nothing.

I lift my hips to help him slide the pants down my legs and he does it with ease. I push my wrists against his hand, I want to be able to use my hands again, I want to free him of his pants too.

I whimper at the need as his mouth is exploring all my exposed skin he can reach, my chest, stomach, neck, mouth. I continue to grind myself against him, letting out a noise of frustration.

"What's wrong, Mel Bell?" He sounds amused, not genuine concern.

He sounds like he knows what's wrong and likes the slight torture he's putting me through.

"Is torture your form of foreplay?" I question, lifting my hips again to encourage him, even though it still hasn't gotten what I wanted.

"Well, is it working?" He nudges my nose with his, acting like he's going to kiss my mouth, but he doesn't, and I sigh in frustration again.

"Find out for yourself," I challenge.

The look in his eyes is darker at my words, even though he

appears to be perfectly restrained I can see him holding on by a thread.

He dips his hand into my soaked panties. I watch his face as he does find out for himself, and his restraint truly snaps. He releases my hands as he pulls off my useless underwear. I'm reaching for his pants automatically, begging to release him.

This time he lets me as his hand continues teasing my center, running along the seam, lightly circling my clit before moving down to my opening. I release his erection from his jeans and he's bigger than I expected.

I swallow at his size, my confidence is wavering now, I want to enjoy this, but I'm afraid it might hurt, yet my pussy clearly isn't getting the memo because it's throbbing at the need.

Zander kicks off his pants and underwear, I'm aware how we are both completely naked and this is really happening. He continues his finger movements at my center, keeping me distracted enough from questioning everything that's happening. I reach down to wrap my hand around his erection and fuck. It is truly massive. My fingers don't fit around it all. I move my hand around it, and he groans into my neck as he plunges a finger inside me.

I gasp and stop my hand's movement on him for a second. He bites down on my neck turning my gasp into a moan.

"I think you like a little bit of torture," He growls into my neck. I think he's right.

He moves his finger in and out of me, the slickness between my thighs increases, beginning to run down my thighs.

He switches to my clit, rubbing harder circles that make my eyes roll back. Keeping his movements, I feel the head of his cock line up at my entrance.

I look up at him, directly in his eyes, the fire that has been there is now a full-blown inferno as he begins to push inside me. His fingers don't stop their movement on my clit, relieving the pressure from the intrusion of his size.

His eyes look down to where he's entering me, the sight of him, defined muscles pushing inside me, watching it happen is almost enough to send me over the edge.

"Fuck," He groans as he pushes deeper inside, slowly so I feel every inch. "You feel so fucking good it's taking everything in me to go slow."

"You don't have to go slow," I breathe out, my hands on his hips encouraging him to push inside me. "I'm not going to break."

"This is about you, Mel, and I'm going to make sure you enjoy it."

He pushes inside more, and I moan, throwing my head back as his movements continue on my clit. I push my hips up to take him deeper myself, I know I'm already close and the feeling of him filling me is only bringing me closer.

"Goddammit, Mel, you look even more perfect with my cock inside you."

I push my hips against him more, so he's completely seated inside me, both of us moaning at the feeling. Zander leans over so our chests are flush against each other, him resting on his forearms on the sides of my head.

He adjusts his hips as I feel him pull out slightly before thrusting back inside, as he does he rubs against the bundle of nerves that is building my impending orgasm. He leans down to kiss my mouth again as he pulls out, and thrusts inside me, harder this time. The feeling of the rubbing and the invasion tears a moan from my throat that is released into his mouth.

He builds up his thrusts becoming harder and faster, I wrap my legs around his waist to keep him continuing the movements, especially as my orgasm continues to build while his thrusts become more frantic.

I'm gasping and moaning probably louder than I should, forgetting where we are as the music downstairs is hopefully masking all our sounds.

"Come for me, Mel, I need to feel you come around my cock."

His words send me over the edge, the sound I make is unlike anything I've ever heard come from my mouth. He kisses me to muffle it and I contract around him.

His movements lose their rhythm as I feel him throb inside me before he spills with a moan that he buries in the crook of my neck.

We are both sweaty, breathing hard, and I'm in absolute bliss. He lifts from me, and I feel empty as soon as he's gone. His body off mine makes me instantly cold as I miss his hot body heat. He takes my hands to stand me up in front of him, both of us still completely naked as he takes my face in his hands and kisses me gently again.

"You're perfect, Mel Bell."

"You're alright, Zander," I smirk at him, and he chuckles before kissing me lightly one more time before gathering our clothes that were strewn across the room.

After pulling on his underwear, he walks around the room that luckily has an attached bathroom, and comes out with a washcloth he found that he doused in warm water before coming back to me. He gently wipes my thighs and my center.

"Are you okay?" He asks me as he tosses the rag in the garbage of the bathroom.

"I'm definitely okay," I smile as he hands me my clothes, my panties seemingly useless now from how soaked they are from my arousal.

As I am silently questioning what I should do with my panties, Zander grabs them from my hand, slides them in his front pocket, and winks at me. I'm not sure if I should be grossed out or turned on again. It ends up being the latter and I shake my head at myself.

We both get dressed, he helps me look less like "I just got fucked" though the ache between my legs keeps reminding me, that, and Zander's constant smile at me. Plus, little kisses on my mouth, and neck every chance he gets.

We emerge from the room, Zander looking out first to make sure there wasn't anyone right outside to avoid an embarrassing confrontation from anyone knowing what we did.

Not that I'm embarrassed I had sex with Zander at all, but I don't need a confrontation about it by classmates. Luckily, we are in the clear, so we make our way back downstairs right away, chuckling together about this secret we share that no one else needs to know about.

Once we get downstairs our laughter stops at who we see. Mark is surrounded by a bunch of his obnoxious friends in the middle of the living room, laughing, clearly drunk, and with people surrounding them begging for attention.

"Shit," I say, turning in front of Zander so his large body hides me completely. He wraps his arms around me, and I look up to his face. "I want to go."

He nods in agreement before looking around to see the best escape route since going out the front door will put us right in Mark's point of view as we try to leave.

Unfortunately, Zander being tall as shit and having a very memorable body makes him hard not to be noticed by many people, in this case it's Mark noticing. Mark knows Zander because of me, he saw us talking at school and ever since we broke up, I know he's seen us together even more.

"Hey man!" Mark calls, Zander cusses under his breath before turning around, keeping me hidden behind him.

"I was just leaving, so if you don't mind," Zander says, trying to walk past Mark who has now blocked our way, but keeping me behind him.

"Zander, right?" Marks says nonchalantly. I roll my eyes; he knows that's his name.

"Yeah, see ya around, Mark," Zander says dismissively, and

tries again to pull me along behind him to get around Mark to the front door.

"Why are you leaving so soon? And who are you trying to hide?" He looks around Zander, but he makes sure I'm still blocked from his view.

"Don't worry about what I'm doing or who I'm with. We are leaving," I can hear the frustration in Zander's voice, and I haven't heard that from him before. He's extremely intimidating.

"Oh, come on, new guy already has a girl. I just want to make you both feel so welcome," Mark laughs, making his fake friendly tone slip a bit.

"Like I said, don't worry about us," Zander continues to walk forward.

I think he's just going to bulldoze through Mark, who is also a big guy, but not as big as Zander and definitely not as tall.

"Come on, I'm just trying to be friendly," Mark says, holding up his hands in surrender. This time when he looks around Zander he catches a glimpse of my hair, the dark red color being pretty unique to me. "Mel?"

Fuck.

Zander steps more in front of me again, "I'll say it one more time, don't worry about us." His voice dropped low, and if he was speaking to me like this, I would be terrified. I feel like Zander has a side that can be scary as shit.

"Don't worry about some shithead sleeping with my ex? Don't worry, I won't. I hope you like my sloppy seconds though; she wasn't even a good lay."

Before I even have time to react, Zander's fist has met Mark's face, and I jump back. The hit was hard enough to knock Mark to his knees, when he looks up there's blood coming from his nose and his lip.

"Say what you want about me, but don't fucking talk about her that way you piece of shit."

The focus of the party has shifted to the two men in front of me, and I'm standing in shock, unsure of what to do. Pull Zander the fuck out of here? Run alone?

Mark chuckles as he stands up, wiping the blood from his face, "Aw, what? You love her or some shit? She'll leave you and move on to the next because that's what whores do."

Just like that Zander has punched him again, this time knocking him to the ground, Zander on him, the punches don't stop. Mark's friends are quick to come over, knocking Zander back, and pulling him away as Mark struggles to hit him from the ground. I catch a couple of hits land, none of which seem to affect Zander at all.

"Zander, stop, let's just go!" I yell as he gets pulled off Mark, still seething.

I run up to him, wrapping my arms around his front, throwing myself between him and his target. He's looking over me at Mark struggling to get up from the ground, breathing hard.

"Zander, please, come on, let's just leave, please," I plead, but he still isn't looking at me, like he doesn't even feel me holding onto him.

It's like he's in another world where nothing exists outside of his anger, not even me.

"Yeah. Zander, leave so you can make your little slut happy," Mark spits blood onto the ground.

I feel Zander start to go toward him again, but I touch his face to have him look at me for the first time.

His gaze softens on mine as I shake my head in a silent plea, tears welling in my eyes, not even from the words Mark is saying, I don't give a shit about his opinion, but my fear for Zander. He nods lightly, I turn around, taking his hand preparing to leave quickly.

"At least he can make me come," I shrug to Mark before Zander pulls me out the front door.

Was that necessary? No.

Am I bit petty? Yes.

We get to Zander's car quickly and jump inside.

As soon as our doors are closed Zander leans over the middle console, taking my face in his hands and kisses me hard. I melt against his lips, his kiss saying so much he hasn't said yet, apologies he doesn't need to make, and his feelings about me he doesn't need to prove. I take it all in before he pulls away, still holding my face.

"Are you okay?" His voice is strained with worry.

"I'm fine, I don't give a shit about what he thinks," I say seriously, then I remember his hands. I grab them from my face to examine his red knuckles. "Are you okay?"

"Yeah, it's not the first time I've punched someone, I'll live," he says, looking into my eyes, searching to make sure I really am okay, and I am. I want to ask about what he just said, but I decide I'll save that for another time.

Zander races away from the neighborhood. I settle back in the seat, looking over at him as he expertly shifts the car, and takes turns so fast that I hang on. But once we are on a longer stretch of road, he rests his hand on my thigh, and rubs his thumb along my leg.

I smile as I rest my hand on top of his. My feelings inside are scary because I've never felt anything so strongly for anyone, and I'm not sure how he's feeling, but I'm so happy and content with him in this moment I just sit back and enjoy the ride.

## 20

**Present**

Once I'm home I change into some comfy clothes. I debate wearing something cute and comfy, but decide, fuck it. If Zander does come over, he's not going to give a shit what I'm wearing. So oversize t-shirt and boy shorts it is.

I haven't heard from him since I was at the store anyway, I assume he's still doing shit for Trent.

I settle on my little loveseat and turn on the TV to look through Netflix for something to watch when my phone rings. I look over at the caller ID to see it's Zander, I answer quickly.

"Hey, what's up?" My voice is higher than it should be.

*Am I okay?*

"Hey Mel, are you back home?" His voice sounds strained like something is wrong.

"Yup, all safe and sound, what's wrong?"

"I wanted to see you so badly tonight, but Trent has me doing a bunch of bullshit I can't go into over the phone. I wanted to let you know this was not my choice, and I *will* see you tomorrow, I promise."

"Oh, okay, that's fine. I told you I had a hot date anyway, it's not a big deal." I keep my voice as even as possible to reassure him.

It really is okay, I understand if he has shit to deal with, and I'm choosing to believe that he's telling me the truth.

"Save that mint ice cream for me, I still want it," I hear the humor start to return to his voice, probably relieved that I'm not mad or upset.

"I don't know, it's looking pretty delicious right about now," I joke.

"You can't just dangle ice cream in front of me and then threaten to take it away like that," his tone sounds more normal, and it makes me smile.

"Fine, it'll be waiting here for you, but if you break your promise and don't see me tomorrow then it won't be here anymore."

"Damn, you drive a hard bargain, I guess if I have to."

I laugh before asking, "You okay?"

"Yeah, I'm fine, just annoyed at this bullshit which isn't new. I just want to be with you tonight. And that ice cream."

"You just want the ice cream."

"You caught me."

"Let me know when you're back home safe, please," I practically whisper.

I may not know exactly what he has to do tonight, but I worry about his safety and him getting caught. I don't know if I'll be able to sleep not knowing that he's not dead in a ditch or sitting in a jail cell.

"I will, but don't worry about me too much, I'll be fine. I always am."

"I'll try, I know you can handle yourself."

We say goodbye before hanging up. He told me not to

worry, but that is so much easier said than done because I know I'm going to worry. I go back to scrolling through Netflix and attempt to lose myself in some mind-numbing entertainment.

I'M startled awake by the loud "ping" of my phone next to me. I look around my pitch-black apartment, unsure of the time, and I don't even remember falling asleep on my little couch. I look at my phone to see it's four in the morning, and the ping was a text from Zander. I let out a sigh of relief when I read it.

> Zander: I hope you're sleeping, but I'm home safe and sound in my very empty bed.

> Mel: Glad you're back home, even though I'm also in my very empty bed too.

I crawl up over the couch that leads right onto the end of my bed and slide under the covers, barely keeping my eyes open as another text comes through.

> Zander: Sounds like we both have a problem that needs to be fixed at some point.

> Mel: Sounds like it. Go to bed!

> Zander: You first!

> Mel: Goodnight!

> Zander: I'll see you tomorrow.

I drift off to sleep easily this time, knowing he's safe at home.

The next morning I'm shocked to see Aylin has texted me, asking to meet her for coffee. I agree and throw on some leggings and a hoodie since it's raining before going down to meet her at the little coffee place that is a few blocks away.

She's already there when I park. I see her in the window with her laptop and a coffee in front of her. She must have had a break in her day because I rarely get to see her during daylight hours anymore.

I go inside, she gives me a wave as I go order my drink. Chai tea latte because I'm switching things up. Once I have my drink, I go sit next to Aylin who's typing away.

"Hey, I was starting to think you may be a vampire since I never see you during the day anymore," I joke as she finishes what she types and closes her computer.

"Oh whatever, you know how busy I am. I had a break in my day and wanted to meet up," she says as she takes a sip of her coffee that I assume is just black. Gross.

"You want to check on me, don't you?" I know her, she can't help herself.

"A little bit, how's it going?" She faces me completely and I know it's one of her therapist things, open body language is open listening, or something like that.

"I have come up with a new story idea that I'm writing, thank you for asking."

I'm avoiding talking about Zander because I can't tell her about the drug dealing stuff.

"That's great! I know you won't tell me what it is, but do you feel good about this one?"

"I do, I think it's going to be a good one."

"Does this inspiration have to do with a certain someone?" She takes a sip of her coffee again, looking at me over the top of her cup.

"Not directly, no, but something about him just makes me so happy." I smile just at the thought of Zander, and she notices.

"Are you being careful?"

No, no I'm definitely not.

"Yes, mom," I roll my eyes. "Anyway, how's everything going? Any new hot clients or anything I should know about?" I wiggle my eyebrows at her.

"That is so not appropriate, Mel!" She exclaims, lightly smacking me on the arm.

"You can acknowledge if someone is hot without acting on it, you party pooper," I fold my arms across my chest.

"I don't think about anyone that way when I'm with clients, that is so wrong," she shakes her head.

We continue hanging out until she says she has to go to class, we part ways and I head back to my apartment to continue to write.

It's early afternoon at this point as I get back into my apartment. I settle into my desk fully prepared to lose myself in my writing when I get a text from the person I wanted to hear from most.

> Zander: What are you doing in like two hours?
>
> Mel: Probably what I'm doing right now, writing. Why?
>
> Zander: Would you like company?
>
> Mel: Hm…is this company, Chris Hemsworth?
>
> Zander: No, but the next best thing?
>
> Mel: Zac Efron?
>
> Zander: How far down am I on this list?
>
> Mel: Definitely my next guess. I guess you can come over in a couple hours. I might let you in.
>
> Zander: I'll settle for a maybe, see you in a little.

I fall back into my writing with a smile on my face as my story develops, though I'm somewhat distracted by the thought of Zander coming over.

After about an hour I give up writing because I feel like I'm too distracted for it to be good. I go into the bathroom to make myself more presentable. I've taken off my hoodie so I'm just in my leggings and a loose T-shirt. My thick hair is laying in waves over my shoulders. I brush my teeth again for good measure.

Once I feel like I'm more presentable I switch my focus to my apartment. I clean up the random garbage around, do the dishes I left in the sink, and make my bed look less like I rolled around all night in it.

Suddenly I realize I should do something for him like he did for me and go to my fridge to see what I have that I could make as a late lunch or dinner. I don't have much so we may end up going somewhere or ordering in. Unless he's down for some rice and/or frozen waffles.

There's a knock at my door, I look through the peephole to double check that it's him because I'm not looking to be kidnapped today. Once I have my confirmation, I open the door to see him standing there like the beautiful God of a man he is.

His brown hair is somewhat disheveled like he's run his fingers through it. Also, his strong jawline is covered in a light layer of scruff like he hasn't shaved in a couple days, I like it. He's wearing a gray zip up hoodie over a black shirt, paired with some dark jeans and Converse I feel will forever be his uniform, but he wears it so well. His arms perfectly filling out the sleeves of his hoodie. He looks at me, those blue/green mixed eyes staring straight into my soul, and I could die right here and now fully content.

"Hey," I say since it's the only word I'm able to squeak out.

I don't know why he makes me so tongue tied when I first see him, it's not like he's changed in the last day or so. I just feel like after so much time apart I'm still in shock he's back in my life.

"Hey yourself," he says smiling as he walks into my apartment.

I shut and lock the front door behind him, once I turn around, he's cupping my face in his hands as he presses his lips to mine. He pulls away way too quickly.

"I've been thinking about when I get to do that again since you left my house," He smiles, his hands not leaving my face.

"What else have you thought about?" My words come out more breathy than I intend.

Zander raises his eyebrow to me, "I've thought about a lot of things so I'm going to need you to be more specific."

"Like... what do you want to do now that you're here?" My words are coming out more sexual than I'm intending, but that could possibly be due to my subconscious taking over. Or maybe it's my vagina. I'm not sure. They have the same intentions.

"Again, Mel, I'm going to need you to be more specific." His deep voice is even lower, and he steps closer into me. I step back.

We continue those movements until I'm backed into my kitchen island.

"Are you hungry?" I ask to be more specific since it's the first thing that popped into my head even though I'm not hungry at all. I'm just hyper aware that he's holding me pinned against the counter.

"Not really," His voice is impossibly low as he speaks into my neck, his breath sending a shiver all the way through my body but settling at my core.

"Did you want to go somewhere?" I barely get the words out as his lips touch my throat, and lightly skim the skin from my collarbone up to my jaw.

"Not really," he says right against my ear, and I feel my

knees give out. I grab onto the counter to stay standing, but his body pressed against me does more than my useless arms.

"Um...do you want...." I start, but he cuts me off as he takes my bottom lip between his teeth. I moan at the action and then his lips are on mine.

"You, Mel, I want you," he says against my mouth, and I'm powerless against this man.

His lips on mine are hungry, unforgiving, and I love it. I meet his hunger with my own. His tongue is on mine and the kiss is messy, all tongues and teeth, and fire as the warmth from him takes over my entire body, his hand on my hip, pulling me to him and his other still on the counter as he pushes me against it.

Suddenly, his hand that is on my waist grips me harder as he flips me around so I'm facing the island and my back is pressed against his chest. I feel him hard against my back. His hand that was on the counter is across my chest, holding me to him. His hand that was on my waist is slowly making circles around my side to my stomach.

His head is dipped next to my face, his breath hitting my ear as he speaks.

"We are all grown up now, so I want to know, does my little Mel Bell like it soft and sweet?" He asks as his hand that was making circles on me descends down to my center, dipping under the tight waistband of my leggings.

He continues his circles lightly grazing where I really want his hand before adding light pressure to my bundle of nerves that makes my hips buck slightly at the sudden touch. His mouth peppers light kisses along my neck and collarbone making my head lull to the side to give him better access.

"Or...do you like it hard and rough?" His hand that was on my chest grabs my throat as he bites my ear lobe and his hand that was making light circles has increased in pressure before he presses two fingers inside me.

I can't stop the moan that escapes. My hips buck more, encouraging his fingers to move, but he leaves them inside me without moving them.

"Oh, my little Mel Bell seems to like it hard and rough, hm?" My head is thrown back against his shoulder as he keeps the pressure on the side of my throat.

He finally moves his fingers inside of me slightly, curling them to hit the spot inside that makes me go temporarily blind.

I nod my head slightly as I try to press against his hand more, but he's staying still again.

"Use your words, Mel," He growls directly in my ear.

"Yes."

"Yes what?"

"Yes, I like it rough."

It was like a switch went off in that moment, I barely register what happens as he pulls his hand from my pants, earning a frustrated yelp from me, though it's short lived as he turns me around so I'm facing him again.

He tears the shirt off my body. Literally tears it. I'm too shocked to say anything, and I don't get a chance anyway because he's ripping my bra down as his mouth descends on one of my nipples while his hand squeezes and molds my other one. His mouth bites down and I gasp, then he's licking and soothing the bite. I throw my head back at the sensation as he presses me harder against the counter, continuing his assault on my breasts. He switches his mouth to my other nipple and mimics the same actions, biting down, then soothing with his tongue.

Zander drops down to his knees in front of me as he pulls down my leggings, then takes my drenched panties and tosses them to the side. He lifts one of my legs and drapes it over his shoulder, completely exposing myself to him.

"Fuck, Mel, suddenly I'm starving," He growls and before I get to say my smart ass comment his mouth is on my center.

I think I might collapse, but his hands on my ass, and this counter are the only things keeping me standing as he assaults my pussy with his tongue.

Zander switches between nipping at my thigh, sucking so hard on my clit I think I might pass out, and licking up my entire seam. He repeats the actions, and feasts on me like he truly is starving.

"Fuck, Zander," I moan as I run my hand through his thick hair and pull slightly.

Suddenly, his tongue is flicking my clit at a speed I wouldn't think is possible. I'm climbing and I couldn't stop it if I wanted to. I pull his hair harder to press him against me. I push my hips harder into his face as I gasp and moan until I'm sent clear over the edge and explode in an orgasm like I've never had before.

Zander stands up as I catch my breath, and his hands on my hips are the only thing keeping me standing as I recover from the orgasm. He brings his mouth close to mine again but doesn't kiss me.

"I'm not even close to being done with you," It almost sounds like a threat and my whore of a pussy reacts accordingly already ready for more. "Go to your couch and kneel, facing your bed."

He reaches around me to unhook my bra so I'm completely naked while he's still fully dressed. I think about challenging him further, but I decide against it. I don't plan on it being the last time this happens between us. Not even close, I'll save my challenging for another time, I want this too badly.

I do what he says, and go to my couch, kneeling on the seat, leaning forward against the back facing my bed.

I feel so exposed like this, but I feel his eyes boring into me as my self consciousness starts to take over slightly. I adjust my position a little, pressing my legs a little closer together and hiding my stomach by pressing more against the back of the couch.

Zander catches what I do, and he's behind me. I can feel his bare chest pressed against my back as his hand is gathering my hair together, pulling my head back toward him so my entire back is pressed against his chest.

"Do not try to hide any of yourself from me ever again, Mel. You are fucking perfect and when I want to worship your whole body, I'm going to do exactly that, understand?"

I nod, and he pulls my hair tighter, "Use your words."

"Yes, I understand."

"Good girl."

He drops my hair and backs up slightly before I feel his mouth trailing across my shoulders, and down my spine, his hands cupping and squeezing my ass. I spread my knees further as they slip on the cushions. His mouth is back to my ear.

"Tell me what you want," He growls before nipping at the sensitive skin between my neck and my shoulder.

"I want you, fuck I want you," I moan, the slickness between my thighs is only getting more obvious and I'm half tempted to start touching myself if he doesn't soon.

"What about me do you want? Specifics, Mel, I like specifics."

"God, you're so annoying, I want you to fuck me, Zander."

He nips at my neck, and I gasp, the pain instantly turning to pleasure as he kisses the same spot, "Tell me I'm annoying while you come around my fucking cock. You won't be able to. You won't even be able to speak."

He might be right about that. I hear his belt and jeans hit the floor and my arousal increases in anticipation.

He wraps one of his arms around my front, cupping my breast as he pulls me against him. He's kneeling by my legs on the couch cushions, his other hand coming around, his fingers teasing my pussy. He circles my clit again briefly before inserting two fingers inside me again. I push my ass back against him at the feeling. I feel him rock-hard against me, and it makes me want him more. I'm painfully reminded of his size, even years later I've never been with anyone as big as him.

"You're so wet for me, Mel."

I really am, I want him so bad I can't even form a full thought. He removes his fingers from me, and lines himself up at my entrance.

I try to lean forward slightly, but his hand across my chest doesn't let me. He pushes inside, and I gasp at the stretch. He doesn't go slow; his head is inside me then in one hard thrust he pushes completely inside me. I yelp at the feeling, the pain from the initial stretch is short lived, taken over by the pleasure of being so full by him.

"Fuck Mel you feel so fucking perfect."

My only response is a whimper and pushing myself back against him to beg him to move.

His hand on my chest moves up to my throat, wrapping around me and pulling me flush against him as he continues his brutal thrusts, and I'm already building again.

He presses his fingers against the side of my throat, the sensation making me see stars. I move my hips to meet his thrusts, wanting all I can get. Each thrust bringing me closer and closer.

"Ah.... Zander...fuck," I moan between his thrusts. He grasps my throat tighter.

"Keep saying my name like that, and this won't last as long as I want it to," He growls into my hair and increases how hard he thrusts into me.

I'm so close, my moans getting louder, and fueled by his grunts behind me. Suddenly, his hand is off my throat, and I want it back. Then he's pulled out of me and I'm about to protest the emptiness, but I don't get the chance. Zander lifts me up and tosses me on my back onto my bed. I squeal at the sudden movement.

Next thing I know, he's on top of me, pressing into me again. I wrap my legs around his waist as he thrusts all the way inside in one deep thrust again and continues his hard thrusts without missing a beat.

I lift my hips up as I wrap my legs tighter and he's hitting a spot deep inside that makes my eyes roll back as I moan, my orgasm building, it's so close, I feel it right there. Zander tucks his hand behind my head and grabs a fistful of my hair, pulling as he speaks, his voice strained from his own lingering orgasm.

"Look at me, Mel, I need to see you come all around me," his thrusts become deeper, harder, faster. I'm screaming his name as I do exactly what he asks and coming all around him. I keep my eyes on him as long as I can until I can't anymore, and my eyes roll back on their own from the pure ecstasy.

Zander continues plowing into me as my orgasm washes through me and I feel him speed up as his breathing becomes heavier, and his groans are more frequent until he's moaning my name with a few more hard thrusts. I feel him inside me throbbing, as his orgasm washes through him and he fills me completely.

We lay like this for a few moments, him still inside me. Chest to chest, both slick with sweat, I'm wet and sticky on my thighs, bliss evident on both of our faces.

After a few beats Zander pulls out of me and rolls onto his side next to me before sliding off my bed and going into the bathroom. When he comes out, he has a wet washcloth and I chuckle at the memory of our first time together, but this is the first time I'm seeing him naked as an adult and holy fuck I want to jump on him again.

He's much bigger now, which I could tell even with clothes on, but his once lean muscles are now bigger and more defined. His arms could crush me. His glorious dick is on full view and even now it's not fully soft yet, and it's still massive. That was just inside me. How?

"This feels like déjà vu," I joke as he leans over and cleans off my legs and presses the warm cloth to my center, there's a slight sting, but the heat relieves it instantly.

"I think there's a few things different this time," He chuckles before removing the washcloth from me and tossing it into my hamper.

"Yeah, I could name at least three," I start to sit up, wincing at the slight ache between my legs, but I like it.

"Yeah? What are the three you're thinking?" He asks as he slips back into my bed behind me.

He pulls me flush against him, forcing me to lay back down and be spooned by him. I settle in, appreciating the feel of his hard muscles behind me and his strong arms around me, holding me close.

"Well first of all we get to do this," I wiggle my hips back against him, and I hear a quiet growl come from him as he presses me harder against him.

"If you do that again, I'm going to fuck you again and it will include a punishment you won't like, what are the other two you're thinking?"

I want to know what he could possibly do that I won't like, but I make a mental note to ask later, "Another is you're not going to get in a fist fight with anyone once we leave this bed."

"That one is not a guarantee, but I'll accept it for now, and the last one?"

I turn around to face him, and I'm a little surprised he lets me, but he keeps his arm wrapped around me. He pulls me against him, so we are chest to chest. His erection is back and pressing against me, almost making me forget my train of thought, but I don't.

"The last one is that you're not leaving me this time." My heart races saying it.

I can't let him leave me this time; we've been apart too long, too many times in our lives. We are finally together again and there has to be a reason for it, but I'm afraid of his reaction. Maybe I'm imagining our entire connection. Maybe it's all in my head and he just wants a reliable fuck.

"You're right, I'm definitely not leaving you this time." He smiles, pressing his lips to mine again. I think he's just going to kiss me sweetly, but his impressive erection bounce back time indicates more.

Zander rolls me onto my back, pressing me into the mattress and proceeds to be anything but gentle with me yet again.

# 21

*Zander*

**Present**

We lay in Mel's bed after hours of fucking. Both of us completely exhausted, sweaty, and still tangled in each other.

I have her wrapped in my arms; her head tucked into my chest as I hold her to me. I can't stop smiling like an idiot into her hair. I can't believe I'm here with her, that we are in her bed right now.

I meant what I said, I will not let her go again, there's no way. She's accepted who I am now, and even though it's not who I want to be, she accepts me. If the last few hours are any indication, I'm pretty sure she has some sort of feelings for me as well.

At some point I drift off to sleep with her still in my arms.

When I wake up it's still dark in Mel's apartment, she's deep breathing next to me so she must still be asleep.

I don't want to wake her up, but I adjust my position so I'm laying further down instead of straining my neck. The slight movement is enough to wake up Mel, she looks up at me through hooded, half asleep eyes.

"Hey beautiful," I say as I move some hair from her face so I can see as much of her green eyes as possible.

"No," she throws her arm over her face, taking away my view again.

"What?" I chuckle as I try to remove her arm from her face again.

I want to see her. I went ten years without her, I'm taking every second of her I can to make up for lost time.

"I'm probably a sleepy mess with drool and all," She rolls away from me, still hiding her face.

I grab her and roll her back over to me, facing me this time. Her face is scrunched up in annoyance at the movement.

"You're always beautiful to me," I nuzzle her to me again, rubbing my nose against hers. "Drool and all."

She gasps and hides her face again.

"I'm kidding. You don't have drool," I laugh, peppering her with light kisses.

"I need a shower," Mel says through her own laughter as I don't stop my kisses all over her face, shoulder, and chest.

"Want company?" I look up into her eyes.

She nods slightly before sliding out of my arms, heading toward the bathroom.

I watch as she walks the short distance to the bathroom appreciating her naked form. Her thick thighs carry her as her round ass sways slightly as she walks, appearing to possibly be a little sore from our hours together.

I smile, proud that is my doing. I hear her start the shower as I rise from bed and follow her into the bathroom. She has a hand stretched out under the water, feeling the temperature.

I raise my hand to rest on her shoulder as I slide it down her outstretched arm and intertwine our fingers.

I watch the side of her face as she watches my movement, a

small smile playing on her lips. The water is warm enough, so I step inside the small shower that's only dwarfed by my size as I pull her in too.

The cramped space is a standing shower only and is a bit smaller than a standard shower with a bathtub and all. It's okay, though, I get to have Mel pressed against me completely as the water hits my back, since the shower head only reaches my shoulder blades.

I hold her against me so she gets the warm water cascading over her body as well. Holding her like this, both of us still completely naked makes my dick react accordingly, even after hours together, I can't get enough of her.

I've never been able to recover so quickly and easily as I can with her. She's also the only woman I've been bare with, ever. Our first time together was the first time I've been bare with anyone, and ever since it's only been her. I was relieved when she told me between our sessions together that she's still on birth control, though I don't even think that would have stopped me. I need her in a way I can't even explain.

I press my lips to the top of her head as I switch our positions so she's under the water enough to wet her hair, and I'm out of the spray.

I take the shampoo from the shelf, squeezing some in my hand as she wets her hair completely. I take the soap and lather it on her head carefully, massaging her scalp as I move my fingers through her thick locks. She closes her eyes, and arches back at the feelings. My dick is pressing into her stomach, but I really do want to give her a break. It's just seeing her head arched back, lips slightly parted, and her breasts with taunt nipples against my chest is making it hard to resist.

Once I'm done lathering her hair she runs it under the water, rinsing out the soap completely before I return my hands to her hair with the conditioner already in my hand.

As I'm lathering her hair for the second time, I feel her

wrap her soft hand around my cock, sending my hips lurching forward. I stop lathering her hair as I bring my hand down to her wrist.

"Mel, I'm trying to take care of *you* right now," I hiss.

"I know, but let me take care of you, please."

I really was going to let this be an innocent shower, but she is making that impossible as her hand continues to squeeze around me, moving up and down my shaft.

I try to focus on my task as I try to finish working my fingers through her hair as she rinses again with just one hand. I help her, but my mind is fuzzy from the movement she hasn't stopped. I thrust my hips into her hand involuntarily, and I see the smirk on her lips like she's proud of what she's doing.

Nope, little Mel Bell, I'm still in charge here.

Her green eyes meet mine and I give her my own smirk before leaning down like I might get on my knees for her again, but instead I take my hands behind her thighs and lift her up. She wraps her legs around my waist instantly with a gasp.

My cock is already perfectly lined up at her entrance in this new position. I turn so I'm pushing her against the shower wall, she yelps as the cold tiles press against her back.

"You started this, now you're going to finish it," I threaten as I press my dick to her warm, soaked core, but not pressing inside her yet.

"Maybe that's what I wanted." Her eyes flicker something dangerous, something I don't think I could ever get tired of seeing.

A challenge. Mel is going to be the death of me.

"You're trouble," I growl before slamming into her in one hard thrust.

She screams out at the invasion, and I feel bad for a second. I should've probably taken it easy considering everything she's already been through with me today, but then she looks at me through her hooded eyes, and moves so her hips grind against me. She clearly wants this just as much as me, and I know my little Mel is tougher than it seems. She's also more dangerous for me than I would've ever guessed.

I slam into her again, continuing with brutal, hard thrusts as the warm water cascades both of us, her moans keeping me going, but bringing me to the edge.

I reach between us to rub that sensitive spot that sends her head back and my name to fall from her lips the way I love to hear. I feel her start to contract around me as she gets close. My name on her lips as she screams out her orgasm sends me over the edge as I spill inside her. I'm throbbing inside her warm, wet heat for a few moments before I pull out and set her on the ground, holding her hips so she doesn't fall.

I kiss her lips softly as I continue to hold her body to me. I so badly want to kiss her harder, show her everything I feel in one kiss, but I decide not to push it. I pull away and finish the shower by cleaning her body fully as I intended to do before getting sidetracked by this perfect little devil in front of me.

Once we are both cleaned thoroughly, and the water has started to become cold I turn it off grabbing a towel and dry off every part of her.

"I am capable of doing that myself, Zander." She protests as I'm knelt down, drying her legs, up between her thighs, and down her other leg.

"I just don't think you'd be as thorough as me," I look up at her, and wink.

I think I see her roll her eyes before I look back down to where I'm drying her.

I wrap her in the towel before grabbing one for myself and drying myself off, less thoroughly than I did to her.

She's already made her way out into the rest of her small apartment. When I leave the bathroom I see her grabbing clothes from her closet, she slips on a large t-shirt over her towel before sliding on cotton looking shorts. I can't help but think about how I wish she was wearing my t-shirt, that's a sight I need to see soon.

I move over to where I discarded my clothes earlier and slide them on, save for my jeans. It doesn't seem like we will be going anywhere so my boxers and my own t-shirt is all I decide to put on.

Mel takes our two towels and brings them back into the bathroom to hang up. I decide to look around her small apartment for the first time since I got here. I wasn't planning on coming over to jump her, but she does something to me. She makes me feel so different I just couldn't help myself.

I'm examining her bookshelves in the dim light seeing if there's anything I recognize. I see her name on a section of books. I still haven't gotten around to reading any of her work, so I pick up the first one on the shelf, reading the back. I'm not a huge reader, but it seems interesting.

Arms wrap around my waist from behind as I feel Mel slide herself against my back pressing her chest and head against me, her head not even reaching my shoulders.

"Whatcha looking at?" Her voice is muffled by my shirt.

"Just admiring your work," I raise the book over my shoulder for her to see.

"Oh wow, I don't know how I feel about you reading my books," I feel her nuzzling her face into my back again.

I turn around to face her. She keeps her arms wrapped around me as I turn and take her chin in between my fingers so she will look up into my eyes.

"Why not?" I wonder. She looks at the book in my hand before looking back into my eyes

"I don't know, it's *you*," she says it like that actually explains anything.

"You let thousands of people read your books, who says I haven't already?" I raise my brow to her.

"I think you would've had comments by now if you had, but

if you want to, I can't stop you." She shrugs, still keeping her arms wrapped around me.

I lean down so our lips are ghosting over each other, not touching, just breathing in each other's air as I whisper, "You could make me do anything if you just ask."

I don't give her a change to reply or say any of her smart-ass comments I know are on her mind as I press my lips against hers.

# 22

**Present**

It's been two weeks since the day Zander came over to my apartment for the first time. It has not been the last, not even close.

He's come over every chance he gets since he insists he doesn't want me to meet Trent if we ever go to his house, plus he says coming over is a way for him to get away anyway.

There was a conversation we had because of how adamantly he doesn't want me to come over to his house and I started getting a little concerned.

"You sure you're *not hiding some wife or live-in girlfriend or something and that's why I can't come over?*" I cross my arms over my chest, staring at Zander as he sits at the island in my kitchen.

He gives me a questioning look, "Mel, if I had some woman waiting for me at home, how would I be here practically every night?"

"Sounds like the words of someone who's thought about this?" I press, but I know I'm being ridiculous.

"Yup, you caught me, that's what's going on and everything I've told you is a lie; I actually work a very basic office job too, dammit."

"I knew it!" I exclaim as he jumps out of the seat, coming over to me.

He then takes me in his arms, proceeding to show me how ridiculous I'm being.

"It's just you, Mel, it will only ever be just you."

IT MAKES A LITTLE SENSE. The little bits, and pieces he tells me about Trent every once in a while, make him sound terrible, and not someone I ever want to meet.

My story that I've decided I'm far enough along to refer to as a book now is coming along really well. I only get the chance to write when Zander is needing to do whatever he has to do on the daily that I decide not to question.

I've gotten slightly more comfortable about his safety, but I still am choosing to be blissfully ignorant to the full extent of everything.

I've kept Aylin up to date with everything, sans details about Zander's "day job". She has yet to meet him, though that's changing tonight and to say I'm nervous would be an understatement.

It's worse than him meeting my parents because, well, they've technically already met him. Zander has asked to see my dad again which has earned him a sideways glance because I'm slightly concerned about that, but I know it will happen eventually.

My feelings for this man have grown every day and it scares the shit out of me. No one should be this perfect. No one *is* this perfect, so I'm still waiting for the other shoe to drop.

. . .

I GIVE Zander questioning looks which make him laugh before asking me, "what?"

"You just can't be real, I refuse to believe it," I said to him, wrapped in his arms one night.

"Shit, I'm not real? Who's going to tell my dad, he might be pretty upset to hear that."

"Shut up, I mean whoever this is," I wave my hand in front of his face in a circular motion, "isn't real, there has to be something wrong with you somewhere."

"Yeah, there is, and I've told you about it already, you're the crazy one still here." He shrugs with his arms around me.

"Okay, you're in my apartment so you're the one that's still here, actually."

"But you let me in, which means you want me around."

"I wouldn't go that far," I joke, but instead of laughing that earns me a sound from his throat and my back pressed down into my mattress.

THERE'S a knock on my door that brings me out of my thoughts.

I answer it to see Zander standing there looking mouth watering as usual, he's dressed up slightly for tonight's adventure. Not that we are doing anything particularly fancy, we are going to some club downtown Aylin wanted to see for the first time. Since it's Friday night she is letting herself have some fun to celebrate another week closer to her degree.

Zander is dressed in a black button down with the sleeves rolled up to his elbows, revealing his muscled forearms, revealing the one covered in tattoos. His shirt tucked into his signature dark jeans with a black belt, and he's switched out his usual converse for some slip-on black Vans.

He looks like the hottest demon to ever emerge from the underworld dressed in almost all black. His light brown hair and bright eyes are a contradiction to his clothes in the perfect way that makes my legs shake beneath me.

"You going to invite me in, or do you want to keep staring?" Zander smirks, bringing my gaze back up to his face since I've been too busy appreciating the way his button up hugs his muscled torso.

"Maybe I want to keep staring," I place my hands on my hips.

"Oh, this is the Mel I'm getting tonight." He rubs his hand down his face before looking back to me again.

I fold my arms across my chest, pushing my very obvious cleavage up higher and I catch his eyes flicker down, "What Mel is that?"

"The one that is *begging* to be put over my knee by the end of the night." His voice drops low as he stalks forward, pushing me back with his body as he enters my apartment and shuts the door behind him with his foot.

"I don't hear any begging." I'm proud my voice isn't shaking more considering what his words have done to the space between my legs.

"Oh, you'll be fucking begging, but that will have to wait since we have places to be." His damn smirk.

"Places? Plural?"

"Possibly, but let's go meet Aylin." He smiles at me.

I know we told her we would meet her there soon I just hoped we could sneak in a quick fuck before we leave.

This man has turned me into a damn sex addict. I've never been this bad, but every time I'm near him I can barely hold back from stripping him naked and jumping on him.

It's a problem.

I purposely didn't wear panties under the navy dress I'm wearing that crisscrosses across my back and falls mid-thigh. I paired it with some black wedges, though I am not usually someone that wears heels I know I can around Zander, even if

I end up taking them off by the end of the night, which is likely.

"Someone is in a hurry," I roll my eyes as I grab my purse from the counter.

"I just want to make a good first impression on your best friend." He kisses my temple as I walk in front of him toward the front door.

As I'm opening it, Zander's hand swings out by my head and pushes it closed. I turn around to face him, "I thought you wanted to leave."

"I couldn't leave this apartment without kissing you first, especially if I have to be around you in that dress all night, unable to really touch you." He dips his head above mine, our lips a breath apart for a second as he looks into my eyes.

I want to ask what he's looking for, but before I get the chance his lips are on mine, his body pressing me against the door. Our tongues battling in each other's mouth and a whimper escapes me as Zander moves his hand up my thigh lightly. He reaches my bare center, a groan escaping his throat into my mouth before he pulls away.

"Oh, you are going to kill me, aren't you?"

I shrug before pressing a quick kiss to his lips and winking then opening my front door again, walking out into the hallway as he slowly follows.

When we reach the elevator, I notice Zander adjust himself slightly in his jeans, making my lips spread in a mischievous smile.

"Don't even think about it, the elevator ride is not anywhere close to long enough for everything I'm planning to do to you tonight." He threatens, and goddammit if that doesn't make me wetter.

I should've worn panties; I'm only torturing myself now.

I shift uncomfortably, crossing my legs, and I see Zander give me a similar smile I gave him. Asshole.

We step inside the elevator, Zander keeping me tucked into his side with his arm around my shoulders tightly. As much as I want to think it's because he wants to hold me, I think it's so I don't do anything he knows he wouldn't stop.

The air is cold as we step outside, and I regret not bringing a jacket, but we will be inside most of the night so I'm sure it'll be fine.

Zander opens the passenger door of his small sports car and holds my hand as I step down into it, thankfully because the heels, while they may only give me a slight height boost, made the step down into the car more intimidating. He slides into the driver's seat and the car is cramped with his huge body taking up so much space as it usually does.

As the car roars to life Zander's phone starts ringing, he looks down at the caller ID and sighs, clenching his jaw.

"You can answer it," I say quietly.

I don't think it's me that's preventing him from answering it, at least that's not what it seems like by the look on his face.

"It's Trent, I really don't want to, but I also don't want him sending anyone to track me down if I don't." He shakes his head, seeming to talk to himself more than me.

I place my hand on his thigh and offer a small smile. "It's really okay, do what you need to do."

With a groan he answers the phone abruptly with a tone I never want directed at me. This Zander is intimidating, scary... oddly sexy, but that's something I'll question later.

"What." It's a statement, not a question from him.

I hear a deep voice on the other side of the call, but I can't quite hear what's being said due to the distance and the roar of the engine.

"No, I can't do that right now, I'm busy." He tells Trent.

I wince as the voice on the other end of the phone clearly gets louder, though I still can't hear what's being said.

"Why don't you do it?" He demands, his voice getting lower, more intimidating.

"Fuck no, Trent, that's not a fucking reason just do it yourself."

I reach my hand back onto his thigh and squeeze. Zander looks at me, his eyebrows furrowed together, clearly pissed, but not at me.

*It's okay* I mouth to him.

Even though I don't know exactly what Trent is asking him to do I'm sure we could just get it done, then go meet Aylin. She probably hasn't even left her place yet.

Zander just shakes his head at me adamantly as Trent continues what I can only assume is yelling on the other end of the phone. I squeeze his thigh harder, and nod to him mouthing the same words again.

Zander closes his eyes, sighing deeply before speaking again, I assume cutting Trent off mid yell.

"Fine, send me the details on the burner." He doesn't open his eyes as he speaks through his teeth.

He's pissed.

The phone call ends, and Zander turns to me, his eyes on fire, but not in the fun way. "I have to do a run; I can come get you after and we can go."

I shake my head at him, "No, it's fine, I'll just come along. I'll stay silent and blend in with the seat, no one will even know I'm here."

"Mel, seriously, this is dangerous. I don't want you in harm's way at all, please just let me come get you afterwards."

"Zander, you won't let anything happen to me, I trust you."

"Exactly, that's what I'm trying to do."

"Come on, let's go," I'm not arguing about this, even though my heart is pounding in my chest at what I just did.

Why the fuck am I going with him? What if he gets arrested? What if *we* get arrested?

I do my best to not show the realized fear on my face as he reluctantly starts driving. I pull out my phone to text Aylin, so she isn't waiting for us. I realize I might have to explain this later, so I'll have to come up with something good.

> Mel: Hey, we are running a little late so can we push this back about an hour?

Her reply is instant and makes me laugh, maybe I won't have to explain anything after all.

> Aylin: Can you two not keep it in your pants for one night?

> Mel: Nope. See you soon!

I guess her assuming we just got caught up in having sex is going to be the easiest explanation.

Zander is getting on the freeway, his face looks like stone as he drives, no look of humor or anything. This is a weird side of him I'm not used to seeing. I feel bad for pushing, but the sound of Trent tracking him down sounded a lot worse than whatever this could be.

We drive to the next town over. I'm confused, but don't say anything because the way Zander looks has me a little afraid, like he's a time bomb waiting to go off. I want to ask if he's mad at me, but I'll wait.

Zander parks in front of a storage center, I look over at him confused, but keep my mouth shut.

He leans over to open the glove box by my legs, once it's open, I notice a gun and a flip phone. My eyes widen at the sight of the gun that's been so casually right by me for who knows how long, and I never knew.

I look over at Zander wide eyed, the seriousness just now settling over me, apparently. Zander takes out the phone, closing the box with the gun still in it. I watch as he turns on the phone and reads something before putting it in his pocket.

"Wait here, please."

It's the first time he's spoken to me the whole drive, and I'm pretty sure my face shows how terrified I am. I just nod.

I watch as he goes inside. The realness of whatever is happening settling over me. I've been living in this happy Zander bubble where he's sweet, rough where it counts, hot as shit, and the same person I knew.

This new side to him, this side I have yet to see is scary, dangerous, and has me questioning if this is the real Zander. If the version of himself around me is fake because it's what he knows I want from him.

I shake my head, no that's so stupid. He was honest about this, he was prepared for me to go running for the hills, and I didn't. I know the real Zander; this one is the one he has to be. He wants to get out of this life, he's said it multiple times.

He comes back quickly, stopping at the trunk before entering the car again. He tosses a large jacket and a hat toward me. They land in my lap; I look at him questioning as he settles back in the driver's seat.

"Put those on please, cover yourself as much as you can, I don't want this low life to see you." He's serious. His tone is stern.

I'm going to seriously have to do some soul searching to find out why that turns me on.

I do what he says, wrapping myself in the huge jacket that covers me pretty well. My thighs are covered by how long it is, and my entire chest is covered as I zip the leather jacket up practically to my neck. I throw my hair back, as I put the base-ball cap on my head.

Zander reaches over again to the glove box, removing the gun. My breath hitches as I watch him tuck the weapon in his waistband.

"Do you trust me?" He asks, looking at me with seriousness in his eyes.

I nod slowly. Zander starts up the car again, driving us to wherever the hell we are going.

I can't stop my spiraling thoughts wondering what in the fuck I really got myself into.

## 23

**Present**

This was not how I saw the night going.

I worried about something like this happening while I'm with Mel, we've been extremely lucky these last few weeks. I've been able to keep Trent at bay and gotten my time with Mel uninterrupted. That is until tonight when that fuck face called demanding I do a run one of his guys couldn't do.

Let me say, the money being made from this run is nothing and not worth interrupting my night with Mel.

I was about to tell Trent to shove it when Mel put her hand on the top part of my thick thigh, and looked at me with those green eyes telling me it's okay. She didn't even know what she was getting into. I was not going to let her, but she reassured me.

Then, she somehow convinced me to let her come along. This woman, this perfect, crazy woman.

We pull up to the meeting spot, I get out of the car, turning to Mel before I shut the door to cover her in darkness, so this guy won't see her. After this we can go enjoy our night.

"Stay here, please stay hidden and whatever happens do not leave this car," I demand.

I watch as her mouth parts slightly in fear. She also looks like she wants to say something but holds back as she nods.

God, I want to say more to her, want to share how I've been feeling even though I know it's too soon, I know she has my heart, but I can't tell her yet.

Plus, I'll have plenty of time to tell her, I've done runs all the time, this isn't something new. This guy is a reliable buyer so I know it's not a set up, it will be fine.

I see him stumble around the corner, rolling my eyes, great.

The man comes closer, he's probably younger than he looks because the man could pass for eighty, but someone doing the hard shit he's doing wouldn't live that long. His hair is a ratty mess, and as he approaches, I see the lost look in his eyes. He stinks, his clothes have probably gone weeks without being washed.

"You Trent's guy?" He asks as he gets closer, examining me.

I stand taller, making my size known.

Many people know not to challenge me or rob me when they see my size. The few that have tried were stupid and didn't get very far.

I barely nod my head, just enough to acknowledge, even though I want to spit at his feet for referring to me as "Trent's guy".

"How much you want?" I ask, quick to get this over with.

I already know his drug of choice from the info Trent sent, plus it's always heroin. That's the popular drug among our buyers apparently.

He tells me the amount, handing over the cash which I count carefully before handing the drugs over to him. It wouldn't be the first time someone has tried to give me fake bills or shorted me. They never get away with it, but I like to be thorough.

I'm satisfied with the amount he gave me, so I hand him over the small baggies that have been carefully measured with the right amount.

The guy examines it himself before nodding that he's satisfied.

Just as he's about to walk away there's a noise from inside my car. My eyes widen as I refuse to look back at Mel and acknowledge that someone is in there in front of this guy. I'm standing in front of the driver's window to block his sight from inside the car. I'm not sure what the sound was, but it seemed like she dropped something, then gasped. I should've kept the car running to block out any potential noise, fuck.

"Who do you have with you there, guy?" The man asks, trying to peek around me.

I'm a brick wall, unmoving.

"No one. You have your shit, move along." I refuse to move because if I open the car door in front of him, he will see Mel.

He continues to try to see around me, and in a moment of clarity for him apparently, he walks around the front of my car and peers in through the windshield.

Son of a bitch. My fists clench at my side. He better keep walking if he knows what's good for him.

"Wow, you guys getting into selling women too?" The man asks, as he tries to get a better view of Mel, and my blood is boiling. "I would pay a pretty penny for that one." He cackles.

"Keep fucking walking before I put a goddamn bullet in your skull." I threaten as I reach for the gun in my waistband.

"Oh, you keeping that one for yourself? Or have to try out the goods first? You know, drugs can only be sold once, but women you can sell over and over."

I snap.

Him talking about any woman this way would make me pissed, but Mel. *My Mel.* No fucking way.

I pull out my gun from my waistband as I take long strides toward him. I grab his collar, suddenly the fear registers in his eyes that I'm serious.

"Hey man, I was just kidding," He tries, but it's too late for me to show him mercy. I warned him.

I lift his scrawny body up by his collar so he's forced to look directly at me, "You're lucky I don't want her to witness a murder tonight, but if I ever see you again, you're fucking dead."

The man is struggling in my grip. I shove my knee up to hit him where I know it hurts before dropping him like he's nothing, kicking him in the ribs a few times, then finally bringing the butt of my gun down on his skull and walk away leaving him writhing on the ground.

He's lucky I didn't knock him out. I wanted him to feel everything so he wouldn't forget.

I walk back to the car, seeing Mel through the windshield looking at me with her jaw dropped, and I can't tell if there's fear in her eyes or just shock.

As soon as I'm in the car I throw open the glove box shoving the gun I never took off safety and the phone I've already turned off inside before closing it and driving away from this place as fast as I can.

Neither of us say anything until we are a good distance away from the scene, I dare a glance at Mel. Her jaw is still dropped. She's staring at me, I'm not sure if she ever looked away.

"Are you okay?" I ask through gritted teeth.

I'm not mad at her, I'm mad at myself for not thinking and leaving the car running.

"Um, yeah...I'm so sorry Zander," She seems terrified, why is she sorry?

"What? Why? I shouldn't have brought you; I knew it would cause trouble," I shake my head, running my hand through my hair.

"No, it's my fault. I made you bring me, then I dropped my stupid phone which that guy clearly heard, and then you...." She seems like she can't even find the words. She shakes her head.

I find a spot and pull the car off to the nearly nonexistent shoulder in the middle of nowhere. I park and turn off the lights before turning toward her.

I can see tears welling in her eyes and I instantly feel guilty. I grab her hands in my own, squeezing hard.

"Do not feel bad, okay?" I squeeze harder. "That wasn't your fault, you didn't hear the shit he was saying. I told you I would keep you safe and I could not handle what he was saying. Everything that happened is on him, not you."

She sniffles, looking at me skeptically, "What was he saying?"

I sigh, I don't want to tell her, but I want her to understand.

"He was asking if we were getting into selling women and assumed you were going to be one." I shake my head, getting angry all over again. If I didn't have her hands in mine, I might need to hit something again.

"Ew, that's so fucked up." Her face skews as she digests the information I just shared with her.

"Yeah, so do you see, now?" I beg her to understand and to stop blaming herself for what happened.

She nods, then a small smile starts to play on her lips as her eyes meet mine. There's something there and I'm confused because it looks like it could be desire.

I must be imagining things. Seeing her in my jacket and hat for some reason is one of the hottest things, like I've staked my claim on her. I guess in a way, I have.

"I don't know why, but I might have been more turned on

than scared, what does that say about me?" She asks softly, and I know what I saw was real, not just my own feelings projected.

"Fuck, Mel," I shake my head, a slight laugh escaping my throat. "You're okay though?"

"I could be better." She shrugs, and there's that look again.

"Mel Bell, as much as I want to do something about that look in your eyes, I stupidly have the world's smallest car and there's no way I can properly fuck you in here."

Her eyes darken as she continues to look at me, "I guess I just have to thank you for defending my honor."

"I wouldn't say that's what I did." I chuckle, but it doesn't matter.

Before I can object Mel is shifting in her seat, leaning over to me, lips on mine, hungry and demanding. I meet her hunger, my tongue demanding dominance over hers and I feel her undo my belt and start to undo my pants.

"Mel," I threaten into our kiss, but she doesn't stop, and I don't think I want her to.

Quickly, she has my stiff erection free from the confines of my pants and boxers. She breaks our kiss, and gives me a mischievous look before dipping down, her hot mouth around the head of my cock.

I throw my head back in a groan as I jerk my hips up. She has her hand wrapped around the base of my shaft, her tongue licking around the head of my dick before dipping her head back down.

I throw off the hat on her head so I can get a better view of her. Her long red hair is draped around her, I gather it in my hands and hold it back as she moves her mouth lower onto me, with her hand meeting her mouth as it moves up while she tests herself on how far she can take me.

I pull on her hair to hold back my urge to thrust my hips up completely, letting her get used to my size in her mouth and take this at her pace so I don't hurt her.

She seems to gain confidence, moving lower onto me, as I let out a low moan, which appears to encourage her to take me further down her throat.

"Fuck, Mel," I hiss between my teeth. It is taking all my willpower to not thrust completely into her mouth.

She hums around me, and I lose it. My grip on her hair tighter as my hips thrust up, I feel the back of her throat and the gag that comes from her, but she doesn't stop. She keeps going, and with faster, harder movements.

Her cheeks hollowed as she sucks on me, her hand gipping me harder. She hums more, earning more thrusts from my hips.

The sight of her bent over the console of my car, mouth around my cock, and her tongue sliding around me perfectly, sends me into a frenzy of thrusting as she takes everything I give. I feel myself at the edge.

"I'm going to fucking come, I want you to fucking swallow all of it," I demand. Normally I would try to take it easy with her like this, but she brings out this part of me, this primal part she seems to really like,

She hums again in approval around me and takes me deeper. I explode into her mouth as she swallows around me, and I watch her throat bob.

It's the hottest fucking thing I've ever seen. She releases me from her mouth, eyes brimmed with tears, lips red and raw, with a smile on her face.

I kiss her hard as I tuck myself away with one hand. She kisses me just as hard before pulling away, settling back on her seat looking over at me with something else in her eyes, like admiration, or maybe more.

I won't let myself believe it's more, not yet, even though I know it. I know I'm in love with this woman and she's going to fucking kill me one day. I just know it.

# 24

*Mel*

**Present**

I fix the appearance of my face after the aftermath of the hottest blowjob I've ever given, while Zander drives us to the club we were supposed to be at way sooner.

I texted Aylin to let her know we were on our way, after the slight delay. I have never been so turned on from giving head, but watching Zander become unhinged is becoming my favorite thing.

When he fucks me, he does so with little to no restraint, and when he's protecting me, he's the same. The fact that I can make him become this feral beast is something truly amazing to see. I love it.

We pull up to the club and Zander has to park down the street due to the packed Portland parking situation. I have his oversize jacket around me as we walk to the club entrance hand in hand. The warmth from his hand could almost keep me warm enough without the jacket. I keep it on though because I like being overwhelmed by his scent and covering my body in it.

The music is pounding as we walk up to the door, the bouncer looking us over before letting us in without any issues.

I wrinkle my face as I look up at Zander, walking into the dark club, "Do I look old or something?"

He shoots his eyes to me, puzzled, "What? You look perfect."

"We didn't get ID'd, I feel like a twenty-seven-year-old grandma now." I'm somewhat joking, it's nice to not have to pull out my ID, but what the fuck?

"I think it has to do more with the scary man on your arm." Zander winks at me and I melt.

How can one simple gesture bring me to my knees so easily?

"You're perfect, Mel, I do not think it had anything to do with you looking old." He smiles at me.

We walk deeper into the club, I'm getting hotter from the crowd of sweat covered people everywhere, the jacket seeming more stupid by the second. I don't want to take it off, it feels like a safety blanket. A Zander smelling safety blanket.

Aylin had let me know she was already here as we parked, and waiting for us on the left side of the bar.

We make our way over to where I see her. Brown wavy hair draped over her shoulders. She's put on a little makeup, and I'm not sure if it was just what she wore during her day or if she put more effort in with the extra time we gave her.

"Hey, love!" I exclaim as we reach her, I release Zander's hand so I can wrap my arms around her.

She returns the hug with a smile on her face.

We separate, and I see her eyes lock onto Zander, giving him a skeptical look. Not one that's meant to be rude, more like she's examining his appearance, trying to get into his head before he even speaks. She's been like that even before she started studying to be a therapist, she always wants to be in people's heads, know what they are thinking and what they won't tell her. Which is why I've been so cautious about talking about Zander to her at all because I know she will see right through any of my lies or omissions.

"Nice to meet you, I'm Zander." He stretches his hand out to her, his winning smile plastered on his face.

"Hi Zander," She takes his hand and shakes it quickly. "I've heard about you a lot recently."

*Jesus.* I roll my eyes, she just had to throw in the "recently" part in didn't she? I watch Zander's face light up more at that confession, his ego taking over.

"Really? All good things I hope." He wraps his arm around my waist, pulling me flush against his side.

"I've definitely heard some positives."

She's straight forward, always right to the point which I generally appreciate. Though, I know if he asks for *specifics* with what I've shared about him, I know she will give them to him. I really don't need that embarrassment from either of them right now.

"Drinks! Who wants what?" I interrupt before Zander gets a chance to dig for more information that I know he will get later anyway, but I want to be drunk for that.

"You know what I always get," Aylin says simply.

"Careful, if I'm ordering then I might make you expand your horizons," I throw her way, and she sticks her tongue out at me.

There's the friend side of Aylin, not the serious one.

Zander leans down to speak right into my ear, "What I want isn't going to be on the menu here."

His words send a shiver down my spine, and Aylin looks over skeptically. She can probably see the flush on my face and guess what he said.

"Okay, so a Jack and Coke, Malibu pineapple, and I already need at least seven shots." I call out as I lean onto the bar, which is pushing my ass out toward Zander. I'm facing Aylin as she leans on her side next to me so we are facing each other.

We get the drinks; I do not order seven shots because as much as I wanted to, I knew that wouldn't be the smartest idea, so Rum and Dr. Pepper it is.

The music is so loud I can feel it in my chest as we all drink and talk more. Zander seems to be doing well winning Aylin over, though I think the man could win over a brick wall he's so charismatic.

I'm thankful she hasn't asked about what he does, she's more focused on his "intentions with me". I roll my eyes at her over protectiveness, continuing to call her "mom" through the night.

I know she's feeling the effects of the alcohol running through her blood after a few more drinks because she's pulling me to dance. I am feeling the buzzing throughout my body as well, but leaving Zander's side tears something within me that I won't admit out loud.

Eventually, I give in and let Aylin drag me closer to the middle of the floor. Before I go, I shed the jacket off and hand it to Zander since the alcohol is making my entire body hot. The dancing will only make that worse and I'm not looking to be drenched in sweat more than I already am.

Aylin and I dance on each other, putting on somewhat of a show, at least I am. I know Zander's eyes are glued to me as Aylin and I run our arms along each other. We switch between her back to my front, swaying her hips to me doing the same.

I feel Zander's gaze on me, making me hotter. I'm sure there's other eyes on us too, but I only feel his.

We continue like this with my back turned to Zander. At one point I feel his large presence behind me. I know it's him from the fire smell, and the familiar electricity that singes my skin as he touches my exposed skin on my back.

Aylin is dancing on my front, and I continue to sway my hips harder. I push my ass back against Zander as I do so. His large hands fall on my hips, following my movement. I'm pressed completely against him behind me, Aylin at my front. I'm sandwiched between them, and just feeling the music around me as we dance. Though, Zander isn't really dancing, just holding me to him, holding my hips to him as I dance against him.

A man approaches Aylin asking to dance with her. It's hard for me to make out the details of his face in the dim lighting from where I'm standing, but what I can see he looks good looking. He's big, not as big as Zander, but definitely muscular. Tan skin, dark hair, and from what I can see, a good face.

Aylin turns around toward me, a question in her eyes. I encourage her with a nod and a smile.

She's skeptical and doesn't go far as the man pulls her against him to dance. I'm glad she's letting loose just a little bit, and not only because this means I can turn my attention back to Zander, which I do.

"Keep your eyes on her, please," I say into his ear as I pull him down closer to me with my arms wrapped around his neck.

"Of course. I would never let anything happen to you or your best friend, you should know this by now."

I'm swaying my hips against him, and I feel his erection pressing against my stomach which is only encouraging my movements. I'm painfully reminded I'm not wearing any panties and I'm soaked.

The drinks in my system taking over my judgment and I'm half tempted to fuck Zander right here on the dance floor, no shame. It would be a show for everyone. Plus, his body being as perfect as it is I'm sure no one would complain, even if mine isn't anything special no one would notice.

Zander must notice something on my face because he leans down, his lips against my ear, "What are you thinking about Mel Bell?"

I have no idea what the face I'm making looks like, but I'm sure with my deep thoughts about Zander's body and fucking on the dance floor it must have been interesting. At least interesting enough for him to ask me about it. The filter I usually have somewhat control over is also gone with my sobriety.

"I'm thinking about what it would be like to fuck you right now in front of all these people." I have no shame admitting this to him.

He laughs, it's low, throaty and sensual. I don't think he's as drunk as Aylin and me. I haven't been paying attention to how much he's been drinking, but he seems way more sober.

"As much as I would love that, especially knowing you're bare under your little dress I'm too selfish for that."

I look up at him skeptically, not sure what he means. That would be the exact opposite of selfish.

He laughs again, clearly seeing the questioning expression all over my face. His lips are against my ear, his breath making me fall into him more as he speaks.

"No one else gets to see how good I make you feel. That's all for me, all of you is for me. Your body, your moans, your screams, everything is *mine*. So, yeah, I'm selfish."

He bites my neck quickly before pulling his head away from me again. I lean into him more, possibly to help keep my balance, but also possibly for that addicting electricity between us.

"Yeah, I guess I'm selfish too," I say, continuing to rub my body against his along the beat of the music all around us.

"Yeah? How's that?" He asks, finally moving his body against mine ever so slightly with his hands on my hips tightly.

"I don't want to share this view with anyone else," I say,

waving my hand around gesturing to his body. "That view is all mine and I'm not sharing."

Zander laughs again, this time into my hair before saying something I can barely hear, but sounds something like, "good".

~

THE NIGHT GROWS LATER.

I get drunker.

Aylin meets back up with us and I want to ask about the mystery guy, but the words don't come to me.

Zander notices that I may have overdone it just a little bit and encourages us to leave. The words are muffled around me, the only grounding thing for me is Zander's arm wrapped around my waist, holding me up.

I'm pretty sure Zander calls Aylin an Uber, we wait all together for it to pull up. With one hand Zander helps Aylin get into the car without face planting. I think he says something about following the car to make sure she gets home safe.

I nod.

I think.

"You're going to have to help me out and tell me where she lives." He chuckles as we are walking back to his car.

I'm struggling as I pull out my phone, pressing it to his chest.

"Her numbers here." My words are so slurred I'm not even sure I make sense.

"Her number won't help much, Mel." I think he's laughing at me. Not nice.

"Her *location* is here," I say, trying my hardest to enunciate my words.

Zander laughs at me again before scooping me up in his

arms. I let out a squeal as he holds me against his chest, holding under my knees and my back like I'm nothing, completely weightless to him.

"You are slowing us down," he says as he walks faster than I was on my own for sure.

He sets me in the low car. I smile, I like this car. I like this man. I loll my head to the driver's side as he climbs in. I appreciate every inch of him as he starts driving, using my phone as GPS to make sure Aylin gets home safe.

"I like you," I say. At least I think I say it, the words don't make it to my ear clearly.

Zander faces me, a smile on his face, he seems entertained by me. I'm a fucking riot.

"I like you too, Mel, careful you might admit shit to me you'll regret in the morning."

I scoff, turning my head away from him, "I can say whatever I want."

"You can, I know you will, I just don't want you mad at yourself in the morning," He's definitely laughing.

"You laughing at me?" I snap, scowling.

"A little," He doesn't stop, and I huff, crossing my arms across my chest, sinking down further in the seat.

"That's mean."

"I don't think so."

"Well, I do."

He doesn't stop laughing. I watch the fuzzy lights as we drive really fast, and I kind of recognize where we are, close to Aylin's place.

There's a car in front of us. Did he really catch up to the Uber? He's so impressive, this sexy, scary man next to me.

"Zander," I say softly, turning my head to face him again.

"Hm?"

"Are you going to hurt me?" My eyes are fluttering closed,

and I think I might fall asleep, the words falling out of my mouth involuntarily.

"Only if you beg me to."

I hum as the sleep takes over my body. I can't tell if that's a threat or a promise, but I assume at some point I'll find out.

## 25

Zander

**Present**

I was able to catch up to the car we put Aylin in, and I watch as the Uber pulls up to her house. I watch as she goes inside to make sure she gets in safely before driving away.

Mel has fallen asleep in the passenger seat. She definitely does not handle her alcohol well, and it makes her pretty entertaining. I meant what I said though, about not wanting her to admit anything she would regret in the morning either positive or negative.

I drive us to Mel's apartment, she stirs a little, but I put my hand on her leg to soothe her every time and she relaxes back into the seat, sleeping.

Once I park my car, I go around to her side, lifting her out of the passenger seat as I carry her into the apartment. She seemed to wake up for a second after I picked her up, looked at me, then nestled her head into my chest. I'm not sure if she then pretended to be asleep or really was after that.

Once inside her apartment I lay her down carefully on her

bed so I can take off her shoes. I debate if I should tuck her in still in her dress, but I know she will be more comfortable in her usual sleeping attire.

I go into her closet to pull out a t-shirt, though I would much rather put mine on her. I also grab some of her sleep shorts. I carefully undress her, once I sit her up as I pull her dress off, she becomes a little more aware, looking up at me with half lidded eyes.

"What are you doing?" Her voice is laced with sleep, her eyes barely staying open.

"I'm just getting you comfortable, baby."

I slip the t-shirt over her head, she helps by pushing her arms through before I carefully lay her back down on her back and pull on the shorts, caressing her soft legs as I pull them up. Appreciating every inch of her skin.

"Do you need anything?" I lean over her once she's dressed, kissing her jaw lightly.

She doesn't say anything, just lifts her arms up slightly to wrap them around me. I chuckle.

"Let me get you comfortable first," I lift her to lay her on the pillows as I pull the blankets around her.

She cuddles in under the blankets as I strip off my jeans and shirt, leaving me in just my boxers as I settle into the bed behind her.

I wrap my arm around her waist, pulling her back against my chest. She sighs, wiggling her hips against me to settle into the spot. The movement makes my erection grow and strain against my boxers.

As difficult as it is to not wake her up in a way I know she will enjoy, she's too drunk and too tired to try anything right now. I hold her to me as I fall asleep myself.

I wake up the next morning, Mel still wrapped around me, our legs tangled together under the sheets, my arms still around her. She's still asleep, I want her to wake up to coffee, probably some painkillers and definitely water.

I carefully slip out of the bed to try my hardest not to wake her. She rolls over, stretching her arms over the empty spot I was laying in, but seems to stay asleep.

First, I go into her bathroom to find some ibuprofen which I set on the nightstand then grab a cup of water from the kitchen to put next to the pills. I start to make some coffee as I hear her ruffle around in the bed. I look up to see her looking around, seeming confused like she's looking for me.

"You okay?" I ask, leaning over the island, watching her.

Her eyes snap up to me, I see her physically relax once she sees I'm still here then presses her hand to her head.

"Yeah, I think I'll survive," she says, not looking at me anymore as she cradles her head.

I pour her coffee with creamer; I've seen how she likes it before bringing it over to her.

"There's ibuprofen and water next to you," I say as I hand her the warm mug she takes carefully.

"Please, be nice to me today and don't tell me any of the dumb shit I said or did," Mel takes a sip of her coffee before setting it down to take the pills.

I get myself my own mug of coffee before sitting down sideways on her little couch, looking at her still on her bed as she nurses her coffee.

"I wouldn't say you *did* anything particularly stupid," I tease, Mel immediately understands what I'm insinuating.

"Goddammit, what did I say?"

She gets up from the bed before sitting down on the opposite side of the couch from me, though it's so small our legs are touching, and we don't have any distance between us.

"You said you didn't want to know," I shrug.

"I changed my mind," Her face is contorted with so much concern. She's cute all worked up like this.

"Hm...well where do I start? The part where you were begging to fuck me in the middle of a club or suggest we run off to Vegas and elope?"

I know the second part I made up will send her in a tailspin. I can't help myself from fucking with her a little bit.

"Shut up, none of that happened," She rolled her eyes at me.

"Okay, the Vegas part didn't, but the begging me to fuck you while we danced did."

She practically choked on her coffee. "No way. This is your fault."

"What's my fault?"

I lean my head on my hand that I've propped on the back of the couch to watch her. Her eyes drift to my exposed bicep. I know I unintentionally flexed. Her eyes burning as she bites her bottom lip that I want to sink my teeth into.

"You know exactly what," she looks away and I chuckle.

Yeah, I do.

"I really want to find out what you're talking about, maybe fuck it out of you, but I need to talk to Trent about what went down yesterday and make sure that guy is taken care of."

I know if I get lost in her I won't leave, and I really want to deal with this bullshit so I can come back to her with a clear mind to take care of her how I need to.

She nods as I stand up and get dressed. She stays seated, drinking her coffee. As I lean over her once I'm fully dressed, she leans her head back to look up at me. She needs more sleep. I need my Mel Bell feeling completely herself.

"I will be back, I promise. And trust me, I would love nothing more than to stay with you curled up right here all day." It's true, I wish life was that simple for us. One day it will be.

Mel nods as I lean down to press my lips against hers. She fists my shirt in her hands, pulling me closer, releasing a groan from my throat. She's not making this any easier for me. I nip at her bottom lip as she pushes her tongue into my mouth as she moans.

Reluctantly, I pull our lips apart before I say fuck everything and push her down onto this miniature couch. Even though she's only trying to push things further, she needs to take care of herself, and I need to deal with Trent.

"Mel, I need you more recovered, I will be back and can properly take care of you," I hate the words I'm saying. I should stay, but I don't want to be distracted with her.

"Stop being nice to me," She pouts, and I laugh.

"I promise you; I'll be back and I will be anything but nice to you, how's that?"

She lights up at my words, my little Mel Bell is so much more than I ever thought and I fucking love it. I place another gentle kiss on her lips before heading out her door. I send her a text right away because I don't want her to think I'm abandoning her, or I didn't mean what I said.

> Zander: I will be back, Mel, you're never getting rid of me, and I hope you know that.

> Mel: Good, I don't plan to, at least not yet.

I smile, climbing in my car. This. Fucking. Woman.

I pull up to my house that is feeling less and less like "home" to me every day. The more time I spend with Mel the more she is my home.

I walk in the door, I know Trent is here because I saw his car parked out front, but he's not sitting in any of his usual spots plotting world domination or whatever the fuck he does in his day-to-day life.

I used to know some of what he does, but in the last year or so I have no idea other than he doesn't do anything to help his own "business" other than bossing other people around.

I call out his name as I go to the fridge to grab a water bottle. I see Trent coming around wearing only pajama pants and no shirt. I roll my eyes, I wonder if he has a girl here, I would rather not deal with that right now, especially if things end in a fight.

"Dude, can you put on a shirt? I don't need to see this." I drink the entire water bottle before crumpling it and throwing it away.

"Chill, you intimidated or something?"

I scoff before muttering, "whatever."

No, I'm not intimidated. Trent works out too, he's muscular, but not as big as me. Not even close. Plus, I have about three inches on him in height, and he's never beat me in a fight. I've never been able to kill him either, but he hasn't won.

"That guy you made me sell to last night is blacklisted, no more selling to him," I say simply, I just want this conversation done with so I can go back to Mel.

"Whoa, why do you say that? We don't stop selling to people unless they steal or hurt our guys. And you look fine." He looks me up and down assessing if I'm hurt, not because he cares but because it would explain this.

I know the truth; he will not be so understanding about it.

"He's an asshole, he's knocking on death's doorstep anyway and I just don't think we should be involved if he shows up dead and it's linked back to us somehow." This is a weak excuse and I know this.

"The fuck, Zander? This isn't new for any of the people we sell to, are you just now getting a conscious or is there something you're not telling me?"

Trent is an asshole, but he's a perceptive asshole, he always has been, which is how he has been able to manipulate so many people into doing shit for him they don't want to do. Myself included.

"I've always had a conscience. I don't want to do this, and you know it."

"Yeah, you have. Wait, Is this about that girl?"

My fists clench, Trent still doesn't even know her name. I have given him very little info about Mel, and I plan to keep it that way.

"It's about some loser asshole that doesn't need to buy from us anymore, we don't need one guy, we have plenty of buyers."

"This is about her. What happened? You know I can find out," He threatens.

I know he can, that guy knows nothing about me other than I kicked his ass after some comments he made, and Trent's not stupid. He would go ask the guy what happened.

"He said shit about her, pissed me off, he got what was coming to him, he doesn't deserve to buy our shit."

"Oh, now it's back to 'our shit', but you want out. What is it Zander? In or out? Plus, when did comments about some girl piss you off so bad?"

I'm fuming, he doesn't get it. I knew he wouldn't, but fuck he's twisting my words around, trying to get me to admit more about Mel than I want him to know.

I know he's going to use any information he gets against me. I barely notice how hard I'm gripping the stone on the island; my knuckles are white and I feel like I'm going to turn into the Hulk or something and break the fucking stone.

"It's 'our shit' until you let me go do what I want to do with my life. Then you don't have to worry about me, what I do and who I do it with. Seems like that would make *your* life a lot easier too."

Trent laughs. He. Fucking. Laughs.

"You know it's not that simple, you're in this with me, we are a team Zander."

"I don't want to be a part of any 'team' with you, especially when it's not."

"Why? Because I tell you what to do? Come on," He rolls his eyes, but there's still that fake humor in his voice. I want to knock the humor right out of him.

"Also, if we are such a 'team' then you'd accept what I'm telling you about not selling to that guy and let it go." He is such a hypocrite. And an asshole.

"Tell me, Zander, what is this all really about? The girl, the guy you sold to, or me?"

"All of the above," I admit.

I know there's no way I'm getting out of any of this without admitting some part of my feelings for Mel, even though he would never understand what it's like to care for a woman.

"Hm, well there's obviously no getting rid of me, we will continue to sell to whoever I say we sell to, so I guess that just leaves not having the girl or not letting her affect you so much." He shrugs like this is the only way. Like that's the easiest solution ever.

"Who says I can't get rid of you," I say through my teeth, and he laughs again.

"You could try, but you know you won't. So, what's it going to be?"

"Those are my options, I guess it will be getting rid of you." I stand up straight, my hands clenched together so hard I'm going to have imprints on my palms.

I stalk toward Trent, who is smirking. He won't back down, so I guess it's going to be a fight.

He speaks before I reach him, and it stops me in my tracks. "Before you do that, you might want to reconsider since I *will* send someone to pay Mel, is it, a little visit if you so much as try *anything* to get rid of me. Which, I know you wouldn't go to the cops since that incriminates yourself and you won't kill me, so your options are limited."

"How the fuck do you know her name?" I stopped moving

as soon as her name came out of his mouth. I have been so careful to never tell him or say it around him.

How?

"Wow, you really do underestimate me. That's pathetic, but yes, I know about Melody James, and I'm going to be really fucking clear with you about this."

I don't think I've ever been so angry in my life. I need to keep it in check by not tackling him to the ground right now. He's right, I have underestimated him, and clearly I have no idea the full extent of what he's capable of.

"You're not going to quit; you're not going to hurt me and you're going to continue to do what I say for however long I say to do it with a smile on your face. If you do that then I'll leave you and Melody alone, but the second you do anything to fuck me over or try *anything* then I'll make sure to pay her a little visit, probably personally."

"Fuck you! I'll do what you want, but threaten me, not her. Leave her out of all of this, she didn't ask to be involved, and I was stupid enough to be," I yell at him. I can't accept any threat toward her, especially because I can't even begin to think about what he would do.

"She didn't ask to be involved, but she is, right? She knows everything?"

He has this stupid smug look on his face that is making the urge to hit him so powerful I don't think I've ever showed so much restraint, but I can't risk Mel getting hurt because I can't control my temper.

"Not everything, leave her out of it. If I fuck up, hurt me, kill me, whatever the fuck you want to do but do not ever touch her."

"How do I know she won't do something with what she does know? You put us both at risk with her knowing anything," He shakes his head.

"She won't, I know her, just leave her alone. I'll keep doing your same errand boy shit, but I'm done with runs."

This is not how I saw this going at all, but him knowing about Mel and threatening her will make me do anything I can to keep him away from her.

"I don't think you're in any place to tell me what you will and won't do, but I'm feeling generous. I can't promise no more runs, but that just means I'll need more guys recruited, which you will be doing a lot of for a while."

"Fine. You're a fucking asshole who's lucky to have your face intact."

Laughing, Trent says, "I might be an asshole, but I own your life and you know it."

He walks away still laughing. I turn and punch a hole through the wall before walking out the door. I can't go back to Mel yet, I'm too pissed, so I go to let off steam before I do something stupid like take my gun and actually kill Trent.

## 26

**10 Years Ago**

That night at the New Year's Eve party changed everything between Zander and me, not only because we slept together, but because of what happened after.

He was protecting me, and Mark is a dick, but it essentially made both of us public enemy number one at school. Of course, I have a couple friends on my side, but anyone that is remotely close or thinks they are close with Mark will not talk to me anymore. I don't even care about that, and neither does Zander because we have each other and when I'm with him I feel like that's all I need.

It's been a couple months since then, and even though we've never said we are officially together it's pretty obvious we are.

Now, it's late March and an unusually sunny day for spring in Oregon. Zander decided we needed to throw caution to the wind a bit and take advantage of it.

We agreed to meet in the school parking lot, but then we

are taking his car to the coast for the day. I know my dad is going to be pissed if he finds out, but we have a plan to call the school for each other and hope they don't suspect anything.

It'll be worth it, plus I don't think Zander could do any wrong in my dad's eyes, and even if he gets mad at me, he will forgive Zander right away. It's really not fair considering I'm his only child, but whatever.

I park in a spot on the far end of the parking lot where Zander and I usually meet before school. I get there before him and wait for a few minutes before I hear his fancy car roaring into the parking lot. He's not very subtle with that, though I don't think he cares.

He pulls into the spot next to me. As soon as I see him through the window looking every bit as perfect as he always does, I can't help the smile that spreads across my face. He's wearing sunglasses, and a t-shirt that hugs his biceps. His light brown hair is slightly a mess on his head and I want to run my finger through it to mess it up more.

I hop into the passenger seat of his car; he pulls me in for a quick kiss as soon as I sit down.

"Ready?" Zander smiles at me, not even waiting for my answer as he throws the car into reverse, speeding out of the parking lot.

I settle into my seat as Zander speeds down the busy roads, weaving in and out of the morning traffic as we make our way to the open roads through the forest that will take us to the coast.

The drive to Seaside would normally take a little less than two hours, but with Zander's insane driving I'm thinking it will take us a little under an hour and a half, assuming he doesn't get pulled over.

I mess with the radio to find some good music to fill the car with. I pick a station with an upbeat song I'm not familiar with playing, but it fits my mood, so I go with it. I subconsciously move my body around, dancing in my seat as I watch the green scenery around me passing by us.

I feel warmth on my thigh, which brings my attention back to the inside of the car where Zander rests his hand on my thigh, rubbing his thumb along my jeans. I smile, placing my own hand on top of his and intertwining our fingers.

"Nervous?" He asks, and I shake my head, then I let out a curse as I remember we haven't called school yet.

I pull out my phone, turning down the music before dialing the school's front office. It rings and I put on my most professional sounding voice as they answer.

"Hello, this is Mrs. Wells, I need to excuse my son Zander Wells from school today, he's not feeling well."

"I'm so sorry to hear that, we hope he feels better soon," The friendly sounding receptionist on the other end of the phone replies.

"Thank you," I hang up quickly as my nerves take over.

"That was a little weird to listen to, I'm not going to lie," Zander says, squeezing my hand.

"Why?" I question, this was his plan.

"Just hearing you refer to me as your son is something weird, but the Mrs. Wells part sounded nice," He winks in my direction and my stomach lurches.

I didn't even think about that.

I shake my head at him, "We are way too young to think that sounds nice."

"That's fine, but I know I'll call you that one day."

I look over at him, his eyes focused on the road, a smirk on his lips. I don't like admitting that I like the way it sounds too, but I won't dare say anything.

∼

THE REST of the drive we don't acknowledge our earlier conversation. Zander called the school for me after a few minutes and then had to make the comment about him "being my daddy", which I just shook my head at him. Though the way he said it with his voice low and sensual did things to me I chose to ignore.

We sang along to some of the songs that played, both pointed out various scenery that we passed along the way through the forest until I saw the coastline come into view. I sit up straighter as we continue down to the road toward the water.

I love the coast, I always have. There's just something about the air around the ocean that makes me so happy. It's all the smells of the ocean, the sound of the waves, the feeling of sand at my feet. The coast is truly my happy place, though I don't come here enough.

Zander finds a small parking lot with a trail that leads down to the beach.

As soon as I step out of the car, I'm hit with the cool ocean breeze, and I take a big inhale. My hair is whipping all around my face, so I tie it back, though it's already a mess.

This is the Oregon coast, cold wind and cool sand, but I love it. I would take this beach over some warm tropical beach any day, my light skin from being a natural redhead doesn't do well with the sun. Zander comes around to the passenger side of his car to take my hand in his, intertwining our fingers as we walk down the sand.

We have to navigate down some rocks to get to the sand. I'm genuinely afraid I might slip and fall a couple times, though Zander keeps me steady.

As soon as we are off the rocks, I take off my shoes. My feet sink into the cool sand as we walk and the wind picks up the closer we get to the ocean.

Once we are close to the water Zander grabs me from behind, lifting me up, "I'm going to throw you in!"

I'm squealing, "No way! Put me down!"

He's laughing hysterically as he keeps me lifted, acting like he's going to throw me in the water. He even goes as far to have his feet in the freezing water as it laps around his ankles, getting his pants wet. My screams become louder as I really start to believe he might drop me into the water.

Finally, he backs out of the water's reach to put me down, keeping his arms around me as he turns me around to face him.

"You really thought I'd throw you in?" His humor is still written all over his face.

"Yeah, I wouldn't put that past you," I try to back out of his arms, but he's keeping me rooted in place.

"Come on, Mel Bell, that's messed up."

"You were so committed you got your pants wet," I point down to his ankles where his jeans are soaked and covered in sand.

"Yeah, it'll dry," He shrugs before throwing his arm around my shoulders as we walk down the beach together.

I sink myself more into his side as he holds me close. His body heat is helping me stay warm as my feet continue to sink in the cold sand as we walk. Once we have walked for a little while there is finally an area that isn't in the direct eye line of someone's house and we sit down together in the sand.

"We should've brought towels or chairs or something," I say as I feel the sand already finding its way into my pants.

"Sand all over you is just a part of going to the coast, you know this," Zander says as he moves his foot to pile up sand around my ankles.

I glare at him, debating if I should dump sand in his lap, but I decide against it. I'm not looking for a war with him right now. He shifts beside me so he's now sitting behind me, his legs stretched out on either side of mine, my back pressed against his front as he wraps his arms around me, holding me to him.

"You looked cold," he says into my hair.

I was, but I wasn't going to complain about it because I didn't want him to suggest we leave.

"Aren't you cold?" I ask because he's not wearing a jacket and his pants are still wet.

"Nope, I'm perfectly fine." He nuzzles his nose into my hair more as I sink back against him completely.

We sit like this, wrapped in each other for I don't know how long. I left my phone in my backpack that is still in Zander's car. I didn't want anything to interrupt this time with him. This perfect time.

Neither of us say anything for a while, the only sound is the dull roar of the ocean. I'm focused on the rise and fall of Zander's chest behind me as he breathes.

"Are you happy?" I mumble, unsure if he can even hear me over the sound of the waves in the distance.

"I'm always happy when I'm with you," he says as he presses his lips gently against my neck.

I sigh as I lean my head to the side slightly as his lips continue to graze my neck, up to my jaw before he presses a gentle kiss on the side of my mouth. I turn my head to face him a bit more.

His eyes seem illuminated by the light reflected in the ocean. His eyes are always bright and a contrast against his tan skin and brown hair, drawing your attention right to them. But in this light, they are hypnotizing, and I forgot what I was even going to say to him as soon as our eyes meet.

I'm too distracted by everything I see in them, the beautiful color and the feelings within them. There's a softness there, like he's trying to really see me and say so much more without saying anything verbally. I wanted to say something more to him, but all I can do in this moment is press my lips against his.

I'm leaning up with my head turned back as our lips meet, his hand moves to the side of my neck to hold me there.

Warmth is spreading all over my body that feels like a fire ignited from where his hand is touching my skin and his lips are on mine.

This kiss is gentle, testing...loving. It's hard to even think of it that way, but It's hard not to. Zander presses his tongue into my mouth, slowly exploring as it tangles with mine. Both of us are just enjoying the feel of each other's mouths and not even pushing it further feeling around our bodies, even though I'm tempted.

We break apart, both breathless, and look into each other's eyes for a moment more before I settle back against him completely. I feel him hard in his pants which makes me smirk.

I am so tempted to do something right here, but it's too public. The sun is shining above us, and there's people around, not many but they are here. There are houses not too far away that could see us outside their window even though they're down the beach a bit.

"Can this be our reality?" I ask after another few minutes of silence between us.

"What do you mean? It is," I hear the confusion in his voice, but I don't turn around to face him again.

"No, like right here at the coast, just us together, nothing else matters. I want this to be our reality."

"So, you want to drop out of school and run away to live on the beach with me?" Now there's humor in his voice.

I groan, "You have no imagination."

"Tell me what you're imagining then," he says against my hair. His breath on my skin sends a shiver down my spine.

Zander must think I just got a chill from the wind because he pulls me closer to him and his warmth.

"I've always wanted to move to the coast when I grow up. I want to have some job I love, live in one of these houses and maybe have you around," I muffle my voice a bit at the last confession, but he hears me anyway.

"I think that's the perfect future. I'm in."

I smile, "You're in?"

"Yup, that's what it will be, one day. I know it. You know how I know it?"

"Hm?" I close my eyes, enjoying the feeling of him around me, the sounds and smells of the ocean, and enjoying his words that make me smile.

"Because I love you," he says softly into my hair, so softly I wasn't even sure I heard him correctly.

My eyes fly open as I turn my head again to see him, "What?"

A nervous smile spreads across his lips, "I love you, Mel. So much."

I'm in shock.

Zander loves me.

Zander. Fucking. Loves me.

It takes a minute for the words to fully sink in before I can respond, and as soon I know I haven't imagined it I respond.

"I love you too, Zander."

His lips meet mine again, this time I know the feeling from before and the look that was in his eyes, it's love. I love him. And he loves me. I didn't think this day could get more perfect, but it did. We break apart, smiles on both our faces as I settle back against him.

I keep smiling as he holds me, his words continuing to swirl around in my head. One day. He knows it.

That's how it will be.

I love him.

He loves me.

# 27

**Present**

It's been a few days since the club with Zander and Aylin. He, yet again, kept his promise to come back, though he was angry about something even though he didn't want to talk too much about it other than it had to do with Trent.

We had a relaxing rest of the day because I needed to recover, and he said taking care of me was helping him forget about the Trent bullshit. I really wanted to know more about what happened, but if he wanted to tell me he would.

Plus, knowing what I already know about Trent, I fear it had something to do with me, and I didn't want to become angry myself.

I'm caught up in writing today as my dad texts me asking to meet for dinner tonight. I think for a second before responding, I decide to say, "fuck it" and hope Zander won't mind.

Mel: Yeah, can I bring someone along?

Dad: Boyfriend?

> Mel: Zander.

I don't confirm or deny because just like last time we don't have a title for whatever we are. Even though we are obviously something I don't know what it is exactly.

> Dad: Of course. Usual spot 1800.

I really hope Zander won't be mad at me for volunteering him to come before asking him, even though I have yet to see Zander actually angry *at me*, which I'm thinking may not be possible and maybe I should try to test that, but not now.

> Mel: Want to go to dinner with my dad tonight?

I'm not sure what Zander is doing right now; I never really know the full extent of anything he does other than the night I was with him. Though, he texts me every morning to tell me he's thinking of me. Then, if he's not able to come over at all he calls me before going to bed.

> Zander: Hell yeah! When and where?

> Mel: Come to my place any time before 5?

> Zander: I won't be later than 4.

I shake my head as I chuckle. I think I can guess his intentions for wanting to be an hour before I told him to be here, not that I mind.

Sometimes, I do feel like a booty call or friends with benefits for him until he looks in my eyes and I see everything there that goes unsaid between us and I know this is more than just sex.

Zander does keep his promise, as usual and is knocking on my door before it's four o'clock. I open the door and will never in my life get tired of seeing him standing there in my doorway, taking up so much of the space, dwarfing the size of my apartment as he steps inside.

"You ready?" He asks as I shut the front door behind him.

"Ready for what?" I look at him confused.

"Ready for your dad to remember how amazing I am?" He clarifies and I shove at his chest lightly as he laughs.

"I really wonder where you hold all that ego, your muscles are big, but not big enough for that." I bite my tongue for what I said.

I never compliment him so openly like that. Partly due to said ego, but also because it feels vulnerable. Though, Zander never shies away from complimenting me whenever he feels like it.

"Oh, please tell me more about my 'big muscles' Mel Bell, my ego needs to be inflated just a little bit more."

He's looking down at me. He always makes me feel so small compared to him, even though I've never felt small in my life.

"I don't think it does, actually." I push past him lightly, headed to my computer to finish what I was working on.

Normally, if Zander is over and I'm needing to finish something he picks a book from my shelves and reads while I finish. This usually leads to me jumping on him not long after because it is the hottest thing I've ever seen to see Zander reading on my small couch that looks even smaller with him sitting on it.

This time he doesn't even let me go over to my computer before he's crowding my space and cornering me against a wall.

"I know there are other parts of my body you enjoy that I think I need to hear about as well." His deep voice brushes against the skin of my cheek as he speaks, and I feel myself getting flushed.

"I never said I *enjoy* anything, I just stated a fact that you have big muscles." I try my hardest to keep my voice steady, though it's shaking from his closeness and the arousal I'm feeling.

"I think you enjoy what I can do." His voice is so low I don't think I would hear him if he wasn't speaking right into my ear.

"What- "

Before I can finish what I'm about to say, Zander wraps his hands around the back of my thighs, and lifts me up, wrapping my legs around his waist so we are face to face.

"You've done this before, not impressed," I challenge as he presses his hips into me against the wall, which sends a shock of electricity through me.

I'm trying my hardest to not seem like I care.

"Oh Mel Bell, I'm not done," He smirks as he pulls away from the wall for a second, my body still wrapped around his.

Zander continues to hold me up with ease, my legs wrapped around his waist, my arms around his neck as one of his arms wraps around my back, his other hand dips between us, into my shorts, moving my panties to the side as his fingers starts to work my center, lightly at first as he teases my clit in small light circles before dipping the tip of his finger inside me. I bite my tongue to stop the whimper that wants to escape.

He's watching my face, watching my reactions that I'm trying to hold back. I'm not sure if he gets sick of me not reacting or he couldn't control himself anymore. He bites my bottom lip, a moan escaping my throat from the feeling as he sucks my lip into his mouth before devouring my mouth with his own.

As his tongue fucks my mouth his fingers begin to imitate the movements as he pushes one finger in completely before introducing another one. I'm panting into his mouth, the sensation of him everywhere taking over my body.

"Fuck my fingers like you want to fuck my cock," He demands into my mouth as his fingers inside me have stopped their movements.

The angle is difficult as I adjust my hips slightly before doing what he says, rolling my hips on his hand, then bringing myself up and back down against his fingers.

He curls them inside me so when I roll my hips against him, he hits the perfect spot that makes me moan as I bury my head in his neck. I continue my movements as I kiss, lick, and bite up his neck. I'm so close, the feeling building so fast, I can feel it about to explode when Zander removes his fingers from me, and I could fucking cry from the loss.

I lift my head from him as I feel his hand slip under my shorts from the back so he's cupping my ass. He maneuvers my body in a way I didn't think would be possible as he holds me up but rips off my shorts and underwear in one swift move, throwing them somewhere in my apartment.

Instead of giving me his hand again, my back hits the wall. I'm pushed up so my legs are draped over his shoulders instead of his waist. My dripping pussy right in Zander's face. He looks up at me with those damn eyes before he looks directly at my center which makes me want to snap my legs closed, though I couldn't with his head in the way. He licks his lips at the sight.

"Your pussy is perfection, the way you grip my fingers as I fuck you with them," He dips his head down, running his tongue along my entire seam as I throw my head back. "The way you fucking taste."

He growls as he licks me in entirety again, "The way you come around my cock. Fucking. Perfection."

Then, he's devouring me like he was with my mouth only minutes ago. His tongue is brutal as he licks, sucks and nips at my center.

His fingers digging into my thighs and I'm hoping I'll have bruises. He sucks so hard on my clit I think I might pass out. His tongue spearing me and then the pressure as he presses against the sensitive bundle of nerves has me reeling.

The impending orgasm I already had from his hand has returned with a vengeance. I'm chanting his name as he continues with his movements, his tongue doing things I wouldn't even believe were possible if they weren't happening to me.

My head is thrown back as I'm begging, "Zander, please, fuck!" I'm pulling at his soft hair as he eats me like I will be his last meal.

The orgasm takes over, white spots take over my vision as I scream out his name, my legs closing involuntarily trapping his head between my legs as he continues to lap me up through the orgasm.

Once it's through, I loosen my legs though they are still shaky and there's no way I can stand on them.

Slowly, Zander slides me down his body until my feet are on the floor, but he's holding my hips to keep me standing. Without his hands on me I would crumple to the floor like jelly.

"So?" He says his smirk back on his face as his lips glisten with my release.

"What?" My voice is shaky, matching every muscle in my body.

"You want to admit you enjoy what I can do?"

"Oh my God," I shake my head, this infuriating man who makes my heart and vagina feel too many things can't be good for my sanity.

"My name is Zander, actually, but thank you for that." He licks his lips and closes his eyes at the taste again. "Double thank you."

I push him away once I feel I can actually stand, "You're too fucking cocky for your own good."

"That's another part of me you enjoy!" He calls out as I walk into the bathroom to take a shower, glaring at his smug, hot as fuck face as I close the door behind me.

Zander can be so sweet I'm not even sure if he's real, and then his ego shows a bit and I know there is balance in the world.

We both antagonize each other in the best way though, it's how it's always been, and I wouldn't change a thing. Plus, he has every right to have an ego about his skills in the bedroom because it's like he was created just for me with a cheat sheet to my entire body.

I'm hoping he will join me in the shower as I strip off my shirt. I wonder if he wants to make me want him in here and will torture me by not showing up. Asshole.

I step in as he opens the door, my eyes meet his as I shut the clear door that is fogged from the hot water. Instead of stripping off his own clothes he props himself against the sink, watching me.

"What are you doing?" I ask, pulling my hair back into a ponytail before it gets wet.

"Enjoying the view, that okay?" He asks, but it's not really a question.

I know he's told me not to be self-conscious with him and to never hide my body from him, but being so vulnerable while he watches makes me want to cover up with something, though I don't have anything to do that with in here. I take the soap and lather myself, trying my hardest to ignore the man watching every single move I'm making.

"I don't think I need anything else in my life if you're in it," Zander says suddenly, pulling me out of my thoughts and my hurried actions of getting clean.

"What do you mean?" I'm confused at his words, especially right now.

"This view, the feel of you, the taste of you on my tongue, it's all I need to survive," he says this like it's the simplest thing in the world.

A nervous laughter comes from me as I shut off the water, and grab a towel to wrap myself in. "That's ridiculous, Zander."

"It's not, and I'm not going to test my theory so you're going to have to trust me." He walks closer as I step out of the shower, bringing his hands to my wet face as I'm in front of him in only a towel. "Do you trust me?"

The playfulness to his voice is gone now and I don't know what happened. This Zander seems worried or something else I can't quite place, especially asking if I trust him. It's more like a plea than a simple question. I bite my bottom lip. Yes, I trust him, of course I do, but there's a hint of fear I feel that made him ask in the first place.

"Yes, I trust you," I say, looking up at him.

"Good," Is his only reply as he presses his lips to mine once again.

As I got dressed Zander continued watching me. While it would seem creepy if anyone else would do this but with him it made me feel worshiped, like he couldn't stand to look away from me for a second while his eyes burned with his desire.

He didn't touch me outside of light kisses for the remainder of time at my apartment before we left to meet my dad. It's okay with me, the last thing I need is post sex anything while meeting with my dad.

Zander insists we take his car. As we are climbing inside of it, I feel I have to warn him, "My dad might ask to take your car for a test drive, this is his dream car I think."

"You think?"

"I know a Porsche is his dream car, but I'm not sure past that," I shrug, buckling the seat belt.

Zander looks amused as he starts up said car, "Do you know what kind of car this even is?"

"What? It's a Porsche, I know that," I look at the emblem on the steering wheel that says it on the logo.

"Yes, but this is one model of many, just because it's a Porsche doesn't mean much." His amused tone is still there.

I wave my hand around, "A car is a car to me."

"You're right, a car is a car, it's about who's driving."

With that he slams on the gas making the car fly down the road as he shifts so smoothly, my eyes are fixated on his hands doing the movement as his veins bulge. I thank whatever Gods there are that he's wearing short sleeves so I can appreciate the way his veins travel up his muscled forearms meeting his perfectly sculpted upper arms. His tattoos accentuating everything about the movements that have no reason to be this erotic to me.

Zander handles the car like a pro race car driver, hardly slowing down at turns as we skid around corners before taking off again. I have no idea how fast he's going, but it doesn't matter.

What I told him is true, I trust him. I trust him with my life, but my heart is taking some time to catch up. I don't know if I trust him with it fully, though it's becoming harder to hold back every day.

We get to the restaurant to meet my dad in about half the time it would take me. As expected, my dad is early, though he's climbing out of his truck as we pull up. As I step out, I look over to him, so he knows it's us.

I see the shock on his face as he sees the car. I guess it is questionable how a twenty-seven-year-old could afford it.

"Hey dad," I say as he approaches us looking between the car, to me, then finally to Zander.

"Hello Mr. James, long time no see," Zander says smoothly. He towers over my dad who's not necessarily short but his five-foot-ten frame is dwarfed by Zander.

"Zander, you look like you're doing well. You know you can call me Dan," My dad says as they grasp hands and shake strongly.

I'm watching the exchange, oddly nervous for some reason. I already know my dad likes Zander, plus he's extremely charismatic it's hard not to like him. If anything, I'm the odd one out here.

"You too, Dan, thank you for letting me come along."

We walk inside, Zander placing his hand on the small of my back as we walk. I'm not sure if my dad notices or not, but he doesn't say anything.

We get led to a table, where Zander pulls out my chair for me. If he hadn't done things like this for me before I would accuse him or trying to show off in front of my dad, though that might still be true.

"So, what brings you back to Portland?" My dad asks once we've sat down.

"None other than this woman right here," Zander says, his arm around my shoulder as he pulls me closer to him.

I scoff, and push at his hard chest, "That's a lie."

My dad looks skeptically between us like he's clearly missing some information, "Have you two kept in touch?"

"Nope," I answer before Zander has the chance to.

The waitress comes over to take our drink orders before Zander says anything else. I never drink in front of my dad, but I feel like I should. I order a glass of white wine; Zander sticks with water which is smart since my dad knows he's driving. My dad orders his iced tea.

"How did you get back in touch?" My dad asks once the waitress walks away.

"Well, Dan, it's a funny story actually…"

"He messaged me on Instagram, I responded, and the rest is history." I cut Zander off because I saw the look in his eye, he was going to tell a very exaggerated version of the story.

"Hm, so then what are you doing for work, Zander?" My dad asks and it feels like a blow to my stomach. I knew it would happen; my dad is someone who cares a lot about success.

I look up at Zander who is calm as can be, his body language relaxed, his arm still draped around the back of my chair and his voice even as he answers.

"My stepbrother and I are in sales, we've expanded out here so I took the opportunity to move back, and hoped Mel and I would be able to catch up." He answers like it's nothing. Like he's said it a hundred times.

"Stepbrother? So, your dad remarried?" He asks, and I am thanking the universe that is the piece of information my dad latched onto. Him and Zander's dad were good friends when we were little.

"Yes, he did, a few years ago. Him and his wife continue to move around for his job and seem happy with that. My stepbrother and I prefer to settle in one place, build the business there and enjoy the company." He squeezes me to him again.

I feel the flush in my face. I've never had a guy be so touchy with me in front of my dad, save for Zander that one time in high school with the medicine debacle.

"He's doing well then?"

"Yes, sir, he's very happy," Zander answers. *Sir.* That's oddly respectful.

"Good, you two look comfortable, so are you dating?" My dad asks suddenly, his voice is always even toned, but him asking so outright makes me choke on the sip of water I was taking.

"Dad, whoa," I widen my eyes at him as if to say, *drop it.*

"We are whatever Mel wants us to be. I'm not going anywhere and she's all mine, so you could call it dating if you want." Zander answers easily, his tone also even through the wide smile on his face.

I want to slide down my chair and under the table. It feels weird to have my dad asking about this and Zander saying the things he will often say to me in private, but it feels more intimate to have him telling someone else.

My dad nods, the smallest smile on his lips. I don't know why that makes me want to curl up more, but it does. I feel like my dad knows about everything we've ever done, and even though I know that's completely irrational I can't stay focused.

The two of them talk through dinner about various topics. Zander's car does come up as I suspected and even though I was wrong the model isn't the exact one that is my dad's dream car. Apparently Zander has something called a Boxster and my dad's dream car is called a 911. Who knew?

I'm not talking much and after we have all finished our meals, I'm on my third glass of wine. At some point Zander moved his arm from my shoulder onto my thigh where he's been moving his strong fingers in circles along my leg as he's engrossed in the conversation he's having with my dad. You would never guess he's touching me at all, even though I can't form a coherent thought outside of what his touch is doing to me.

We sit at the table a little longer as I finish my wine, and because the two of them are so into their conversation I don't think they want to leave.

I also don't think I've ever seen my dad more talkative. We don't exactly have the same interests, so our conversations aren't usually more than surface level.

Zander has this way about him that people are drawn to

him, he can talk to anyone, and he always has, which is how we became friends in the first place.

I was a scared little kid on the first day of kindergarten and he pulled me into his little world, no matter how much time or distance has been between us I never left that world. It grew and changed, but we've always been in this world together.

# 28

**Present**

The dinner with Mel and her dad was weeks ago, and ever since then Trent has me doing more and more for him.

I haven't had as much time with Mel, which I think has weighed on me more than it has her, since she's thrown herself completely into the book she's writing. I'm so happy she's able to write since she told me about the slump she's been in for a while. It makes me so happy for her, but I'm selfish and I don't like not having a lot of time with her.

Trent has made me recruit like crazy which consists of being around a lot of people, going to parties I don't want to be at, and socializing with people I don't want to be around. I pretend like they have qualities that interest me enough to bring them in on the business.

It's exhausting, and annoying. I would rather be intimidating people to get them to do what I want than pretending to be their friend.

Unfortunately, trust is a big part of this world since you

have to trust people before you bring them in and continue to trust them afterwards.

I hate every minute I'm away from Mel, but at least she's safe because as long as I'm doing what Trent wants me to, he's not going to touch her. Though, the more time I am away from her the more my resentment for Trent grows since this is all his fault.

I'm stashing every single dollar I get away in my secret account because I'm more motivated to leave than ever. I know it's more complicated to leave now that I'll have to bring Mel along with me. It will have to be strategic and quick.

It's now been a week since I've been able to see Mel. I've been kept so busy and when I finally get the chance, she's asleep or I've somehow ended up in my bed though I'm pretty sure I drove asleep.

I always make sure to call her when I can just to hear her voice. That keeps me going, and also her reassurance that she understands and really, she's okay. I text her when I'm not able to call, I need her to know I'm always thinking about her because I'm not fucking this up again.

I sit in my car, it's dark as I'm about to go to this underground party to do more recruiting when my phone rings with a Facetime from Mel.

Sometimes she Facetimes me, but I can't always answer or talk long due to service issues or the risk of someone seeing her. I'm safe in my car so I answer.

"Just the face I was thinking about," I say as soon as the call connects, and her face covers my screen.

Her green eyes are the center of my attention, but her straight nose and plump lips draw my attention next. I miss those lips. I miss everything about her.

"Yeah? What were you thinking?" She asks, taking her bottom lip between her teeth and I know that look. My cock already hardening in my pants, so I adjust a bit.

"I was thinking about how much I miss you and what I will do the next time I see you," My voice drops lower.

"And when will that be?" She questions.

She's never bugged me about not being able to see her as much lately, but this is something else. Something needy as desire laces her voice.

"I'm hoping soon, especially when you're looking at me like that." Her cheeks are flushed, pupils blown and I can see her need even through the phone screen.

"How about tonight? My hand isn't enough for me, I need you here and I need to know what you have planned for me," Her voice is breathy.

I question for a second if she's been drinking since she's usually only this forward when she's drunk, but I think she's just drunk with desire at this moment.

"Fuck, Mel, I will do everything in my power to see you tonight," I hate what I'm saying. I hate it, but I can't risk her.

"Hm, what if I had a challenge for you?" She says, and I catch a glimpse of her shoulder that only has a thin strap over it. I'm not sure if she's just in a tank top or a bra and I'm desperate to see all of her. My dick is straining my jeans, and I don't even think fucking my fist will help.

"What challenge?" My voice is so gravely I barely recognize it.

"My front door is unlocked for you, I'm touching myself imagining it's you and if you can get here before I finish, I'll let you in, if not then my door will be locked."

My jaw drops, who is she? I'm also paranoid about her door being unlocked. She lives in a pretty secure building, but it still makes me uncomfortable knowing anyone could walk in on her like that.

Only I can, she's mine. A growl escapes my throat, I can't say no, I can't leave her vulnerable like this, I need to get to her.

"What do you say?" I notice her shift around and I think she might have started touching herself before she even called me, a light moan leaving her lips, but nothing like when she's with me.

"I'm on my way, but no matter what I will break your door if I have to. I need to touch you."

Just at my words her moans become louder. I throw my car into drive to make my way to her apartment.

I don't dare hang up the phone as I drive, but I'm focused on getting to her as fast as possible. Her little mewling noises coming through the phone are driving me insane, making my foot hit the gas harder and turn the wheel faster.

"I'm so fucking wet for you, Zander. I need you to fuck me so bad." She moans, and I get a glance at the phone that's being held unsteady above her beautiful face contorted in pleasure.

She's wearing a white tank top that is practically see through, her nipples hard, peeking through the fabric. God, I want to see what she's doing, how she's touching herself.

I want it to be my finger, not hers. My tongue. My cock inside her. I let out a frustrated groan as I continue speeding down the streets.

"What are you thinking about, Mel Bell?" I ask because I can't help myself, I need to hear more of her. I need to know she wants me there, inside of her as much as I do.

"I'm thinking about you holding me down so hard I have bruises from your hands, ah," She moans, cutting off her words for a moment before resuming. "I'm thinking about your giant cock sliding inside of me so hard it makes me scream, your hand around my throat fucking me so fucking good, God, Zander."

She calls out my name and I swear to fuck I could come right now without even touching myself at the sound of my name on her lips like this.

I'm so close to her apartment, even if she finishes before I get there, I meant what I said. I will break down her fucking door. I am going to fuck her so hard she won't remember her Goddamn name.

"I'm almost there, Mel, I swear to fucking God, I will give you everything you need and more. You're going to come so much you'll forget what it feels like to not have me inside you."

Mel throws her head back with another loud moan as her grip on her phone shakes.

"Zander, I need you here right now, fuck!" It seems like she can barely get the words out of her perfect lips.

I round the last corner to pull into her apartment parking. I practically forget to turn off my car as I'm flying out of the seat and running up the entrance.

I don't even want to wait for the elevator, I fly up the stairs taking two at a time all five levels up to her apartment. I turned the volume down so her sounds wouldn't be heard by anyone I passed.

"I'm here, Mel, I'm almost to your fucking door and you better be ready," I growl into the phone as I'm flying up the stairs. Cardio is not my strong suit, but I'm solely focused on getting to her.

"Oh God Zander, I'm so fucking close," She gasps, her head thrown back in pleasure and I think she's dropped the phone as I finally get to the fifth floor, racing to her door.

I continue to hear her sounds quietly through the phone speaker, but I'm at her door. I throw it open to reveal her on her bed, she snaps her head up toward me as I slam the door making sure I lock it behind me as I unbuckle my belt, staring at her.

"Stand up," I command as my belt comes undone. I unbutton my pants, leaving them open, but still completely clothed.

Mel listens, standing up on shaky legs, still just in her thin tank top, no bottoms of any kind and I can see the glistening from her dripping pussy on her legs even in the dull light.

"Good girl. Get over here," I drop my voice so low I know she likes; it's covered in lust.

I pull my shirt over my head as she makes her way over to me, watching every move I make. Her eyes scan the length of my body, my jeans low on my hips. She reaches me, standing in front of me on legs that seem like they may give out underneath her any second.

I place my hands on her waist as she looks up at me.

"Do you think you're cute getting me to come over here to give you what you want?" My gravelly voice asks as she looks up at me through her lashes, her fingers dancing lightly at my waistband.

Mel bites her bottom lip with a tiny smirk on her face as she nods her head subtly. I tighten my grip on her waist, my own restraint slipping.

"Do you think you have all this control because you got me here?" I start pushing her back, slowly toward her island.

She seems to think for a second because her smirk gets more obvious on her face, and she nods again.

"I guess I'm going to have to prove to you who's really in control here." I lift her quickly to set her ass on top of the island. She squeaks as her bare ass touches the cool stone.

I rip her useless tank top over her head before latching my mouth to one of her nipples, as my hand grabs her other breast, rubbing, squeezing and molding to my hand as she yelps.

I bite down on her nipple before licking and sucking to soothe the bite. I move to her other nipple and repeat my process as she's writhing under my touch, her hands in my hair pulling me to her.

"Did you come, Mel Bell?" I ask as I pop her tit from my mouth.

She shakes her head, looking down at me, still tugging at my hair.

"Do you want to?"

"God, yes!" She finally speaks and it's practically a scream.

I push my hips that are between her thighs harder into her soaked pussy as she moans from the slight friction, I give her.

"Do you *deserve* to come after that show you put on for me?" I thrust my hips into hers again because I need her moan in my ears again.

She nods furiously, her thick hair falling over her face. I brush it back behind her ears as I press my hips into her, but don't move. I just keep them there so she can feel my erection as I hold her head to mine, our foreheads touching, her breath touching my lips.

I slam my lips into hers, tasting and taking everything I want from her. She moans into my mouth immediately as she tries to rub her bare pussy against me, but I keep my hips completely still. I move my hand to her back, pushing her tightly against me so she can't move.

She lets out a frustrated groan I swallow into my mouth as I devour her mouth with my tongue. She meets my intensity with her own as she continues to try to rub against me, and I don't let her.

She makes more frustrated noises from her throat; I bite her lip before breaking away. I need to be inside her. I push down my pants and boxers in one swift motion as she lets out an exasperated noise along with a soft, "yes."

I pull her to the edge of the counter as she wraps her legs around my waist, and I line up at her entrance.

"You're mine, Mel," I say, as I thrust into her, hard. She screams as she throws her head back, but I continue to hold her to me. "All. Fucking. Mine."

I thrust into her hard, but steady strokes because I'm going to make this last and I was already ready to explode when I stepped into this apartment.

I tangle my fingers in the back of her hair, pulling her hair back as I begin to attack her neck with my mouth. I'm biting, sucking and kissing down her neck to her collarbone as she moans and gasps.

"Tell me you're fucking mine, Mel," I demand into her neck with a particularly brutal thrust.

"I'm yours, Zander," She yelps at another thrust. "All yours."

I slide my hand up to grasp her throat as I continue ramming into her. I guide her gently down so she's lying flat on the island, keeping my hand around her throat as I claim her with my cock.

She starts to arch her back, I use my free hand to press her hips down, so I'm holding her down completely as I slam my cock inside her over and over. Her screams take over all around us mixed with my groans and growls that I can't stop.

"I'm so close Zander, please," She begs. I continue my thrusts into her as I feel her contract around me, building until she explodes with a scream, clamping around my dick so hard it takes everything in me not to finish right now, but I'm not done with her, not yet.

Once she comes down, I ease her back up to a sitting position, my thrusts slowed as she came. I wrap her thighs around my waist again, this time picking her up to walk her over to her bed. I continue slow, less brutal thrusts as we get to her soft bed. I pull out of her as I lay her down.

"On your hands and knees," I demand, my voice doesn't sound like my own. I stroke my cock once, using her come all over to slide my hand up and down, she watches me over her shoulder as she gets in the position.

"Fuck, that shouldn't be so hot," She mutters, her voice raspy.

"You like watching me fuck my fist?" I ask, leaning over as I push into her again.

"Yeah," The word comes out as a moan as I enter her fully. "You do that thinking about me?" She asks through my slow thrusts, as she pushes her ass back against me.

"Every. Fucking. Day," I growl into her ear, my chest pressed against her back. "I think about this pussy, how you taste, how you feel on my cock, how you sound screaming my name."

She moans again, pushing herself back against me harder like she's begging me to move more.

"Tell me what you want, baby girl," I say against her cheek.

"Harder, Zander, please!" She begs.

I slam into her hard again as she screams again, leaning her face down into the mattress so the sound is muffled.

I fuck her until she comes again, this time I'm not able to hold back as I spill inside of her with my own loud groan.

I don't think I've ever come so hard in my life. I roll off her, pulling her against my chest as we lay back on her bed, both covered in sweat, sticky, and in euphoric bliss. I want to clean her up, but I can't have her out of my arms, not right now.

The reality hits me once the euphoria has faded a bit. Trent is going to fucking kill me for not going to that party. I'll just lie and say there wasn't anyone worth recruiting, whatever.

I needed this time with Mel. I need tonight. We haven't had a night together in so long. We need this.

We lay in silence for a while, both breathing heavily, she's trailing her finger over my chest, down my abdomen, tracing the muscles there. I'm moving my fingers along her back in light circles. I see the little tattoo on the inside of her wrist as she's tracing, and I ask about it for the first time. She also has one on her shoulder blade I've noticed every time I fuck her from behind, but always forget to ask after it's over.

"What are your tattoos from?" I ask, taking her hand in my own, turning it over to get a better view of the tiny key she has tattooed.

"It's stupid, they both are, yours are probably more interesting." She waves me off as she takes my hand in hers, holding our hands up together appearing to examine the vast difference in size.

"Mine aren't all that interesting, but I'll tell you if you tell me yours first," I negotiate.

Mine really aren't all that interesting, I've drawn them all and done a few on myself as practice.

"Fine, this one is because I was feeling really lost at one point in college and thought if I could just find the 'key to my life' it would get better, so I got this to remind me what I was working toward. Aylin got this one with me."

I really want to ask more about what she said about feeling lost in college, and I feel guilty I wasn't there to help her through it, I should have been.

"Did you find it? What do you think your key to life is?"

She's seemed so happy all the time I've seen her, and I don't want her to feel whatever she felt back then again, no matter the reason.

"I don't think we have just one, but yeah I think writing and being creative is one of my keys."

I decide not to push that one more, though I desperately want her to consider me as one of her keys to her life because she's one of mine. We also share that being creative is another, I feel like when I'm able to draw everything is complete. I feel a similar feeling when I'm with her, that everything is complete.

"What about the one on your shoulder?"

In all honesty when I've seen it, I've been pretty distracted so I'm not completely sure what it is. It looked floral, like a rose with an essence of darkness almost like it was burned.

"I got that one after publishing my first book, it's just a little nod to that story, it's dark roses with one red one, the edges burnt, but it's the prettiest one in the bunch because damage doesn't make you ugly, it makes you strong. It makes you beautiful."

She begins examining my own artwork on my arm, starting with my sleeve, clearly signaling she's done talking about her own.

"I drew all of these, a couple of them I tattooed on myself which is a lot harder than it looks," I point out some of the swirls and intricate details running through the ink that covers the skin on my arm to point out the ones I did. "Everything else I didn't do was done by an artist I trusted in Arizona who I know would honor my own art. I was supposed to work with him as his apprentice until he was in a really bad accident, and never recovered."

I haven't talked about what happened to Jeremy in forever, it still hurts. He was one of my best friends, and someone who really understood the situation I'm in with Trent. He was going to help me until we were stupid, and it cost him gravely.

"Did he survive?" Mel asks quietly.

"No, Mel Bell, he didn't." I pull her closer to me, needing to feel her heat and her body against mine as I relive the memory. "He was in a coma for a few weeks, there was one time we thought that maybe he would get out of it. He didn't, he was brain dead and there was nothing we could do for him."

I feel the tears threatening to fall, but I just hold her tighter against me to fight the urge, which helps. She holds me too. I never needed someone's touch as much as I need hers. She's everything. She's my comfort, my passion, my life, my love. She's all of it. I need her.

"I'm sorry, Zander," she says softly again, holding me as she presses light kisses along my chest. "Does it help to think you have a piece of him ingrained on your skin? Sure, it's your art, but he helped you put it there."

"I never thought of it that way, I guess that is one of the best ways to remember him," I smile a little.

I always felt a little guilty that I never let him put some of his own art on me, I only wanted my own.

"I'm pretty smart, guess you should keep me around." She jokes, and I can tell she wants to bring the mood up again due to the somber turn it took.

"I guess I should," I joke back, holding her to me, pressing a kiss to her hair.

As we lay in silence, bodies tangled in each other, I can't help the nagging worry that's taking over the back of my mind if Trent finds out about this, and if he tries to do anything to Mel.

I know I can be a good liar so he shouldn't, but I can't shake the lingering fear that he's going to try something to hurt me through Mel.

# 29

## Mel

**10 Years Ago**

It's the week before school is out, and to say I'm ready for the school year to be over would be an understatement.

Next year we are Seniors and I already have Senioritis; I have no idea how I'll mentally get through next year.

Even with all the drama and unexpected arrival of Zander I've gotten through the most important year of my high school career with decent grades. I'm not too worried about getting into the schools I want for college.

I have big dreams of going to NYU or somewhere else far away, but I know it's not what is going to be in the cards for me. I'll likely stay in Oregon attending University of Oregon, Oregon State, or Portland State.

I'm lying in bed thinking about all the things I don't need to be worried about yet. I shake it off as I look over to my phone where Zander has texted me, this happens more often than I'd ever admit to anyone.

We meet up in the middle of the night because neither of us can sleep, which can be caused by any number of reasons.

Stress, anxiety, just missing each other, there's not always a rhyme or reason, it's just us.

> Zander: Our park?

> Mel: Already on my way.

The night is warm enough I don't think I'll need a jacket, so I just throw on some leggings under my oversize t-shirt, not worrying about putting up any appearances with him at this point.

He clearly loves me for me no matter what I look like. Thinking about that sends a flutter through my stomach. Zander loves me. It's been weeks since he's first said it, but it still hits me with a rush of happiness when I think about him loving me.

I drive the short distance to the park; he beat me here as usual. He greets me with a searing kiss as he always does, making my legs feel like they might go out from underneath me. It doesn't matter how many times this man kisses me; every time feels like it could be the first time.

"Any particular reason tonight?" I ask, knowing full well there likely isn't one.

"Yeah, actually," I look at him with a raised eyebrow. "It was a full six hours since I kissed you and I couldn't stand another second."

I scoff at him, "Shut up."

He kisses me hard again, and I groan when he pulls away. I don't want the loss of contact, not right now.

Sometimes I'm content with Zander just holding me, or when we spend almost the whole night just swinging and talking, but not tonight. Tonight, there's something else that makes me want him. Need him.

"What will it be tonight?" He asks, still holding me to him.

I'm only focused on his lips I can't reach, even on my tip toes without him leaning down.

"What do you mean?" I flick my eyes up to meet his finally.

I think he notices where my attention has been as the amused look on his face is evident.

"Swings, stargazing, late night drive somewhere, or something else?"

"If I want something else?" I test, pressing myself tighter against his strong body.

"Like?" He still has that stupid amused look on his face. It makes me want to mess with him just a bit since he thinks he knows what I'm thinking. Even though he likely does, I don't want him to have that over me.

"Like...playing tag and you're it," I swat at his chest before ducking out of his embrace and running toward the playground.

I'm running and regret not wearing a bra instantly, but I figured it would just get in the way, I didn't anticipate running. My tits are pretty big, so I'm having to hold them as I run since the pain was already starting.

Zander is way faster than me with his long ass legs, and with my unstrapped chest slowing me down he catches up to me quickly. Arms wrap around my waist, lifting me up from behind as I squeal.

"Got you! What do I win?" He exclaims as he spins me around in his arms.

"There's no prize, have you never played tag before?" I ask as he sets me down. I look at him skeptically.

"Of course, I have, pretty sure I taught you when we were kids," he says proudly.

"I don't think that happened at all. The knowledge of tag is just something ingrained in our brains, I don't think you taught me," I challenge, my hands on my hips.

"Pretty sure I taught you, I probably remember more about

when we were young than you do." He presses forward, crowding my space again without touching me.

"What makes you so confident about that?"

I do have a decently bad memory, only a few key moments stand out vividly while smaller details from the past seem to fade easily. Painful memories stick around the strongest, and it's the cruelest thing my brain does to me.

"Because I can tell you the exact moment, I knew I liked you more than just a friend," he says confidently.

He's never told me that before. Things were different when he came back, but I don't think I could pinpoint one exact moment I knew I had more feelings for him, I just knew.

"When was that? Five Minutes ago?" I try to joke, but he's serious as he reaches his hands out to cup my face, keeping my eyes locked on his.

"Try like eleven years ago. Remember the sleepover?" I'm shocked by this confession.

"Yeah, I remember the sleepover, but we were like five or six, Zander!" I shake my head. He keeps me in place, not releasing his hold on me.

"Yeah, but you and I were always the closest, and when we snuck into my room to play shadow puppets something just changed. I didn't know at the time, but now I know it was when I knew there was more between us. We weren't just best friends, we had to be more someday."

I'm shocked, I wish I had something similar to tell him, but I really don't have a distinct moment, I just had no idea that's how he felt.

"You felt that way the whole time we were friends?" I just can't believe it.

"I knew we were kids, and the feeling wasn't going to go away. I knew I'd end up with you again." He's so confident as he holds my face. He seems like he wants to say more, but instead he seals his lips to mine. "I love you."

I smile against this mouth, "I love you too, dummy."

The memory of how my stupid not nickname came to be from him is something I remember, along with my reply of saying I'll call him "dummy". I don't use it that often, it's not as fitting anymore.

I pull my lips away from his for a second, smirking.

"We are still playing tag, and you're it again," I swat at his chest, using his shock as my advantage to escape again.

This time I have a purpose, I run back toward our cars because I wanted him before that conversation, and now I need him desperately.

I need every part of him because now we can.

Now, we can be together.

Now we know how each other feels and I never want to go back to how it was before. Zander was right, we couldn't be just best friends, we always needed to be more.

I push myself to run back to our cars before Zander catches up to me. I hop up on the hood of his car as soon as I reach it, watching as he approaches. He slows his run as soon as I do that, and he's watching me intensely.

"I don't think I've ever seen a more perfect sight." He makes his way over to me, his eyes not leaving mine.

"What? Your precious car?" I pat the hood next to me like I'm petting it.

"No, my beautiful Mel Bell *on* my precious car." He reaches me, leaning over me.

"Well, I think I know something even better." I slide off the hood, his eyes watching my movements as I go around to open the back door and slide inside all the way to the other side.

The back is not very spacious, I just know once he's back here with me the space will be limited, but that's okay. There's room for what I want.

Zander slides in, shutting the door behind him. I crawl the small distance over to him before straddling his lap. His hands instinctively go to my hips, holding me against him as I bring our lips together.

I kiss him like we have forever, softly. He parts my lips with his tongue as we tangle them together. Nipping at each other's lips. The kiss becomes hungrier, my need growing and my arousal increasing, dampening my leggings since I opted to not wear any underwear. My nipples are hardening and scraping against the fabric of my t-shirt so I'm painfully aware of the lack of undergarments.

I grind my hips against him, letting out a moan into his mouth as his hands slide down my back into the back of my leggings, cupping my ass and pulling me against him harder.

I run my hands down his hard chest to his waistband as I grip his hard length through his sweatpants. He groans as I rub my hand against him. Zander moves his hands lower on my backside, pulling my leggings down further. I lift up to my knees to remove my leggings completely, our lips not breaking apart for even a second.

I'm naked from the waist down as I settle back on his lap and grind myself against him harder, I'm probably soaking his pants with my arousal. I continue my movements against his erection still contained in his pants until he lets out a growl, lifting me slightly as he rips his pants down his legs.

"I need to be inside you," Zander growls against my lips as his erection springs free.

His size always impresses me, no matter how many times we have sex. I always anticipate the slight pain I feel when he first pushes inside me, stretching me until he fills me, and I'm filled with pleasure.

I continue rubbing myself against him, spreading my arousal along the thick length of him until he grabs my hips, stopping the movement to lift me up and slowly lowering myself onto him. I'm gasping as he fills me. I hold onto his strong shoulders as I lower down onto him.

Once I'm fully seated on him, I adjust my hips so I can comfortably move against him. I circle my hips around him as he trails his lips down my neck, licking and sucking as I continue my movements. I bring myself up and then back down on him with a moan at the feeling.

Zander stops trailing my neck, moving one hand to the back of my neck tangling his fingers in my hair bringing our foreheads together as he thrusts upward.

"I love you so fucking much," He groans, his minty breath hitting my lips as I gasp at another upward thrust.

"I love you, Zander." His lips are on mine again as he thrusts harder into me.

I meet his thrusts, lifting myself up, then bringing myself down on me, circling my hips periodically. Zander's hand in my hair tightens a bit so my head is pulled back for him to run his mouth along my throat again.

His other hand is on my hip guiding my movements. Each thrust hits a spot inside me, so deep that I can't stop the noises escaping my throat as my orgasm builds stronger and more powerful with each movement of our hips.

Zander is getting close too, his movements become faster and more frenzied as our hips meet over and over. I'm gasping and moaning, feeling like I can't get enough air.

Zander's groans become louder against me until we both explode; I clench around him as stars take over my vision as my orgasm takes over my entire body. I feel Zander throb inside me as he spills inside me, only adding to my sensation.

We are just holding each other, neither of us moving for a few moments before I sit up to move next to him. I slip my leggings back on as he slides up his own pants. It's uncomfortable to feel the mix of my wetness with Zander's come falling down my thighs in my pants, but it's kind of what I get for this.

"Are you okay?" Zander asks as he watches me wince adjusting my pants.

"Yeah, I'm great." I smile up at him as he takes me, bringing me back onto his lap, holding me close to his chest.

I breathe him in, his smoky scent of a bonfire with a hint of spice mixed in, as I nuzzle my nose into his chest more.

We sit like this in silence for a while, just holding each other. I love his warmth, his strength, the way we fit together. I love him so much. I close my eyes focusing purely on his scent and the feeling of his chest rising and falling as he runs his hand through my hair. I never want to move from this spot with him.

I never want to be without him. I don't know what I would do if I couldn't see him every day. I'm excited for what is going to be the best summer ever, I know it.

# 30

**Present**

I do not know what got into me last night when I decided to call Zander.

We hadn't seen each other in a while because Trent has made him so busy recently, he never has time to see me. I just needed him here with me.

I'm glad he came over, though I could tell something was bothering him the rest of the night. I did my best to try and distract him multiple times, which he always accepted. I just felt like there's something he's not telling me. Something he's scared of, and I don't know if it has to do with Trent or me.

I don't even want to entertain the idea that it might have to do with me since everything between us seems perfect.

Too perfect.

I can't believe how easy it was to fall back into something with him. I can't believe how strong my feelings for him came back, like I was hit by a train.

Zander had to leave this morning after we woke up, he said he had to make up a story to Trent as to where he was and say he was working since that's what he was supposed to be doing before I lured him over here.

Reluctantly he left, and the little bit I was able to sleep was the best sleep I've had in a while. There's just something about being wrapped in his arms that comforts me to a point of contentment that is unlike anything else.

It's always felt like that with him. I don't know why because with anyone else I've been with I hate cuddling, like *hate* it.

I sit on my loveseat, mug of coffee in my hand while I think about everything with him, all the way back when we were kids.

There has to be some reason we always come back together, I don't necessarily believe in fate or anything like that, but something about us feels like it could be. Especially since I know I love him. I never stopped loving him, no matter how hard I tried to forget about him. I tried to move on, albeit unsuccessfully every single time.

Zander is different.

Zander is for me.

Zander is one of the keys in my life.

I thought of saying that to him last night when he asked about my tattoos, but I held back. Maybe I'll let him know someday.

I DON'T HEAR from Zander throughout the day. I want to check on him to make sure he's okay, but I don't want to come across as crazy or clingy, so I throw myself into writing.

I'm almost done with my first draft, and I'm so beyond proud of this story I feel like my creativity is regenerated. I don't want to give Zander credit for that, but he may have helped a bit. Especially the air of mystery he still has about him.

I feel like I know everything, though not the nitty gritty

details he keeps hidden from me which I'm sure is for the best. He didn't even want to tell me what that guy said the night I came along for a drug deal. Not my proudest moment, but I knew he would keep me safe as long as we didn't get arrested.

The day fades around me as I'm fully enthralled in writing, music playing softly around me. I'm not even paying attention to my phone or the fading daylight when there's a knock on my door.

I jump in my chair because the noise is jarring against the soft music I've had playing all day. I smooth down my hair since I tend to mess with it subconsciously as I write because the only person that would be here right now is Zander. I'm excited he actually got more time to come see me and surprise me.

I stroll over to my door, swinging it open with a big smile on my face until I see who's standing there.

It's not Zander.

My heart begins pounding in my chest as I go to slam the door in this mystery man's face. I take a second to examine him quickly, assessing the risk and all the alarm bells in my head are going off.

This man is big, not as big as Zander by any means, but he towers over my short frame. I can tell he is packed with lean muscle even through the button up and slacks he's wearing. His dark black hair and light brown eyes look like a contradiction against each other. I can just feel that I should be scared of this man.

I quickly slam the door shut, but it's caught by the man's hand. I try pushing it closed despite him pushing it open. He's much stronger than me, so I end up being pushed back completely as the door flies open to let him in.

I'm scrambling backwards looking around for anything I can use as a weapon as he stalks into my apartment, shutting my one escape behind him.

My phone is on my desk and the only place I could run into

to lock the door would be the bathroom. I couldn't grab my phone and get there without him catching me, I know it.

I'm glancing around for anything I can use to protect myself, but of course my apartment is decently clean, no knives in the sink or anything I can use.

I put distance between us using the kitchen island as he finally speaks. I haven't even screamed, but I'm thinking I should have.

"So, you're the famous Melody James," The man says, his voice deep and smooth.

*Great, my first stalker.*

"Get the fuck out of my apartment," I say weakly. My voice is so shaky I can barely get the words out.

"I'm not going to hurt you, I've come to talk," he says. It's terrifying how smooth his voice is, like breaking into women's apartments is a daily occurrence for him. Like he feeds off the fear. "I'm Trent, you know my stepbrother, Zander."

*What?*

*This is Trent.*

*Why is he here in my apartment?*

I don't know why, but I did not picture him looking like this.

He looks like a successful businessman who just got off work at his nine to five at the office, and if it weren't for the glimmer of something sinister in his eyes, he would be pretty good looking. Which makes him all the more terrifying since everyone knows the Devil isn't red with horns, he's beautiful because he was an angel first.

"What are you doing here?" My voice is like a squeak.

I'm slightly comforted by the fact that he's not completely random, but also more terrified that he's here in the first place.

Where the fuck is Zander?

There has to be a reason he's never wanted me to meet him.

"Like I said, I've come to talk. Zander sent me here."

What the fuck? Zander wouldn't send him here. I know that for a fact.

"Okay, say what you need to say, then leave." My confidence is coming back slightly just at the thought that Zander would not be okay with this. I'm hoping he knows and is already planning on storming in here any minute.

Also, my brain decided to wake up and remind me I'm only a few inches from my knife drawer.

"Come on, Mel, I want to get to know the woman that has my brother so head over heels for her. Let's get to know each other a bit and I'll let you know why I'm here." He is so calm it makes me more uneasy.

"I think I'm good, is Zander, okay? Why would he send you here?"

He better not have done something to Zander.

I'm examining his hands and clothing for any signs of a struggle, but I don't see any. He looks put together, no sign of a fight, nothing. Though, he could have had someone else do the dirty work for him since it seems like that person is usually Zander.

"Your boyfriend is fine, don't worry about him. He didn't *directly* send me here, but he's the reason I'm here. I know he saw you last night when he was supposed to be doing things for *me*."

I swallow the hard lump that's in my throat. How? How did he know? How did he find out where I live? I have so many questions.

"See, him and I had a deal. He seemed to forget how important our business is as soon as you came into his life. He used to be my best guy back in Arizona; reliable, hardworking to a fault and the best I had. Then, we came here, and he got...distracted." Trent looks me up and down like he's assessing me. I instinctively wrap my arms around myself at the feeling of his eyes on me.

This earns me a light laugh from him, not one out of humor, it's dripping with intimidation as he continues, "I did my research as I always do, had you both followed just a little to gain the information I needed. Then, I reminded Zander what really matters and that's the business. He knows this, he's always known this he just forgot a little bit. Because of you."

"That's not fucking true, and you know it. Zander wants out. He wants away from you, he doesn't give a shit about your 'business.'" I spit the words at him, he's not going to act like he knows what Zander wants more than I do.

Trent laughs, and there's still no humor there, the sound is booming especially in the small space of my apartment.

"That's what he told you? Wow, I have been giving you a lot of credit to think you were pretty smart, but clearly I was wrong."

I clench my jaw, this guy is a real asshole, I understand Zander's obvious hatred for him now.

"What else has he told you, or not told you? Let's see you know about our business, and yet haven't gone to the cops which means you really love Zander, because he would get it worse than me, his past and all." Trent says this like I should know something as he looks at me waiting for a reaction.

I try my hardest not to show one, but clearly fail as I see the look on Trent's face light up a bit at my confusion.

"So, he didn't tell you that then? He is pretty ashamed of it, it shows failure which he doesn't do well with which is why he's my best guy."

"Didn't tell me what?" I regret asking. I know I shouldn't. I can ask Zander later; I just want Trent out.

"He got caught once, had a decent amount of product on him, and ended up in jail for a year because of it. Once he got out, he was more motivated than ever to prove himself to me and the business. This is his life; this is what he's good at."

My heart stops in my chest, Zander didn't tell me he went to jail, that seems like a pretty significant thing to leave out. I'm starting to question everything.

Is anything he said true if he didn't tell me this? Is Trent, right? Is this really what he wants, and he just lied to me to make himself look better to me? No, I can't believe that.

"Let's see, what else did he not tell you? You know about his friend Jeremy?" I can't speak, I just nod slightly. I don't know who to believe here. "Zander killed him."

My stomach drops completely. I shake my head, "No, that's not true at all. I know Zander, he didn't kill anyone."

Trent laughs again, "Wow, he has you seriously brainwashed, doesn't he? Zander is the reason Jeremy got in that accident that killed him, and trust me Zander isn't a fucking saint, he has more blood on his hands than you could ever know."

I don't believe this; I can't believe any of this.

Though, I'm questioning everything Zander has said to me, he has been super secretive about this part of his life. I don't know the full extent of it.

I saw what he did to that guy, I've seen his tempter, even when we were younger. He can be intense. He can be violent.

What if Trent is actually telling the truth?

I can find out about the jail part. If that isn't true then obviously all of this is a lie, but if it is...I'm realizing maybe I don't even know Zander.

The boy I knew, the man I loved, my best friend, he's different. He's not who he once was.

"Now, I never got to tell you about our deal, I got too distracted. You seem to have a way of doing that don't you?"

I hold back a gag; I think Trent distracts himself because he likes the sound of his own voice too much.

"I told Zander to make sure he remembers what is important and put the business first and I would leave you both alone. You made sure that didn't happen yesterday, so now I'm following through on my end of the deal."

I'm standing completely still anticipating what he's going to do next.

I watch as he pulls out a gun from his waistband, similar to the one I saw in Zander's car, and I hold my breath as he sets it down on the island separating us.

"You're going to stay out of my way. You're going to stay out of Zander's way. If you don't then I'll make sure this gun gets used on both of you. But don't worry, you won't die. You'll both get to watch each other suffer so much you'll be wishing you were dead."

"No!" I scream, I can't take it, the fear explodes out of me, "You can't do that, you can't hurt him."

"Even now all you care about is me hurting him more than yourself? That's cute." He laughs again, the sound giving me the same reaction as nails on a chalkboard.

"I won't distract him from what you need anymore, just don't fucking hurt him." I feel like I'm about to cry, but I refuse to show weakness right now.

"I'm sure he had his fun with you, but the fact that he wasn't completely honest with you tells me all I need to know. He doesn't care about you. I'm sure you're real fun. He might miss part of you, but he's always been good at going through women." I feel like my heart is tearing in my chest at everything that's happened.

Zander lied, maybe Trent is right, and he won't miss me.

"Just don't hurt him," I say softly as my heart breaks in my chest at his words. Maybe, he really did mean more to me than I did to him.

"I won't. If I find you, you went to the cops or do anything to fuck me over though, I will see you again. It won't be as pleasant as this conversation," he says, tucking the gun back into his waistband.

I scoff as I hold back my tears threatening to make a strong appearance any second. I don't know what part of this conversation was pleasant.

I watch as Trent turns around, seemingly not even concerned about me throwing something at the back of his fucking head as he walks to my front door and leaves without another word.

I run over to lock the door so he can't come storming back in here. As soon as I turn the deadbolt I drop down to the floor, the hot tears flow freely down my cheeks.

I sit on the floor, holding my knees to my chest as I sob at what just happened.

I'm so conflicted, I feel like I don't know who Zander is anymore.

Out of everything he's told me, what was true? What wasn't?

I also can't put his life at risk with Trent, even if I'm pissed at him for not being completely honest with me about everything, I don't want him hurt or dead.

I don't know what to feel. The worst part about all of this is I want to run into his arms, to hold me and whisper into my hair that everything is okay. But it's not. Nothing is okay.

Once my sobs have slowed down slightly, I get up on shaky legs to go to my phone.

Nothing from Zander. I wonder who Trent threatened first, or if he didn't even need to threaten Zander to stay away from me and he did so willingly because what Trent said is true. I'm disposable to him since he's "always been good about going through women". The reminder hits me in the chest again, the thought that he doesn't care about me at all.

I dial Aylin, it's time I tell her the full truth. I need my best friend before I do something really stupid.

∼

As soon as Aylin answered, the tears came out freely yet again. I could barely say anything, but she knew it had to do with Zander, because of course she did.

She said she would come over, and not even fifteen minutes later she was at my door. I checked to make sure it was her before answering this time. I became too complacent just assuming who was at my door, but I won't do that again.

We settle on my loveseat, as I continue to cry. I feel like a faucet that can't shut off. Aylin is patient as she waits for me to be able to form words.

Once I'm able to speak I tell her everything. I tell her about what Zander really does, I tell her about what really happened before we met up with her. I tell her about all my feelings for him, even the ones I feel stupid to admit.

Then, I finally tell her about Trent. I relay everything I can, the threat, and what he said about Zander. I don't leave anything out. I feel guilty I hid any of this from her in the first place, but she doesn't say anything to make me feel bad about any of it. She doesn't judge. She just listens.

Once I'm done, she finally speaks, "Do you want to know what I think?"

I nod. I really do.

"I think you might have been caught up in the nostalgia with Zander and it may have blinded you a bit to some red flags."

I will admit I don't like where this is going.

"You said he never told you much about what he was doing, but maybe a part of you didn't want to know the truth?"

I guess that's one way of saying it. I enjoyed my blissful ignorance.

"You pictured Zander as you last saw him, the guy you fell in love with and you wanted him, so that's who you chose to see. Though ten years changes people a ton, he just isn't who you thought he was." She speaks sympathetically, and I know she's not trying to hurt me, she's trying to make me understand. She's trying to wake me up.

"I still love him, Aylin, even knowing all of this whether it's true or not I fucking love him. What is wrong with me?" I'm trying my hardest not to keep crying.

"Of course, you do. He was your first love. He will always have your heart. It sounds like even if you want to forgive him there's other things preventing that now." Concern is in her voice now, and I know it's because of the not-so-subtle threat to my life that occurred.

"What if I kill Trent first?" I say a little too excitedly.

Aylin looks at me skeptically, "I don't think that's a road you want to go down, love."

She's right. I'm not a killer, even if in this moment I would like to be.

"What do you want to do?" She asks softly.

I think silently for a few moments before taking my phone that has not received a single message from Zander and block his number. I show Aylin what I did.

"I guess I do the smart thing and protect both of us," I say reluctantly. I feel an instant pang of guilt at blocking his number.

What if something is wrong with him? Trent may have threatened me, but actually hurt Zander, I would never know.

I guess I just have to trust that he's okay.

At least while I figure out if there's another way out of this.

# 31

**Present**

That motherfucker.

Trent made me go to Washington as soon as I got back home in the morning and had a whole list of shit for me to do for him up there.

I barely had time to eat between the demands he made before I left the house. I told him I wasn't able to recruit anyone at the party the night before, so I feel like this is my punishment.

Later that night, I'm finally walking back into the house I've come to hate with every fiber of my being when I see Trent dressed like he just attended an actual legitimate business meeting sipping on his whiskey as he stands in the living room like he was waiting for me or some shit.

"Tell me again, Zander, why weren't you able to recruit anyone at that party last night? I had a few guys lined up that had been primed and were ready to prove themselves there."

This isn't a real question. He knows something.

"I was there all night, so whatever guys you're talking about must not have showed. I need to go to bed, I'm exhausted from all the shit you made me do today." I start to walk up the stairs before I stop in my tracks.

"You sure you're not exhausted from spending the whole night with Mel?" I hear him set the glass down before I look over at him.

He's rolling up his sleeves, he's preparing for my anger. Which means he's about to piss me off even more than usual.

"What the fuck are you talking about?" I try to keep my voice level, but I'm quick to anger. He knows this.

"I know you didn't go to the party. You were with her. We had a deal, and you broke it. You couldn't even handle one simple thing." He shakes his head as he rolls up his other sleeve.

"You've been making me do shit for you day and night, yeah I took a fucking night off to see her, Trent! I did what you wanted today, *all fucking day*." I clench my jaw so hard I might chip a tooth.

"She's pretty, even prettier in person," he says simply.

I ball my fists, "What the fuck did you just say?"

"Mel, she's pretty, I told you I would pay her a visit personally." He faces me fully, challenging me. He knows what he's doing.

As much as I want to hold back, I explode.

I charge toward him, grabbing the collar of his shirt, holding tightly as I imagine it's his fucking throat.

He looks at me with a smirk on his face, his eyes meeting my challenge.

"What did you do?" I ask through clenched teeth, holding his shirt so tight I think it might rip.

"We had a little chat, I told her all the things you never bothered to, plus a little extra to make sure she will stay away since I can't trust you not to."

I don't hold back anymore; I cock back my fist before

bringing it down onto his face to knock the smirk right off.

He's knocked out of my grasp by the hit, but when he turns his head back toward me his nose and gums are bleeding as he smiles at me.

He smiles because this is exactly what he wanted.

He wanted me unhinged.

I go to punch him again, this time he puts in effort to block me while coming at me with his own fists.

We continue the all-out brawl, fists flying everywhere.

Trent is one of the only people that is actual competition for me, but I'm seeing red. I could kill him.

I want to kill him.

We end up on the floor, I get the advantage, plunging my fists into his face repeatedly until he knocks me back, catching me off guard enough to get behind me to put me in a choke hold.

I'm fighting against his strong arm around my throat. I'm covered in blood, and I know it's both of ours, but I don't care. He's cutting off my oxygen I need to get him the fuck off me. My one piece of optimism is he doesn't want me dead; he needs me too much for that.

"She was more than happy to stay away from you after I told her how disposable she is to you. She was just an easy fuck to you." His words burn as he says them right into my ear.

I throw my elbow back into his groin, he doubles over as he lets me go. I'm gasping for air.

"She didn't believe you; she trusts me more than you," I spit blood pooling in my mouth at his feet.

"Maybe, but taking out my gun really made her listen." Trent is still bent over, I must have gotten a good shot in.

Good, I hope his balls fall off.

"Did you fucking hurt her?"

If he did, I will kill him.

"Not yet, but I did tell her if she didn't stay away, you both would get to watch each other suffer, wouldn't that be a sight?" Trent is standing up straighter as he recovers. I want to hit him there again, but I know he won't let me get another easy shot in.

"I'll kill you. This is over, I'm done, I'm out, Trent. You've gone too far. I'm. Done."

He laughs. I hate his stupid fucking laugh.

"You're not done. You will have to kill me to be done, and you won't, you're weak. You always have been. You may look big and strong, but you're fucking weak."

I rush at him again, but he deflects my next blow, he's not holding back anymore.

I grab hold of his head as I bring it down onto my knee, resulting in blood spilling from his face. He acts like it doesn't faze him as he continues charging at me, fists everywhere.

I dodge his blows but a few still land. He's trying to choke me again. I won't let him get that advantage again.

We've fought before, but this is the worst.

Neither of us slow down nor stop our fists flying at each other. I get him on the ground again, this time I kick him while he's down until he grabs my leg from under me to make me fall.

He tries to get on top of me, but I fight him off so he's not able to pin me down.

"I'm not fucking weak," I say finally once I have him pinned under me, this time unable to knock me off. "But that's not why I'm not going to kill you. If I do, I know I wouldn't get to see her again and I would have to die to let you come between us."

With that Trent is smiling, but I send one last punch into his face so hard it knocks him out cold.

I know he's not dead, he's gone through worse, but it's enough that I'm able to stumble out of the house to get over to Mel.

I need to see her. I need to explain everything.

I need to protect her.

I'm covered in blood, and bleeding from so many places I'm

not even sure where it's coming from as I speed down the street to her apartment.

My head is throbbing, I'm limping, my fists are burning, but I don't let any of it slow me down as I make my way up to her apartment.

It's so late, well past midnight and I might be waking her up, but I need to see her. I need to make sure Trent didn't hurt her.

I need her.

I pound on her door, "Mel, it's me please answer!"

There's no noise I can hear on the other side of the door.

She better be here. She better be okay. I continue pounding my fist on the door which is sending a searing pain down my arm from how fucked up it already is from the fight.

"Mel, please!" I don't care if I wake up her neighbors, I don't care about anything else but her right now.

Finally, I hear her voice on the other side of the door, but she doesn't open it.

"Zander, please go away." Her voice is soft, but I can hear the sadness.

"Mel, open the door please, I need to make sure you're okay," I beg, resting my forehead against the door.

"I'm fine, please leave, we are done." Her voice cracks, and it mimics the cracking I feel in my chest at her words.

"No, we aren't. If this is about Trent I'll deal with him, we are not done," I demand.

"It's not about Trent. You lied. You didn't tell me you went to fucking jail, what the fuck Zander?"

That shithead.

"Let me in and I'll explain, please, Mel."

"So, it's true?" Her voice cracks and I feel like I'm breaking her heart.

I sigh, "Yes, but I guarantee he didn't tell you the whole story, please let me in."

"No. Go away, you've always been good at going through women, I'm no one to you. Leave."

"I meant everything I've ever said to you, there is no one else, there could never be anyone else ever again. You are mine, and I am yours, Trent was just trying to piss you off whatever he told you. Please believe me, you know me." I never beg, but I'm begging.

I need her.

I can't lose her.

"I thought I did, but I don't." I can barely hear her through the door, and it makes this hurt so much more. "Please leave, it's for the best. For both of us."

"Mel...I love you, please," I choke back tears as I feel them. I haven't told her I love her in ten years, but I've known it. I never stopped loving her.

"You ruined me for anyone else the first time we kissed ten years ago. I've always been yours and you've always been mine so if you think this is it for us, you're wrong."

"Goodbye Zander." I barely hear her words.

I stand there in her hallways, my head against her door for I don't know how long just waiting, hoping she will open the door.

I debate staying out here until she leaves. She has to come out at some point, then she will talk to me face to face.

As my adrenaline comes down and my emotions take over the pain all over my body becomes apparent and I look down at myself, if any of her neighbors come out to see me, they will likely call the cops on some psychopath in the hallway.

That's when I have an idea. It's stupid, but it's something. I feel like I have nothing left to lose at this point.

Mel won't talk to me while Trent is a threat. I can't kill him. I have to do something I never in a million years thought I would do, but it's my last resort. It's the only shot I have to get a chance at a life with Mel.

## 32

**10 Years Ago**

I'm pacing around my room; Zander didn't sound like his normal self when he asked to come over to talk to me, so naturally now I'm freaking out.

My dad is at work, so normally Zander coming over would be something to look forward to, but not this time.

I hear a knock at the door and run over to answer it to see him standing there with his head looking down, hands in his pockets.

"What's going on with you?" I ask, stepping aside so he can come in.

He looks up at me, and I see something foreign in his eyes, sadness, regret, anger?

A mix of all three, possible.

He looks around a second before stepping inside, still not answering me.

I shut the door behind him and step in front of him again, looking up to meet his eyes, but he's still not looking directly at me.

"We are leaving again," he says softly, and I swear the words felt like a punch to my gut.

"What? When?" I squeak out.

I know it's been a possibility, we both did. I think we both just chose to forget about it so we could enjoy our time together, and I think we both figured it would be best to not think about it.

Zander shifts on his feet, and he's still not fucking looking at me. I think one of the stages of grief is anger so I'm jumping right to that one, "Zander, would you fucking look at me?"

His eyes finally meet mine and there's tears along the edge. I've never seen him cry, not even once in all our years of friendship as kids.

"When are you leaving?" I ask again, my hands on my hips, holding onto the anger so I don't start crying too.

"The day after tomorrow." He's looking at me, his voice still low and it sounds like he's trying to hold back those tears I saw.

I'm shocked.

I step back from him, and he takes a step forward. I see his hand lift like he's going to reach for me, but he stops himself.

That's too soon, they can't leave that soon, no they had to have more notice than that, that's ridiculous.

That's when a question comes to me that I don't think I want to ask because I'm afraid of what the answer is going to be.

"How long have you known?"

"Mel..." He steps closer to me again, but I back up out of his reach. My anger is just getting worse.

Why won't he tell me?"

"How long have you known, Zander?" I fold my arms over my chest. I feel my own tears threatening to make their appearance now, but I need to stay strong for myself.

I do not want to cry.

He sighs.

"I've known for a little while."

"How long is 'a little while'?"

"I've known since we moved back, we would be leaving in June."

I feel like my heart just jumped off a cliff and took my brain with it.

He's known the entire time.

He's known and never told me.

I can't breathe.

I feel like I'm about to pass out.

I feel my heart actively ripping itself into shreds in my chest and there's nothing I can do to stop it.

"You've known the entire time you've been back? You knew when you kissed me, when you fucked me, when you said you love me, when you *promised* you were here for me?!" I'm screaming, and I feel the tears coming out.

Dammit, I don't want to cry.

"Mel, please let me explain, I didn't mean for this, I really didn't." He walks toward me, reaching for me. I pull my arm away from him and back up more.

I don't want him to touch me because if he touches me, I might do something stupid like forgive him.

"No, there's no explaining. You fucking lied to me! This whole time you were lying to me! You said you weren't going to come in and ruin my life and do the same shit you've done in the past, but you *lied!* All the shit that happened with Mark and you stood up for me, stood by me all while you were *lying!*" Tears are pouring down my face, I can't stop them even if I tried.

"I meant everything I told you, Mel, I meant every word I just didn't want our time together ruined by you knowing I was leaving, please don't hate me." He tries reaching for me again, but I keep my distance. "We could make this work, it's only one year until I'm eighteen and can move out on my own."

"Fuck you, Zander. You said it yourself long distance doesn't work so that's bullshit and you know what? I do hate you. You're fucking selfish, you didn't want our time together ruined, and now it is. Every single thing. I regret everything I ever did with you, and I regret everything I ever fucking said to you because you didn't deserve shit from me. Get the fuck out and never talk to me again. This is me telling you to fuck off for real."

His own tears have fallen, but he doesn't seem like he notices or even cares. Before I'm able to stop him, he quickly pulls me into a tight hug that normally would have me melting into his arms.

"I meant every word, especially when I told you I love you." He whispers into my hair.

I push against his chest, and he lets me go.

"Don't. Don't fucking say that to me, if you loved me, you would've told me."

"I wanted to, there were so many times I wanted to so bad, I just couldn't."

"Why not?"

"Because it would have ruined everything," He shakes his head.

"Well congratulations, it's ruined anyway. Get out."

He turns around and starts walking back to the front door. I watch him as he walks away and I think he's going to leave without saying anything else, but after he opens the door he turns around, the tears still streaming down his face.

"I love you, Mel, and I always will even if you don't believe me."

And then he walks out the door.

I drop down to my knees, not even trying to contain my tears anymore.

I'm sobbing, my face in my hands while the hot tears come out of my eyes like two faucets I can't shut off.

I'm crying loudly and I don't even care. I end up laying on the floor when I feel like I can't walk because my hysterical crying has taken everything out of me. I'm going to stay here forever.

I don't even know how much time passes that I'm lying on the floor sobbing. Eventually tears stop coming out and I think about what my mom used to say, I never truly believed you could run out of tears, but I think I actually did.

I push up off the floor and attempt to make my legs work to go to my room because the last thing I want is my dad to come home and find me passed out on the living room floor and I have to explain what happened, I can't do that right now.

Once in my room I see my phone I left on my nightstand and I look to see if Zander tried to call or text me, not that I expected him to, not that I even want him to.

Right?

There are no notifications. I lay in bed, and just stare at the wall, replaying everything in my head.

Maybe I should've let him explain.

No, there's no excuse for what he did, he's had months to tell me, and he hadn't.

He just wanted to do the same shit he said he always did, ruin other people's lives because he's going to leave, and it doesn't affect him in the long run. Just me. I'm the only one that got hurt.

Though, he looked pretty sad when he was leaving, and he might be, but he brought this upon himself. He just said all that shit to try and make himself feel better, especially about loving me.

Maybe I shouldn't have said I didn't mean everything; I do love him. I really do, which is why this hurts so fucking bad. But he doesn't deserve that. He doesn't get my love as he breaks my fucking heart.

I spend the rest of the night staring at nothing, but deep

down I am really hoping he will try calling or texting to check on me or make me listen to him.

Something, I want something from him, but it never comes.

He doesn't reach out again. And I won't reach out first, he probably hates me for the shit I said to him, he doesn't want to hear from me anyway, he got what he wanted.

Jokes on me though, he got even more than he bargained for, since he got my fucking heart and just left with it.

## 33

**Present**

I'm numb.

I'm lying in bed, silence surrounding me as the sun rises and I don't move.

I can't sleep.

I can't cry anymore.

I feel nothing.

The thought of getting out of bed physically pains me.

I can't move.

This feels like when he left last time, but this is worse.

So much worse.

I was so sure this would be it for us, and it was ripped away. There's nothing we can do about it, not if we want to live.

When Zander came over, I wanted to rip open that door so fast, fly into his arms and beg him to tell me the truth about everything.

But after everything Trent told me I just couldn't do that. I couldn't continue putting him at risk for something bad to happen.

I'm scared something will happen anyway.

Even after everything, I'm hoping Zander won't give up on me as easily. I know that's ridiculous like when I wanted him to call me after he left, after everything I said. I wasn't mean this time. Just hurt.

I couldn't even look out to see him in front of my door because I know if I saw his eyes I would cave. I was close anyway. I grabbed the door handle multiple times.

I needed him.

I still do.

He lied, because lies of omission are still lies.

He didn't tell me about going to jail.

I still don't know the full story about Jeremy, and about everything Zander has done.

I want to be mad at him.

If I'm mad this is easier.

Instead, I'm nothing. I'm not sad anymore. I'm not mad. I'm just fucking numb, and that's almost scarier than if I was feeling something.

AYLIN COMES over at some point, I'm not paying attention to the time. She told me she would be back today when she left yesterday. Letting her in is the first time I roll out of bed.

As soon as I open the door, I turn around to flop back onto my bed.

"He showed up here last night," I say dryly as I throw myself face down onto my bed once again.

"What happened?" She asks softly without a tone of judgment. She's good at keeping her tone even.

"He came here. I told him to leave. He begged me to let him explain. I said no."

"How do you feel about that?" She asks. This is therapist Aylin, not friend Aylin.

"Fucking terrible. I don't like that he lied, but I also don't believe Trent and I don't want anything to happen to him. I *want* him to explain. I *want* him to fight for me, for us. I'm sad, I'm scared, I'm mad, I'm all of it and I'm also nothing."

My words spill out, I don't even know what I'm saying. I don't know what I want. I just want things to be back how they were.

Aylin comes over to sit on my bed by me.

"Ideally, what do you want to happen?" She asks so gently it makes me want to cry again.

"I don't know."

"You do know. In your perfect world what do you want?"

I turn over so I'm looking up at the ceiling, taking a breath before I answer, "I want Zander happy. That's all, whether I'm in his life or not, whatever he's doing as long as he's happy."

"Do you think he's happy now?"

I think back to last night, how he sounded at my door. How he begged for me. How he told me he loved me. My heart stopped in that moment, and I needed to see him. I needed to feel him.

It took everything in me not to open the door and scream that I love him too.

"No, I don't think he is," I shake my head. "But I don't know what to do about any of it, he's stuck."

"I know it seems like he's stuck, but there's always a way out of things. Even things as complicated as this," She continues to speak so calmly.

"Doctor, please share your ideas then because I got nothing." I throw a pillow over my face.

Aylin scoffs, "Don't call me that. I don't have any great ideas. I just think that maybe you both have the same goal, so working together might be best. Even if it's dangerous."

I remove the pillow from my face to look at her skeptically.

"Hold on," I start, pausing to make sure I processed what she just said correctly. "you're telling me *not* to be careful? You're not my best friend, you're an imposter."

"I'm glad your humor is coming back. Do you think this is something worth fighting for or not?"

"Before I answer that, I have a question," I sit up to look at her. "Are you pro Zander now because yesterday you were telling me he had red flags I chose to ignore and only wanted to see the person I *wanted* to see. Now you're all about me risking my life? What side are you on?"

"I never said I was on a side, I told you what I thought. Now, I'm telling you what I think again *if* you're wanting to help him."

"So, you don't hate him?" I'm so confused.

"No? I never said I did."

I squint my eyes at her, "You had me block him."

"No, I asked what you wanted to do, and you did that all on your own."

"God, you're good."

Aylin chuckles.

These mind games she's playing on me while I'm already vulnerable are making my head spin.

I should unblock Zander. Even though I'm pissed at this situation, and I'm upset how things were left, that was a bit dramatic. It was for my own good to prevent myself from reaching out.

Now, I want to help him, even at a distance. Even if he doesn't want to be with me anymore, I want to help him get free. I want him to be happy.

I glare at Aylin again, waiting to see if she will spout anymore wisdom. She just watches me intently, waiting for me to say anything else. I think for a second before I do.

"Help me come up with a plan," I say as a smile spreads across her mouth.

Aylin may appear professional and perfect, but I know there's something in her I get glimpses of that is a little more reckless. She went through hell as a kid, and I think she likes to pretend it didn't alter who she is, but there's a fire within her that was caused by her trauma, and even she doesn't realize it.

## 34

Zander

**Present**

I cannot believe I just did that.

I reluctantly left Mel's apartment building, feeling completely defeated, but also more determined than ever to get what I want, freedom. Now that Mel is roped into this, and her safety threatened by Trent I needed to do something. I needed to take a chance, even if it's stupid.

I took both my phone and the burner phone out, drove into the forest and smashed them to shit. I don't know if Trent uses them to track me, but I wouldn't put it past that fucking psychopath.

I also searched my car for any sign of a tracker, though Trent tends to go for the easy way out and a phone would be the easiest option for him.

I parked in a parking lot down the street from the police station just in case, then hyper aware of my surroundings making sure no one is following me, I hid myself with a hood as I walked in. I didn't get a chance to get cleaned up after the fight with Trent, I looked like shit. I'm limping, but I needed to do this.

By the time I left the sun has been up for a while. I didn't expect that to take so long. Apparently when you're trying to bargain immunity for information, they want to make you squirm and then get all the info they can.

I mostly talked to a cop named Nate who started off our encounter by asking what the hell happened to me, and assumed I was there to report an assault. I didn't bring up the fight with Trent, focusing purely on his crimes and leaving myself out of it as much as I could.

It's not enough. They need proof.

I'm immune on the drug charges as long as they get Trent, but if anything else comes up against me, I might not be as lucky. And of course, there are things that could come up. The only thing I'm immune to is drug dealing right now, plus they want to use me as a confidential informant from here on out.

There's a plan in place and I'm supposed to frame Trent. I told them no wires; they won't work, he won't admit to shit in front of me. He's always careful with what exactly he says.

They want a setup, an undercover to buy from him. I told them good luck, he won't do that, and they will get to arrest one of his runners instead.

Nate asked me about anything else he's done that could bring him down. Anything in Arizona, anything more serious.

That's the problem.

Either I don't know, or Trent has had someone else do this dirty work for him.

Usually me, and I'm not about to admit that shit.

This may be the stupidest thing I've ever done, but I'm not about to go to prison for life.

I know that even if this does work and Trent gets arrested it won't be for very long, not for the charges they are trying to get him on. Which is why I know I have to have my escape plan in place.

My plan is including Mel, even if she doesn't want to come with me, I need to have something in place with her too since she's not going to be safe from his wrath. She's not going to be safe without me.

I want to check on her.

I want to call her, but I smashed my phone and for the time being it's probably best not to have one. It's also probably best to not draw any more attention to her. Trent is only using her to get to me, he won't seek her out if she's not a threat to him.

My head has too many thoughts going at once. I just keep thinking about everything that needs to happen. My lack of sleep from the last two days is not helping.

Nate gave me his number to give him any information we can use, including any potential setup.

I have to get my escape in place.

I also have to not kill Trent.

All of these things are easier said than done.

First thing I do is cash out my entire bank account.

I'll need all the money to my name for this to happen, and I don't want to run the risk of Trent being able to track me anywhere. The next part of my plan is a bit riskier.

I remember where Aylin lives in some small off campus apartments, driving there I debate on actually talking to her or leaving a note.

A note is easy to rip up but talking to her might not happen since she's likely not even home. Or she will refuse to open the door like Mel.

I cleaned up my face in a gas station bathroom, so I'm not covered in blood. I'm still wearing my dark jacket to cover my ruined shirt. It's really warm out, but I'm too focused to even care.

I knock on Aylin's door, no answer.

I try a few more times before accepting that she isn't here.

I didn't see or hear any movement inside, so I don't think she's just refusing to talk to me.

I search my car for something to write with, but I don't have anything, dammit. No note either. I don't like the idea of not being able to tell someone to make sure Mel stays safe while I fix this.

I debate for about two minutes if I should tell her dad, but that might not bode well for me later when I ask his permission to marry his daughter. Because we will get out of this, and I *will* be with her forever.

My one happy thought is that Mel may not leave her apartment much, I'll check on her periodically from a distance. I won't linger too long, just enough to make sure she's okay. At least until it's safe to have her in my arms again.

ALL THESE PLANS are taking way too long to come together.

It's been over a week since I went to the cops, and nothing has changed.

Later that day I went to the house and pretended like I just blew off steam and things were back to normal. It's not the first time Trent and I fought, then got back to business as usual.

I've continued to have to do what Trent asks, though nothing has been so extreme. I berate him constantly to try and get him to do a run so we can set him up. Then he can at least get a distribution charge.

When I was caught with the drugs in my car, I didn't have enough for anything more than possession. Plus, I had a good lawyer who got me off pretty light with the year I got. I try not to think about that time very often.

It was the darkest time of my life. The confined area, shared with too many men cramped in there. Gangs based on racism; everything was awful.

I felt like I didn't have any support on the outside. My dad was so pissed at me, though he helped me with a lawyer we hardly talked that whole year.

Things have been better now, we worked it out. I told him I truly don't know how the drugs were in my car. I figured maybe it fell out of my asshole friends' pockets since it was tucked into the passenger seat. I didn't surround myself with the best people in Arizona, even before Trent sucked me into this life. I really struggled after we left Portland the last time, and I'm not proud ot eh man I became during that time, outside of helping my Nanna.

I didn't think any of them did the hard shit though, just drank too much, smoked weed, and on occasion some coke. I only ever drank and smoked weed, coke never appealed to me.

That's when it hits me for the first time.

Trent planted the drugs in my car.

He had to.

He was into dealing back then, a lot lower level than he is now, and he wanted me involved. He knew how tough I am, he told me all the time how much use he could have for me. How helpful I would be. How good I could be at it.

He was the one to put the drugs there, I don't know when. It's not a mystery that I drive outside the rules of the road a bit. He must have figured sooner or later I would've been caught. Unless he set me up too, made a call in as a tip.

I'm fuming, why have I never thought of this before?

Am I that stupid?

Of course, it was him, and he got me exactly where he wanted me. Roped into the life, stuck because of my criminal history, and once Jeremy died, I had no clear out since he was willing to help me with our plan to open a tattoo shop together.

If I didn't already know Jeremy's death was due to our pure stupidity, I would blame Trent for that too. The sadistic motherfucker would kill the one person willing to help me get away from him.

I know what I need to do. I just have to get my escape plan together because once everything starts it'll be too late to back out or change anything.

IT TAKES another two weeks for me to finally get things into place.

I haven't talked to Mel in over three weeks, and I'm dying. I drive by her apartment every night to get a glimpse of her window. Sometimes I see the faint light inside, sometimes it's dark.

When it's dark I check the parking lot for her car which is always there. I don't know what I would do if she wasn't at home, and I couldn't find her. My mind would spin wondering if she's with a guy, wondering if she's hurt.

I would tear the whole city apart to find her. If she was with a guy, I would tear him apart next. I hope she doesn't think I gave up on her, on us. I haven't. Not even close.

The part of my plan that took the longest is where we are going to run away. It's not perfect, but it's somewhere safe, and it's somewhere Trent has no idea about.

One day we will be able to have everything we both dreamed of, and I will promise her that as long as she will take me back.

I will admit all my planning has included Mel willingly going along with it. I do know there's still the chance she doesn't want anything to do with me anymore. I try not to think about that, she might be mad, but I will win her back. I haven't failed yet; I will tell her everything she wants to know about me. I will share every single part of me and my history so I'm completely bare to her emotionally.

The other part of my plan that has been complicated was finessing enough product without Trent knowing, for me to plant on him.

The final part is when I can actually set it in motion. I knew I couldn't plant anything on him too soon, risking him finding it before everything is ready.

I've contacted the cop, Nate, a couple times with any information I have that could help with the setup.

Admittedly this plan is weak.

It could be easy for Trent to get off with minimal or no charges, though this is how he got me so I have some confidence. Nate has been surprisingly helpful for a cop, he gives me tips to help without saying too much. I'm not sure if he's even supposed to help me like this, but he has. He also said he can be the one to catch Trent once the time comes.

It's been a month since this all started, and tonight is the night everything is going to go down.

Trent has finally agreed to come to a party to recruit since I haven't been doing as well as I should be. I haven't been trying on purpose, often standing off to the side, not engaging much.

Trent was pissed, but I must have been right about him tracking me because he hasn't brought up Mel again. From what I can see her lights turn on and off so I'm hoping she's okay.

I just got a new phone for the plan because I don't want to risk Trent tracking me again. It'll be destroyed as soon as this is over, and I'll have Mel with me. Even though it's been the hardest month being away from her, and unable to contact her it will be worth it.

I have a bag packed in my trunk, ready to go. I had to pack and load it in my car while Trent was sleeping a couple nights ago.

That was also the night I planted everything in his car.

I put a bunch of wrapped blocks in the trunk where the spare tire is kept. I also taped some under the seats for good measure. I've been nervous about him finding any of them, but so far, it's been okay.

I'm cursing my tiny car yet again because I know it doesn't have enough room for much of Mel's stuff when I get there.

We will have to come back at some point, I know this. I just want this to work so I can get her alone and beg for her forgiveness. Neither of us leaving the safe space until she forgives me.

Trent has me run another stupid errand for him, saying we will meet at the party after I'm done. I think he may not want me there anyway.

We barely speak, we haven't fought again, but we are even more distant than we've ever been. It works in my favor, though. I just want to know how Mel has been doing this whole time, and I feel like I should've seen her, should've contacted her somehow, but I couldn't. This has to happen first.

I watch Trent leave, waiting until his headlights are out of view before I pull out the flip phone to call Nate.

"Trent's on the move with product in his car," I say simply. We've discussed the plan a few times, he knows where Trent is going and where I hid the product.

"On it."

We hang up. I run downstairs, jumping in my car ready to get a front row seat to the show that is about to begin.

# 35

**Present**

My motivation to help Zander disappeared after about a week of him ignoring me.

I tried reaching out, leaving so many messages his voicemail ended up full so I couldn't leave anymore.

I told him I would hear him out.
I told him I wanted to help.
I begged for him to come back.
I heard nothing back.

It was like my heart was broken all over again. I started to feel like he really did give up on me, on us. Even though he told me he wouldn't.

After two weeks of no contact, I was paranoid that something was wrong, maybe Trent did hurt him and that's why he hasn't contacted me. I knew I couldn't go by his house in my car, that was a death wish.

So, I had Aylin drive. She was hesitant about the field trip but agreed after telling me she wouldn't get too close, just enough to get the answers we need before hightailing it out of there.

I hid on the floor of the backseat, peaking my head out when we got close to the house hidden by the forest. My heart raced seeing the house that confines Zander with the enemy. The bright lights were on, shining even brighter in the dark forest.

I pointed out Zander's car in the driveway, and begged Aylin to stay for a second longer to see if we could see anything in the window.

A figure appeared, and we panicked. I've never seen her drive like that, it reminded me of Zander. I was flung around in the backseat as she turned the car in a complete one-eighty before flooring the gas pedal.

Her car is not as capable as Zander's so the ride was not smooth, especially after my back hit the back door.

I climbed back into the front seat as we watched behind us to make sure no one followed. Neither of us got a good look at the figure so I couldn't be certain if it was Zander or Trent. We left without any real answers, but I tried to keep my hope that he is okay.

After three weeks I've given up all hope.

He hasn't contacted me, there's been nothing.

The positive I have is that neither has Trent. I debate for a second going to the cops, but I know that will just end badly for both Zander and me. I can't do that.

One night I'm about to go to sleep, as I go to my window to close the blinds my eyes are drawn to the parking lot.

There, I see a familiar black sports car. I don't think he can see me from up here, I can't see inside it at all. My heart flutters in my chest as I watch him drive away quickly.

Maybe all hope isn't lost. I sleep better that night, clinging to the tiny hope that seeing his car gave me. I know it's him.

He's checking on me because he did mean what he said to me that night he came here.

*"I've always been yours and you've always been mine so if you think this is it for us, you're wrong."*

AFTER THAT NIGHT I was never able to catch another glimpse of Zander's car outside, but I can't help the feeling that something is going to happen.

It's been a week and I'm starting to think maybe it might be me doing something, who knows?

I'm close to snapping and showing up at his doorstep, consequences be damned.

I continue to try and distract myself, every day that passes. I try to write, but the words don't come as easily as they did before. I'm almost done with my first draft, but it's missing something, and I'm stuck.

I move between reading, playing music too loud and dancing like an idiot, watching ridiculous movies, and even resort to taking a walk a couple times which is when I know I've truly lost it because I detest exercise.

I'm sitting at my desk trying to push through the writer's block, trying to pull from all my emotions I'm feeling for *anything* to finish my first draft. I've been sitting here longer than I would care to admit, but after feeling practically useless for the last month I'm forcing myself to do something.

I'm biting at my nails when there's a pounding at my door. I jump, instantly panicked.

The last time this happened it was Trent. I stand up slowly, cautious of what might be just on the other side of the door. It's locked, but it's also my only escape unless I want to try and survive a five-story jump.

"Mel, it's me," A deep voice says from the other side of the door, knocking again.

My heart lurches. I know that voice, every emotion I've had for the last month comes rushing back.

I don't want to give in to him so easily.

I'm mad.

I may be happy he's here, but I'm also fucking pissed at him.

"Mel, please, we don't have a ton of time," Zander says, a hint of uncertainty in his voice.

I have a fleeting thought that this might be some sort of set up, but I don't think he would do that.

I feel like my feet can't move. I feel like I've been cemented in my spot.

"I will explain everything, please just open the door," He sounds desperate, strained and...scared.

My head begins functioning enough to realize this is real. This is happening.

I stride over to the door quickly, opening it to reveal Zander with an arm stretched above his head, holding onto the door frame as he slouches over.

I can't form words.

Did he get more attractive in the last month, or are my memories just not doing him justice?

His arms bulge in the sleeves of his t-shirt as he grasps the door frame. His light brown hair is hanging in his face and I want to push it back. Then, his eyes meet mine, and for just a moment I forget about all the negative feelings and the hurt, as I look into those bright blue/green eyes that make my knees weak.

Unfortunately, as he steps into my apartment the negative feelings come back as I watch him move with purpose, looking around like he's looking for something. I remember that he lied to me, he has a lot to explain, and I need to stand my ground with this.

I fold my arms across my chest as I watch Zander go into my closet pulling out a duffel bag.

"What do you think you're doing?" I ask finally.

He isn't saying anything which is adding to my anger. He doesn't get to come in here without an explanation and start packing me a bag.

He finally looks up at me again as he strides over to me quickly without touching me, "I will explain everything on the way, and then I'll continue to explain once we get there. Just trust me right now that we need to leave."

My jaw drops, "Go where? What the fuck are you talking about?"

"We have to leave, I promise I will explain it *all* just please don't fight me right this second," He goes back to grabbing handfuls of my clothes and shoving them in the bag he grabbed.

I watch him, stunned, "No, this isn't happening. I'm not going anywhere with you right now, not when you disappeared for a month, no contact, nothing and then think you can come in here to make me go somewhere with you. No."

I grab the bag from him and throw it off my bed, where he was packing it.

He sighs loudly, running his hand down his face.

I try to stop myself from staring at the veins bulging in his arms as he does that, but I can't help it. I bite the corner of my lip to prevent a smile because I'm still mad, pissed even.

Zander's eyes land on me again, this time he might be a bit mad too. I've seen that look in his eyes, but it's never been directed at me.

Not until now.

I back up away from him, but he steps closer, our chests touching as he looks down to me. I have to arch my neck back completely to meet his gaze.

"Mel Bell, you have no idea what has been going on the last

month, I don't give a shit if you hate me right now you are coming with me even if I have to throw you over my shoulder and carry you out myself. We need to leave sooner rather than later. I need you out of here right now."

As he speaks, I realize his anger may not be directed at me, his voice is strained, but somehow soft as it always is towards me.

What he's saying makes me panic.

"Did you do something? Why do we need to leave?" My mouth suddenly feels dry, I try to lick my lips to help, but it does nothing.

Zander's eyes watch the movement as my tongue swipes across my bottom lip, and I think for a moment he might kiss me, but he doesn't. My heart sinking a little lower because a part of me was hoping he would.

He turns back around, grabbing the bag I threw onto the floor, stuffing my stuff back inside before closing it.

"I told you I'd explain on the way, grab whatever you might need and let's go."

I don't think I've ever heard Zander's voice so emotionless. He always has humor, his charisma shining through like a beacon of light. This Zander is like a robot, emotionless and cold.

I want to fight this more.

I know I should.

I need to ask the million questions swimming around my mind, but I just can't.

I can't, he wouldn't be doing this unless he had a good reason. Plus, I'll have plenty of time to fight him if he doesn't explain like he said he would.

"I need to know how long this excursion is for me to know what I might need," I look around at what might be a necessity or not.

"I don't know, but we will be back," He's standing by the front door impatiently.

I grab my laptop and a couple books I shove into my backpack before going to him at my door.

"Happy?" I ask, not a hint of happiness in my own voice.

"You have no idea," he says in the same robot tone he's had.

It's making it extremely difficult to distinguish any emotion he's really having in this moment.

We get down to his car, he throws my duffel in the small trunk as he tells me to put my backpack in the front trunk.

I do as he says, growing more concerned by the minute.

We both climb into his car. I almost forgot how small it is in here with Zander, and I feel more suffocated by the tension that's in the air all around us.

He still doesn't say anything as he speeds off, maneuvering the car like a pro. I become fixed on his arms, how they move and what veins will appear as he shifts the gear and turns the wheel. He's driving with a purpose and I'm trying to figure out where we are going.

He still hasn't said anything. Once we are outside the Portland city limits, I finally demand for some answers. I need something.

"I'm going to need you to start from the beginning and tell me what the fuck is going on," I demand, turning in my seat to face him

Zander's jaw clenches, his strong jawline accentuated by the action as he prepares to speak, "The beginning was a long time ago. Are you sure you want me to start there?"

I raise my eyebrow to him. "You said you'd explain. So, explain."

# 36

Zander

**Present**

I will admit how I showed up to Mel's apartment is not how I intended to.

I thought I would be happy, relieved, throw my arms around her, kiss her senseless and tell her we are running away together before literally sweeping her off her feet.

That's definitely not what happened.

After Trent left our house I followed far behind him, but I knew the route he was taking.

Eventually I saw the police lights. I pulled up behind the cop car, a decent distance behind to not be obvious.

I watched the interaction which included a frustrated Trent getting pulled out of his car when I assume he refused to consent to a search. I hear him yelling, but I'm too far to hear what he's saying.

Another police car comes up at some point, this one has a K-9. I watch the dog sniff all around his car, signaling something was found.

I become excited watching everything unfold.

The plan is working.

I'm about to be free.

There's more yelling, they continue to search the car as Trent is handcuffed sitting on the ground.

I bet he's more pissed about having to sit in the dirt than any of this.

After a while they begin to put the drugs in bags, and I think they are going to take Trent away, that's when I decide to make my presence known.

I get back into my car, driving up next to the commotion. I see Nate, the cop I've been talking to as he gives me a slight nod before Trent's gaze fixates on me. He fights against the officer that was leading him to the back of one of those cars.

"Zander, what the fuck?" Trent spits at me, fighting against the officer trying to pull him along.

"Nothing you don't deserve," I shrug. I see Trent's face drop as realization sets in that this was all me.

"I'll be out on bail in no time and then I'm coming after Mel first so you can fucking watch. This isn't over."

He's shoved into the car, I'm hit with some paranoia at his words, but I know I'm about to get her far from here to a place he will never know about.

Nate comes up to my passenger side window, leaning in as he speaks quietly, "He's probably right just so you know. He likely won't get a high bail and won't be in custody long since this is a first offense."

"What? What do you mean? I thought this would be done," I shake my head trying to remember my own experience which is all a blur as I've tried my best to block it all out.

"Sorry, man, until he's actually sentenced, he will likely still be a problem for you," Nate moves away from my car probably not wanting to seem too obvious.

I'm grateful for his help, I know he has done more than he's supposed to, but now I'm still terrified of what comes next.

I speed away and go straight for Mel's apartment.

The whole way there I'm thinking of what we can do. We are going to get away tonight, but this isn't going to be it for us.

Trent doesn't know where we are going. It will take a huge effort to find us, he won't be that vengeful, will he?

All my joy from the victory is gone because it's not a victory at all yet.

The worst part about all of this is Trent could still be found not guilty and come after us. I plan for us to be long gone by then.

Once I'm at her apartment I'm so desperate to see her I'm begging her to open the door.

Once she does, I'm hit with everything all at once. Her thick red hair falling over her shoulders, she's in leggings and a sweatshirt, she looks like she's tired and I wonder if she's had issues sleeping this whole time like me.

I grip the door frame harder to prevent myself from reaching out and grabbing her to bring her against me. That's the only thing I want right now.

I need to hold her.

I need to touch her, but I know I can't. Not yet.

She deserves an explanation first.

We have to leave. She argues as I throw together a bag for her before she throws it on the ground. I'm frustrated, she doesn't understand yet, but we have to go.

"Mel Bell, you have no idea what has been going on the last month, I don't give a shit if you hate me right now you are coming with me even if I have to throw you over my shoulder and carry you out myself. We need to leave sooner rather than later. I need you out of here right now."

I don't know how long we have; it doesn't even matter we just need to leave and once we are gone I can figure out our next steps, but I'm not risking Trent getting released quickly and coming right here.

"Did you do something? Why do we need to leave?" Mel asks as she licks her bottom lip. I watch, dying to take that lip in my teeth, dying to have that tongue in my mouth. Dying to feel her everywhere.

I turn back to packing her bag before I do something stupid, like grab her and do exactly what I want to do before she's ready.

"I told you I'd explain on the way, grab whatever you might need and let's go," I stand by the front door, holding onto her duffel.

I'M DRIVING to our destination. I still haven't told Mel where yet, but she asked for an explanation from the beginning. And we have about a two-and-a-half-hour drive.

I start by telling her Trent planted drugs in my car which led to me getting arrested and spending the following year in jail. She looks terrified as I tell her the details of what I saw while I was locked up, but she doesn't speak.

I tell her how I got out, and because my options were so limited Trent manipulated me into helping him out for some good money. His requests were easy at first, nothing too bad. Then, they got worse and more involved until I was too stuck to do anything about it.

I tell her about Jeremy, how we met when I was looking around to find an artist that would tattoo my designs on me. We became good friends, and hung out outside of me getting tattooed. We were friends for years, he wanted me to be his apprentice and then at some point we would open our own shop together.

It was the perfect plan. I tell Mel about it all, I'm not holding back any details anymore.

The next thing I tell her is the hardest, and I do everything I can to hold back my emotion.

"We liked racing, we both had nice cars that we would race on side streets, and just fuck around," I start, needing to pause as I relive the memory. "One night we decided to race as usual, but this time it had just rained a lot. It wasn't raining anymore so we figured it would be fine. Arizona is notorious for having shitty drainage systems since it rains so rarely. Jeremy got in front of me, and it was too late for him to notice the lake caused by the rain that overtook the road..."

I feel Mel place her hand on mine. I look over to see her silently comforting me. I squeeze her hand as I intertwine our fingers. I never thought such a simple gesture could have such a huge impact on someone. But with her hand in mine, I feel like everything will be okay.

"Anyway, it wouldn't have happened if I didn't want to race that night. You know the rest of the story," I clear my throat as if that can clear the lump in my throat.

"It's not your fault," Mel finally says softly.

"No, it is. It was my idea; I know it's my fault."

"No, Zander it's not and I don't think he would want you to blame yourself. I never met him, but a good friend wouldn't want you to carry this guilt with you."

She's right. He wouldn't.

"He would've liked you, I know it," I look over at her again with a small smile on my lips.

I continue telling her everything as we get closer to our destination. I tell her how I was trying to move to Portland by myself, but Trent came along instead and the hell it's been outside of her. I tell her everything I've had to do while I've been here.

She now knows everything. Including everything that happened tonight and why we have to get away.

"So, it's not done yet?" She asks, her fear evident in her voice.

I give her hand a comforting squeeze since neither of us has let go.

"No, but I'm done being away from you. We are in this together," I tell her confidently.

I mean it. Whatever is going to happen we will handle together.

"Good, now where the fuck are we going?"

I chuckle, oh yeah, she still doesn't know that yet.

"I want this to be the last secret between us, and I want it to be a surprise," I feel lighter having everything off my chest.

I feel like there's no barrier between us and for the first time in a month I feel like everything is going to be okay.

# 37

**Present**

The majority of our drive was filled with Zander telling me everything. I'm still trying to wrap my head around it all, and I'm still not completely convinced this isn't a dream I'm about to wake up from.

I continued to hold his hand because the warmth and his strength is the only thing reassuring me at this moment. Especially because I don't think either of us know what is going to happen next. We just know we will be by each other's side the whole time.

Finally, I realize where we are by the distinct landscape and bridges.

"Why are we in Newport?" I ask, looking around at the scenery barely lit by the streetlights reflecting in the water of the river, and the lights on the bridge.

"Because I know it's some place we will be safe for a little while," Zander squeezes my hand once.

We continue driving through some side streets and around

curves that are only illuminated by the lights on Zander's car. It's scary, yet I've never felt so safe with him.

He pulls up to a little house that is held up on stilts, the first level being the small one car garage with wooden stairs outside leading up to the front door.

"Whose house is this?" I ask.

It's dark. I barely make out anything specific about where we are or the details of the house. I don't know anyone that lives in Newport, and I didn't think Zander did either, even though I feel like I'm just getting to know him again.

"Ours for the time being," he says as he shuts off the car surrounding us in complete darkness. "It was really hard to find something. I found this; it's owned by a really nice older woman. I told her I would help fix it up if she let us stay here for a little while."

"Ours? Wait, what? I feel like there's so much going on I can't even keep up," I shake my head. "You want us to live here? What about my apartment?"

"That's up to you, I told you we could go back to get more of your things when it's safer, but if you want to go back there to stay when this is all over, I'll understand that too," He's looking at me, his eyes almost glowing in the dim light.

I don't even know if I'll want to go back. This is what I wanted forever, and he knows that. A house on the coast...with him.

I get out of the car without saying anything else because I'm too curious about this house. Zander follows close behind as we climb the stairs. I look around, the surroundings barely lit by the moonlight. I see it's in a secluded location, only one neighbor on the left. We are up on a hill, far from the main roadways and I don't think we are close to any of the more popular beach areas. It's perfect.

Zander opens the front door to let us in. The first thing I notice is almost the entire back of the house that faces out to the ocean is floor to ceiling windows. This provides the greatest view I've ever seen, it's like a picture. Especially at night, the moon reflecting the water. Light waves rolling and crashing. Rocks jut out of the water closer to the shoreline, the waves crashing into them.

I didn't even notice myself walk over to the window, mesmerized by the view. I haven't noticed anything about the house around us except this wall of windows.

I feel warmth at my back as Zander stands behind me, his broad figure covering me completely before I feel his hands lightly slide around my waist. I lean back against him, my head leaning back against his hard chest as I continue to stare out at the view.

"I'm sorry, Mel Bell. I'm sorry for everything," he says softly, his lips lightly touching the top of my head.

I don't say anything, I close my eyes enjoying the feel of him again. I sink into the warmth and hardness of his chest as he holds me against him. I enjoy being surrounded by his scent again. That fire-tinged spice that is so unique to him.

I missed him. He didn't want any of this to happen, I know he never meant to put us in danger. I don't think he ever meant to hurt me.

I turn around in his arms to look into his eyes again, the shadows of his face illuminated by the light from the ocean. His jawline is sharp and strong. Eyes just as bright as the water outside. His hands around me strong and capable but holding me with softness.

I flick my eyes from his down to his mouth. I want to kiss him. I run my hands up his muscled chest up to his neck. I'm on my tiptoes as I move my hands around the back of his neck. He presses me harder against him as he presses his lips onto mine.

The kiss is soft, I let out a sigh into his mouth. Everything feels like it's supposed to again. Our kiss deepens, both of us becoming more desperate by the moment.

Desperate for the time we lost, yet again.

Desperate to feel each other.

Desperate to hold each other.

Zander lifts me up with ease, I wrap my legs around his waist as he walks us into a room off to the right.

He sets me down on a soft bed, I glance around as his mouth moves across my jaw, and down my neck. There's a window looking out to the ocean in here too, that's all I get to notice when Zander's hand is lifting my shirt up. He removes it, while ripping my bra down so his mouth can latch onto my breast.

I let out a moan at the feel of his hot mouth on my nipple. I arch my back up as he swirls his tongue around the point before moving to the other one to repeat the movement.

I grasp at his shirt, yanking it over his head as he continues his descent down my body because I want to enjoy the view as Zander worships me. Zander's hands reach my hips as he pulls down my pants and underwear together. He slides his hands up the inside of my thighs, holding my legs open as his mouth latches onto my dripping cunt.

I throw my head back from the feeling of his tongue on me. He licks me everywhere, like he's trying to taste every single part of me he can. I wrap my hands in his soft hair, pulling his mouth against me as he licks and sucks.

"You have no idea how much I missed this," He growls against me before licking my entire seam as I feel my orgasm beginning to take over my body.

Zander slips a finger inside me, curling up to the sensitive spot on my inner walls. I buck against him, but he uses his other hand to hold me down, completely at his mercy.

My orgasm hits me like a tidal wave, my entire body shakes

as I pull Zander's head against me, his movements not slowing, extending my pleasure.

Once I'm limp from the pleasure Zander lifts himself up over me, a smirk on his face. I grab his neck to bring his lips to mine to kiss off that look.

I taste myself on my tongue as he dominates my mouth. I reach down to his erection through his jeans, palming and squeezing it as he moans into my mouth.

I wrap my legs around his waist, lifting myself up against him before using all my strength to flip him onto his back. I know the only reason I was able to was because he wasn't expecting it.

I'm straddling his hips, completely naked as I fumble around with his jeans to get them off. My hands still shaking from my orgasm.

"Someone isn't very patient tonight," he says, eyeing my struggling hands.

"I've been patient long enough," I groan in frustration.

Zander chuckles as he helps me, lifting me up with his hips as he slides them down. I reach behind me to push them off his legs.

His cock is hard and throbbing beneath me, I wrap my hand around him, pumping my hand around his shaft as he hisses through his teeth. I take his erection, and rub myself with his length, not putting it inside me yet. I rub against him, rubbing all my wetness along him. He's groaning, gripping my hips tighter by the second.

"Now who's not being patient?" I taunt, continuing my movements against him.

"Mel," He growls. "Ride my fucking cock right now or I swear- "

His words are cut off with a moan as I lower myself onto him, filling myself completely with him. I adjust my position to accommodate his size before I swivel my hips around him.

His hands on my hips are gripping me hard enough to leave bruises as he lifts me slightly, then back down on himself. I fall into the rhythm, bringing myself up then back down on him hard, hitting the farthest part inside me. The room is filled with our groans and moans as the rhythm increases.

Zander is lifting his hips up to fuck me from below. I'm close to another orgasm when suddenly our positions are switched, I'm underneath him as he slams his hips into mine, my moans turn into screams. My second orgasm hits harder than the first from the force of him driving his cock into me.

As soon as I'm exploding around him Zander can't hold back, I feel him throb with a groan as he spills inside me.

We both lay there, sweaty, breathless, looking into each other's eyes. Zander's still inside me, it's like neither of us want to move, we don't want to break away from this moment.

Zander rests his forehead on mine before speaking softly, "I love you."

The last time he said this there was a door between us. The time before that was ten years ago when he was leaving. My heart begins hammering in my chest. I haven't told him I love him in so long, even though I know I never stopped.

"I love you, Zander," I say just as softly.

His lips are on mine again, I feel his cock still inside me hardening again as we kiss, both overtaken with this scary, but familiar emotion between us.

He starts to move his hips against me again, this time it's softer, feeling every inch of him as he pulls out slowly, then back in powerful, strong, but lovingly. We make love like this for what feels like forever, and as the sun rises over the ocean, we never leave each other's arms.

I don't know what is about to happen with the potential danger waiting for us, but I do know that I love this man. We are going to get through this together. No one can get between us again.

# 38

**Present**

Having Mel in my arms again makes me feel complete. I don't want to let her go, ever.

We can function attached at the hip because that's what I'm about to do. I need to touch her at all times.

We slept into the late morning after being up basically all-night alternating between fucking and making love, everything feels right with her. She hasn't even really seen the house, but I hope she likes it.

I know she likes the view, that was what made me continue to fight for this place.

Mrs. Carter is a nice older woman whose husband passed away a few years ago. She told me this was their first house together and could never stand to sell it. She wanted to restore it for herself but is unable to do any of the work and paying someone would be way too expensive.

That's where our deal came into play. Even though this isn't the dream house on the coast I want to give Mel for our life together, it's something. It's also safer than staying in Portland right now because I have no idea what Trent is going to do when he can't find me.

Especially since he knows I set him up.

I continue to stare at Mel's sleeping form, wrapped around my body, illuminated by the sunlight reflected off the ocean outside. I run my fingers through her hair softly. Her wavy thick hair is so soft through my fingers.

She stirs before opening her eyes, looking up at me, smiling instantly. I'm beyond happy she's here with me, and that she doesn't hate me. She could have, I've fucked up enough to warrant it. It makes me love her more that she cares enough to not hold a grudge.

"Waking up here suits you," I say, pressing my lips softly against hers.

"Here in this house, or here in your arms?" She asks, snuggling closer into my chest.

"Both," She hums against my bare chest in response as I continue to hold her.

Eventually, we pull ourselves out of bed. I want to show her around the small house. It's only two bedrooms, one bathroom, right around a thousand square feet.

Mel's face lights up looking everywhere. She's smiling so wide I can't take my eyes off her as she explores every inch of it.

Everything is outdated, the cabinet doors are practically falling off, and the floor needs to be replaced, it's old and neglected, but Mel looks like she's in heaven. She doesn't see the flaws. She sees her dream coming to life. I can't help but just watch her joy, smiling at her.

Mel goes to take a shower and I decide to check my phone to see if there's any updates from Nate. I call him when there's no messages or missed calls. I'm hoping that means Trent is still stuck at the police station or locked in a holding cell, but I want to double check.

"Greene," He answers with his last name, I only know because of the card he gave me.

"Nate, it's Zander," I say simply. I know this is still uncharted territory with him helping me so much since he's overstepping what he normally should.

"Hey, I was going to call you, but some other shit came up," I hear some shuffling and I wonder if he's moving away from other people to continue. "He got out this morning. Court is next week for him."

Shit. I'm not surprised, but I'm on alert.

"Thanks," I hang up the phone. My mind instantly running through any possibility.

We are safe here; I know we are. We can handle a week here until Trent goes to court, then he will be gone for a while, right?

If they decide to keep him.

They could just let him go.

I run my hand through my hair, I have to do something. Hiding out here is fine, but it's not a solution, not a real one.

Mel comes out of the bathroom, wrapped in a towel. As soon as she sees me, she can see the distress on my face because her own falls in concern.

"What happened?" She asks, clearly scared.

"Trent was released, he doesn't have court until next week," I tell her even though I wanted to hide it, keep her in this happy bubble with just us. I can't do that to her again, though. I can't lie to her anymore.

"What are we going to do?" She stands up taller, Mel is tough. I know this.

"We are going to stay here where it's safe," I stride over to her, cupping her face in my hands. "And I'm going to do everything I can to protect you."

She leans into my touch, smirking, "Maybe I'll be the one protecting you."

I smile at her, pulling the towel off her still wet body, she squeals as I throw her over my shoulder into the bedroom again.

~

THE FEW DAYS go by without any issues, and it's almost too good to be true that we haven't heard anything from Trent in any way. Maybe he gave up. I laugh at that thought, there's no way.

Mel and I are caught up in each other, we started some projects at the house, Mel picking out designs we should do. Paint colors, what floor we should use, all of it I leave up to her. She seems to enjoy it, her face lighting up as her creativity spirals.

"Do you paint?" She asked me one day while looking up design ideas on Pinterest.

"I've painted walls and stuff, yeah," I wondered if she was just questioning my ability to do the projects this house requires.

"No, like on canvases," She clarified. "You're a good artist from what I've seen, so I thought maybe it would be nice if you painted a mural over there."

She pointed out a big empty wall in the entryway, "I'll do anything you ask me to."

She smiled as I kissed her. I meant that, I will do anything she asks me to, she has all of me. She always has.

~

IT'S ALMOST BEEN A WEEK, I'm anxious to know what happens with Trent, but Mel has kept me distracted when she sees me getting into my head too much.

We continue to work on the house. I try to get all my worries out by working, and when that doesn't work, I distract myself with Mel's body. That works every time.

I wake up before Mel most mornings, and this morning I'm sitting on the floor in front of the giant window in the living room watching the colors from the sky reflect into the ocean as the sun rises. I want to do something like that for the mural Mel wants me to paint because I know she will love it.

My phone rings form across the room, and I'm cautious about answering it. No one really has this new number for me, plus it's really early. It could be Nate or some scam call. I stand up to grab the phone to answer. Before I'm even able to say a word the voice on the other end speaks. My jaw drops, fists clench, I feel my face getting hot with fury.

"Hello little brother."

# 39

**Present**

When I wake up, I reach my arm out to the other side of the bed to find that it's empty. Zander usually wakes up before me, but usually stays in bed holding me.

I hear him speaking to someone in the living room, so I go out there to see what's going on. The tension in his voice makes me uneasy.

Once I see him, he's clearly angry. His knuckles are white from gripping his phone, he's pacing while his other fist is clenched at his side.

"Just give up and let it go!" He yells into the speaker, and I am pretty sure I know who is on the other end of the phone.

My heart is racing as I stand there and watch Zander.

"Fuck you, Trent, it's done!" He looks up to see me standing there finally.

I want to go over to him. I want to hold him, but I can't move.

"If you think I'm going to meet up with you, you're insane.

You won't find us so just give up and take your punishment like a man. Just like I had to." There's a beat of silence while Trent says something on the other end before Zander hangs up the phone and throws it across the room, shattering.

"What happened?" I'm panicked. Whatever Trent said couldn't be good, I don't think anything he says could be good.

Zander strides over to me quickly, wrapping his arms around me completely, and holding me to his chest tightly.

He doesn't speak right away, as he holds me. I feel his breathing slow beneath my cheek as I rest my head on his chest.

"He says he wants to talk to me, man to man to settle everything once and for all," He finally says. His deep voice is lower as I can sense the hesitation in his tone.

"Maybe he really does want to settle everything," I try to be optimistic, though I know how naïve I sound. There's no way a guy like Trent just wants to talk to Zander.

He sighs before speaking again, "He says if I don't he will come here. He knows we are in Newport, not exactly where we are, but at this point I wouldn't put it past him to be able to find out."

I look up at him, "What do you mean?"

"He got my new number somehow; I never gave it to him. I never told anyone where we were going. He's got some way to find out the information he wants."

My breath hitches. He is so much worse than I thought, I knew Trent was dangerous, but fuck, this is a new extreme.

"What do we do?" I ask because we are in this together.

"I'm going to meet him; you're going to see your dad, so you aren't alone. After that, you and I will come back here and finally move on with our lives," He cups my face in his hands as he speaks, looking so deeply into my tear rimmed eyes.

"You're not going alone, I'm coming with you," I'm adamant. We said we would do this together.

He shakes his head, "No, I need to do this alone. I need to know you're safe with your dad. It'll be okay."

I don't like it. I don't like any of this.

I CAN'T BELIEVE we are in Zander's car driving back to Portland right now. He told me Trent said to meet at midnight at this old library that hasn't been used in our lifetime. There used to be stories that circulated about that place when we were kids. Stories like if you stepped foot in you'd be cursed for seven years or some shit. I feel like adults just told kid's that so we wouldn't be tempted to go there. In reality I'm sure it is just full of homeless people.

Apparently, Trent said if Zander doesn't show then he would find us before sunrise.

I called my dad and asked if I could stay the night at his house tonight, making up an excuse about work being done at my apartment. He said I could, but that he's working the night shift. Plan B is going to Aylin's place to stay the night there.

She was more than okay with it as long as I promise to give her the full run down.

Zander is going to drop me off with her before going to meet Trent. He gave me the cop he's been in contact with (Nate I think?) number to call. He told me if he's not back at Aylin's place to get me in an hour, then I need to call. I think an hour is too long, but he made me promise.

The drive is tense, we are both nervous. I'm practically shaking, Zander's hand on my thigh is the only thing grounding me as we make our way back to familiar territory.

Without the looming danger around us I have never been so happy as I was these last few days with Zander. Just us, a little house on the coast and nothing else mattered.

I almost started to believe it was all real until I was forced to remember that our perfect world isn't all that perfect. At least not yet.

Before I know it, we are at Aylin's small off campus apartment. Zander walks me up to her door, I already feel the tears threatening to fall down my cheeks when he turns to face me. As soon as our eyes meet a tear falls out, Zander catches it with his finger on my cheek, wiping it away.

"Everything is going to be fine, Mel Bell. Do you trust me?" He runs his knuckle along my cheek.

"Of course, I just don't want you to get hurt," My voice is shaky as I'm still trying to hold back sobs.

"Baby, it takes a lot to hurt me, I can handle myself," He smiles, but it's not because he's happy. I can tell he's just smiling to ease my mind.

Zander captures my mouth with his in a soft, loving kiss. I melt into him like it's the first time kissing him.

I want to keep kissing him forever.

I want him with me forever.

I just have to believe this will be okay, everything will be okay. He reaches above me to knock on Aylin's door before parting from me, but not stepping away.

Aylin opens the door, I don't want to look away from Zander, I don't want him to leave.

"Keep her here, and both of you stay safe," Zander says to Aylin, but he's looking at me.

"Don't worry, she will be here impatiently waiting for you to come back," Aylin says, and I finally turn to look at her.

Zander leans down to whisper in my ear, "I love you," before turning to go back to his car.

I watch him drive away before heading into Aylin's apartment. As soon as I'm inside we shut and lock the door. She looks at me with a questioning look.

"You have so much to catch me up on," She leads me to her

couch so I can tell her everything that's happened since we last saw each other before Zander and I left.

AYLIN WAITS until I've told her everything, yet again, before she speaks, "If you don't turn this into your next book then you're missing out."

I chuckle before looking at the clock in her kitchen to see it's only ten minutes past midnight. I begin to fidget in my seat. I don't like the idea of waiting an hour before getting help. I don't like not being there to make sure Zander is okay. Aylin notices my uneasiness.

"What's wrong?"

"I think we should go help," I say simply, even though I know it sounds crazy.

"Help with what?" She tilts her head, genuinely confused even though I told her what Zander is going to do right now.

"We should go make sure Zander is okay and call for help if needed. He told me to give him an hour, but I have a bad feeling about waiting that long," I twist my fingers around my hair, thinking of the many possibilities of this going very sideways.

Aylin is quiet for a few seconds, seriously considering what we should do before she says, "Fine, let's go."

I've always said Aylin is my ride or die, tonight just proves it.

Aylin knows where this old library is as she drives us there, carefully. I'm keeping my eye out for anything that could stand in our way as we approach the run-down building that looks like it's hardly standing anymore.

I'm not sure there's even a roof, walls are broken down and there's a chain-link fence around the whole place. I don't know where Zander's car is, my anxiety spiking as I don't see anything.

"Turn off your lights so we can get closer," I tell Aylin as she continues to circle the fence to look for any opening.

She turns off her lights as the car rolls slowly while we both strain, looking for any sign of life.

Finally, around the back of the building I see Zander's car parked across the street. Aylin parks behind the sports car while we just sit for a second.

"Do you think they climbed the fence to get in?" She asks, breaking the silence that had surrounded us.

I look around, we have yet to see any sort of opening. Unless the fence is loose in some spot that we can't see then I think she's right.

"Zander's so tall, he just had to step over it," I shrug. I'm exaggerating but trying to lighten the mood a bit. Especially because we still can't see or hear anything going on inside, and I want to be closer.

Aylin laughs, "What's your plan?"

"Let's go in," I am hesitant, but I also can't sit here and wait.

I half expect Aylin to argue, to try and stop me from going in, convincing me it's a bad idea.

That doesn't happen.

"Let's go."

She climbs out of the car before me, frankly, I'm a little surprised at how willing she is to jump into danger like this. As I meet her gaze outside, I narrow my eyes at her.

"What?" She asks quietly.

"I don't know what's gotten into you lately, but I like it."

She shakes her head at me.

Once we get to the gate there aren't any holes or loose parts for us to slip through so climbing it is going to be our only option. I don't like the idea that if we have to run away quickly, we are essentially fucked because there's no way I'm getting over this thing quickly.

My fingers hurt as the chain digs into my skin as I hoist

myself up to the top, swinging my leg over and jumping down onto the other side. Aylin waits until I'm over to do the same. I'm proud of us, for two curvy girls we are agile as fuck.

We make our way to the creepy building, trying to keep our footsteps as quiet as possible. We reach a side with a door, but I know if we try to open it anyone inside will hear.

We scope around for any openings or holes we could climb through that are not up at the top, and out of our reach.

This building is huge up close, and they could be inside anywhere.

Finally, we get to a window with a panel knocked out so we can see inside. There, I see four large figures. One is clearly Zander as he is the tallest and biggest of the bunch, but the other three that are standing across from him aren't much smaller. I know one of them is Trent.

Both Aylin and I are looking in through the small opening, it's hard to hear what's being said, but it doesn't matter because suddenly two of the figures across from Zander rush at him, grabbing him, forcing him down to his knees, hard.

I throw my hand over my mouth to hide my gasp as I watch. They are holding him there, his arms restrained when the third figure-who I assume is Trent- approaches him, punching Zander across the face. I hold back my scream behind my hand. I know I can't draw attention to us.

I can't look at Aylin, but I know she's watching in horror along with me, both helpless and terrified. We can't hear anything they are saying, we are too far away. Trent hits Zander a few more times, and Zander isn't doing anything. Why isn't he doing anything? I've seen him fight multiple people when he was a teenager. I know he should at least *try*.

Next thing I see is Trent holding something, the minimal light shining inside creates a shine on what it is.

A knife.

I want to rush in, we need to do something he's going to kill him!

I know if we rush in, we will just get killed as well. We have to strategic about this.

My mind is racing, trying to think of what to do when the knife is brought down across Zander's face. I can't hold back my scream as I shout, "NO!"

My hand slaps up to my mouth, but it's too late. They are looking over here.

Aylin and I crouch down, out of view of the window, but we have to run. I can't leave, not without Zander.

"Go help him, I'll divert them," Aylin says suddenly as she starts to stand up and run back the way we came.

"No, we need to stick together," I whisper-yell at her, but she's already on her feet, ready.

"We got this, Mel," she says, surprisingly calm as she starts making more noise as she runs back around the building.

I watch in horror, and shock at her. I couldn't stand if something happened to her. I couldn't lose Aylin and Zander, even if I somehow made it out of this I wouldn't survive without them. I'm not going to let her down. I won't let either of them down. I have to get to Zander. I stand up to peek in the window again, one of the figures is gone, but there's still someone holding Zander from behind, Trent still standing in front of him.

I need to get inside. As I continue to circle the massive building searching for an opening, I take out my phone to call Nate. Maybe if they catch Trent red handed trying to fucking murder Zander, they won't let that monster out.

"Greene," He answers, a gruff voice that takes me off guard.

"Come to the abandoned library off Burnside, shit's going down," I whisper since I don't have time to get into the details.

All I can hope is that he will actually show up.

At this moment I'm on my own, hoping Aylin got away and hoping Zander is okay.

After what feels like forever, I find an opening. It's not big, I'm not sure if I'm going to be able to squeeze through, but I have to try. My back and chest scrape across the stone as I slide my body through the opening until I'm inside.

I breathe a sigh of relief that I'm in.

Then, the fear takes over again because I'm inside with some dangerous people, and I don't know how badly injured Zander is. The air is musky and stale; it's hard not to gag at the overwhelming weight in the air.

The walls are lined with old wooden bookshelves, some have books on them still at the very top that can't be reached without a ladder.

The place is riddled with vandalism and is practically destroyed. Books are ripped up, papers and garbage are scattered everywhere with spray-paint decorating almost every surface.

Carefully, I make my way closer to the area I saw Zander in. Finally, I hear the voices getting louder as I round the last corner. My back is to a wall, I know they are on the other side. I can finally hear what Trent is saying.

"You think my friend has caught up to Mel? What do you think he's doing to her now, little brother?" Trent says in that same calm tone he used when he spoke to me.

I risk a peek around the wall to see Zander.

I peek out slightly to see him on his knees, restrained by the man behind him, a slash across his cheek is bleeding heavily. He looks pale and blood soaked.

I hold back my cry.

His eyes are looking directly at Trent, refusing to look away. I want to run in there, I could tackle Trent and buy some time, I debate it, readying my feet when Zander's eyes flick to mine so briefly I'm not sure if it was real.

Then he shakes his head in the most subtle way like he knows exactly what I was thinking. His facial expression doesn't change as he continues glaring at Trent, but he saw me.

"It's probably just some kids looking to come here to do drugs or something. Mel isn't here," Zander snarls at Trent.

"Either way, she will be next. I just have to finish with you first," I hear another slash, it sounds like he ripped through clothing, and Zander grunts. I don't want to see what he did.

"Then stop playing with me and finish me then!" Zander yells, taunting him and I don't get why.

*Why isn't he fighting back? What is he doing?*

I hear another smack; the sound of Zander being hit across the face again. I flinch on instinct like I'm the one taking the hit.

"It's too bad it came down to this, we could've been something great, but you decided fucking me over was better for you," Trent sighs like he is actually disappointed. "You chose some girl over your fucking family and now you'll never get to see her again."

Another slash, and more smacks. I can't look, I want to scream.

I want to run, throw myself in front of Zander.

I want to do *something*, but I'm stuck in place because I don't know what the fuck to do.

"You were never my fucking family," Zander spits at Trent. I can hear the struggle in his voice, and it only fuels my fire, I need to help him.

Suddenly, I hear the sirens in the distance and my head perks up. *Yes.*

"Leave him, we should get the fuck out of here," Another voice says that I don't recognize. I assume it's the guy that's restraining Zander.

"One last thing," Trent says as I hear the flick of a lighter before a hard thud which I think is Zander being dropped onto the floor, and then footsteps walking away.

I peek out again, seeing Zander's large body slumped over

on the floor, either unconscious or too weak from the blood loss to move.

That's not even the most concerning part of what I see, there's a pile of loose ripped out book pages on fire less than six feet away from him, the flames spreading quickly from the old paper everywhere.

Trent and the other guy aren't completely out yet, but I don't care. I rush out from behind the wall, straight to Zander.

I turn him over, seeing the full extent of the damage. The sharp cuts across his face, and chest bleeding profusely.

He's unconscious, I'm panicking as the flames are taking over the space around us.

"Zander, come on, you need to get up, we have to get out of here!" I run my hand across his cheek, smearing his blood, but I don't care.

He doesn't stir, I can't lift him. I need to move him as far from the inferno as I can.

I put my arms under his armpits, hoisting him up as much as I can, which I don't even think lifts his hips from the ground as I drag him across the floor. My goal is to get to the door we passed, though I know it's far.

I keep trying to rouse Zander as I'm dragging his heavy body. The building is filling with smoke quickly, burning my lungs, but I keep pushing through.

"Zander, please! It's Mel, please!" I feel myself getting weaker as my lungs are filling with smoke. The sirens outside have gotten louder, but the fire has spread exponentially.

I don't know how far we are from the door. I can barely see anything through the thick, black smoke. I'm gasping for air, my arms growing heavier and I can't pull Zander along anymore. I can't even move my own body any further. This isn't how this is supposed to happen.

I fall onto my knees, gasping for air, but my lungs are filled with the black smoke from the fire instead. Zander is on his back; I collapse onto his chest.

I can't breathe.

I can't move.

Everything grows darker around us as I realize we aren't getting out of here. We aren't getting saved. I failed us both, and this is it.

"I love you, I'm sorry," I say to Zander before everything goes dark.

# 40

**Present**

There's a beeping noise that's annoying me, I never set an alarm so what the fuck is that? Did Mel set an alarm for some reason?

*Mel.*

The memories start flooding back, meeting with Trent, his threats to deal with me and he will leave Mel alone, the blood, the smoke, Mel was there.

She showed up.

I saw her, I know I did.

I was waiting for my time to go after Trent, but I was outnumbered. When the one guy left to check out the noise, I felt slightly more confident. I can handle myself in a fight, and I can take a beating.

The knife Trent pulled out complicated my plan.

Seeing Mel complicated my plan even more.

I kept feeling weaker, I saw Mel's face. She wanted to intervene, and I know if I went after Trent she would have.

I couldn't risk anything happening to her, but I kept getting weaker from the blood loss. The more I tried to hang on, the more I faded until I couldn't feel much anymore. The cuts Trent inflicted were too deep, I was losing too much blood.

I open my eyes, I don't know where I am, but I'm weak and in pain everywhere. There's a tube around my head under my nose giving me oxygen, and IVs connected to my arms.

I'm alone in the room, the beeping increases as I realize I don't know where Mel is, if she's okay.

If she's not okay I'm going to set the world on fire as I let it consume me. Finish the job it started.

Two people walk into the room, I assume due to the increase in my heart rate indicated on the stupid machine I want to throw across the room, if only I had the strength to do so.

"Mr. Wells, how are you feeling?" The man wearing a white jacket asks. I assume he's the doctor.

"I'd be better if I knew where Melody James was," I don't give a shit about myself, I'm alive, but I can't live without her.

"She was the woman you were found with?" He asks, going to the computer the woman behind him wheeled in the room.

"Yes, I need to see her," I try to sit up, but the stinging in my chest prevents me from going very far.

"I can only provide information to family, who is she to you?" Suddenly, I don't like this guy very much.

She's my forever? My everything? That's more than family, "She's my fiancé."

The guy looks at me skeptically. He's lucky I can't move much because if I could he wouldn't be looking at me like that.

"She's fine, she's down the hall and will be released tomorrow," His words give me a wave of relief as I sink back down onto the bed. "You need to continue to rest, I'm sure she will come in here when she's released."

"No, I need to go see her," I fight against the pain to try and stand up; the doctor pushes me back down onto the bed.

The nurse comes over and puts something into my IV that makes my eyelids heavy.

I'm not done talking, I have too many questions, but I'm drifting away again. That doctor better not show his face to me again because I promised no one would come between Mel and me again, and he just did.

When I wake up again, I'm in a little less pain, but as I slowly open my eyes, I see I'm still in the same hospital room.

I look over to the recliner where I see Mel curled up under a blanket, her hair fanned out, and I smile at the sight of her. Alive. Sleeping peacefully.

She doesn't look hurt, she got released from the hospital before me so I'm hoping she didn't have anything really wrong with her.

I stare at her until she stirs, turning over to face me, her green eyes locking with mine. I see the tears instantly appear in her eyes as she throws the blanket off, coming to my side.

"Zander, oh my God," She cries, her hand on my cheek, forehead resting against mine. "I was so fucking worried."

"They didn't tell you I was fine?" I'm about to be mad at that doctor all over again.

"They did, but I didn't believe it since you've been passed out since I got released yesterday," She presses her lips to mine lightly. I'm holding her hand to my face.

*Yesterday? I was asleep for two fucking days?*

I slide over in the small bed that is barely big enough for me, but I need her next to me. I need to hold her. I need to feel that she's really here.

"Come here," I instruct. She looks at me skeptically before I pull her arm down.

She gives in, climbing into the bed, curling up next to me

carefully avoiding my chest. I assume she saw the damage more than I did.

"Nate came to talk to me," she says softly. "Well, he was coming to talk to you, but I was the only one awake in this room."

I give her a small squeeze, the simple action sending pain through my body, but it was worth it.

"What did he say?" I ask, my eyelids already feeling heavy again, but I've slept long enough. I want to leave. With Mel.

"He told me what went down after I passed out," She shudders at the memory, but I continue to hold her against me. "He said we are lucky to be alive, by the time they got to us the smoke was so bad we should've died from smoke inhalation alone, plus you lost so much blood, they have no idea how you're alive."

I can hear her voice straining as she tells me this. I know I lost a lot of blood, Trent knocked me out, and I faded in and out of consciousness. I have a flash memory of being dragged, I assume by Mel. I'm impressed she was able to move me at all, I'm so much bigger than her, but my Mel Bell is strong.

"I'm not that easy to kill, Mel Bell," I press my lips to the side of her head lightly.

She snuggles closer into me. "Anyway, they caught up to Trent and those two guys with him, Aylin actually hit one with her car. That's a story for another time," She chuckles lightly. I should've guessed Aylin was with her but imagining her hitting someone with her car is something I can't picture.

"Nate told me Trent won't be getting out as quickly this time, now he's got all sorts of charges against him because of this. He said we should be good for a while," She looks up at me, relief written all over her face.

I wrap both my arms around her, not caring about the pain in my chest, she makes me feel better in every single way.

Finally, We get to have peace. We can have our life together. I let out a sigh of relief I feel like I've been holding in for ten years.

"I love you so much, Zander."

"I love you, Mel Bell."

# EPILOGUE

**Mel**

**6 Months Later**

We've been living in the little house on the coast since Zander got released from the hospital.
He's back to himself with some additional scars that, in all honesty, make him even sexier. We have made some serious improvements to the little house; I never want to leave.

I finished my book, which will be released in a month. Zander is so supportive and excited for me. I let him read it, afraid of what he might think.

He said it's amazing and not only because I wrote it, though I don't believe his opinion. He's blind when it comes to me. Somehow, I'm perfect in his eyes and I don't know how, but I'll take it.

We got the rest of my things from my apartment to bring here. I got to meet Mrs. Carter; Zander wasn't kidding when he said she was so nice. She really is, we let her come see the improvements we've made on the house.

She started crying, and I thought she hated it. I felt so guilty we ruined this house that meant so much to her. She then told us it's better than she could've ever imagined.

Her favorite part is the mural Zander painted in the entryway that's an abstract interpretation of a sunrise or sunset over the ocean. It's vibrant, powerful and beautiful. It's my favorite part of the house too, even more than the windows that look onto the ocean.

Zander's been drawing more, always sketching when we have the time. Sometimes we go down to the beach, and I cuddle up against him as he draws. I love watching him work. I love seeing what he creates with his hands. Watching the blank piece of paper come to life with designs. I told him I want him to tattoo something on me.

HE LOOKS AT ME SKEPTICALLY, *pausing his sketch,* "Let me get more practice in, I don't want to fuck it up and you hate me."

"I would never hate you for that, I want your art on me," *I look at his arms, examining the art on his skin I know he designed. Even if he didn't put it all on himself, he still drew it and it's beautiful.*

"I will, one day, I promise. We have forever, right?"

*I smile up at him,* "Yeah, we have forever."

HE FOUND someone in Newport that was willing to take him on as an apprentice. It's only been about two months since he started so he has a lot to learn, but he's loving it so far, and I have never been so happy.

Trent was also sentenced to five years on all counts. It should've been longer, the motherfucker had good lawyers that got the sentence reduced. It still could be reduced more for "good behavior" which I choose to think he's incapable of showing. We choose not to think about it, he has that time to cool off, hopefully realizing coming after us won't even be worth it at that point.

I hear the front door open behind me, so I turn away from the window to face Zander just walking into the door, the biggest smile on his face.

"What were you doing?" I ask because I know he wasn't at the shop today.

He was gone when I woke up, which of course suddenly sent me into a panic until I saw the note, he left me.

The note told me not to worry, he would be back soon and that he wasn't doing anything dangerous. I scoff because I still think we have different definitions of dangerous, but I trust him. He's not going to risk losing me again, I know that for a fact.

"Come here, I'll show you," His bright smile takes over his entire face as he holds his hand out to me.

I take it in my own as we go outside. I'm confused when I look around and I don't see his Porsche. There's a Jeep parked next to my car in the driveway. I look up at Zander, "Where's your car?"

"I sold it for that, you don't like it?" He asks, clearly excited, but I'm still confused. He loves his sports cars, this is not him.

"I do, but why?"

"Oh, I sold it for more than that," He turns, outstretching his arms to the side, "I sold it for this too."

My eyes flicker to his, to the house.

No, this is a prank. Mrs. Carter couldn't part with this house, she loved it too much. Same with Zander and that car, he loved that thing too much to sell it.

"How? What?" I can't speak because I refuse to believe what he's trying to tell me.

He laughs, pulling me against his chest, "Mrs. Carter

wanted to give us this house after she saw what we did to it, she said she couldn't imagine better people to have it. I told her she couldn't just give it to us, we would pay her for it. So, I sold my car to buy it from her. She refused to let me get a mortgage for what it's really worth; she just wants us to be happy here."

I can't believe what he's telling me. I shake my head, and I'm about to tell him to go get his car back when he scoops me up, holding behind my knees and cradling my back. I squeal at the sudden movement, throwing my arms around his neck.

He walks us back into the house, "Welcome home, Mel Bell."

∼

## Zander

I lied to her.

Well, I didn't tell her the entirety of what I did. I didn't *just* pay Mrs. Carter for the house with the money I got for my car.

At least this time what I'm hiding is a good thing, and she's going to know tonight because I can't stand to wait on this any longer. The ring I bought is burning a hole in my pocket, and I'm dying to see it on her finger.

We decided to go out to dinner tonight to celebrate our new home, but my plan is to take her to the lighthouse afterwards, which should be right at sunset, the perfect backdrop for the perfect proposal.

I'm sitting in the living room, bouncing my leg as I stare out the large windows while Mel finishes getting ready in our room. I'm nervous, even though I know I shouldn't be. I love her. She loves me. It's us against the world, and yet I'm still worried for some reason.

"You ready?" She asks, stepping in front of me with her

wide smile pasted on her beautiful face. My nerves quickly dissipate from the sight.

"More than you know," I beam at her.

As I stand up I wrap her in my arms to plant a kiss on her mouth. Mel instantly melts into me, and it makes me want to drop to my knees right now to ask her then worship her in every way possible. Instead, I take her hand in mine as we leave the house, and I know when we return she will be more than just my girlfriend.

AFTER DINNER we drive the short distance to Hacenta Head lighthouse. It's a bit of a staple, and yet we haven't had the chance to go together, even though we can see it on a clear day out in the distance from our house.

The timing is perfect, and I want to pat myself on the back. The sun is setting in the distance giving the entire area an orange glow. Mel is mesmerized, I see it reflected in her green eyes and it makes my heart leap in my chest. I love this woman. I want forever with this woman. I've wanted her to be mine since we were kids, and now she will. Finally, after all we've been through.

We both get out of the car, I come around to her side to take her hand in mine as we walk up the path to the white lighthouse on top of the hill. I want to take in some of the scenery, but I can't bring myself to look away from her. The light brings out the shades of red in her hair, her green eyes practically glowing against her pale skin, and her face reflects her pure joy as we walk along the path.

Once we get to the top of the hill we go to the railing that looks out into the expanse of water. The waves crashing against the rocks beneath us. Mel leans against the railing, I step up behind her to wrap my arms around her front, holding her against me.

We are silent for a few moments. I just hold her, the sound of the waves mingled with our breathing and heartbeats. The sun is disappearing in the distance, and I need to ask her, I can't wait any longer for her to be mine, wholly and fully.

I press my lips against the side of her head, "Mel, you know how much I love you."

I feel her chuckle as she turns around in my arms with a smile, "No, I don't think I do."

I smile back before continuing, "Well, then you should know that I love you more than I've loved anyone. I've loved you since we were five years old, and didn't even know what love could be. You've always had my entire heart, and I want to prove it to you every day for the rest of our lives."

I slide one hand into hers as I drop down to one knee in front of her. Mel's face turns from joy into shock, her mouth agape as I begin to pull the little black box from my pocket.

"Melody James, my Mel Bell, will you marry me and make me the happiest man in the entire world?"

She gasps, and I see the tears start streaming down her cheeks, but she's smiling as she exclaims, "Yes!"

I jump up to wrap her in my arms as she jumps up, wrapping her legs around my waist, kissing me. I kiss her back feverishly.

Mel.

My Mel.

My *fiancé*.

I feel like everything has come full circle, and that in this moment I officially have everything I could have ever asked for.

**THE END**

# WHAT'S NEXT?

Want a Mel and Zander spicy <u>BONUS SCENE</u>?

**Read Aylin's story now in "Who They Are"**
A dark forbidden romance

*How far can you bend until you finally break?*

**Blurb:**
She's a LIAR to everyone around her.
Lying is the only way to protect herself.
She can never trust anyone, not after what she's been through.
If no one knows her then she can never truly be hurt.
Then when they leave her it's because she pushed them away.

He PRETENDS he's okay to everyone around him.
Pretending to be someone he's not every day is easy.
Pretending nothing affects him makes him feel invincible.
When they meet they both know there's more than meets the eye, but neither will admit it.
LYING and PRETENDING is easier until it becomes too much.
There's no choice left but to figure out WHO THEY ARE.

<u>READ NOW ON KU</u>

# ABOUT THE AUTHOR

Madi is 20 something trying to figure out what "adulting" is. Madi has been writing stories since she was a teenager she continues to express all her emotions in her writing. She's also an avid reader, especially of dark romance. Madi lives in the PNW where she attended college after moving from the unforgiving heat of Arizona. Madi spends her free time with her husband and family of pets (4 dogs and 2 cats).

As an indie author reviews are everything so if you loved Mel and Zander please leave a review, I appreciate it!

Follow my Instagram for updates! @Madidaniellewrites

You can also follow on Tiktok @Madidaniellewrites

Join my Facebook reader group! Madi Danielle's Reader Group

# ACKNOWLEDGMENTS

I'm going to try not to make this long winded because most of the people that I want to thank I have done so over...and over... and over again, but I doing it one more time!

First of all, thank you to my best friends Ashley and Julia who encouraged me this entire process. Julia, specifically for unlocking the memory that triggered this entire story, I don't know how or why it happened, but it did. Now, here we are! Also, for flying to see me so we could have an adventure along the coast and take beautiful shots of the perfection that is the Oregon coast. Ashley, for always being my booha, and my smut reading buddy.

Thank you Kelly Boudreaux for proofreading and giving me feedback, I am so beyond thankful for everything you did for me reading this story that was hard for me to put out there. It's like sharing a diary, but it's fiction. For some reason even though it's a story I made up it feels almost more personal than sharing a real life experience,

Thank you Cat from TRC Designs the cover artist GENIUS for the cover of this book! I swear, she is amazing, and the cover is better than I could have ever imagined for my book, so thank you!